To my family

Zhang R. C.

To my parents, my wife, and my son

Zhao S. L.

To my parents, my wife, my son, and my daughter

Li P. F.

统计与数据科学丛书 6

A Theory on Optimal Factorial Designs

（最优因析设计理论）

Zhang Runchu   Zhao Shengli   Li Pengfei

（张润楚　赵胜利　李鹏飞）

Science Press
Beijing

Responsible Editors: Li Xin, Li Yueting

Copyright© 2024 by Science Press
Published by Science Press
16 Donghuangchenggen North Street
Beijing 100717, P. R. China

Printed in Beijing

ISBN 978-7-03-077668-6

"统计与数据科学丛书" 序

统计学是一门集收集、处理、分析与解释量化的数据的科学. 统计学也包含了一些实验科学的因素, 例如通过设计收集数据的实验方案获取有价值的数据, 为提供优化的决策以及推断问题中的因果关系提供依据.

统计学主要起源于对国家经济以及人口的描述, 那时统计研究基本上是经济学的范畴. 之后, 因心理学、医学、人体测量学、遗传学和农业的需要逐渐发展壮大, 20 世纪上半叶是统计学发展的辉煌时代. 世界各国学者在共同努力下, 逐渐建立了统计学的框架, 并将其发展成为一个成熟的学科. 随着科学技术的进步, 作为信息处理的重要手段, 统计学已经从政府决策机构收集数据的管理工具发展成为各行各业必备的基础知识.

从 20 世纪 60 年代开始, 计算机技术的发展给统计学注入了新的发展动力. 特别是近二十年来, 社会生产活动与科学技术的数字化进程不断加快, 人们越来越多地希望能够从大量的数据中总结出一些经验规律, 对各行各业的发展提供数据科学的方法论, 统计学在其中扮演了越来越重要的角色. 从 20 世纪 80 年代开始, 科学家就阐明了统计学与数据科学的紧密关系. 进入 21 世纪, 把统计学扩展到数据计算的前沿领域已经成为当前重要的研究方向. 针对这一发展趋势, 进一步提高我国的统计学与数据处理的研究水平, 应用与数据分析有关的技术和理论服务社会, 加快青年人才的培养, 是我们当今面临的重要和紧迫的任务. "统计与数据科学丛书" 因此应运而生.

这套丛书旨在针对一些重要的统计学及其计算的相关领域与研究方向作较系统的介绍. 既阐述该领域的基础知识, 又反映其新发展, 力求深入浅出, 简明扼要, 注重创新. 丛书面向统计学、计算机科学、管理科学、经济金融等领域的高校师生、科研人员以及实际应用人员, 也可以作为大学相关专业的高年级本科生、研究生的教材或参考书.

朱力行

2019 年 11 月

Preface

Experimental design is a scientific approach used to investigate the relationship between variables in real-world scenarios. Typically, there is a dependent variable (outcome) that varies in response to certain input variables or factors. Through observation or experimentation, researchers aim to understand the underlying rules governing these changes. When multiple variables are involved, an experiment designed to observe and explore the governing rules is referred to as a multi-factor experiment.

In 1926, R. A. Fisher introduced factorial design as a method for agricultural experiments, and since then, it has become an important tool for studying multi-factor experiments. Yates (1935, 1937) made significant contributions to its early development. When we deal with a large number of factors in a multi-factor experiment, conducting a complete/full factorial experiment can be impractical due to the enormous number of runs (experimental combinations) and associated costs. In such cases, researchers often opt for a fractional factorial design, which involves selecting a subset of runs from the complete/full factorial design. This approach was introduced by Box and Hunter (1961a, b). Fractional factorial designs are particularly useful when the experimenter is primarily interested in estimating lower-order factorial effects. They offer an economical and efficient means of conducting multi-factor experiments.

In the estimation of factorial effects, the following effect hierarchy principle is often emphasized (Wu and Hamada, 2000, 2009):

(i) Lower-order effects are more likely to be significant than higher-order effects.

(ii) Effects of the same order are equally likely to be significant.

The accuracy of factorial effect estimation is highly dependent on the chosen experimental design, making the selection of factorial designs a critical step. Consequently, the identification of optimal designs becomes a key issue in the study of modern experimental designs across various situations. At present, several criteria exist to aid in the selection of these optimal factorial designs.

The first classification pattern that has been considered for regular designs is the wordlength pattern (WLP), introduced by Box and Hunter (1961a, b). Based on the WLP, several criteria were proposed. The first criterion is the maximum resolution criterion, also proposed by Box and Hunter (1961a, b). It suggests that a fractional factorial design with higher resolution leads to less confounding between lower-order factorial effects. However, since there are many designs with maximum resolution, this criterion alone cannot determine which one is the best. As a result, a more refined criterion called the minimum aberration (MA) criterion was proposed by Fries and Hunter (1980). Subsequently, the maximum estimation capacity (MEC) criterion was introduced by Cheng, Steinberg, and Sun (1999) and Cheng and Mukerjee (1998). The MA criterion gained significant attention in the 1990s and early 2000s, leading to a substantial number of papers being published on this topic.

From an application standpoint, the estimability of factorial effects in a design, particularly the lower-order effects, is of great interest. Recognizing this, Wu and Chen (1992) proposed the clear effects (CE) criterion, which aims to maximize the number of clear main effects and two-factor interactions (2fi's). In this context, a main effect or 2fi is considered "clear" if it is not aliased with any other main effect or 2fi. A clear main effect or 2fi is estimable under the assumption that interactions involving three or more factors are negligible.

While the literature demonstrates alignment between the MA and CE criteria in many cases, there are instances where the optimal designs identified by the MA criterion differ from those determined by the CE criterion. This raises the question: both MA and CE criteria are based on the same effect hierarchy principle and aim to minimize the confounding of lower-order effects, so why do they select different optimal designs? The distinction arises from the fact that the MA criterion is based on the classification pattern WLP and selects the design that sequentially minimizes the components of WLP. In contrast, the CE criterion is not based on the WLP, and is only based on the number of clear main effects and 2fi's. Obviously, the number of clear main effects and 2fi's is not enough as a complete alias measure to elaborately classify and rank all the regular designs.

Furthermore, in recent decades, investigators of experimental design have continuously raised several additional questions. For instance, they have explored the relationships between existing criteria and their corresponding optimal designs. They have also investigated whether a more general alias classification pattern exists that can unify all the existing criteria and generate a broader range of practical and useful criteria. Motivated by these inquiries, Zhang, Li, Zhao, and Ai (2008) introduced a new classification pattern and criterion known as the aliased effect-number pattern (AENP) and the general minimum lower-order confounding (GMC) criterion. This proposal aimed to address the aforementioned questions and provide a fresh perspective in the field of experimental design.

It has been demonstrated that the classification pattern WLP used in the MA criterion, the number of clear main effects and 2fi's in the CE criterion, and the number of models containing all the main effects and a specified number of 2fi's in the MEC criterion can be expressed as specific functions of the AENP. This implies that all the existing criteria are determined by respective functions derived from the AENP.

Since their first introduction, the AENP and GMC criterion have undergone significant development and extension. This book aims to provide a comprehensive account of the modern theory of factorial designs, with the GMC approach serving as its core. Our intention is for this book to be utilized as a textbook for graduate courses in design theory within the field of statistics. Additionally, we hope that it will serve as a valuable reference for researchers in the area of experimental design.

The writing of this book is partially supported by the National Natural Science Foundation of China (Grant Nos. 10871104, 11171165, 11771250, 12171277), the Specialized Research Fund for the Doctoral Program of Higher Education of China (Grant No. 20050055038), the Natural Sciences and Engineering Research Council of Canada (RGPIN-2020-04964), and funding from the Faculty of Mathematics Research Chair at the University of Waterloo. We have greatly benefited from the encouragement and valuable comments/suggestions provided by Professors C.F. Jeff Wu, Cheng Chingshui, Rahul Mukerjee, Narayanaswamy Balakrishnan, Chen Jia hua, Tang Boxin, Xu Hongquan, Wu Changbao, and Dr. Qin Jing. Additionally, we are sincerely grateful for the contributions of many colleagues and former students, including Ai Mingyao, Narayanaswamy Balakrishnan, Cheng Yi, Guo Bing, Hu Jianwei, Rohana J. Karunamuni, Li Peng, Li Zhiming, Dennis K.J. Lin, Liu Minqian, Rahul Mukerjee, Ren Junbai, Sun Qing, Sun Tao, Tan Yili, Wang Dongying, Wei Jialin, Yang Jianfeng, Ye Shili, Zhang Tianfang, Zhao Qianqian, Zhao Yuna, Zhou Qi, and Zhou Zhiyang. Their support and assistance throughout the process are highly appreciated.

Lastly, we would like to express our deepest gratitude to our respective families for their unwavering support of our research activities over the years.

Tianjin, China	*Zhang Runchu*
Qufu, China	*Zhao Shengli*
Waterloo, Canada	*Li Pengfei*

Contents

1 Introduction

Statistical experimental design and data analysis is an important branch of statistics, and serves as the foundation of modern statistics. Today, modern experimental design theory is widely used across various scientific and practical fields, including industry, agriculture, medical science, physics, chemistry, aviation, spaceflight, and creature-imitating techniques, among others. When the number of factors is large, conducting a complete/full factorial experiment can be prohibitively expensive for experimenters. In such cases, experimenters prefer to use fractional factorial designs, which are subsets of the full factorial design. This chapter aims to provide an introduction to the basic concepts of fractional factorial designs and discuss the optimality criteria used for selecting such designs.

1.1 Factorial Designs and Factorial Effects

Experimentation is a powerful tool for understanding and improving products (Wu and Hamada, 2000, 2009). In many experiments, researchers investigate how changes in input variables, or *factors*, affect the experimental outcome, also known as the response. These experiments are called *factorial experiments*, where each factor typically has at least two different settings, known as *levels*. Any combination of factor levels is referred to as a *treatment combination* or *run* in industrial experimentation. To better illustrate the concepts, this book primarily focuses on factorial experiments where all factors have two levels. The last two chapters, Chapters 9 and 10, will discuss multi-level factorial experiments and general orthogonal designs, respectively.

A primary objective of factorial experiments is to identify the significant factors that have a substantial impact on the response and determine the optimal treatment combination involving these factors. To accomplish this task, we rely on the concept of *factorial effects*. Consider an experiment with n two-level factors, where the total number of treatment combinations is 2^n and the two levels of each factor are denoted as "-1" (low level) and "1" (high level). The *full factorial design* encompasses all $N = 2^n$ treatment combinations in the experiment. Let z_i ($i = 1, \cdots, N$) denote the treatment effect associated with the ith treatment combination in the experiment. These treatment effects serve as the basis for defining the factorial effects in full factorial experiments.

To quantify the average impact of a two-level factor, denoted as d_1, we compute the difference between the average treatment effect in the experiment at the high level of d_1 (represented as $\bar{z}(d_1 = 1)$) and the average treatment effect at the low level of d_1 (represented as $\bar{z}(d_1 = -1)$). This difference is called the *main effect* of d_1. Mathematically, the main effect $ME(d_1)$ can be expressed as:

$$ME(d_1) = \bar{z}(d_1 = 1) - \bar{z}(d_1 = -1). \tag{1.1}$$

To assess the joint effect of two two-level factors, such as d_1 and d_2, the $d_1 \times d_2$ *interaction effect* can be defined in two equivalent ways:

$$
\begin{aligned}
INT(d_1, d_2) &= \frac{1}{2}\{ME(d_1|d_2 = 1) - ME(d_1|d_2 = -1)\} \\
&= \frac{1}{2}\{ME(d_2|d_1 = 1) - ME(d_2|d_1 = -1)\}. \tag{1.2}
\end{aligned}
$$

Here, $ME(d_1|d_2 = 1)$ is the *conditional main effect* of d_1 given that d_2 is at the high ("1") level, and similar definitions apply to other terms. Specifically,

$$ME(d_1|d_2 = 1) = \bar{z}(d_1 = 1|d_2 = 1) - \bar{z}(d_1 = -1|d_2 = 1),$$

where $\bar{z}(d_1 = 1|d_2 = 1)$ denotes the average treatment effects in the experiment with both d_1 and d_2 are at the high level, and $\bar{z}(d_1 = -1|d_2 = 1)$ is defined similarly. It is important to note that a significant interaction indicates that the effect of one factor, such as d_1, is dependent on the level of the other factors, such as d_2.

Higher-order interaction effects can be defined in a similar manner. For k ($\leqslant n$) two-level factors, $d_1, \cdots, d_k$, their interaction effect is defined in terms of $(k-1)$-factor interactions as follows:

$$INT(d_1, \cdots, d_k) = \frac{1}{2} \{INT(d_1, \cdots, d_{k-1}|d_k = 1)$$
$$- INT(d_1, \cdots, d_{k-1}|d_k = -1)\}. \tag{1.3}$$

In the case of $k = 2$, $INT(d_1, \cdots, d_{k-1}|d_k = 1)$ corresponds to the previously defined $ME(d_1|d_2 = 1)$. When $k > 2$, $INT(d_1, \cdots, d_{k-1}|d_k = 1)$ represents the *conditional interaction effect* of $d_1, \cdots, d_{k-1}$ given that d_k is at the high ("1") level. The definitions for other terms are similar to the previous ones.

For an experiment with n two-level factors, we can define n main effects and

$$\binom{n}{2} + \cdots + \binom{n}{n} = 2^n - 1 - n$$

interaction effects. Throughout this book, the main effects and the interaction effects of all orders together are referred to as the *factorial effects*. In total, there are $2^n - 1$ factorial effects for an experiment with n two-level factors. For simplicity, we may omit the symbol "$\times$" in $d_1 \times d_2$. When there is no confusion, we may also omit "d" in the factor label and use $1, 2, \cdots, n$ to directly represent the factor labels. By doing these, the notation "12" means the interaction effect between the first factor and the second factor.

The factorial effects defined above are closely connected to the coefficients of a linear regression model. Let Y represent the experimental outcome and $x_1, \cdots, x_n$ denote the covariates for n two-level factors, where x_i $(i = 1, \cdots, n)$ is 1 when the ith factor is at the high level and -1 when the ith factor is at the low level. The linear regression model assumes the following form:

$$E(Y) = \alpha_0 + \sum_{i=1}^{n} \alpha_i x_i + \sum_{i<j} \alpha_{ij} x_i x_j + \cdots + \alpha_{1\ldots n} x_1 \cdots x_n, \tag{1.4}$$

where α_0 is the intercept or the grand mean of the experimental outcome, and the meanings of other α's will be explained later.

In the full factorial experiment, Wu and Hamada (2009) showed that

Each factorial effect $= 2 \times$ corresponding coefficient in (1.4). $\tag{1.5}$

For instance,

$$ME(d_1) = 2\alpha_1 \text{ and } INT(d_1, d_2) = 2\alpha_{12}.$$

This property also holds when we consider the fractional factorial experiment in next section.

Full factorial experiments have many nice properties. For example, the factorial effects obtained from the 2^n full factorial experiments have the property of *reproducibility*. Additionally, all columns in the model matrix of the linear regression model (1.4) are orthogonal to each other. We refer to Wu and Hamada (2009) for more details.

Full factorial experiments, however, have a limitation: the run number $N = 2^n$ grows exponentially as n increases, making it impractical for experiments with a large number of factors. As a result, experimenters commonly use a fraction of the full factorial design that consists of 2^q runs, where $q < n$, to reduce the number of treatment combinations. The natural question then becomes how to select this fraction of the full factorial design. In Section 1.2, we introduce the formal definition of fractional factorial designs, and in Section 1.3, we discuss some optimality criteria for selecting such designs.

1.2　Fractional Factorial Designs

A 2^{n-m} *fractional factorial design* is an experimental design with n two-level factors and 2^{n-m} runs, which is a 2^{-m} fraction of the full 2^n factorial experiment. We can represent a 2^{n-m} design using a $2^q \times n$ matrix, where $q = n - m$. Each element in the matrix takes the values of either -1 or 1, with the rows corresponding to the 2^{n-m} runs and the columns representing the n two-level factors in the design. The -1 and 1 values in each row indicate the level assigned to each factor for that specific run. Throughout this book, we will use column and factor exchangeably.

One convenient method for selecting a 2^{n-m} design is to use the saturated design, which we will discuss in detail below. Let H_q be the $2^q \times (2^q - 1)$ matrix generated by q independent columns with each column having 2^q elements of entries -1 or 1, given by:

$$H_q = (1, 2, 12, 3, 13, 23, 123, \cdots, q, 1q, 2q, 12q, 3q, \cdots, 123 \cdots q)_{2^q}. \qquad (1.6)$$

The q independent columns of H_q are of the form:

$$1_{2^q} = (-1, 1, -1, 1, \cdots, -1, 1, -1, 1)',$$

$$2_{2^q} = (-1, -1, 1, 1, \cdots, -1, -1, 1, 1)',$$

$$3_{2^q} = (-1, -1, -1, -1, 1, 1, 1, 1, \cdots, -1, -1, -1, -1, 1, 1, 1, 1)',$$

$$\cdots$$

$$q_{2^q} = (-1, -1, \cdots, -1, 1, 1, \cdots, 1)'.$$

The remaining columns, $(12)_{2^q}$, $(1q)_{2^q}$, $(2q)_{2^q}, \cdots$, $(123\cdots q)_{2^q}$, are generated by these q independent columns. As an example, consider $(12)_{2^q}$. It can be obtained as the component-wise product of the independent columns 1_{2^q} and 2_{2^q}, i.e.,

$$(12)_{2^q} = (1, -1, -1, 1, \cdots, 1, -1, -1, 1)'.$$

Without confusion, we will omit the subscript 2^q hereafter. The matrix H_q is a well-known design called the *saturated design*, which is generated by q independent columns and is given in Yates order in (1.6). Table 1.1 gives the saturated design $H_3 = (1, 2, 12, 3, 13, 23, 123)$ in Yates order as an example. In the following, for a vector a and a matrix $B = (b_1, \cdots, b_l)$, let $aB = (ab_1, \cdots, ab_l)$ be the matrix obtained by taking the component-wise products of a and b_i for $i = 1, \cdots, l$. Further, for $1 \leqslant r \leqslant q - 1$, let H_r be the design consisting of the first $2^r - 1$ columns of H_q, which is generated by the first r independent columns, $1, \cdots, r$. Then we have

$$H_1 = \{1\} \quad \text{and} \quad H_r = \{H_{r-1}, r, rH_{r-1}\} \text{ for } r = 2, \cdots, q. \tag{1.7}$$

Table 1.1 Saturated design H_3 in Yates order

1	2	12	3	13	23	123
-1	-1	1	-1	1	1	-1
1	-1	-1	-1	-1	1	1
-1	1	-1	-1	1	-1	1
1	1	1	-1	-1	-1	-1
-1	-1	1	1	-1	-1	1
1	-1	-1	1	1	-1	-1
-1	1	-1	1	-1	1	-1
1	1	1	1	1	1	1

A 2^{n-m} design D can be obtained from the saturated design H_q by selecting n columns that contain q independent columns. Designs of this type are referred to as *regular* 2^{n-m} designs. In this book, we will use the term "n-projection of H_q" to describe the resulting design D. It is important to note that the factorial effects for regular 2^{n-m} designs can be defined in a similar manner as shown in (1.1)–(1.5).

To illustrate the above construction method, consider the 2^{4-1} design in Table 1.2, which is taken from H_3 in Table 1.1. In this design, columns 1, 2, and 3 are independent columns, while the fourth column is the component-wise product of columns 1, 2, and 3. Notionally, we write

$$4 = 123 \text{ or } I = 1234.$$

Here, I denotes the column of all 1's, and the equation $I = 1234$ means that the component-wise product of columns 1, 2, 3, and 4 results in a column of all 1's.

Table 1.2   A regular 2^{4-1} design

1	2	3	4(= 123)
−1	−1	−1	−1
1	−1	−1	1
−1	1	−1	1
1	1	−1	−1
−1	−1	1	1
1	−1	1	−1
−1	1	1	−1
1	1	1	1

Following the definition of factorial effects in Section 1.1, the equation $4 = 123$ indicates that

$$ME(4) = INT(1, 2, 3).$$

We refer to this as the main effect of the fourth factor being *aliased* with the interaction effect 123 involving factors 1, 2, and 3. The equation $I = 1234$ implies that the two columns in the model matrix of the linear model (1.4) for the intercept and the four-factor interaction 1234 are identical. We say that the intercept is aliased with the interaction 1234 and call $I = 1234$ the *defining relation* of the 2^{4-1} design, where "1234" is called a *word*. Since the 2^{4-1} design only has 7 degrees of freedom for estimating factorial effects, it cannot estimate all $15 = 2^4 − 1$ factorial effects. As shown below, out of 15 factorial effects, 14 can be estimated in 7 pairs of aliased effects. Applying the rules that

$$11 = 22 = \cdots = I \text{ and } Ii = i \text{ for any factor } i,$$

the equation $I = 1234$ can be used to determine which effects are aliased together.

By multiplying both sides of $I = 1234$ by column 1, that is,

$$1 = 1 \times I = 1 \times 1234 = 234,$$

the relationship $1 = 234$ is obtained. By following the same approach, we can infer all 7 aliasing relations:

$$1 = 234, \ 2 = 134, \ 12 = 34, \ 3 = 124, \ 13 = 24, \ 23 = 14, \ 123 = 4.$$

The previous example provides a good illustration of an equivalent way to generate the n columns in a 2^{n-m} design. First, we choose q independent columns to be $1, \cdots, q$ which generate $2^q = 2^{n-m}$ runs. Each of the remaining $m = n - q$ columns can be generated as a component-wise product of some independent columns, which corresponds to a defining word. Here, a "*word*" consists of letters which are the names of factors/columns denoted by $1, 2, \cdots, n$. For a 2^{n-m} design, we need m defining words to generate the m columns that are not part of the q independent columns. These defining words are called independent defining words and can be used to form a group, called *defining contrast subgroup*. This group consists of I (called the *identity element*) and $2^m - 1$ words, which are aliased with I. Suppose that the words v_i for $i = 1, \cdots, m$ are used to define the 2^{n-m} design, that is,

$$I = v_1 = \cdots = v_m.$$

The remaining words in the defining contrast subgroup can be obtained by multiplying the v_i's, for example,

$$I = v_1 v_2 = v_1 v_3 = \cdots = v_1 v_2 \cdots v_m.$$

Put together, the defining contrast subgroup of the 2^{n-m} design is

$$I = v_1 = \cdots = v_m = v_1 v_2 = v_1 v_3 = \cdots = v_1 v_2 \cdots v_m.$$

Each term in the defining contrast subgroup except for I is called a defining word.

For example, consider the 2^{5-2} design D_0 with the first three factors being 1–3, which generate an 8-run full factorial design. The fourth factor is determined by $4 = 12$, and the fifth factor is determined by $5 = 13$, resulting in two defining words: $I = 124$ and $I = 135$. Taking the product of the two defining words gives $I = 124 \times 135 = 2345$, the third word aliased with I. Therefore, the defining contrast subgroup for D_0 is given by

$$I = 124 = 135 = 2345.$$

Note that the 2^{5-2} design has only 7 degrees of freedom to estimate the factorial effects. The remaining $28 = (2^5 - 1 - 3)$ factorial effects, which are not aliased I, can be partitioned into 7 groups, with each group containing 4 effects that are aliased with one another. By multiplying all the 7 factorial effects generated by factors 1–3 to each term in the defining contrast subgroup, we get the following aliasing relations for D_0:

$$1 = 24 = 35 = 12345,$$
$$2 = 14 = 1235 = 345,$$
$$12 = 4 = 235 = 1345,$$
$$3 = 1234 = 15 = 245, \qquad (1.8)$$
$$13 = 234 = 5 = 1245,$$
$$23 = 134 = 125 = 45,$$
$$123 = 34 = 25 = 145.$$

In general, a 2^{n-m} design consists of $2^n - 1$ effects. Among these effects, $2^n - 2^m$ effects are not aliased with the identity element I, and they are divided into $2^q - 1$ groups, also known as *alias sets*. As illustrated earlier, the $2^q - 1$ alias sets can be obtained by multiplying all $2^q - 1$ factorial effects generated by the q independent factors with each term in the defining contrast subgroup. Each effect corresponds to one alias set, which contains 2^m effects that are aliased with each other.

It can be verified that the columns in the model matrix of the linear model (1.4) for any two factorial effects are either orthogonal to each other when they are not in the same alias set or identical when they are in the same alias set. This characteristic is unique to a regular 2^{n-m} design.

Among the 2^m effects in the same alias set, only one can be estimated while assuming that all the other $2^m - 1$ effects can be ignored (Mukerjee and Wu, 2006). Hence, a "good" fractional factorial design should avoid the aliasing of important effects.

1.3   Optimality Criteria

For given n and m, there may exist multiple 2^{n-m} designs. An important question is how to choose a "good" 2^{n-m} design and what criteria should be used to judge "goodness". The existing optimality criteria are driven by the *effect hierarchy principle* (Mukerjee and Wu, 2006; Wu and Hamada 2000, 2009), which is as follows:

(i) Lower-order effects are more likely to be significant than higher-order effects.

(ii) Effects of the same order are equally likely to be significant.

It is worth mentioning that two 2^{n-m} designs are considered isomorphic (or equivalent) if one defining contrast subgroup can be obtained from the other by permuting the factor labels. In the process of ranking and selecting designs, isomorphic designs are treated as identical and indistinguishable from each other.

1.3.1   Maximum Resolution Criterion

The first criterion for judging the goodness of 2^{n-m} designs is the maximum resolution criterion, proposed by Box and Hunter (1961a, b). Recall that there are $2^m - 1$ defining words in the defining contrast subgroup. The number of "letters" in each defining word is referred to its *wordlength*. Let $A_i(D)$ be the number of defining words of length i in a 2^{n-m} design D, $i = 1, \cdots, n$. Further, let

$$W(D) = (A_1(D), A_2(D), A_3(D), \cdots, A_n(D)),$$

which is called the *wordlength pattern* (WLP) of D. The *resolution* of a 2^{n-m} design is defined to be the smallest r such that $A_r(D) \geqslant 1$ (Box and Hunter, 1961a, b). In this book, we use the Roman letter to denote the resolution.

A design D with resolution R keeps all its effects involving c or fewer factors estimable, i.e., not aliased with each other, under the absence of all effects involving $R - c$ or more factors, where $1 \leqslant c \leqslant (R-1)/2$ (Mukerjee and Wu, 2006). For given n and m, under the effect hierarchy principle, a design with maximum resolution is preferable. This is called the *maximum resolution* criterion. It should be noted that designs with resolutions II or less may fail to estimate certain main effects, even when all interactions are absent. Since the main effects are typically of primary interest to the experimenter, we focus on designs with resolution III or higher. In this context, the WLP can be reduced to

$$W(D) = (A_3(D), A_4(D), \cdots, A_n(D)).   \qquad (1.9)$$

1.3.2   Minimum Aberration Criterion

Note that a design cannot be judged solely by its resolution (Wu and Hamada, 2009). To illustrate this, consider the following example. Table 1.3 gives two 2^{7-2} designs, both with resolution IV. However, they have different WLPs:

$$W(D_1) = (0, 2, 0, 1, 0),   \quad W(D_2) = (0, 1, 2, 0, 0).   \qquad (1.10)$$

Table 1.3   Two 2_{IV}^{7-2} designs

Designs	Definition relations	Aliasing relations among two-factor interactions
D_1	I=1236=1457=234567	12=36, 13=26, 14=57, 15=47, 16=23, 17=45
D_2	I=12346=12357=4567	45=67, 46=57, 47=56

The design D_1 has six pairs of aliased two-factor interactions (2fi's), while the design D_2 has three pairs. This difference arises from the fact that the design D_1 has two defining words with length four, while D_2 has only one. It appears that having more defining words of length four leads to an increased number of aliasing relations among 2fi's. In general, when there are more defining words with shorter lengths, we can anticipate a higher occurrence of aliasing relations among the lower-order effects. This observation motivates the following minimum aberration (MA) criterion, proposed by Fries and Hunter (1980).

Definition 1.1   *Let D_1 and D_2 be two 2^{n-m} designs. Let r be the smallest integer such that $A_r(D_1) \neq A_r(D_2)$. If $A_r(D_1) < A_r(D_2)$, D_1 is said to have less aberration than D_2. A design is called an MA design if no other design has less aberration than it.*

We would like to emphasize that, according to Definition 1.1, the MA 2^{n-m} design sequentially minimizes the WLP (1.9) among all 2^{n-m} designs. Consequently, an MA 2^{n-m} design must have the maximum resolution among all the 2^{n-m} designs. For the two 2^{7-2} designs in Table 1.3, their corresponding WLPs in (1.10) and Definition 1.1 together tell that the design D_2 has less aberration than D_1. In fact, D_2 is the MA 2^{7-2} design (Mukerjee and Wu, 2006).

Since the seminal work of Fries and Hunter (1980), there has been significant attention on the theory and construction of MA designs in the literature over the past few decades. See, for example, Franklin (1984), Chen and Wu (1991), Chen (1992), Chen, Sun, and Wu (1993), Chen and Hedayat (1996), Tang and Wu (1996), Suen, Chen, and Wu (1997), Zhang and Park (2000), Zhang and Shao (2001), Butler (2003), Ai and Zhang (2004a), Zhu and Zeng (2005), Cheng and Tang (2005), Chen and Cheng (2006), Xu and Cheng (2008), and Zhao, Li, and Karunamuni (2013). For a comprehensive overview and further discussions on MA designs, we refer to Mukerjee and Wu (2006), Wu and Hamada (2009), and Cheng (2014).

1.3.3 Clear Effects Criterion

Since the first introduction, the MA criterion has become the most commonly used one for judging the goodness of 2^{n-m} designs. Nevertheless, there are situations in which MA designs may not necessarily be optimal according to other sensible criteria. To better understand this, let us first introduce the concept of clear effect.

Definition 1.2 *A main effect or 2fi is called clear if it is not aliased with any other main effects or 2fi's.*

A clear main effect or 2fi can be estimated under the assumption that interactions involving three or more factors can be ignored. So, a "good" design should have as many clear effects as possible. However, an MA design may not have the largest number of clear effects. To see it, consider the following two 2^{9-4} designs with defining contrast subgroups:

$D_3: \quad I \quad = 1236 = 1247 = 1258 = 13459 = 3467 = 3568 = 24569 = 4578 = 23579$
$\qquad\qquad = 23489 = 12345678 = 15679 = 14689 = 13789 = 26789,$

$D_4: \quad I \quad = 1236 = 1247 = 1348 = 23459 = 3467 = 2468 = 14569 = 2378 = 13579$
$\qquad\qquad = 12589 = 1678 = 25679 = 35689 = 45789 = 123456789.$

The WLPs of the two designs are respectively

$$W(D_3) = (0, 6, 8, 0, 0, 1, 0) \text{ and } W(D_4) = (0, 7, 7, 0, 0, 0, 1).$$

Clearly, D_3 has less aberration than D_4. The aliasing relations of the 2fi's of the two designs are as follows:

$D_3:$ $12 = 36 = 47 = 58, 13 = 26, 14 = 27, 15 = 28, 16 = 23, 17 = 24, 18 = 25,$
$34 = 67, 35 = 68, 37 = 46, 38 = 56, 45 = 78, 48 = 57,$

$D_4:$ $12 = 36 = 47, 13 = 26 = 48, 14 = 27 = 38, 16 = 23 = 78, 17 = 24 = 68,$
$18 = 34 = 67, 28 = 37 = 46.$

The two designs respectively have eight and fifteen clear 2fi's. Wu and Hamada (2009) pointed out that the concept of clear estimation of effects has a more direct and interpretable meaning than the length of defining words from an operational point of view. Based on this perspective, we would conclude that D_4 is better than D_3 due to its higher number of clear effects.

In a design with a resolution of at least V, all main effects and 2fi's are clear. However, there are cases where the experimenter cannot afford a design with such a high resolution. In such situations, designs with resolutions of III or IV are often considered as viable alternatives. For designs with a resolution of IV, where all main effects are clear, it is preferable to choose the design with the maximum number of clear 2fi's. This design is referred to as a *MaxC2 design* . In the case of designs with a resolution of III, it is assumed that the magnitude of the main effects is much larger than that of the 2fi's. Although the 2fi's aliased with a main effect can introduce bias in estimating the main effect, this bias is not expected to be substantial. Therefore, a resolution III design with the maximum number of clear 2fi's is sometimes preferred over a resolution IV design. This additional criterion for design selection, known as the *clear effects* (CE) *criterion*, was proposed by Wu and Chen (1992) and Chen, Sun, and Wu (1993). For further advancements in this area, refer to Mukerjee and Wu (2006), Wu and Hamada (2009), and Cheng (2014).

1.3.4   Maximum Estimation Capacity Criterion

To analyze the impact of factors on the response variable, the linear model is commonly used. This model assumes that the response is a linear function of the factorial effects. For more details, please refer to Section 1.1. In situations where effects involving three or more factors are considered negligible, Sun (1993) introduced the concept of estimation capacity. The goal is to select a design that allows for the estimation of the maximum number of linear models containing all main effects and certain 2fi's. In other words, in (1.4), only the terms $x_1, \cdots, x_n$, and $x_i x_j$ for some $i < j$ are included.

For $1 \leqslant r \leqslant n(n-1)/2$, let $E_r(D)$ be the number of models containing all the main effects and r 2fi's that a 2^{n-m} design D can estimate, i.e., the columns in the model matrix of the linear model (1.4) for these r 2fi's are not identical. It is important to emphasize that one effect can be estimated if and only if all the other effects within the same alias set can be ignored (Mukerjee and Wu, 2006). Therefore, only one effect in an alias set can be included in the model.

Let us consider the 2^{5-2} design D_0 mentioned in Section 1.2 with the aliasing relations given by (1.8). When $r = 1$, assuming that other two-factor interactions in the same alias set and interactions involving three or more factors can be ignored, the design D_0 can estimate four models. In addition to the five main effects $1, \cdots, 5$, these models respectively include the 2fi's 23, 45, 25, and 34. Thus, we have $E_1(D_0) = 4$. Similarly, when $r = 2$, the design D_0 can estimate four models. In addition to the five main effects $1, \cdots, 5$, these models respectively include two 2fi's: $(23, 25)$, $(23, 34)$, $(45, 25)$, and $(45, 34)$. Hence, $E_2(D_0) = 4$. Clearly, if $3 \leqslant r \leqslant 10$, $E_r(D_0) = 0$.

A design D is said to have the *maximum estimation capacity* (MEC) if it maximizes $E_r(D)$ for all $r = 1, \cdots, n(n-1)/2$. The construction of MEC designs has been studied by Cheng and Mukerjee (1998) as well as Cheng, Steinberg, and Sun (1999), who developed general theory in this area. It has been shown that in many situations, MEC designs are consistent with MA designs. More theories and developments on MEC designs can be found in Mukerjee and Wu (2006) and Cheng (2014).

1.4   Organization of the Book

When considering the criteria discussed in Section 1.3, several questions arise:

(i) What relationships exist among these criteria?

(ii) Why do criteria that originate from the same ideas, such as the MA and CE criteria, often lead to different optimal designs?

(iii) What fundamental information is contained in the defining contrast sub-group?

To address the aforementioned questions, Zhang, Li, Zhao, and Ai (2008) introduced a new pattern called the aliased effect-number pattern (AENP). They showed that the WLP in (1.9) for the MA criterion, the number of clear main effects and the number of clear 2fi's for the CE criterion, and $E_r(D)$ for the MEC criterion can be expressed as specific functions of the AENP. Building on the AENP, Zhang, Li, Zhao, and Ai (2008) further proposed the general minimum lower-order confounding (GMC) criterion. This criterion aims to select a "good" design that minimizes the aliasing between the lower-order effects. Since its first introduction, there has been substantial development and extension of the AENP and the GMC criterion. This book aims to provide a comprehensive account of the modern theory of factorial designs, with the GMC approach as its core.

The organization of the book is as follows. Chapter 2 introduces the AENP and GMC criterion, and discusses the relationship between the GMC and the four criteria mentioned in Section 1.3. Chapter 3 provides methods and results for constructing 2^{n-m} GMC designs. Chapter 4 discusses three different GMC criteria and construction methods for blocked two-level designs. To effectively implement GMC designs in practical applications, Chapter 5 introduces the factor aliased effect-number pattern (F-AENP) and the blocked factor aliased effect-number pattern (B-F-AENP). These patterns are used to rank the columns of regular designs and blocked regular designs, respectively. The concept of the AENP and GMC criterion is further extended to different design types in subsequent chapters: split-plot designs in Chapter 6, compromise designs in Chapter 7, robust parameter designs in Chapter 8, multi-level designs in Chapter 9, and general orthogonal designs in Chapter 10.

2 General Minimum Lower-Order Confounding Criterion for 2^{n-m} Designs

In this chapter, we first introduce the aliased effect-number pattern (AENP), which provides a more explicit description of the aliasing relations of the effects of a 2^{n-m} design compared to the wordlength pattern (WLP). Building upon the AENP, we further define the general minimum lower-order confounding (GMC) criterion for 2^{n-m} designs. Additionally, we will discuss the connections and differences between the GMC criterion and other criteria, namely the maximum resolution criterion, the minimum aberration (MA) criterion, the clear effects (CE) criterion, and the maximum estimation capacity (MEC) criterion, which are discussed in Section 1.3.

2.1 GMC Criterion

Let us begin by defining the concept of AENP for a 2^{n-m} design, where the details of its defining contrast subgroup can be found in Section 1.2, and the corresponding WLP is provided in (1.9).

To describe how the ith-order effects are aliased with the jth-order effects for a given ordered pair (i, j), we need to consider two key elements. Firstly, we must assess the severity with which the ith-order effect is aliased with the jth-order effects and measure the degree of aliased severity. If the ith-order effect is aliased with k

jth-order effects simultaneously, we say that the degree of the ith-order effect being aliased with the jth-order effects is k. Secondly, we consider the number of ith-order effects that are aliased with the jth-order effects at a given aliased severity degree k. We use ${}_i^\#C_j^{(k)}$ to denote this number. For a 2^{n-m} design, we have the following set

$$\{{}_i^\#C_j^{(k)}, i, j = 0, 1, \cdots, n, k = 0, 1, \cdots, K_j\}, \tag{2.1}$$

where $K_j = \binom{n}{j}$. The set reflects the overall confounding between effects in a design. It is worth mentioning that the numbers ${}_i^\#C_j^{(k)}$ in (2.1) are not symmetric with respect to i and j when $i \neq j$.

The numbers in (2.1) are not equally important and should be arranged appropriately. Estimation of an ith-order effect becomes easier as its degree of aliasing with other effects decreases. If an ith-order effect is aliased at degree 0 with lower-order effects and higher-order effects are negligible, it can be estimated without confounding. Furthermore, since the total number of ith-order effects in a 2^{n-m} design is $\binom{n}{i}$, a larger value of ${}_i^\#C_j^{(0)}$ indicates the less severe confounding of the ith-order effects by jth-order effects. When maximizing the number ${}_i^\#C_j^{(0)}$, a larger value of ${}_i^\#C_j^{(1)}$ also indicates the less severe confounding of the ith-order effects by jth-order effects, and so on. Since the larger the degree k, the more severely the effect is aliased, we should rank the numbers of aliased ith-order effects with jth-order effects in $\{{}_i^\#C_j^{(k)}, k = 0, 1, \cdots, K_j\}$ from degree 0 to the most severe degree. This ranking can be represented as the order given by the vector:

$$_i^\#C_j = ({}_i^\#C_j^{(0)}, {}_i^\#C_j^{(1)}, \cdots, {}_i^\#C_j^{(K_j)}), \tag{2.2}$$

which simply shows a distribution of the numbers of ith-order effects aliased with jth-order effects on the degrees $k = 0, 1, \cdots, K_j$. Note that the 0th-order effect corresponds to the identity element I in the defining contrast subgroup. To save space, for a vector ${}_i^\#C_j$, we use 0^s to denote s successive zero components in it, and if it has a tail with successive zero components we cut the tail part hereafter.

Next, we consider the ranking of the different vectors ${}_i^\#C_j$'s. First we ignore ${}_0^\#C_0$, ${}_0^\#C_1$, and ${}_1^\#C_0$ since ${}_0^\#C_0 = (1)$, ${}_0^\#C_1 = (1)$, and ${}_1^\#C_0 = (n)$ for the 2^{n-m} designs. According to the effect hierarchy principle, we should rank ${}_1^\#C_1$ first, and then consider the vectors related to 2fi's. For every $i \geqslant 2$, consider the two vectors ${}_0^\#C_i = (0^{A_i}, 1)$

and $^{\#}_iC_0 = (^{\#}_iC_0^{(0)}, ^{\#}_iC_0^{(1)})$, where A_i denotes the numer of words with length i in the defining contrast subgroup. Obviously, $^{\#}_0C_i$ should be placed before $^{\#}_iC_0$ because the 0th-order effect is more important. Since the latter can be determined by the former for every i, we can ignore all $^{\#}_iC_0$'s. Next, if the 2fi's are not negligible, then we should rank the vectors $^{\#}_0C_2$, $^{\#}_1C_2$, $^{\#}_2C_1$, and $^{\#}_2C_2$ in order as $(^{\#}_0C_2, ^{\#}_1C_2, ^{\#}_2C_1, ^{\#}_2C_2)$. The reason for placing $^{\#}_0C_2$ first is related to whether the grand mean effect can be estimated under the assumption that 2fi's cannot be neglected; putting $^{\#}_1C_2$ before $^{\#}_2C_1$ is due to the fact that the main effects are more important than 2fi's; $^{\#}_2C_2$ should be placed last. If the third-order effects are not negligible, following the similar arguments, we should rank the vectors $^{\#}_0C_3$, $^{\#}_1C_3$, $^{\#}_2C_3$, $^{\#}_3C_1$, $^{\#}_3C_2$, and $^{\#}_3C_3$ in order as $(^{\#}_0C_3, ^{\#}_1C_3, ^{\#}_2C_3, ^{\#}_3C_1, ^{\#}_3C_2, ^{\#}_3C_3)$, and so on. The general rule can be described as follows:

(i) if $\max\{i,j\} < \max\{s,t\}$, then $^{\#}_iC_j$ is placed ahead of $^{\#}_sC_t$;

(ii) if $\max\{i,j\} = \max\{s,t\}$ and $i < s$, then $^{\#}_iC_j$ is placed ahead of $^{\#}_sC_t$;

(iii) if $\max\{i,j\} = \max\{s,t\}$, $i = s$ and $j < t$, then $^{\#}_iC_j$ is placed ahead of $^{\#}_sC_t$.

Therefore, according to the effect hierarchy principle, we rank the numbers in (2.1) as

$$^{\#}C = (^{\#}_1C_1, ^{\#}_0C_2, ^{\#}_1C_2, ^{\#}_2C_1, ^{\#}_2C_2, ^{\#}_0C_3, ^{\#}_1C_3, ^{\#}_2C_3, ^{\#}_3C_1, ^{\#}_3C_2, ^{\#}_3C_3,$$

$$^{\#}_0C_4, ^{\#}_1C_4, ^{\#}_2C_4, ^{\#}_3C_4, ^{\#}_4C_1, ^{\#}_4C_2, ^{\#}_4C_3, ^{\#}_4C_4, \cdots). \qquad (2.3)$$

We call the ordering (2.3) an *aliased effect-number pattern* (AENP). Such a pattern, as well as (2.1), contains the basic information of all effects aliased with other effects at varying degrees in a design.

A main purpose of experimental design is to estimate as many factorial effects as possible, especially the lower-order effects, e.g., the main effects and 2fi's. So, a "good" design should minimize the confounding between the lower-order effects and hence should maximize the entries of $^{\#}C$ sequentially (Zhang, Li, Zhao, and Ai, 2008).

As discussed in Section 1.3.1, our focus is on designs with a resolution of at least *III*. Then $^{\#}_1C_1 = (n)$ and $^{\#}_0C_2 = (1)$. Note that some of the terms in (2.3) are uniquely determined by others that precede them and hence are redundant under the GMC criterion (Zhang and Mukerjee, 2009a). In a design of resolution III or higher, any jth-order effect $(j \geqslant 2)$ is aliased with at most one main effect, and the number of jth-order effects that are aliased with one main effect equals $\sum_{k \geqslant 1} k \, {}^{\#}_1 C_j^{(k)}$. Hence,

$$
{}^{\#}_j C_1^{(1)} = \sum_{k \geqslant 1} k \, {}^{\#}_1 C_j^{(k)}, \quad {}^{\#}_j C_1^{(0)} = K_j - {}^{\#}_j C_1^{(1)} - A_j, \quad {}^{\#}_j C_1^{(k)} = 0 \quad (k \geqslant 2).
$$

Furthermore, an inspection of the manners in which a defining word can entail aliasing of a main effect with a jth-order one shows that

$$
\sum_{k \geqslant 1} k \, {}^{\#}_1 C_j^{(k)} = (n - j + 1) A_{j-1} + (j + 1) A_{j+1},
$$

where A_j is the number of defining words with length j in the defining contrast subgroup for $j = 1, \cdots, n$, and $A_{n+1} = 0$. Thus, the ${}^{\#}_0 C_j \, (j \geqslant 3)$ in (2.3) can be dropped as they are uniquely determined by the preceding terms ${}^{\#}_1 C_u, 2 \leqslant u \leqslant j - 1$. Similarly, the ${}^{\#}_j C_1 \, (j \geqslant 2)$ are redundant because of the terms ${}^{\#}_1 C_u, 2 \leqslant u \leqslant j$. As a result, the GMC criterion is defined on a simpler version of (2.3), as given by

$$
{}^{\#}C = ({}^{\#}_1 C_2, {}^{\#}_2 C_2, {}^{\#}_1 C_3, {}^{\#}_2 C_3, {}^{\#}_3 C_2, {}^{\#}_3 C_3, \cdots). \tag{2.4}
$$

Definition 2.1   *Let ${}^{\#}C_l$ be the l-th component of ${}^{\#}C$, and ${}^{\#}C(D)$ and ${}^{\#}C(D')$ the AENPs of designs D and D', respectively. Suppose that ${}^{\#}C_l$ is the first component such that ${}^{\#}C_l(D)$ and ${}^{\#}C_l(D')$ are different. If ${}^{\#}C_l(D) > {}^{\#}C_l(D')$, then D is said to have less general lower-order confounding (GLOC) than D'. A design D is said to have general minimum lower-order confounding if no other design has less GLOC than D, and such a design is called a GMC design.*

The following result follows directly from the definition of GMC design.

Theorem 2.2   *A GMC 2^{n-m} design must have maximum resolution among all 2^{n-m} designs.*

Fries and Hunter (1980) proved that the defining contrast subgroup of an MA design contains all the letters of the design. In the following, we will prove that a GMC design also possesses this property (Guo, Zhou, and Zhang, 2014). To begin with, we introduce a helpful lemma.

Lemma 2.3   *Consider two 2^{n-m} designs D and D' with resolution R. Let $G_i(D)$ denote the set of defining words with length i in the defining contrast subgroup of D, and let $G_i(D')$ be similarly defined for D'. If $G_R(D)$ is a subset of $G_R(D')$ and*

$G_R(D) \neq G_R(D')$, *then D has less GLOC than D'.*

Proof. For all the pairs (i, j)'s with $i + j < R$, we have

$$\overset{\#}{i}C_j(D) = \overset{\#}{i}C_j(D') = (K_i, 0, \cdots, 0),$$

where $K_i = \binom{n}{i}$. Consider the two cases of $i + j = R$: (a) $(i, j) = (R/2, R/2)$ when R is an even number; (b) $(i, j) = ((R-1)/2, (R+1)/2)$ when R is an odd number.

The proofs for (a) and (b) are similar and we only prove (a). Recall that

$$\sum_{k=0}^{K_j} \overset{\#}{i}C_j^{(k)} = \binom{n}{i}$$

and note that $G_R(D)$ is a proper subset of $G_R(D')$. Denote $i_0 = j_0 = R/2$. There is at least a defining word of length R of D' which is not a defining word of D and attributes to $\overset{\#}{i_0}C_{j_0}^{(k)}(D')$ for some $k > 0$. Then we have

$$\sum_{k=1}^{K_{j_0}} \overset{\#}{i_0}C_{j_0}^{(k)}(D') > \sum_{k=1}^{K_{j_0}} \overset{\#}{i_0}C_{j_0}^{(k)}(D)$$

and thus $\overset{\#}{i_0}C_{j_0}^{(0)}(D) > \overset{\#}{i_0}C_{j_0}^{(0)}(D')$. The result follows immediately. $\square$

Using Lemma 2.3, we can get the following theorem.

Theorem 2.4 *For a GMC 2^{n-m} design, its defining contrast subgroup must contain all the factors.*

Proof. We need only to prove that a 2^{n-m} design whose defining contrast subgroup does not contain all the factors is not a GMC design.

Suppose D is a 2^{n-m} design with resolution R and v_1 is a defining word with length R. Denote the factors of D as $d_i, i = 1, \cdots, n$. Without loss of generality, suppose its defining contrast subgroup does not contain d_n. Suppose $v_1, v_2, \cdots, v_m$ are m independent defining words of D. Consider another 2^{n-m} design D' with $d_n v_1, v_2, \cdots, v_m$ as its m independent defining words. Clearly, we have $R(D) \leqslant R(D')$. If $R(D) = R(D')$, then $G_R(D)$ is a subset of $G_R(D')$ and $G_R(D) \neq G_R(D')$. Hence, D' has less GLOC than D by Lemma 2.3. If $R(D) < R(D')$, then D' has less GLOC than D obviously. Both results mean that the design D must not be a GMC design and hence the theorem is proved. $\square$

Theorem 2.4 serves as a valuable guideline when searching for GMC designs. Taking advantage of this property, Guo, Zhou, and Zhang (2014) successfully constructed all GMC 2^{n-m} designs with $m \leqslant 4$. For the convenience of presentation, we defer the details of these constructions to Appendix A. Zhang, Li, Zhao, and Ai (2008) tabulated all GMC designs of 16 and 32 runs, and the GMC designs of 64 runs with $n \leqslant 32$. Some of these designs are provided in Appendix B.

In the following three sections, we explore the relationship between the GMC criterion and other existing criteria.

2.2　Relationship with MA Criterion

In order to study the relationship between the GMC and MA criteria, we need to establish the relationship between the WLP and AENP as the cores of MA and GMC, respectively. Recall that A_j $(j = 1, \cdots, n)$ is the number of defining words with length j in the defining contrast subgroup for a 2^{n-m} design.

Theorem 2.5　*For a 2^{n-m} design with resolution at least III, its WLP in (1.9) is a function of $\{{}^{\#}_i C_j^{(k)}, i, j = 0, 1, \cdots, n, k = 1, \cdots, K_j\}$ in the following forms:*

(a) ${}^{\#}_i C_0^{(0)} = \binom{n}{i} - A_i$ *or* ${}^{\#}_i C_0^{(1)} = A_i$;

(b) *For any i, A_i is a function of ${}_s C_t, s, t = 1, \cdots, n$, in (2.5) in the proof, where ${}_s C_t$ is a function of $\{{}^{\#}_s C_t^{(k)}, k = 1, \cdots, K_t\}$ as in (2.7) in the proof, and sequentially minimizing A_i's in (1.9) is equivalent to sequentially minimizing ${}_s C_t$'s of C in (2.6);*

(c) *More specifically,*

$$A_3 = \frac{1}{3} \sum_{k=1}^{K_2} k \, {}^{\#}_1 C_2^{(k)}, \quad A_4 = \frac{1}{6} \sum_{k=1}^{K_2} k \, {}^{\#}_2 C_2^{(k)},$$

and

$$A_5 = \frac{1}{6} \left\{ \sum_{k=1}^{K_3} k \, {}^{\#}_2 C_3^{(k)} - (n-3) \sum_{k=1}^{K_2} k \, {}^{\#}_1 C_2^{(k)} \right\}.$$

Proof.　By the definition of the AENP, Part (a) is trivial.

For a 2^{n-m} design with resolution at least III, Zhang and Park (2000) defined ${}_i C_j$ as the number of alias relations of ith-order interactions which are aliased by jth-order interactions in a design, and obtained, for $i \leqslant j$,

$${}_i C_j = \sum_{l=0}^{i} \binom{n - (j - i + 2l)}{i - l} \binom{j - i + 2l}{l} A_{j-i+2l}, \quad i, j = 1, 2, \cdots, n, \qquad (2.5)$$

where $\binom{x}{0} = 1$, $\binom{x}{y} = 0$ for $x < y$ or $x < 0$, and $A_i = 0$ for $i \leqslant 2$ or $i > n$.

Furthermore, they proposed using the sequence

$$C = (_1C_1,\ _1C_2,\ _2C_2,\ _1C_3,\ _2C_3,\ _3C_3,\ _1C_4,\ _2C_4,\ _3C_4,\ _4C_4,\ \cdots) \tag{2.6}$$

to choose optimal designs. Based on (2.5), they showed that sequences (1.9) and (2.6) can be determined from each other, and that sequentially minimizing (2.6) is equivalent to sequentially minimizing (1.9).

By the definition of $_iC_j$, and comparing with the definition of alias sets for a regular design, it is easy to get the following relations for all i, j:

$$_iC_j = \sum_{k=1}^{K_j} k\ {}_i^{\#}C_j^{(k)}. \tag{2.7}$$

Thus, Part (b) is proved.

By using (2.5) and (2.7), Part (c) follows directly.   □

From Theorem 2.5, we have the following corollary.

Corollary 2.6 *The designs with different WLPs must have different AENPs.*

The converse of the corollary does not hold; designs with different AENPs may have the same WLP. The following example illustrates two such designs.

Example 2.7 Consider the two 2^{12-7} designs:

$$D_1 : I = 126 = 137 = 238 = 12349 = 1235t_0 = 45t_1 = 12345t_2,$$

$$D_2 : I = 126 = 137 = 248 = 349 = 125t_0 = 135t_1 = 145t_2,$$

where t_0, t_1, and t_2 denote the factors 10, 11, and 12, respectively. The designs D_1 and D_2 have the same WLP

$$W = (8, 15, 24, 32, 24, 15, 8, 0, 0, 1),$$

but their AENPs are different. In particular, they first differ at ${}_2^{\#}C_2^{(1)}(D_1) = 60$ and ${}_2^{\#}C_2^{(1)}(D_2) = 54$.   □

Consequently, the AENP is a more refined pattern than the WLP for judging designs; the WLP is only related to the part $\{{}_i^{\#}C_0^{(1)}, i = 1, \cdots\}$ of the AENP.

On the other hand, from Part (b) of Theorem 2.5, we can see that the MA criterion only uses the information from

$$\{{}_i^{\#}C_j^{(k)}, i, j = 0, 1, \cdots, n, k = 1, \cdots, K_j\}$$

without $\{{}_i^{\#}C_j^{(0)}, i, j = 0, 1, \cdots, n\}$. We note that although ${}_i^{\#}C_j^{(0)}$ can determine the sum $\sum_{k=1}^{K_j} {}_i^{\#}C_j^{(k)}$, it cannot determine the vector $({}_i^{\#}C_j^{(1)}, \cdots, {}_i^{\#}C_j^{(K_j)})$ and

$$_iC_j = \sum_{k=1}^{K_j} k \, {}_i^{\#}C_j^{(k)}.$$

Therefore, it is possible for two designs D and D' with

$$_i^{\#}C_j^{(0)}(D) > {}_i^{\#}C_j^{(0)}(D')$$

to have

$$\sum_{k=1}^{K_j} {}_i^{\#}C_j^{(k)}(D) < \sum_{k=1}^{K_j} {}_i^{\#}C_j^{(k)}(D'),$$

and at the same time to have

$$_iC_j(D) = \sum_{k=1}^{K_j} k \, {}_i^{\#}C_j^{(k)}(D) > {}_iC_j(D') = \sum_{k=1}^{K_j} k \, {}_i^{\#}C_j^{(k)}(D').$$

Example 2.8 Consider the two 2^{9-4} designs in Section 1.3.3:

$D_3:$ I $= 1236 = 1247 = 1258 = 13459 = 3467 = 3568 = 24569 = 4578 = 23579$

$= 23489 = 12345678 = 15679 = 14689 = 13789 = 26789,$

$D_4:$ I $= 1236 = 1247 = 1348 = 23459 = 3467 = 2468 = 14569 = 2378 = 13579$

$= 12589 = 1678 = 25679 = 35689 = 45789 = 123456789.$

Although

$$_2^{\#}C_2^{(0)}(D_3) = 8 < {}_2^{\#}C_2^{(0)}(D_4) = 15,$$

we still have

$$_2C_2(D_3) = (1 \times 24 + 3 \times 4)/2 = 18 < {}_2C_2(D_4) = (2 \times 21)/2 = 21.$$

Thus, by sequentially minimizing (2.6), the MA criterion suggests that D_3 is an MA design and therefore superior to D_4 according to this criterion. On the other hand, based on the effect hierarchy principle, the GMC criterion suggests that D_4 is a GMC design and hence superior to D_3 according to this criterion.

In fact, although both have 9 clear main effects, D_4 has 15 clear 2fi's while D_3 has only 8. Perhaps using only partial information in the AENP is a reason why sometimes the best design obtained by the MA criterion is inferior to the best one obtained by the GMC criterion under the principle above. $\square$

From (2.7), we can see that ${}_iC_j$ is a linear function of the components of ${}_i^{\#}C_j$ with k as the weight of ${}_i^{\#}C_j^{(k)}$, and sequentially maximizing the components of ${}^{\#}C$ tends to sequentially minimize the components of C. Hence, the optimal designs under the

MA and GMC criteria are often consistent especially for designs with small runs (see Tables 2.2 and 2.3 in Appendix B). But there are a significant number of cases where the two criteria yield different optimal designs. More details can be found in Section 3.5. The following is one more example.

Example 2.9 Consider the three 2^{13-7} designs with 64 runs:

$$D_5 : I = 12347 = 34568 = 2459 = 1456t_0 = 256t_1 = 136t_2 = 235t_3,$$

$$D_6 : I = 12347 = 3458 = 2459 = 356t_0 = 256t_1 = 456t_2 = 346t_3,$$

$$D_7 : I = 12347 = 34568 = 2459 = 1456t_0 = 246t_1 = 12356t_2 = 256t_3.$$

The WLPs of D_5, D_6 and D_7 are, respectively, $(0, 14, 28, 24, 24, 17, 12, 8, 0, 0, 0)$, $(0, 26, 12, 24, 28, 13, 20, 0, 4, 0, 0)$, and $(0, 14, 33, 16, 16, 33, 14, 0, 0, 0, 1)$, and the most important parts of their AENPs are shown in Table 2.1.

Table 2.1　Some $^\#_i C_j$'s of designs D_5, D_6, and D_7

	D_5		D_6		D_7	
	$j = 1$	$j = 2$	$j = 1$	$j = 2$	$j = 1$	$j = 2$
$i = 1$	13	13	13	13	13	13
$i = 2$	78	$20, 36, 18, 4$	78	$23, 0, 24, 16, 15$	78	$36, 0, 42$

According to the MA criterion, D_5 is the best one and D_7 follows. However, from Table 2.1, one sees that they all have 13 clear main effects, D_5 has 20 clear 2fi's, D_6 has 23 clear 2fi's, and D_7 has 36 clear 2fi's. Therefore, according to the GMC and CE criteria, their order of optimality should be D_7, D_6, and D_5. The best design D_5 under the MA criterion is not the best one among the three. □

2.3 Relationship with CE Criterion

In order to study the relationship between the CE criterion and the GMC criterion, we first present two formulas for calculating the numbers of clear effects via the AENP.

Lemma 2.10 *Consider the 2^{n-m} designs with resolution at least III. Then $^\#_1 C_2^{(0)}$ is the number of clear main effects in a design, and $^\#_2 C_2^{(0)} - ^\#_1 C_2^{(1)}$ is the number of clear 2fi's in a design.*

Based on Lemma 2.10 and the related results of Chen and Hedayat (1998), we can easily obtain Theorem 2.11, which shows that the CE criterion is the one maximizing the special functions of the AENP in Lemma 2.10.

Theorem 2.11   (a) When $n \leqslant 2^{n-m-1}$, the CE criterion selects the 2^{n-m} designs sequentially maximizing $\#_1 C_2^{(0)}$ and $\#_2 C_2^{(0)}$ as the optimal ones;

(b) when $2^{n-m-1} < n < 2^{n-m} - 1$, there exist only the designs with resolution at most III, and any 2^{n-m} design with resolution III has neither any clear main effect nor any clear 2fi;

(c) for given n and m, if optimal designs under the clear effects criterion exist, then the GMC design must be the best one among all optimal designs under the CE criterion, where the meaning of "best" is under the comparison in Definition 2.1 of the GMC criterion.

Now let us discuss the links between the MA and CE criteria. Consider the designs with resolution at least III. From the analysis in Section 2.2 and Theorem 2.11, we have found that the MA criterion only uses the information from $\{\#_i C_j^{(k)}, i, j = 0, 1, \cdots, n, k = 1, \cdots, K_j\}$ at (2.1), and choosing optimal designs by the CE criterion only uses the information from $\{\#_i C_j^{(0)}, i, j = 0, 1, \cdots, n\}$. This implies that the information used comes from the two separate parts of the set (2.1). As mentioned above, the two parts have the relation

$$\#_i C_j^{(0)} + \sum_{k=1}^{K_j} \#_i C_j^{(k)} = \binom{n}{i}$$

for any i and j. Thus the larger $\#_i C_j^{(0)}$ we choose, the smaller the number $\sum_{k=1}^{K_j} \#_i C_j^{(k)}$ we obtain. In many cases, when $\#_i C_j^{(0)}$ is large, the weighted sum $_i C_j = \sum_{k=1}^{K_j} k \#_i C_j^{(k)}$ tends to be small. Thus sequentially maximizing the sequence $(\#_1 C_2^{(0)}, \#_2 C_2^{(0)}, \cdots)$ tends to sequentially minimize the sequence (2.6). Perhaps this is the reason why, in many cases, the two criteria would give the same optimal designs. However, although the relationship between the number $\#_i C_j^{(0)}$ and the sum $\sum_{k=1}^{K_j} \#_i C_j^{(k)}$ is rather clear, the same cannot be said for $\#_i C_j^{(0)}$ and the weighted sum $_i C_j = \sum_{k=1}^{K_j} k \#_i C_j^{(k)}$. Therefore, conflicting results from the two criteria may appear, as shown in the examples given.

Return to consider the relationship with CE criterion. While the CE criterion cannot distinguish between designs with the same numbers of clear main effects and

2fi's, the GMC criterion can. The following example illustrates this point.

Example 2.12   Consider the 2^{18-12} designs with 64 runs. According to the CE criterion, there are 33 best designs with 18 clear main effects and no clear 2fi. Two of them are listed in Table 2.4 in Appendix B. Among the 33 designs, under the GMC criterion the best one has

$$_2^\#C_2 = (0, 60, 0^3, 84, 0^2, 9),$$

i.e., it has 60 2fi's each aliased with only one 2fi. The worst one has

$$_2^\#C_2 = (0^3, 36, 75, 42),$$

i.e., every 2fi of the design is aliased with at least three 2fi's, and there are seven such designs. There are 14 designs for which every 2fi is aliased with at least two 2fi's, and 2, 2, 2, 1, and 4 designs that have 32, 8, 6, 4 and 2 2fi's, respectively, each aliased with one 2fi. Obviously, for the best design under the GMC criterion, one can easily de-alias up to 60 2fi's through the least follow-up experiments if needed. But for the other designs, one only can de-alias very few 2fi's by some follow-up experiments, or it is difficult to de-alias any 2fi.   □

Accordingly, in some sense, the GMC criterion can be viewed as a refinement of the CE criterion. Note that the CE criterion cannot be used when there are no clear effects. However, there is no limitation on the use of the GMC criterion, and it provides more information than the CE criterion.

2.4   Relationship with MEC Criterion

Recall that for $1 \leqslant r \leqslant n(n-1)/2$, $E_r(D)$ is defined to be the number of models containing all the main effects and r 2fi's that can be estimated by the design D. A design D is said to dominate design D' if $E_r(D) \geqslant E_r(D')$ for all r with strict inequality for at least one r. Furthermore, a design that maximizes $E_r(D)$ for all r is said to have the MEC.

Clearly, there are $_2^\#C_2^{(k)}/(k+1)$ alias sets containing $k+1$ 2fi's and $_1^\#C_2^{(k+1)}$ alias sets containing $k+1$ 2fi's and one main effect. Moreover, an alias set contains at most $l = \min\{\lfloor n/2 \rfloor, 2^m\}$ 2fi's. Here, $\lfloor x \rfloor$ denotes the integer part of x. Then all the alias sets containing 2fi's but none of the main effect can be partitioned into l classes.

The i-th class consists of the alias sets that contain $i+1$ 2fi's, $i = 0, 1, \cdots, l-1$. Let $\mathcal{C}_i$ be the i-th class. Then,

$$|\mathcal{C}_i| = {}_2^\#C_2^{(i)}/(i+1) - {}_1^\#C_2^{(i+1)}.$$

Hereafter, $|\cdot|$ denotes the cardinality of a set. Note that $|\mathcal{C}_i|$ may be zero for some i's. Theorem 2.13 follows from the definition of $E_r(D)$ immediately.

Theorem 2.13 $E_r(D)$ *can be expressed as a function of* ${}_1^\#C_2$ *and* ${}_2^\#C_2$ *as*

$$E_r(D) = \begin{cases} \displaystyle\sum_{r_0+\cdots+r_{l-1}=r} \prod_{i=0}^{l-1} \binom{|\mathcal{C}_i|}{r_i}(i+1)^{r_i}, & \text{if } r \leqslant f, \\ 0, & \text{otherwise,} \end{cases} \tag{2.8}$$

where $0 \leqslant r_i \leqslant |\mathcal{C}_i|$, $f = 2^{n-m} - 1 - n$.

Thus, the MEC criterion can be treated as the one that optimizes a special function of the AENP. The following discussion further illuminates this point.

Using the notation in Cheng and Mukerjee (1998), it has been shown that a design D will behave well under the MEC criterion if $\sum_{i=n+1}^{n+f} m_i(D)$ is large and $m_{n+1}(D), \cdots, m_{n+f}(D)$ are close to one another, where $m_i(D)$ is the number of 2fi's in the i-th alias set not containing any main effect. In other words, a design D does well under the MEC criterion if $\sum_{i=n+1}^{n+f} m_i(D)$ is large and $\sum_{i=n+1}^{n+f} m_i^2(D)$ is small. Since

$$\sum_{i=n+1}^{n+f} m_i(D) = \sum_{i=0}^{l-1} |\mathcal{C}_i|(i+1) \quad \text{and} \quad \sum_{i=n+1}^{n+f} m_i^2(D) = \sum_{i=0}^{l-1} |\mathcal{C}_i|(i+1)^2,$$

it follows that a design D that maximizes $\sum_{i=0}^{l-1} |\mathcal{C}_i|(i+1)$ and minimizes $\sum_{i=0}^{l-1} |\mathcal{C}_i|(i+1)^2$ does well under the MEC criterion.

Appendix A: GMC 2^{n-m} Designs with $m \leqslant 4$

In this appendix, we present the results for constructing GMC 2^{n-m} designs with $m \leqslant 4$. The detailed proof can be found in Guo, Zhou, and Zhang (2014).

For $m = 1$, it is evident that the design with the defining relation $I = 12 \cdots n$ corresponds to the GMC 2^{n-1} design. This is because a GMC design must possess maximum resolution, and $I = 12 \cdots n$ is the unique defining relation of the maximum resolution 2^{n-1} design.

For $m = 2$, we first recall the result of constructing MA 2^{n-2} designs due to

Robillard (1968). Let $n = 3u + l$, where $0 \leqslant l < 3$, and define

$$
\begin{cases}
B_1 = 1 \cdots (2u) \text{ and } B_2 = (u+1) \cdots (3u), & \text{if } l = 0, \\
B_1 = 1 \cdots (2u+1) \text{ and } B_2 = (u+1) \cdots (3u+1), & \text{if } l = 1, \\
B_1 = 1 \cdots (2u+1) \text{ and } B_2 = (u+1) \cdots (3u+2), & \text{if } l = 2.
\end{cases}
\tag{2.9}
$$

The following theorem can be used to construct the GMC 2^{n-2} design.

Theorem 2.14 *The 2^{n-2} design D with the defining contrast subgroup*

$$
I = B_1 = B_2 = B_1 B_2,
$$

where B_1 and B_2 are given in (2.9), is a GMC 2^{n-2} design.

Next, we consider the case $m = 3$. Let $n = 7u + l$, where $0 \leqslant l < 7$. Following Chen and Wu (1991), for $i = 1, \cdots, 7$, we define

$$
B_i =
\begin{cases}
((i-1)u+1) \cdots (iu)(7u+i), & \text{for } i \leqslant l, \\
((i-1)u+1) \cdots (iu), & \text{for other } i\text{'s.}
\end{cases}
\tag{2.10}
$$

We have the following theorem:

Theorem 2.15 *Let D be the 2^{n-3} design with the defining contrast subgroup*

$$
I = B_7 B_6 B_4 B_3 = B_7 B_5 B_4 B_2 = B_6 B_5 B_4 B_1
$$

$$
= B_6 B_5 B_3 B_2 = B_7 B_5 B_3 B_1 = B_7 B_6 B_2 B_1 = B_4 B_3 B_2 B_1,
$$

where the B_i's are given in (2.10). Then, D is a GMC 2^{n-3} design if the resolution of D is at least III.

Now, we consider the case $m = 4$. Similar to the case $m = 3$, write $n = 15u + l$, where $0 \leqslant l < 15$. Divide the n letters into 15 approximately equal blocks, denoted by $B_1, \cdots, B_{15}$, as follows:

$$
B_i =
\begin{cases}
((i-1)u+1) \cdots (iu)(15u+i), & \text{for } i \leqslant l, \\
((i-1)u+1) \cdots (iu), & \text{for other } i\text{'s.}
\end{cases}
$$

When $l \neq 5$, define the four words as

$$
\{B_{15} B_{14} B_{12} B_9 B_8 B_7 B_6 B_1, \quad B_{15} B_{13} B_{11} B_9 B_8 B_7 B_5 B_2
$$

$$
B_{15} B_{14} B_{11} B_{10} B_8 B_6 B_5 B_3, \quad B_{15} B_{13} B_{12} B_{10} B_7 B_6 B_5 B_4\}.
\tag{2.11}
$$

When $l = 5$, switch B_{15} and B_5 in (2.11). Recall that the 2^{9-4} GMC design is given in Example 2.8. When $n \neq 9$, we have the following theorem.

Theorem 2.16 *When $n \neq 9$, the 2^{n-4} design D generated by the four words in (2.11) is a GMC design if D has the resolution at least III.*

Appendix B: GMC 2^{n-m} Designs with 16, 32, and 64 Runs

In this Appendix, we tabulate some GMC 2^{n-m} designs with 16, 32, and 64 runs. We also include some simple comparisons with the results of the MA and CE criteria. Some explanations are given below.

For simplicity, in the first part of the table, we use n-m.i to denote the i-th good design, according to the GMC criterion, among all 2^{n-m} designs.

A 2^{n-m} design can be obtained by selecting a subset of n columns from the saturated design H_q, consisting of $n - m$ independent columns, $1, \cdots, q$, and m additional columns. In the second part ("Additional Columns") of the table, the column numbers for m additional columns correspond to those in H_q in Yates order.

Table 2.2 **16-run GMC designs and comparisons with the MA and CE criteria**

Design	Additional Columns	AENP $^{\#}_1C_2; {}^{\#}_2C_2$	WLP $A_3, \cdots, A_6$	Cs c_1, c_2	Order G,M,C
6-2.1	14 7	6; 0,12,3	0,3,0,0	6,0	1,1,1
6-2.3	12 6	1,4,1; 9,6	2,1,0,0	1,5	3,4,3
6-2.4	12 3	0,6; 15	2,0,0,1	0,9	4,3,4
7-3.1	14 7 11	7; 0^2,21	0,7,0,0	7,0	1,1,1
7-3.3	12 6 10	1,0,6; 6,12,3	4,3,0,0	1,6	3,5,3
7-3.5	12 6 3	0,5,2; 9,12	3,2,1,1	0,4	5,3,4
8-4.1	14 7 11 13	8; 0^3,28	0,14,0,0	8,0	1,1,1
8-4.2	14 7 3 5	2,0,6; 0,24,0,4	4,6,4,0	2,0	2,4,2
8-4.3	14 7 11 3	1,6,0,1; 7,0,21	3,7,4,0	1,1	3,2,4
8-4.4	12 6 10 14	1,0^2,7; 7,0,21	7,7,0,0	1,7	4,6,3
8-4.5	14 7 3 12	0,4,4; 4,18,6	4,5,4,2	0,0	5,3,-
9-5.1	14 7 11 13 3	0,8,0^2,1; 8,0^2,28	4,14,8,0	0,0	1,1,-
9-5.2	14 7 11 3 6	0,2,5,2; 2,12,18,4	6,10,8,4	0,0	2,3,-
9-5.3	12 6 10 14 3	0,2,0,6,1; 2,12,18,4	8,10,4,4	0,0	3,5,-
9-5.4	14 7 3 12 9	0^2,9; 0,18,18	6,9,9,6	0,0	4,2,-
9-5.5	14 7 3 12 6	0^2,6,3; 0,18,18	7,9,6,6	0,0	5,4,-
10-6.1	14 7 11 13 3 6	0^2,8,0,2; 0,16,0,24,5	8,18,16,8	0,0	1,1,-
10-6.3	12 6 10 14 3 5	0^2,3,4,3; 0,6,27,12	10,16,12,12	0,0	3,4,-
10-6.4	14 7 3 12 6 15	0^3,10; 0^2,45	10,15,12,15	0,0	4,3,-
11-7.1	14 7 11 13 3 6 12	0^3,8,3; 0^2,24,16,15	12,26,28,24	0,0	1,1,-
11-7.2	14 7 11 13 3 6 5	0^3,8,0,3; 0^2,24,16,15	13,26,24,24	0,0	2,3,-
11-7.3	14 7 3 12 9 6 5	0^3,5,6; 0^2,15,40	13,25,25,27	0,0	3,2,-
12-8.1	14 7 11 13 3 6 12 9	0^4,12; 0^3,48,0,18	16,39,48,48	0,0	1,1,-

The third part of the table is the AENP of the design. Here, we only list $^{\#}_1C_2$ and $^{\#}_2C_2$. We also list the WLP (A_3 to A_6) and the numbers $\{c_1, c_2\}$ of clear main effects and clear 2fi's for comparison in the fourth and fifth parts of the table, respectively. In the last part, the optimality order-numbers of the designs under the GMC, MA, and CE criteria, respectively, in all the non-isomorphic 2^{n-m} designs are listed, where the subscript s of r_s in this part indicates the number of non-isomorphic designs which have the same order-number r under its corresponding criterion, and "-" means no clear main effects and 2fi's. For parameters $n = 2^{n-m} - i$, $i = 1, 2, 3$, the design is unique up to isomorphism and hence is omitted.

Table 2.3 32-run GMC designs and comparisons with the MA and CE criteria

Design	Additional Columns	AENP $_1^{\#}C_2; {}_2^{\#}C_2$	WLP $A_3, \cdots, A_6$	Cs c_1, c_2	Order G,M,C
7-2.1	30 7	7; 15,6	0,1,2,0	7,15	1,1,1
8-3.1	30 7 11	8; 13,12,3	0,3,4,0	8,13	1,1,1
9-4.1	30 7 11 13	9; 15,0,21	0,7,7,0	9,15	1,2,1
9-4.2	30 7 11 19	9; 8,24,0,4	0,6,8,0	9,8	2,1,2$_2$
9-4.3	28 14 22 26	9; 8,0^2,28	0,14,0,0	9,8	3,5,2$_2$
10-5.1	30 7 11 19 29	10; 0,40,0^2,5	0,10,16,0	10,0	1,1,1$_4$
11-6.1	28 14 22 26 7 11	11; 0^2,24,16,15	0,26,0,24	11,0	1,2,1$_2$
11-6.2	28 14 7 19 25 11	11; 0^2,15,40	0,25,0,27	11,0	2,1,1$_2$
12-7.1	28 14 22 26 7 11 13	12; 0^3,48,0,18	0,39,0,48	12,0	1,2,1$_2$
12-7.2	28 14 7 19 25 11 13	12; 0^3,36,30	0,38,0,52	12,0	2,1,1$_2$
13-8.1	28 14 22 26 7 11 13 19	13; 0^4,60,18	0,55,0,96	13,0	1,1,1
14-9.1	28 14 22 26 7 11 13 19 21	14; 0^5,84,7	0,77,0,168	14,0	1,1,1
15-10.1	28 14 22 26 7 11 13 19 21 25	15; 0^6,105	0,105,0,280	15,0	1,1,1
16-11.1	28 14 22 26 7 11 13 19 21 25 31	16; 0^7,120	0,140,0,448	16,0	1,1,1
17-12.1	28 14 22 26 7 11 13 19 21 25 31 3	0,16,0^6,1; 16,0^6,120	8,140,112,448	0,0	1,1,-
18-13.1	28 14 22 26 7 11 13 19 21 25 31 3 6	0^2,16,0^5,2; 0,32,0^5,112,9	16,148,224,560	0,0	1,1,-
19-14.1	28 14 22 26 7 11 13 19 21 25 31 3 6 12	0^3,16,0^4,3; 0^2,48,0^4,96,27	24,164,344,784	0,0	1,1,-
20-15.1	28 14 22 26 7 11 13 19 21 25 31 3 6 12 9	0^4,16,0^3,4; 0^3,64,0^3,96,0,30	32,189,480,1120	0,0	1,2,-
20-15.2	28 14 22 26 7 11 13 19 21 25 31 3 6 12 24	0^4,16,0^3,4; 0^3,64,0^3,72,54	32,188,480,1128	0,0	2,1,-
21-16.1	28 14 22 26 7 11 13 19 21 25 31 3 6 12 9 24	0^5,16,0^2,5; 0^4,80,0^2,64,36,30	40,221,640,1600	0,0	1,2,-
21-16.2	28 14 22 26 7 11 13 19 21 25 31 3 6 12 24 17	0^5,16,0^2,5; 0^4,80,0^2,40,90	40,220,641,1608	0,0	2,1,-
22-17.1	28 14 22 26 7 11 13 19 21 25 31 3 6 12 9 24 18	0^6,16,0,6; 0^5,96,0,64,0,60,11	48,263,832,2224	0,0	1,1,-
23-18.1	28 14 22 26 7 11 13 19 21 25 31 3 6 12 9 24 18 23	0^7,16,7; 0^6,112,64,0^2,77	56,315,1064,3024	0,0	1,1,-
24-19.1	28 14 22 26 7 11 13 19 21 25 31 3 6 12 9 24 18 23 29	0^8,24; 0^7,192,0^3,84	64,378,1344,4032	0,0	1,1,
25-20.1	28 14 22 26 7 11 13 19 21 25 31 3 6 12 9 24 18 23 29 5	0^9,24,0^2,1; 0^8,216,0^2,84	76,442,1656,5376	0,0	1,1,-
26-21.1	28 14 22 26 7 11 13 19 21 25 31 3 6 12 9 24 18 23 29 5 10	0^{10},24,0,2; 0^9,240,0,72,13	88,518,2032,7032	0,0	1,1,-
27-22.1	28 14 22 26 7 11 13 19 21 25 31 3 6 12 9 24 18 23 29 5 10 20	0^{11},24,3; 0^{10},264,48,39	100,606,2484,9064	0,0	1,1,-
28-23.1	28 14 22 26 7 11 13 19 21 25 31 3 6 12 9 24 18 23 29 5 10 20 27	0^{12},28; 0^{11},336,0,42	112,707,3024,11536	0,0	1,1,-

Table 2.4   64-run GMC designs and comparisons with the MA and CE criteria

Design	Additional Columns	AENP $_1^{\#}C_2; _2^{\#}C_2$	WLP $A_3, \cdots, A_6$	Cs c_1, c_2	Order G,M,C
8-2.1	60 15	8; 28	0,0,2,1	8,28	1,1,1
9-3.1	60 15 22	9; 30,6	0,1,4,2	9,30	1,1,1
10-4.1	60 15 22 39	10; 33,12	0,2,8,4	10,33	1,1,1
11-5.1	60 15 22 39 21	11; 34,18,3	0,4,14,8	11,34	1,1,1
12-6.1	60 15 22 39 21 59	12; 36,24,6	0,6,24,16	12,36	1,1,1
13-7.1	60 15 22 39 21 59 19	13; 36,0,42	0,14,33,16	13,36	1,2,1
13-7.2	60 14 22 11 19 7 13	13; 23,0,24,16,15	0,26,12,24	13,23	2,37,2
13-7.7	60 15 22 39 19 41 26	13; 20,36,18,4	0,14,28,24	13,20	7,1,7
14-8.1	60 14 22 11 19 7 13 21	14; 25,0²48,0,18	0,39,16,48	14,25	1,42,1₂
14-8.17	60 15 22 35 26 37 19 46	14; 8,52,18,8,5	0,22,40,36	14,8	17,1,17
15-9.1	60 14 22 11 19 7 13 21 26	15; 27,0³60,18	0,55,22,96	15,27	1,40,1
15-9.27	60 15 22 35 26 37 19 46 59	15; 0,60,30,0,15	0,30,60,60	15,0	27,1,27
16-10.1	60 14 22 11 19 7 13 21 26 25	16; 29,0⁴84,7	0,77,28,168	16,29	1,45,1
16-10.20	60 15 22 35 26 37 19 46 59 29	16; 0,36,66,0²18	0,43,81,96	16,0	20,1,19₃₀
17-11.1	60 14 22 11 19 7 13 21 26 25 31	17; 31,0⁵105	0,105,35,280	17,31	1,38,1
17-11.17	60 15 22 35 26 37 19 49 29 55 41	17; 0,18,81,16,0²21	0,59,108,150	17,0	17,1,17₂₄
18-12.1	60 14 22 11 19 7 13 21 26 25 31 58	18; 0,60,0³84,0²9	0,92,112,280	18,0	1,3,1₃₃
18-12.6	60 15 22 35 26 37 19 49 29 55 41 50	18; 0,6,75,48,0³24	0,78,144,228	18,0	6,1,1₃₃
19-13.1	60 15 22 35 26 49 37 55 19 50 29 46 41	19; 0²48,96,0⁴27	0,100,192,336	19,0	1,1,1₂₅
20-14.1	60 15 22 35 26 49 37 55 19 50 29 46 41 59	20; 0³160,0⁵30	0,125,256,480	20,0	1,1,1₂₄
21-15.1	56 28 44 52 14 22 26 38 42 50 62 7 11 19 13	21; 0⁴80,0²64,36,30	0,221,0,1600	21,0	1,16,1₁₆
21-15.16	56 11 22 37 7 59 28 42 14 49 19 38 21 41 26	21; 0⁵60,126,24	0,204,0,1680	21,0	16,1,1₁₆
22-16.1	56 28 44 52 14 22 26 38 42 50 62 7 11 19 13 21	22; 0⁵96,0,64,0,60,11	0,263,0,2224	22,0	1,15,1₁₅
22-16.14	56 11 22 37 7 59 28 42 14 49 19 38 21 41 26 44	22; 0⁵6,105,120	0,250,0,2304	22,0	14,1,1₁₅
23-17.1	56 28 44 52 14 22 26 38 42 50 62 7 11 19 13 21 25	23; 0⁶112,64,0²77	0,315,0,3024	23,0	1,9,1₉
23-17.8	56 11 22 37 7 59 28 42 14 49 19 38 21 41 26 44 13	23; 0⁶28,144,81	0,304,0,3105	23,0	8,1₂,1₉
23-17.9	56 11 22 37 7 59 28 42 14 49 13 26 47 50 19 21 35	23; 0⁶21,168,54,10	0,304,0,3105	23,0	9,1₂,1₉
24-18.1	56 28 44 52 14 22 26 38 42 50 62 7 11 19 13 21 25 31	24; 0⁷192,0³84	0,378,0,4032	24,0	1,8,1₈
24-18.8	56 11 22 37 7 59 28 42 14 49 13 26 47 50 19 21 35 38	24; 0⁷48,198,30	0,365,0,4138	24,0	8,1,1₈
25-19.1	56 28 44 52 14 22 26 38 42 50 62 7 11 19 13 21 25 31 35	25; 0⁸216,0²84	0,442,0,5376	25,0	1,5,1₅
25-19.5	56 11 22 37 7 59 28 42 14 49 13 26 47 50 19 21 35 38 52	25; 0⁸90,210	0,435,0,5440	25,0	5,1,1₅
26-20.1	56 28 44 52 14 22 26 38 42 50 62 7 11 19 13 21 25 31 35 37	26; 0⁹240,0,72,13	0,518,0,7032	26,0	1,4,1₄
26-20.4	56 11 22 37 7 59 28 42 14 49 13 26 47 50 19 21 35 38 52 25	26; 0⁹160,165	0,515,0,7062	26,0	4,1,1₄
27-21.1	56 11 22 37 7 59 28 42 14 49 13 26 47 50 19 21 35 38 25 31 44	27; 0¹⁰264,48,39	0,606,0,9064	27,0	1,2,1₂
27-21.2	56 11 22 37 7 59 28 42 14 49 13 26 47 50 19 21 35 38 52 55 25	27; 0¹⁰231,120	0,605,0,9075	27,0	2,1,1₂
28-22.1	56 11 22 37 7 59 28 42 14 49 13 26 47 50 19 21 35 38 25 31 44 41	28; 0¹¹336,0,42	0,707,0,11536	28,0	1,2,1₂
28-22.2	56 11 22 37 7 59 28 42 14 49 13 26 47 50 19 21 35 38 52 55 25 31	28; 0¹¹300,78	0,706,0,11548	28,0	2,1,1₂
29-23.1	56 11 22 37 7 59 28 42 14 49 13 26 47 50 19 21 35 38 52 55 25 31 44	29; 0¹²364,42	0,819,0,14560	29,0	1,1,1
30-24.1	56 11 22 37 7 59 28 42 14 49 13 26 47 50 19 21 35 38 52 55 25 31 44 41	30; 0¹³420,15	0,945,0,18200	30,0	1,1,1
31-25.1	56 11 22 37 7 59 28 42 14 49 13 26 47 50 19 21 35 38 52 55 25 31 44 41 62	31; 0¹⁴465	0,1085,0,22568	31,0	1,1,1
32-26.1	56 11 22 37 7 59 28 42 14 49 13 26 47 50 19 21 35 38 52 55 25 31 44 41 62 61	32; 0¹⁵496	0,1240,0,27776	32,0	1,1,1

3 General Minimum Lower-Order Confounding 2^{n-m} Designs

In this chapter, we first present several useful results and the structure of 2^{n-m} designs with resolution IV and $N/4 + 1 \leqslant n \leqslant N/2$, where $N = n^{n-m}$. With these preparations, we present some general methods for constructing GMC 2^{n-m} designs. These methods can be utilized to obtain all GMC 2^{n-m} designs with $N/4 + 1 \leqslant n \leqslant N - 1$. Additionally, we discuss the situations in which GMC designs differ from MA designs.

3.1 Some Preparation

3.1.1 Several Useful Results

Recall that $q = n - m$, H_q is the saturated design in (1.6), and H_r in (1.7) is the design consisting of the first $2^r - 1$ columns of H_q for $1 \leqslant r \leqslant q - 1$. As discussed in Section 1.2, the columns of a 2^{n-m} design D can be taken from H_q. The design consisting of the columns in H_q but not in D is called its *complementary design*, and is denoted as $\bar{D} = H_q \backslash D$.

For the sake of clarity, we introduce some new notations. Given a design $S \subset H_q$ and a column γ in H_q, we define

$$B_2(S, \gamma) = |\{(d_1, d_2) : d_1 \in S, d_2 \in S, d_1 d_2 = \gamma\}|. \tag{3.1}$$

According to this definition, $B_2(S, \gamma)$ is the number of 2fi's in S aliased with γ.

Additionally, we find it useful to define:

$$\bar{g}(S) = |\{\gamma : \gamma \in \bar{S}, B_2(S,\gamma) > 0\}|, \tag{3.2}$$

which is the number of main effects in $\bar{S}$ aliased with at least one 2fi of S.

For example, consider $q = 3$, $S = \{1,2,3,12,23\}$, $\gamma_1 = 12 \in S$, $\gamma_2 = 13 \in \bar{S}$, and $\gamma_3 = 123 \in \bar{S}$. Among the 10 2fi's in S, there are one 2fi (between 1 and 2), two 2fi's (between 1 and 3, and between 12 and 23), and two 2fi's (between 1 and 23, and between 3 and 12), which are aliased with γ_1, γ_2, and γ_3, respectively. Hence, $B_2(S,\gamma_1) = 1$ and $B_2(S,\gamma_2) = B_2(S,\gamma_3) = 2$. Note that $\bar{S} = \{12,123\}$. By the definition of $\bar{g}(S)$ in (3.2), $\bar{g}(S) = 2$.

The following theorem, taken from Zhang and Mukerjee (2009a), investigates the relationships of the key terms of the AENP of D and that of $\bar{D}$.

Theorem 3.1　　*Let D be a 2^{n-m} design and $\bar{D} = H_q \backslash D$ be its complementary design with the number of columns being $f = 2^{n-m} - 1 - n$. We further assume that $n \geqslant N/2$, i.e., $n - 1 \geqslant f$. Recall that $B_2(\cdot, \cdot)$ is defined in (3.1). Then, we have*

(a) *for any $\gamma \in D$,*

$$B_2(D,\gamma) = \frac{1}{2}(n - f - 1) + B_2(\bar{D}, \gamma), \tag{3.3}$$

and for any $\gamma \notin D$,

$$B_2(D,\gamma) = \frac{1}{2}(n - f + 1) + B_2(\bar{D}, \gamma); \tag{3.4}$$

(b) $_1^\# C_2^{(k)}(D) = |\{\gamma : \gamma \in D, \frac{1}{2}(n - f - 1) + B_2(\bar{D}, \gamma) = k\}|$;

(c) *the design D sequentially maximizes $_1^\# C_2$ only if it minimizes $\bar{g}(\bar{D})$, where $\bar{g}(\bar{D})$ is defined in (3.2) with S being replaced by $\bar{D}$.*

Proof.　For any $\gamma \in H_q$, there are $(2^q - 2)/2$ 2fi's aliased with γ. Among these, $B_2(D,\gamma)$ 2fi's have both factors from D, and $B_2(\bar{D},\gamma)$ 2fi's have both factors from $\bar{D}$. The remaining 2fi's consist of one factor from D and the other from $\bar{D}$. Hence, for $\gamma \in D$,

$$n - 1 - 2B_2(D,\gamma) = f - 2B_2(\bar{D},\gamma),$$

which implies that

$$B_2(D,\gamma) = \frac{1}{2}(n - f - 1) + B_2(\bar{D},\gamma);$$

for $\gamma \notin D$,

$$n - 2B_2(D, \gamma) = f - 1 - 2B_2(\bar{D}, \gamma),$$

which implies that

$$B_2(D, \gamma) = \frac{1}{2}(n - f + 1) + B_2(\bar{D}, \gamma).$$

This finishes (a).

For (b), by the definition of ${}_1^{\#}C_2^{(k)}(D)$ in Section 2.1, we get

$${}_1^{\#}C_2^{(k)}(D) = |\{\gamma : \gamma \in D, B_2(D, \gamma) = k\}|.$$

By using (3.3), we have

$${}_1^{\#}C_2^{(k)}(D) = |\{\gamma : \gamma \in D, \frac{1}{2}(n - f - 1) + B_2(\bar{D}, \gamma) = k\}|.$$

This finishes (b).

For (c), we notice that ${}_1^{\#}C_2^{(k)}(D) = 0$ when $k < (n - f - 1)/2$ and ${}_1^{\#}C_2^{(k)}(D) = n - \bar{g}(\bar{D})$ when $k = (n - f - 1)/2$. Hence, to sequentially maximize ${}_1^{\#}C_2$, we need to minimize $\bar{g}(\bar{D})$ first. This finishes (c). □

As we can see in Theorem 3.1, minimizing $\bar{g}(\cdot)$ is an important step in the search for a GMC design. Li, Zhao, and Zhang (2011) gave a general result which describes the structure of designs that minimize $\bar{g}(\cdot)$ and plays a key role in the construction of GMC designs in this chapter. We need some additional notations. Define

$$S_{pr} = H_p \backslash H_r, \tag{3.5}$$

$$F_{jr} = (j, jH_{r-1}) \tag{3.6}$$

for $p = r + 1, \cdots, q$, $j = r, r + 1, \cdots, q$, and $r = 2, \cdots, q$. Clearly, when $j = r$, $(H_{r-1}, F_{jr}) = H_r$. We also denote $S_{r(r-1)}$ as S_r and F_{rr} as F_r for simplicity. Clearly, $S_r = F_r$. Note that the designs F_{qr} and F_r with $r \geqslant 3$ are isomorphic and the unique saturated resolution IV design with r independent columns. Introducing both notations F_{qr} and F_r is for convenience of presentation.

Theorem 3.2　*Let $S \subset H_q$ be a design with s factors (columns). Under isomorphism, we then have the following conclusions.*

(a) if $2^{r-1} \leqslant s \leqslant 2^r - 1$ for some $r \leqslant q$ and $\bar{g}(S)$ is minimized among all the designs with s factors, then S has r independent factors and $S \subset H_r$;

(b) if $2^{r-2} + 1 \leqslant s \leqslant 2^{r-1}$ for some $r \leqslant q$ and $\bar{g}(S)$ is minimized among all the designs with s factors and resolution at least IV, then S has r independent factors

and $S \subset F_{qr}$ (or F_r);

(c) if $2^{r-2} + 1 \leqslant s \leqslant 2^{r-1}$ for some $r \leqslant q$, then S sequentially maximizes the components of

$$(-\bar{g}(S), {}_2^{\#}C_2(S)) \tag{3.7}$$

among all the designs with s factors and resolution at least IV if and only if S is any one of the following four isomorphic designs: that consisting of the first s columns of F_{qr}; that consisting of the last s columns of F_{qr}; that consisting of the first s columns of F_r; that consisting of the last s columns of F_r. Here F_{qr} and F_r are defined in (3.6) and have Yates order.

The proof of Theorem 3.2 is quite lengthy; we refer to Li, Zhao, and Zhang (2011) for more details.

Combining Theorem 3.1 (b) and Theorem 3.2 (a), we conclude that if $\bar{g}(\bar{D})$ is minimized and the number of columns in $\bar{D}$, $f = 2^{n-m} - 1 - n$, satisfies $2^{r-1} \leqslant f \leqslant 2^r - 1$, then $\bar{D}$ should have r independent factors. A similar observation is also made in Zhang and Mukerjee (2009a) and Hu and Zhang (2011).

3.1.2　Structure of Resolution IV Design with $N/4 + 1 \leqslant n \leqslant N/2$

As indicated in Theorem 2.2, the GMC design should also have the maximum resolution. The following result summarizes the maximum resolution for a 2^{n-m} design with $N/4 + 1 \leqslant n \leqslant N/2$. More details can be found in Wu and Wu (2002).

Lemma 3.3　For a 2^{n-m} design,

(a) the maximum resolution is IV when $N \geqslant 16$ and $N/4 + 1 < n \leqslant N/2$;

(b) the maximum resolution is IV when $N \geqslant 32$ and $n = N/4 + 1$.

In the following, unless explicitly specified, we assume that $N \geqslant 16$ and $N \geqslant 32$ for the two cases: $N/4 + 1 < n \leqslant N/2$ and $n = N/4 + 1$, respectively. In these cases, the maximum resolution of a 2^{n-m} design is IV.

Based on the previous discussion, it is evident that the structure of a resolution IV design plays an important role in constructing GMC 2^{n-m} designs. In the following, we will present a summary of several useful results regarding the structure of a resolution IV design.

Block and Mee (2003) introduced a class of 2^{n-m} factorial designs with resolution *IV*, known as *second-order saturated* (SOS) *designs*. These designs make use of all their degrees of freedom to estimate main effects and 2fi's. Chen and Cheng (2006) proved that SOS designs are *maximal designs*, where a regular design of resolution *IV* or higher is called *maximal* if its resolution reduces to *III* whenever an extra factor is added. For simplicity, unless specifically stated otherwise, we will use the term *SOS design* to refer to both SOS resolution *IV* designs and maximal designs with resolution at least *IV*.

Zhang and Cheng (2010) gave an equivalent definition of SOS designs in terms of the AENP.

Definition 3.4 *A 2^{n-m} design D of $N = 2^{n-m}$ runs is an SOS design if and only if ${}^{\#}_{1}C_2^{(0)}(D) = n$ and $\sum_{k=0}^{K_2} {}^{\#}_{2}C_2^{(k)}(D)/(k+1) = N - n - 1$.*

The following are two examples of SOS designs.

Example 3.5 Consider the 2^{5-1} design with 1, 2, 3, and 4 being independent factors and 5 being determined by $5 = 1234$. This design is a maximal design of resolution *V* (Chen and Cheng, 2006). □

Example 3.6 Consider the 2^{9-4} GMC design in Example 2.8 with the following defining contrast subgroup:

$$I = 1236 = 1247 = 1348 = 23459 = 3467 = 2468 = 14569 = 2378 = 13579$$

$$= 12589 = 1678 = 25679 = 35689 = 45789 = 123456789.$$

This design is the unique 2^{9-4} SOS design or maximal design with resolution *IV* (Chen and Cheng, 2006; Zhang and Cheng, 2010). □

Doubling plays an important role in the construction of maximal designs. To help understand the doubling method, we introduce some further notation. For $1 \leqslant r < s \leqslant t \leqslant q$, let

$$H_{r,s}^t = (r, (r+1), r(r+1), \cdots, s, rs, (r+1)s, \cdots, r \cdots s)_{2^t} \tag{3.8}$$

be the closed subset generated by the independent columns $r_{2^t}, \cdots, s_{2^t}$ in Yates order. That is, $H_{r,s}^t$ consists of the independent columns $r_{2^t}, \cdots, s_{2^t}$ and all their possible component-wise products. If $t = q$, we may omit the superscript if it does not cause confusion. That is,

$$H_{r,s} = H_{r,s}^q. \tag{3.9}$$

Let $X = (x_1, \cdots, x_{n_x}) \subset H_{1,t}^t$ be a $2^t \times n_x$ matrix, and denote $\mathbf{J}_0 = (1,1)'$ and $\mathbf{J}_1 = (-1,1)'$. The double of X, $D(X)$, called a *doubled design*, can be written as the $2^{t+1} \times (2n_x)$ matrix:

$$D(X) = \begin{pmatrix} X & -X \\ X & X \end{pmatrix} = (\mathbf{J}_0 \ \mathbf{J}_1) \otimes X, \tag{3.10}$$

where $\otimes$ is the Kronecker product.

We use $D^{q-t}(X)$, also called a *doubled design*, to denote the matrix obtained by repeatedly doubling X $q-t$ times. That is,

$$D^{q-t}(X) = \underbrace{(\mathbf{J}_0 \ \mathbf{J}_1) \otimes (\mathbf{J}_0 \ \mathbf{J}_1) \otimes \cdots \otimes (\mathbf{J}_0 \ \mathbf{J}_1)}_{q-t \text{ times}} \otimes X = (I_{2^{q-t}}, H_{1,q-t}^{q-t}) \otimes X, \tag{3.11}$$

where $I_{2^{q-t}}$ denotes the column with length 2^{q-t} and all elements being 1. Then, $D^{q-t}(X)$ becomes a $2^q \times (2^{q-t} n_x)$ matrix. Sometimes, we may also write $D(X)$ and $D^{q-t}(X)$ as

$$D(X) = (D(x_1), \cdots, D(x_{n_x})) \quad \text{and} \quad D^{q-t}(X) = (D^{q-t}(x_1), \cdots, D^{q-t}(x_{n_x})).$$

The following are some simple rules to express $D^{q-t}(x_i)$'s in terms of the columns of H_q. Suppose a column in $(I_{2^{q-t}}, H_{1,q-t}^{q-t})$ is labelled as $(1^{a_1} \cdots (q-t)^{a_{q-t}})_{2^{q-t}}$ for some $a_1, \cdots, a_{q-t} \in \{0,1\}$, and a column in X is labelled as $(1^{b_1} \cdots t^{b_t})_{2^t}$ for some $b_1, \cdots, b_t \in \{0,1\}$. After some algebra, it can be verified that

$$(1^{a_1} \cdots (q-t)^{a_{q-t}})_{2^{q-t}} \otimes (1^{b_1} \cdots t^{b_t})_{2^t} = (1^{b_1} \cdots t^{b_t}(t+1)^{a_1} \cdots q^{a_{q-t}})_{2^q}$$
$$= 1^{b_1} \cdots t^{b_t}(t+1)^{a_1} \cdots q^{a_{q-t}} \tag{3.12}$$

and

$$D^{q-t}((1^{b_1} \cdots t^{b_t})_{2^t}) = ((1^{b_1} \cdots t^{b_t})_{2^q}, (1^{b_1} \cdots t^{b_t})_{2^q} H_{t+1,q}^q)$$
$$= (1^{b_1} \cdots t^{b_t}, 1^{b_1} \cdots t^{b_t} H_{t+1,q}). \tag{3.13}$$

For instance,

$$D^{q-4}(1_{2^4}) = (1, 1H_{5,q}) \quad \text{and} \quad D^{q-4}((1234)_{2^4}) = (1234, 1234H_{5,q}).$$

We refer to Chen and Cheng (2006) and Zhang and Cheng (2010) for more details about the properties of the doubling method.

The following theorem summarizes some existing results for SOS designs or maximal designs (Bruen, Haddad, and Wehlau, 1998; Davydov and Tombak, 1990; Chen and Cheng, 2006; Butler, 2007).

Theorem 3.7   (a) *For* $n = N/2$, F_{qq} *or* F_q *is the unique SOS design, up to isomorphism.*

(b) *For* $n = 5N/16$, *the SOS design is unique up to isomorphism, and can be obtained by doubling the* 2^{5-1} *maximal design in Example 3.5* $q - 4$ *times.*

(c) *For* $n \geqslant N/4 + 1$, *an SOS design must have*

$$n \in \{N/2, 5N/16, 9N/32, 17N/64, \cdots, N/4 + 1\}.$$

Conversely, for each integer $n = (2^{t-2} + 1)N/2^t$ *with* $5 \leqslant t \leqslant q$, *there exists at least one* N-*run SOS design with* n *factors, and can be obtained by doubling some maximal design* X *with* $2^{t-2} + 1$ *factors and* 2^t *runs* $q - t$ *times.*

(d) *For* $n > N/4 + 1$, *every regular design of resolution IV is a projection of an SOS design.*

Example 3.8   Let $X = (1, 2, 3, 4, 1234)_{2^4} = (x_1, x_2, x_3, x_4, x_5)$, which is the 2^{5-1} maximal design in Example 3.5.

By using Part (b) of Theorem 3.7, the SOS design with $5N/16$ runs is given by $S_{(5N/16)} = D^{q-4}(X)$. By rearranging the columns, we can write $S_{(5N/16)}$ as

$$S_{(5N/16)} = (D^{q-4}(x_1), D^{q-4}(x_2), D^{q-4}(x_3), D^{q-4}(x_4), D^{q-4}(x_5)). \tag{3.14}$$

We refer to $S_{(5N/16)}$ in (3.14) as having rechanged Yates order (RC Yates order, for short). By using the rule in (3.13), each part of $S_{(5N/16)}$ can be written as

$$D^{q-4}(x_1) = (1, 1H_{5,q}),$$
$$D^{q-4}(x_2) = (2, 2H_{5,q}),$$
$$D^{q-4}(x_3) = (3, 3H_{5,q}), \tag{3.15}$$
$$D^{q-4}(x_4) = (4, 4H_{5,q}),$$
$$D^{q-4}(x_5) = (1234, 1234H_{5,q}).$$

For example, when $q = 6$,

$$D^2(x_1) = (1, 15, 16, 156)_{2^6},$$
$$D^2(x_2) = (2, 25, 26, 256)_{2^6},$$
$$D^2(x_3) = (3, 35, 36, 356)_{2^6},$$

$$D^2(x_4) = (4, 45, 46, 456)_{2^6},$$

$$D^2(x_5) = (1234, 12345, 12346, 123456)_{2^6}.$$

In RC Yates order, the SOS design with 20 columns/factors and 64 runs is

$$S_{(5N/16)} = (1, 15, 16, 156, 2, 25, 26, 256, 3, 35, 36, 356,$$
$$4, 45, 46, 456, 1234, 12345, 12346, 123456)_{2^6}. \tag{3.16}$$

□

Example 3.9 Let

$$X = (1, 2, 3, 4, 5, 123, 124, 134, 2345)_{2^5} = (x_1, x_2, x_3, x_4, x_5, x_6, x_7, x_8, x_9),$$

which is the 2^{9-4} SOS in Example 3.6.

By using Part (c) of Theorem 3.7, the SOS design with $9N/32$ runs is given by $S_{(9N/32)} = D^{q-5}(X)$. With a rearrangement of columns, we can write $S_{(9N/32)}$ as

$$S_{(9N/32)} = (D^{q-5}(x_1), D^{q-5}(x_2), D^{q-5}(x_3), D^{q-5}(x_4), D^{q-5}(x_5),$$
$$D^{q-5}(x_6), D^{q-5}(x_7), D^{q-5}(x_8), D^{q-5}(x_9)). \tag{3.17}$$

We say $S_{(9N/32)}$ in (3.17) to have RC Yates order. Again, using the rule in (3.13), we have

$$D^{q-5}(x_1) = (1, 1H_{6,q}),$$
$$D^{q-5}(x_2) = (2, 2H_{6,q}),$$
$$D^{q-5}(x_3) = (3, 3H_{6,q}),$$
$$D^{q-5}(x_4) = (4, 4H_{6,q}),$$
$$D^{q-5}(x_5) = (5, 5H_{6,q}), \tag{3.18}$$
$$D^{q-5}(x_6) = (123, 123H_{6,q}),$$
$$D^{q-5}(x_7) = (124, 124H_{6,q}),$$
$$D^{q-5}(x_8) = (134, 134H_{6,q}),$$
$$D^{q-5}(x_9) = (2345, 2345H_{6,q}).$$

When $q = 7$, the SOS design with 36 columns/factors and 128 runs in RC Yates order is

$$S_{(9N/32)} = (1, 16, 17, 167, 2, 26, 27, 267, 3, 36, 37, 367, 4, 46, 47, 467,$$
$$5, 56, 57, 567, 123, 1236, 1237, 12367, 124, 1246, 1247, 12467, \tag{3.19}$$
$$134, 1346, 1347, 13467, 2345, 23456, 23457, 234567)_{2^7}.$$

□

3.2 GMC 2^{n-m} Designs with $n \geqslant 5N/16 + 1$

3.2.1 Main Results and Examples

In this section, we present the main results for constructing GMC 2^{n-m} designs with $n \geqslant 5N/16 + 1$ and provide some illustrative examples. For convenience of presentation, the detailed proof will be provided in Section 3.2.2.

Theorem 3.10 *Suppose the columns in H_q and F_q are written in Yates order.*

(a) *For $5N/16 + 1 \leqslant n \leqslant N/2$, the GMC 2^{n-m} design is the design that consists of the last n columns in H_q or F_q.*

(b) *For $n > N/2$, the GMC 2^{n-m} design is the design that consists of the last n columns in H_q.*

The first example illustrates the application of Part (a) of Theorem 3.10.

Example 3.11 Suppose that we require a GMC design with $N = 32$ runs and n factors, where $11 = 5/16N + 1 \leqslant n \leqslant N/2 = 16$. The design F_5 with Yates order can be written as

$$F_5 = \{5, 5H_4\}$$

$$= \{5, 15, 25, 125, 35, 135, 235, 1235, 45, 145, 245, 1245, 345, 1345, 2345, 12345\},$$

where the columns of F_5 correspond to the last 16 columns of H_5.

According to Part (a) of Theorem 3.10, to get a 2^{n-m} design with $n - m = 5$, we only need to take the last n columns (or delete the first $16 - n$ columns) from F_5. For example, by taking the last 13 columns of F_5, we obtain the GMC 2^{13-8} design:

$$D_1 = F_5 \backslash \{5, 15, 25\}$$

$$= \{125, 35, 135, 235, 1235, 45, 145, 245, 1245, 345, 1345, 2345, 12345\}.$$

By taking the last 12 columns of F_5, we get the GMC 2^{12-7} design:

$$D_2 = F_5 \backslash \{5, 15, 25, 125\}$$

$$= \{35, 135, 235, 1235, 45, 145, 245, 1245, 345, 1345, 2345, 12345\}. \qquad \square$$

Next, we use an example to illustrate the construction method in Part (b) of Theorem 3.10.

Example 3.12 Suppose we want a GMC design with 32 runs and more than 16 factors, i.e., $N = 32$ and $n > 16$. The design H_5 with Yates order can be written as

$$H_5 = \{1, 2, 12, 3, 13, 23, 123, 4, 14, 24, 124, 34, 134, 234, 1234\} \cup F_5.$$

Here, F_5 is given in Example 3.11.

According to Part (b) of Theorem 3.10, if we take the last n columns or delete the first $31 - n$ columns from H_5, then we get the GMC 2^{n-m} design. For example, taking the last 20 columns or deleting the first 11 columns from H_5, we get a GMC 2^{20-15} design

$$D_3 = \{34, 134, 234, 1234, 5, 15, 25, 125, 35, 135, 235, 1235, 45, 145, 245, 1245, 345,$$

$$1345, 2345, 12345\}. \qquad \qquad \square$$

3.2.2　Proof of Theorem 3.10

We start with Part (a) of Theorem 3.10, in which $5N/16 + 1 \leqslant n \leqslant N/2$.

By Lemma 3.3 and Theorem 3.7, the GMC 2^{n-m} designs should have resolution IV and be a subset of F_q when $5N/16 + 1 \leqslant n \leqslant N/2$. Let D be a 2^{n-m} design of resolution IV with $5N/16 + 1 \leqslant n \leqslant N/2$. Then, the number of factors in $F_q \backslash D$, which is $N/2 - n$, is less than that of D, which is n.

The roadmap of the proof of Part (a) of Theorem 3.10 is as follows. We first establish the relationships between the AENP of D and that of $F_q \backslash D$ in Lemma 3.13, which implies that the GMC 2^{n-m} design should maximize

$$(-\bar{g}(F_q \backslash D), {}^{\#}_2 C_2(F_q \backslash D)).$$

After that, we apply Part (c) of Theorem 3.2 to finish the proof.

Lemma 3.13　*Let $D \subset F_q$ be a 2^{n-m} design with $q \geqslant 4$ and $n > N/4$. Then*

(a) $B_2(D, \gamma) = \begin{cases} 0, & \text{if } \gamma \in F_q, \\ B_2(F_q \backslash D, \gamma) + n - N/4, & \text{if } \gamma \in H_{q-1}; \end{cases}$

(b) ${}^{\#}_1 C_2^{(k)}(D) = \begin{cases} n, & \text{if } k = 0, \\ 0, & \text{if } k \geqslant 1; \end{cases}$

(c) ${}^{\#}_2 C_2^{(k)}(D) = \begin{cases} 0, & \text{if } k < n - N/4 - 1, \\ -(k+1)\bar{g}(F_q \backslash D) + (k+1)(N/2 - 1), & \text{if } k = n - N/4 - 1, \\ \frac{k+1}{k+1-(n-N/4)} {}^{\#}_2 C_2^{(k-n+N/4)}(F_q \backslash D), & \text{if } k \geqslant n - N/4. \end{cases}$

Proof. Recall that $B_2(D, \gamma)$ is the number of 2fi's in D that are aliased with γ. From the structure of F_q, any $\gamma \in F_q$ will not be aliased with the 2fi's in F_q. Therefore, the first equality in (a) and the two equalities in (b) follow.

For the second equality of (a), first note that for any $\gamma \in H_{q-1}$, there are $N/4$ pairs of factors in F_q such that the interaction formed by each pair is aliased with γ. These $N/4$ pairs can be partitioned into three groups: $B_2(D, \gamma)$ with both factors from D, $B_2(F_q \backslash D, \gamma)$ with both factors from $F_q \backslash D$, and $n - 2B_2(D, \gamma)$ with one factor from D and the other from $F_q \backslash D$. Therefore

$$B_2(D, \gamma) + B_2(F_q \backslash D, \gamma) + n - 2B_2(D, \gamma) = N/4,$$

which implies the second equality of (a).

For (c), note that Part (a) and the definition of ${}_2^{\#}C_2^{(k)}(D)$ together imply

$$\begin{aligned}{}_2^{\#}C_2^{(k)}(D) &= (k+1)|\{\gamma : \gamma \in H_q, B_2(D, \gamma) = k+1\}| \\ &= (k+1)|\{\gamma : \gamma \in H_{q-1}, B_2(F_q \backslash D, \gamma) = k+1 - (n - N/4)\}|.\end{aligned}$$

The first and third equalities in (c) follow directly from the above equation and the definition of ${}_2^{\#}C_2^{(k)}(F_q \backslash D)$. To get the second equality, use Part (a), $k = n - N/4 - 1$, and $|H_{q-1}| = N/2 - 1$ to obtain

$$\begin{aligned}{}_2^{\#}C_2^{(k)}(D) &= (k+1)|\{\gamma : \gamma \in H_{q-1}, B_2(F_q \backslash D, \gamma) = 0\}| \\ &= (k+1)(N/2 - 1) - (k+1)|\{\gamma : \gamma \in H_{q-1}, B_2(F_q \backslash D, \gamma) > 0\}| \\ &= (k+1)(N/2 - 1) - (k+1)|\{\gamma : \gamma \in H_q \backslash (F_q \backslash D), B_2(F_q \backslash D, \gamma) > 0\}| \\ &= (k+1)(N/2 - 1) - (k+1)\bar{g}(F_q \backslash D).\end{aligned}$$

This completes the proof. □

From Lemma 3.13, it follows that maximizing the first two terms $\{{}_1^{\#}C_2(D), {}_2^{\#}C_2(D)\}$ of the sequence (2.4) is equivalent to maximizing the sequence

$$(-\bar{g}(F_q \backslash D), {}_2^{\#}C_2(F_q \backslash D)). \tag{3.20}$$

Next, we apply Part (c) of Theorem 3.2 to finish the proof. Suppose $2^{r-2} + 1 \leqslant N/2 - n \leqslant 2^{r-1}$ for some r. By applying Part (c) of Theorem 3.2 with $S = F_q \backslash D$ and $s = N/2 - n$, we observe that the design $F_q \backslash D$ consisting of the first $N/2 - n$ columns of F_{qr} uniquely maximizes the sequence (3.20). When H_q and F_q are written in Yates order, the first $N/2 - n$ columns of F_{qr} are also the first $N/2 - n$ columns of F_q. Consequently, the GMC design D consists of the last n columns of F_q, which are the same as the last n columns of H_q. This completes the proof of Part (a) of Theorem 3.10.

Now, let us consider the proof of Part (b) of Theorem 3.10, in which $n > N/2$.

We still use D to denote the regular 2^{n-m} fractional factorial design and $q = n - m$. Recall that $S_{qr} = H_q \backslash H_r$. By Theorem 3.1 and Part (a) of Theorem 3.2, if D has GMC and the number of columns in $H_q \backslash D$ satisfies $2^{r-1} \leqslant N - 1 - n \leqslant 2^r - 1$ for some $r \leqslant q - 1$, then $H_q \backslash D$ has r independent factors. Therefore $H_q \backslash D \subset H_r$ and $S_{qr} \subset D$.

If $N - 1 - n = 2^r - 1$, which equals the number of columns in H_r, then $H_q \backslash D = H_r$ and $D = S_{qr}$ has GMC. If $2^{r-1} \leqslant N - 1 - n < 2^r - 1$, then it is convenient to use $D \backslash S_{qr}$ to construct GMC designs because the number of columns in $D \backslash S_{qr}$ is much smaller than that in D.

The proof of Part (b) of Theorem 3.10 follows the roadmap below. We first establish the connection between $B_2(D, \gamma)$ and $B_2(D \backslash S_{qr}, \gamma)$ in Lemma 3.14. With the help of Lemma 3.14, we identify the relationship between the AENPs of D and $D \backslash S_{qr}$ in Lemma 3.15, which implies that the GMC design should sequentially maximize the sequence

$$({}^{\#}_1 C_2(D \backslash S_{qr}), -\bar{g}(D \backslash S_{qr}), {}^{\#}_2 C_2(D \backslash S_{qr})).$$

After that, Part (c) of Theorem 3.2 is applied to finish the proof.

Lemma 3.14　*Suppose D is a 2^{n-m} design with $S_{qr} \subset D$.*

(a) *If $\gamma \in S_{qr}$, then $B_2(D, \gamma) = n - N/2$.*

(b) *If $\gamma \in H_r$, then $B_2(D, \gamma) = B_2(D \backslash S_{qr}, \gamma) + N/2 - 2^{r-1}$.*

Proof.　Again note that $B_2(D, \gamma)$ is the number of 2fi's in D aliased with γ.

(a) For any $\gamma = d_1 d_2 \in S_{qr}$, there are two possibilities: both d_1 and d_2 are in S_{qr}, or d_1 and d_2 are respectively in $D \backslash S_{qr}$ and S_{qr}. Therefore

$$B_2(D, \gamma) = |\{(d_1, d_2) : \gamma = d_1 d_2, d_1 \in D \backslash S_{qr}, d_2 \in S_{qr}\}|$$
$$+ |\{(d_1, d_2) : \gamma = d_1 d_2, d_1 \in S_{qr}, d_2 \in S_{qr}\}|.$$

For any $d_1 \in D \backslash S_{qr}$, we can uniquely determine $d_2 = d_1 \gamma$ in S_{qr}. Therefore, we have

$$|\{(d_1, d_2) : \gamma = d_1 d_2, d_1 \in D\backslash S_{qr}, d_2 \in S_{qr}\}| = n - (N - 2^r).$$

For any $\gamma \in S_{qr}$, there are $N/2 - 1$ pairs of factors in H_q whose interaction is aliased with γ. Among these pairs, there are $2^r - 1$ with one factor from H_r and another one from S_{qr}; for the remaining $N/2 - 2^r$ pairs, both factors are from S_{qr}. Part (a) follows from

$$|\{(d_1, d_2) : \gamma = d_1 d_2, d_1 \in S_{qr}, d_2 \in S_{qr}\}| = N/2 - 2^r$$

and

$$B_2(D, \gamma) = n - (N - 2^r) + N/2 - 2^r = n - N/2.$$

(b) For any $\gamma = d_1 d_2 \in H_r$, there are two possibilities: both d_1 and d_2 are in $D\backslash S_{qr}$ or both are in S_{qr}. Now we have

$$
\begin{aligned}
B_2(D, \gamma) =& |\{(d_1, d_2) : \gamma = d_1 d_2, d_1 \in D\backslash S_{qr}, d_2 \in D\backslash S_{qr}\}| \\
& + |\{(d_1, d_2) : \gamma = d_1 d_2, d_1 \in S_{qr}, d_2 \in S_{qr}\}| \\
=& B_2(D\backslash S_{qr}, \gamma) + |\{(d_1, d_2) : \gamma = d_1 d_2, d_1 \in S_{qr}, d_2 \in S_{qr}\}|,
\end{aligned}
$$

where the second equality is from the definition of $B_2(D\backslash S_{qr}, \gamma)$. For any $\gamma \in H_r$, there are $N/2 - 1$ pairs of factors in H_q whose interaction is aliased with γ. Among these pairs, $(2^r - 2)/2 = 2^{r-1} - 1$ are from H_r and $N/2 - 2^{r-1}$ are from S_{qr}. Part (b) follows from

$$|\{(d_1, d_2) : \gamma = d_1 d_2, d_1 \in S_{qr}, d_2 \in S_{qr}\}| = N/2 - 2^{r-1}$$

and

$$B_2(D, \gamma) = B_2(D\backslash S_{qr}, \gamma) + N/2 - 2^{r-1}.$$

This completes the proof. $\qquad\square$

Lemma 3.14 describes the connection between $B_2(D, \gamma)$ and $B_2(D\backslash S_{qr}, \gamma)$. The relationship between the leading terms of AENPs of D and $D\backslash S_{qr}$ is given in the following lemma.

Lemma 3.15 *Suppose $D = \{S_{qr}, D\backslash S_{qr}\}$.*

(a) ${}^\#_1 C_2^{(k)}(D) = \begin{cases} constant, & if \ k < N/2 - 2^{r-1}, \\ {}^\#_1 C_2^{(k-N/2+2^{r-1})}(D\backslash S_{qr}) + constant, & if \ k \geqslant N/2 - 2^{r-1}, \end{cases}$

$$(b)\ {}^{\#}_{2}C_2^{(k)}(D) = \begin{cases} constant, & if\ k < N/2 - 2^{r-1} - 1, \\ -(k+1)\bar{g}(D\backslash S_{qr}) + (k+1)\,{}^{\#}_{1}C_2^{(0)}(D\backslash S_{qr}) \\ \quad +constant, & if\ k = N/2 - 2^{r-1} - 1, \\ \frac{k+1}{k-N/2+2^{r-1}+1}\,{}^{\#}_{2}C_2^{(k-N/2+2^{r-1})}(D\backslash S_{qr}) \\ \quad +constant, & if\ k \geqslant N/2 - 2^{r-1}, \end{cases}$$

where the constants are non-negative values depending only on n, k and N.

Proof. For (a). From the definition of ${}^{\#}_{1}C_2^{(k)}(D)$, we have

$$ {}^{\#}_{1}C_2^{(k)}(D) = |\{\gamma : \gamma \in S_{qr}, B_2(D, \gamma) = k\}| + |\{\gamma : \gamma \in D\backslash S_{qr}, B_2(D, \gamma) = k\}|.$$

Part (a) follows from an application of Lemma 3.14:

$$ {}^{\#}_{1}C_2^{(k)}(D) = I(n - N/2 = k) \times (N - 2^r)$$
$$ + |\{\gamma : \gamma \in D\backslash S_{qr}, B_2(D\backslash S_{qr}, \gamma) + N/2 - 2^{r-1} = k\}|,$$

where $I(\cdot)$ is the indicator function.

For (b). By the definition of ${}^{\#}_{2}C_2^{(k)}(D)$, we have

$$ {}^{\#}_{2}C_2^{(k)}(D) = (k+1)|\{\gamma : \gamma \in S_{qr}, B_2(D, \gamma) = k+1\}|$$
$$ + (k+1)|\{\gamma : \gamma \in H_r, B_2(D, \gamma) = k+1\}|.$$

Applying Lemma 3.14, this reduces to

$$ {}^{\#}_{2}C_2^{(k)}(D) = I(n - N/2 = k+1) \times (k+1)(N - 2^r)$$
$$ + (k+1)|\{\gamma : \gamma \in H_r, B_2(D\backslash S_{qr}, \gamma) = k+1 - N/2 + 2^{r-1}\}|.$$

The first and third expressions of (b) follow directly from the above equation and the definition of ${}^{\#}_{2}C_2^{(k)}(D\backslash S_{qr})$.

To derive the second expression of (b), put $k = N/2 - 2^{r-1} - 1$. We have

$$ {}^{\#}_{2}C_2^{(k)}(D) = (k+1)|\{\gamma : \gamma \in H_r, B_2(D\backslash S_{qr}, \gamma) = 0\}| + constant$$
$$ = (k+1)|\{\gamma : \gamma \in D\backslash S_{qr}, B_2(D\backslash S_{qr}, \gamma) = 0\}|$$
$$ + (k+1)|\{\gamma : \gamma \in H_q\backslash D, B_2(D\backslash S_{qr}, \gamma) = 0\}| + constant.$$

From the definition of ${}^{\#}_{1}C_2^{(k)}(D\backslash S_{qr})$ and $\bar{g}(\cdot)$ in (3.2), we obtain

$$ |\{\gamma : \gamma \in D\backslash S_{qr}, B_2(D\backslash S_{qr}, \gamma) = 0\}| = {}^{\#}_{1}C_2^{(0)}(D\backslash S_{qr})$$

and

$$ |\{\gamma : \gamma \in H_q\backslash D, B_2(D\backslash S_{qr}, \gamma) = 0\}|$$

$$= (N - 1 - n) - |\{\gamma : \gamma \in H_q \backslash D, B_2(D\backslash S_{qr}, \gamma) > 0\}|$$

$$= (N - 1 - n) - |\{\gamma : \gamma \in S_{qr} \cup (H_q\backslash D), B_2(D\backslash S_{qr}, \gamma) > 0\}|$$

$$= (N - 1 - n) - |\{\gamma : \gamma \in H_q\backslash(D\backslash S_{qr}), B_2(D\backslash S_{qr}, \gamma) > 0\}|$$

$$= (N - 1 - n) - \bar{g}(D\backslash S_{qr}).$$

The second equality above follows from the structure of S_{qr} and $D\backslash S_{qr}$. A re-arrangement of terms yields the desired result. $\square$

Lemma 3.15 implies that the GMC design should maximize

$$({}^{\#}_1C_2(D\backslash S_{qr}), -\bar{g}(D\backslash S_{qr}), {}^{\#}_2C_2(D\backslash S_{qr})). \tag{3.21}$$

If $2^{r-1} \leqslant N-1-n \leqslant 2^r - 1$, then there are r independent factors in H_r and $n+2^r - N$ $(< 2^{r-1})$ factors in $D\backslash S_{qr}$. We can thus find a design with resolution at least IV and with $n + 2^r - N$ factors in H_r. Note that ${}^{\#}_1C_2(D\backslash S_{qr})$ is maximized if $D\backslash S_{qr}$ has resolution at least IV. The two terms following ${}^{\#}_1C_2(D\backslash S_{qr})$ in (3.21) are $-\bar{g}(D\backslash S_{qr})$ and ${}^{\#}_2C_2(D\backslash S_{qr})$.

Let $f_r = n + 2^r - N$, which is the number of columns in $D\backslash S_{qr}$. We then have $0 \leqslant f_r \leqslant 2^{r-1} - 1$. If $f_r = 0$ or 1, then $D = S_{qr}$ or $S_{qr} \cup \{12 \cdots r\}$, and the result is obvious.

Next, consider $2^{l-2} + 1 \leqslant f_r \leqslant 2^{l-1}$ for some $2 \leqslant l \leqslant r$. Let $S = D\backslash S_{qr}$, $s = f_r$ and apply Part (c) of Theorem 3.2. If $D\backslash S_{qr}$ consists of the first f_r columns of F_l, then $D\backslash S_{qr}$ uniquely maximizes the sequence (3.21). Here, F_l is defined in (3.6). When H_q is written in Yates order, the design consisting of the first f_r columns of F_l is isomorphic to the one consisting of the first f_r columns of F_r. Part (c) of Theorem 3.2 shows that the design consisting of the first f_r columns of F_r is isomorphic to the one consisting of the last f_r columns of F_r. Therefore, if $D\backslash S_{qr}$ consists of the last f_r columns of F_r, then $D\backslash S_{qr}$ uniquely maximizes the sequence (3.21) under isomorphism. Combining the last f_r columns of F_r with S_{qr}, we can conclude that the design consisting of the last n columns of H_q has GMC.

3.3   GMC 2^{n-m} Designs with $9N/32+1 \leqslant n \leqslant 5N/16$

3.3.1   Main Results and Example

In this section, we begin by summarizing the construction method proposed by Zhang and Cheng (2010) for the GMC 2^{n-m} designs with $9N/32 + 1 \leqslant n \leqslant 5N/16$.

Recall that in Example 3.8, the SOS design with $5N/16$ runs and RC Yates order is given by

$$S_{(5N/16)} = D^{q-4}(X) = (D^{q-4}(x_1), D^{q-4}(x_2), D^{q-4}(x_3), D^{q-4}(x_4), D^{q-4}(x_5)),$$

where $X = (1, 2, 3, 4, 1234)_{2^4} = (x_1, x_2, x_3, x_4, x_5)$. The detailed forms of $D^{q-4}(x_i)$ for $i = 1, \cdots, 5$ are given in (3.15). According to Theorem 3.7, the SOS design with $5N/16$ runs is unique up to isomorphism. Now, we present the following construction result by Zhang and Cheng (2010).

Theorem 3.16   *The GMC 2^{n-m} designs with $9N/32 + 1 \leqslant n \leqslant 5N/16$, up to isomorphism, consist of the last n columns of $S_{(5N/16)}$ with RC Yates order.*

The following is an illustration of Theorem 3.16.

Example 3.17   Recall that when $q = 6$ and $N = 2^6$, in (3.16), the SOS design with 20 columns/factors and 64 runs is given as

$$S_{(5N/16)} = (1, 15, 16, 156, 2, 25, 26, 256, 3, 35, 36, 356,$$
$$4, 45, 46, 456, 1234, 12345, 12346, 123456)_{2^6}.$$

If we delete the first column of $S_{(5N/16)}$, the design consisting of the remaining 19 columns is a GMC 2^{19-13} design.   □

3.3.2   Outline of the Proof of Theorem 3.16

The proof of Theorem 3.16 follows similar ideas to those in Part (a) of Theorem 3.2, but it is more technically involved. Here, we provide an outline of the main steps in the proof, while referring to Zhang and Cheng (2010) for more details.

By Theorem 3.7, any 2^{n-m} design D with resolution IV must be a projection of F_q or $S_{(5N/16)}$. Considering the structures of F_q and $S_{(5N/16)}$, we need to analyze the following three cases:

Case I: $D \subset F_q$;

Case II: $D \subset S_{(5N/16)}$ and $S_{(5N/16)} \backslash D$ contains columns from at least two $D^{q-4}(x_i)$'s;

Case III: $D \subset S_{(5N/16)}$ and $S_{(5N/16)} \backslash D \subset D^{q-4}(x_p)$ for some $1 \leqslant p \leqslant 5$.

The proof of Zhang and Cheng (2010) consists of two steps. In Step 1, they showed that the GMC design must belong to Case III. This observation aligns with the findings of Chen and Liu (2011). The formal result is presented below.

Theorem 3.18 *A GMC 2^{n-m} design D with $9N/32 < n \leqslant 5N/16$ must be an n-projection of $S_{(5N/16)}$ with $S_{(5N/16)} \backslash D \subset D^{q-4}(x_p)$ for some $1 \leqslant p \leqslant 5$.*

By Theorem 3.18, up to isomorphism, a design D with $9N/32+1 \leqslant n \leqslant 5N/16$ has GMC only if $S_{(5N/16)} \backslash D \subset D^{q-4}(x_1)$.

In Step 2, Zhang and Cheng (2010) argued that for all the possible choices of $D \subset S_{(5N/16)}$, sequentially maximizing the components of $^{\#}_2 C_2(D)$ is equivalent to sequentially maximizing the components of

$$(-\bar{g}(S_{(5N/16)} \backslash D), \,{}^{\#}_2 C_2(S_{(5N/16)} \backslash D)). \tag{3.22}$$

Using Theorem 3.2 (c), it can be concluded that $S_{(5N/16)} \backslash D$, up to isomorphism, sequentially maximizes the components of (3.22) if and only if $S_{(5N/16)} \backslash D$ consists of the first $5N/16 - n$ columns of $D^{q-4}(x_1)$. The results stated in Theorem 3.16 follow from these findings.

3.4 GMC 2^{n-m} Designs with $N/4+1 \leqslant n \leqslant 9N/32$

Cheng and Zhang (2010) presented a construction method for GMC 2^{n-m} designs with $N/4+1 \leqslant n \leqslant 9N/32$. In this section, we summarize their main results.

3.4.1 Some Properties of MaxC2 2^{n-m} Designs with $n = N/4+1$

Let D be a 2^{n-m} design with $n = N/4+1$. We define $\mathcal{N}_i$ as the number of 2fi's in the ith alias set, where $i = 1, 2, \cdots, N-1$. Furthermore, we assume that the last $N-1-n$ alias sets do not contain main effects. Based on the definition of the AENP, we can express the AENPs of D as follows:

$$\begin{cases} {}^{\#}_1C_2^{(k)}(D) = |\{\mathcal{N}_i : \mathcal{N}_i = k, \text{ for } i = 1, \cdots, n\}|, \\ {}^{\#}_2C_2^{(k)}(D) = (k+1)|\{\mathcal{N}_i : \mathcal{N}_i = k+1, \text{ for } i = 1, \cdots, N-1\}|. \end{cases} \tag{3.23}$$

Recall that in Section 1.3.3, a design is called of MaxC2 if it has resolution IV and the maximum number of clear 2fi's. Wu and Wu (2002) showed that D is a MaxC2 design if and only if

(i) $\mathcal{N}_i = 0$ for $i = 1, \cdots, N/4 + 1$;

(ii) $|\{\mathcal{N}_i : \mathcal{N}_i = 1, \text{ for } i = N/4 + 2, \cdots, N - 1\}| = 2(N/4 - 1) + 1$;

(iii) $|\{\mathcal{N}_i : \mathcal{N}_i = N/8 - 1, \text{ for } i = N/4 + 2, \cdots, N - 1\}| = N/4 - 1$.

According to (3.23), we can directly obtain the values of ${}^{\#}_1C_2$ and ${}^{\#}_2C_2$ of a MaxC2 2^{n-m} design with $n = N/4 + 1$:

$$\begin{cases} {}^{\#}_1C_2^{(k)} = \begin{cases} N/4 + 1, & \text{for } k = 0, \\ 0, & \text{for other } k\text{'s}; \end{cases} \\ {}^{\#}_2C_2^{(k)} = \begin{cases} 2(N/4 - 1) + 1, & \text{for } k = 0, \\ (N/4 - 1)(N/8 - 1), & \text{for } k = N/8 - 2, \\ 0, & \text{for other } k\text{'s}. \end{cases} \end{cases} \tag{3.24}$$

As discussed in Lemma 3.3, the maximum resolution of 2^{n-m} designs with $n = N/4 + 1$ must be IV when $q \geqslant 5$. It follows from Theorems 2.2 and 2.11 that any GMC design must have maximum resolution, and any GMC design with resolution IV must be a MaxC2 design. Therefore, the GMC 2^{n-m} design with $n = N/4 + 1$ must be a MaxC2 design and satisfies (3.24). Furthermore, we have the following theorem, the detailed proof of which can be found in Cheng and Zhang (2010).

Theorem 3.19 *For $q \geqslant 5$, the 2^{n-m} design with $n = N/4 + 1$ satisfying (3.24) is unique up to isomorphism.*

For $4 \leqslant t \leqslant q$, let

$$\Phi(t) = (t, t(t-1), (t-1)H_{1,t-2}^t)_{2^t} = (a_1, \cdots, a_{2^{t-2}+1}). \tag{3.25}$$

Cheng and Zhang (2010) showed that the $\Phi(q)$ satisfies (3.24) and is a MaxC2 design or a GMC design. According to Definition 3.4 and (3.24), $\Phi(q)$ is also an SOS design. The above discussion can be generalized for $5 \leqslant t \leqslant q$. That is, the $\Phi(t)$ for $5 \leqslant t \leqslant q$ is an SOS design and a GMC design with $2^{t-2} + 1$ columns and 2^t runs. Tang, Ma, Ingram, and Wang (2002) constructed the 2^{n-m} MaxC2 design with $n = N/4 + 1$.

By Theorem 3.19, their design is isomorphic to the $\Phi(q)$. We summarize the results as follows.

Theorem 3.20   For $5 \leqslant t \leqslant q$, $\Phi(t)$ is an SOS design and is the unique (up to isomorphism) MaxC2 or GMC design with $2^{t-2}+1$ columns and 2^t runs.

Here are two examples that illustrate $\Phi(q)$:

Example 3.21   Consider $\Phi(4) = (4, 34, 13, 23, 123)_{2^4}$, which is a 16×5 matrix. We denote the first four columns/factors by $d_1, \cdots, d_4$ and the last column by d_5. It can be easily verified that the first four columns $d_1, \cdots, d_4$ are independent, and the last column satisfies $d_5 = d_1 d_2 d_3 d_4$. Hence, $\Phi(4)$ is isomorphic to the 2^{5-1} maximal design in Example 3.5.   □

Example 3.22   Consider $\Phi(5) = (5, 45, 14, 24, 124, 34, 134, 234, 1234)_{2^5}$, which is a 32×9 matrix. Let

$$d_1 = 14, \ d_2 = 24, \ d_3 = 34, \ d_4 = 234, \ d_5 = 5$$

and

$$d_6 = 1234, \ d_7 = 134, \ d_8 = 124, \ d_9 = 45.$$

It can be easily verified that $d_1, \cdots, d_5$ are five independent factors/columns. Further,

$$d_6 = d_1 d_2 d_3, \ d_7 = d_1 d_2 d_4, \ d_8 = d_1 d_3 d_4, \ d_9 = d_2 d_3 d_4 d_5.$$

Hence, $\Phi(5)$ is isomorphic to the 2^{9-4} SOS design in Example 3.6.   □

3.4.2   GMC 2^{n-m} Designs with $N/4+1 < n \leqslant 9N/32$

With the above preparation, we now present the construction result when $N/4+1 < n \leqslant 9N/32$. For the given n, we can find a t with $5 \leqslant t \leqslant q-1$ such that

$$N(2^{t-1}+1)/2^{t+1} < n \leqslant N(2^{t-2}+1)/2^t.$$

Recall that

$$\Phi(t) = (t, t(t-1), (t-1)H^t_{1,t-2})_{2^t} = (a_1, \cdots, a_{2^{t-2}+1}).$$

Let

$$S_{((2^{t-2}+1)N/2^t)} = (D^{q-t}(a_1), \cdots, D^{q-t}(a_{2^{t-2}+1})), \tag{3.26}$$

where $D^{q-t}(a_i)$ for $i = 1, \cdots, 2^{t-2} + 1$ can be obtained by using the rule in (3.13). Then, $S_{((2^{t-2}+1)N/2^t)}$ is an SOS design with $(2^{t-2} + 1)N/2^t$ factors and $N = 2^q$ runs in RC Yates order.

Theorem 3.23   *For $5 \leqslant t \leqslant q - 1$ and $N(2^{t-1} + 1)/2^{t+1} < n \leqslant N(2^{t-2} + 1)/2^t$, up to isomorphism, the design consisting of the last n columns of $S_{((2^{t-2}+1)N/2^t)}$ in (3.26) is the unique GMC 2^{n-m} design.*

The following example illustrates the construction method in Theorem 3.23.

Example 3.24   Consider $q = 7$, and let $1, \cdots, 7$ be seven independent columns. Suppose our interest is to construct a 2^{35-28} GMC design. In this case, we have $N = 2^7$, $n = 35$, and $t = 5$ in Theorem 3.23.

Recall that when $q = 7$ and $t = 5$, the SOS design with $(2^{t-2} + 1)N/2^t = 36$ columns/factors and 128 runs in RC Yates order is given in (3.19). That is,

$$S_{(9N/32)} = (1, 16, 17, 167, 2, 26, 27, 267, 3, 36, 37, 367, 4, 46, 47, 467,$$
$$5, 56, 57, 567, 123, 1236, 1237, 12367, 124, 1246, 1247, 12467,$$
$$134, 1346, 1347, 13467, 2345, 23456, 23457, 234567)_{2^7}.$$

By deleting the first column of $S_{(9N/32)}$, we obtain a GMC design with 35 factors. The remaining 35 columns of $S_{(9N/32)}$ form this GMC design.   □

3.4.3   Outline of the Proof of Theorem 3.23

In this section, we provide an outline of the proof of Theorem 3.23. The details can be found in Cheng and Zhang (2010).

By Theorem 3.7, we know that an SOS design with $N(2^{t-2} + 1)/2^t$ factors and 2^q runs can be obtained by doubling some SOS design with $2^{t-2} + 1$ factors and 2^t runs $q - t$ times. Let

$$\mathscr{L}(t) = \{D^{q-t}(X) : X \text{ is an SOS } 2^{(2^{t-2}+1)-(2^{t-2}+1-t)} \text{ design}\}$$

denote the set of all the SOS designs with $N(2^{t-2} + 1)/2^t$ factors and 2^q runs. For a given t, consider all the n-projections of $\mathscr{L}(t)$:

$$\mathscr{P}(n, t) = \{D : D \text{ is an } n\text{-projection of } S, S \in \mathscr{L}(t)\}. \tag{3.27}$$

The proof of Theorem 3.23 consists of three steps. In the first step, Cheng and

Zhang (2010) showed that the GMC 2^{n-m} design should be in $\mathscr{P}(n,t)$.

Theorem 3.25　*For $5 \leqslant t \leqslant q-1$ and $N(2^{t-1}+1)/2^{t+1} < n \leqslant N(2^{t-2}+1)/2^t$, if $\Psi(n,t)$ is the one with the least GLOC in $\mathscr{P}(n,t)$, then $\Psi(n,t)$ has GMC among all the 2^{n-m} designs.*

Theorem 3.25 implies that, for $5 \leqslant t \leqslant q-1$, the construction of a GMC 2^{n-m} design with $N(2^{t-1}+1)/2^{t+1} < n \leqslant N(2^{t-2}+1)/2^t$ is equivalent to finding $\Psi(n,t)$ with the least GLOC among designs in $\mathscr{P}(n,t)$.

Recall that $\Phi(t)$ is defined as in (3.25). As summarized in Theorem 3.20, $\Phi(t)$ is an SOS $2^{(2^{t-2}+1)-(2^{t-2}+1-t)}$ design. Hence, $S_{((2^{t-2}+1)N/2^t)}$ in (3.26) is an element of $\mathscr{L}(t)$. In the second step, Cheng and Zhang (2010) showed that the one with the least GLOC in all the n-projections of $\mathscr{P}(n,t)$ should be an n-projection of $S_{((2^{t-2}+1)N/2^t)}$, and further the design consisting of the last n columns of $S_{((2^{t-2}+1)N/2^t)}$ has the least GLOC in all the n-projections of $S_{((2^{t-2}+1)N/2^t)}$.

Theorem 3.26　*For $5 \leqslant t \leqslant q-1$ and $N(2^{t-1}+1)/2^{t+1} < n \leqslant N(2^{t-2}+1)/2^t$, up to isomorphism, the design consisting of the last n columns of $S_{((2^{t-2}+1)N/2^t)}$ is the one with the least GLOC in all the n-projections of $\mathscr{P}(n,t)$.*

In the third step, Cheng and Zhang (2010) combined Theorems 3.25 and 3.26 to conclude the results in Theorem 3.23.

3.5　When Do the MA and GMC Designs Differ?

As we discussed in Section 2.2, the MA and GMC criteria differ. It is natural to ask: under what circumstances do the two criteria yield different optimal designs? Cheng and Zhang (2010) and Li, Zhao, and Zhang (2011) provided some partial answers.

Theorem 3.27　*The MA and GMC designs differ in the following three parameter settings:*

(a) $4 \leqslant n+2^r - N \leqslant 2^{r-1}-4$ *with* $4 \leqslant r \leqslant q-1$ *when* $2^{r-1} \leqslant N-1-n \leqslant 2^r-1$ *for some r and $n \geqslant N/2$;*

(b) $5N/16+1 \leqslant n \leqslant N/2-4$;

(c) $N/4+1 \leqslant n \leqslant 9N/32$ *and* $q \geqslant 5$.

The proof of Parts (a) and (b) can be found in Li, Zhao, and Zhang (2011), while the proof of Part (c) is available in Cheng and Zhang (2010). Zhang and Mukerjee (2009a) discovered that the GMC and MA designs are different when $N - 1 - n = 11$. This finding corresponds to a special case of Part (a) of Theorem 3.27 with $r = 4$. The following example provides another application of Part (a) of Theorem 3.27.

Example 3.28　Suppose $N = 32$ and $n = 20$. According to Butler (2003), the MA 2^{20-15} design is isomorphic to

$$D_4 = \{124, 134, 234, 1234\} \cup F_5.$$

Note that the four columns $\{124, 134, 234, 1234\}$ joined into the design D_4 are independent. Now, for the GMC 2^{20-15} design D_3 in Example 3.12, the four columns $\{34, 134, 234, 1234\}$ joined into D_3 with the same F_5 are not independent. As a result, among regular 2^{20-15} designs, the GMC and MA designs are different.　　　□

The next example is used to illustrate the result in Part (b) of Theorem 3.27.

Example 3.29　Let us consider the case when $N = 32$ and $n = 12 \leqslant 32/2 - 4$. According to Butler (2003), the MA 2^{12-7} design is isomorphic to

$$D_5 = \{125, 135, 235, 1235, 45, 145, 245, 1245, 345, 1345, 2345, 12345\}$$

$$= F_5 \backslash \{5, 15, 25, 35\}.$$

Note that the design D_5 is obtained by deleting the four columns $\{5, 15, 25, 35\}$ from F_5 and the deleted four columns are independent. From Example 3.11, $D_2 = F_5 \backslash \{5, 15, 25, 125\}$ is the GMC 2^{12-7} design up to isomorphism. However, the deleted four columns $\{5, 15, 25, 125\}$ are not independent. Thus, the MA design D_5 is different from D_2 and does not have GMC.　　　□

The last example illustrates the result in Part (c) of Theorem 3.27.

Example 3.30　Let us consider the two 2^{9-4} designs presented in Example 2.8, where one corresponds to an MA design and the other to a GMC design. In this case, the MA design and the GMC design differ when $q = 5$ and $n = N/4 + 1$. This scenario corresponds to a specific case covered by Part (c) of Theorem 3.27.　　　□

4 General Minimum Lower-Order Confounding Blocked Designs

Fractional factorial designs typically involve a completely random allocation of selected treatment combinations to experimental units. However, this kind of allocation is appropriate only if the experimental units are homogeneous. In practice, experimental units are often inhomogeneous, particularly when the experiment's size is relatively large. This inhomogeneity can cause systematic variation and decrease the precision of effect estimation. To address this problem, blocking is an effective method. This chapter focuses on establishing the GMC theory for two-level blocked designs.

4.1 Two Kinds of Blocking Problems

According to Bisgaard (1994), there are two types of blocking problems: those with a single block variable and those with two or more block variables. These types are commonly referred to as the "single block variable problem" and the "multi block variable problem", respectively.

In recent decades, many researchers have investigated the single block variable problem, including Sitter, Chen, and Feder (1997), Chen and Cheng (1999), Zhang and Park (2000), Cheng and Wu (2002), Xu (2006), Xu and Mee (2010), and Zhao, Li, and Karunamuni (2013). However, practical experiments often encounter scenarios involving multiple block variables in blocked designs. As Bisgaard (1994) highlighted in the agricultural context, when designs are implemented in rectangular schemes, both row and column inhomogeneity effects are likely to exist in the soil. To illustrate this point further, consider another example where the experiment aims to compare two gasoline additives by testing them on two cars with two drivers over two days. In this case, it is necessary to consider three variables–cars, drivers, and days–in order to appropriately allocate the experimental units.

We assume that the experimenters are solely interested in estimating the treatment factor effects and that all interactions between treatment and block factors are negligible. Additionally, we assume that the treatment factor effects follow the effect hierarchy principle outlined in Section 1.3. The key difference between the two types of blocking problems lies in the effect hierarchy principles associated with the block factors (columns), which can be summarized as follows:

$(AS)_s$: For the single block variable problem, the main effects of block columns and any order interactions of block columns are equally likely to be significant.

$(AS)_m$: For the multi block variable problem, lower-order block factor effects are more likely to be significant than higher-order block factor effects, and the same order block factor effects are equally likely to be significant.

To select two-level blocked designs, the GMC criteria are established in the subsequent section, taking into account the aforementioned two effect hierarchy principles.

4.2   GMC Criteria for Blocked Designs

Zhang and Mukerjee (2009b) extended the GMC idea to address the single block variable problem and introduced the blocked GMC (B-GMC) criterion for selecting regular blocked designs at the s-level. In a different perspective from Zhang and Mukerjee (2009b), Wei, Li, and Zhang (2014) further extended the GMC idea and proposed the blocked GMC (B^1-GMC) criterion for selecting optimal two-level blocked designs with a single block variable. Furthermore, for the selection of two-level regular blocked designs with multiple block variables, Zhang, Li, and Wei (2011) proposed the blocked GMC (B^2-GMC) criterion. The remainder of this section provides a detailed introduction to these three criteria.

We start by considering the single block variable problem. In the following, we use $(D_t : D_b)$, taken from the saturated design H_q in (1.6), to denote a blocked $2^{n-m} : 2^r$ design, where D_t is a $2^q \times n$ matrix with each column representing a treatment factor, and D_b is a $2^q \times (2^r - 1)$ matrix for blocking. Of the n factors in D_t, $q = n - m$ are independent, and the remaining m are expressed by the q independent factors and determine m defining words, called *treatment-defining words*. Of the $2^r - 1$ columns in D_b, r are considered to be independent block factors, which are also expressed by the q independent treatment columns and determine r independent block-defining words.

For example, the $2^{4-1} : 2^2$ design $D = (1, 2, 3, 123 : 12, 23, 13)$ is taken from $H_3 = \{1, 2, 12, 3, 13, 23, 123\}$. When an experiment with four factors and eight runs must be blocked into four blocks, the experimenter can assign the treatment factors to the four columns $1, 2, 3$, and 123, and block the eight runs into four blocks by assigning the columns 12 and 23 as two independent block factors.

For a $2^{n-m} : 2^r$ design $D = (D_t : D_b)$, all possible products of the m treatment-defining words constitute a subgroup, called the treatment-defining contrast subgroup. Each element in this subgroup is called a treatment-defining word. The number of letters in a treatment-defining word is referred to its length. For $1 \leqslant i \leqslant n$, let A_{i0} be the number of treatment-defining words of length i in D_t, and A_{i1} be the number of ith-order treatment effects aliased with a block effect.

With the above preparation, we now introduce the B-GMC criterion proposed by Zhang and Mukerjee (2009b) for the single block variable problem. For $1 \leqslant i \leqslant n$, let $_i^{\#}C_0(D)$ denote the number of ith-order treatment effects which is neither the treatment-defining words nor aliased with the block effects. Then

$$_i^{\#}C_0(D) = K_i - A_{i0} - A_{i1},$$

where $K_i = \binom{n}{i}$. Further, among the $_i^{\#}C_0(D)$ effects which might be estimated, let $_i^{\#}C_j^{(k)}(D)$ denote the number of those aliased with k jth-order effects, and let

$$_i^{\#}C_j(D) = (_i^{\#}C_j^{(0)}(D), _i^{\#}C_j^{(1)}(D), \cdots, _i^{\#}C_j^{(K_j)}(D))$$

for $1 \leqslant i, j \leqslant n$. Throughout this chapter, we focus on the blocked designs with no treatment main effect being aliased with other treatment main effects and block effects. In other words, we assume that $A_{10} = A_{20} = A_{11} = 0$.

Let

$$^{\#}C(D) = (^{\#}_1C_2(D), ^{\#}_2C_0(D), ^{\#}_2C_2(D), ^{\#}_1C_3(D), ^{\#}_2C_3(D), ^{\#}_3C_0(D), \cdots), \qquad (4.1)$$

which is called the *aliased effect-number pattern* of the blocked designs (B-AENP). A design D is said to *have B-GMC* if it sequentially maximizes the components of (4.1). When all the treatment effects involving three or more factors are negligible, (4.1) is reduced to

$$^{\#}C(D) = (^{\#}_1C_2(D), ^{\#}_2C_0(D), ^{\#}_2C_2(D)). \qquad (4.2)$$

Then a design D is said to have B-GMC if it sequentially maximizes the components of (4.2).

Deleting $^{\#}_2C_0(D)$ in (4.2), we get the following pattern, denoted as B^1-AENP,

$$^{\#}C(D) = (^{\#}_1C_2(D), ^{\#}_2C_2(D)), \qquad (4.3)$$

which is equivalent to that given by Wei, Li, and Zhang (2014). A design D is said to have B^1-GMC if it sequentially maximizes the components of (4.3).

Both the B-GMC and B^1-GMC criteria mentioned earlier are for the single block variable problem. Next, we will introduce the GMC criterion for the multi block variable problem. It is important to note that the key difference between these two types of blocking problems lies in the effect hierarchy principles. In the case of the single block variable problem, it is assumed that all block factor effects are equally likely to be significant. However, for the multi block variable problem, lower-order block factor effects are assumed to be more likely to be significant compared to higher-order effects. As a result, some higher-order block factor effects, such as those involving three or more block factors, may be assumed to be negligible. Consequently, treatment factor effects that are aliased with these negligible block factor effects can be estimated.

We will continue to use the notation $2^{n-m} : 2^r$ to denote a blocked design $D = (D_t : D_b)$ for the multi block variable problem. However, the difference now is that D_b represents a $2^q \times r$ blocking scheme matrix, where each column corresponds to a block factor. Furthermore, in the case of multi block variable problem, for $1 \leqslant i \leqslant n$, let A_{i1} be the number of ith-order treatment effects aliased with a potentially significant block effect. The AENP in (4.3) is referred to as B^2-AENP for multi block variable problem, which is equivalent to that given by Zhang, Li, and Wei (2011). A design D is said to *have B^2-GMC* if it maximizes the components of (4.3) sequentially.

4.3 Construction of B-GMC Designs

Tan and Zhang (2013), Zhao, Lin, and Li (2016), and Zhao and Zhao (2018) considered the construction of B-GMC $2^{n-m} : 2^r$ designs with $5N/16 + 1 \leqslant n \leqslant N - 1$. This section summaries their main results.

To present the results, we introduce the concept of isomorphism in blocked designs. Suppose $D^1 = (D_t^1 : D_b^1)$ and $D^2 = (D_t^2 : D_b^2)$ are two $2^{n-m} : 2^r$ designs. These designs are considered *isomorphic* (or *equivalent*) if there exists an isomorphism mapping that maps each column of D_t^1 to a corresponding column of D_t^2, and each column of D_b^1 to a corresponding column of D_b^2.

Let $D = (D_t : D_b)$ be a $2^{n-m} : 2^r$ design. Recall that in Chapters 2 and 3, we use ${}_i^\#C_j^{(k)}(D_t)$ to denote the number of ith-order effects aliased with k jth-order effects in the unblocked 2^{n-m} design D_t. From the definition of ${}_1^\#C_2^{(k)}(D)$ for the blocked design D, we have

$$ {}_1^\#C_2^{(k)}(D) = {}_1^\#C_2^{(k)}(D_t) $$

for any k. Therefore, based on (4.1) or (4.2) and the B-GMC criterion, if a blocked design $D = (D_t : D_b)$ has B-GMC, we need to maximize ${}_1^\#C_2(D)$, which is the first component of (4.2). Since ${}_1^\#C_2(D) = {}_1^\#C_2(D_t)$, it is clear that ${}_1^\#C_2(D)$ depends solely on D_t. Therefore, we can and should treat D_t as an unblocked design and select it optimally first. This observation plays an important role in the next three subsections.

Note that when $r = q - 1$, up to isomorphism, we may choose $D_b = H_{q-1}$ and $D_t \subset F_q$. In this scenario, any 2fi in D_t is aliased with a block effect in D_b. Consequently, all elements in the AENP of blocked designs, as defined in (4.2), become constants. We may simply choose D_t to be the design consisting of the last n columns of F_q. The resulting design $D = (D_t : D_b)$ has B-GMC.

In the next three subsections, we focus on the case where $r \leqslant q - 2$.

4.3.1　B-GMC $2^{n-m} : 2^r$ Designs with $5N/16 + 1 \leqslant n \leqslant N/2$

In this section, we discuss the construction method for B-GMC $2^{n-m} : 2^r$ designs with $5N/16 + 1 \leqslant n \leqslant N/2$. For convenience of presentation, we first provide an overview of the main results, followed by an outline of the major steps in the proof.

As we discussed above, the GMC $2^{n-m} : 2^r$ designs should maximize ${}^\#_1C_2(D)$ or ${}^\#_1C_2(D_t)$ first. By Lemma 3.3 and Theorem 3.7 or the discussion in Section 3.2.2, if D_t maximizes ${}^\#_1C_2(D_t)$, then the D_t must have resolution IV and can be taken from $F_q = F_{qq}$ up to isomorphism, where F_{qq} is defined in (3.6). In the following, we present the structure of GMC $2^{n-m} : 2^r$ designs with $D_t \subset F_q$.

For ease of presentation, we need some new notation. Let $\alpha_0 = \beta_0 = I$, the column with all entries being 1. Denote

$$H_{r+1,q-1} = \{\alpha_1, \cdots, \alpha_{2^{q-r-1}-1}\} \tag{4.4}$$

be the subset of H_q, which consists of the independent columns $r + 1, \cdots, q - 1$ and all their possible component-wise products, and

$$H_{r,q-1} = \{\beta_1, \cdots, \beta_{2^{q-r}-1}\} \tag{4.5}$$

be the subset of H_q, which consists of the independent columns $r, \cdots, q - 1$ and all their possible component-wise products. It is important to note that $H_{r+1,q-1}$ and $H_{r,q-1}$ are consistent with the notation in (3.9). Further, assume that the elements α_i and β_j are in Yates order, respectively. For example, $\alpha_1 = r + 1$, $\alpha_2 = r + 2$, $\alpha_3 = (r+1)(r+2)$, $\beta_1 = r$, $\beta_2 = r+1$, and $\beta_3 = r(r+1)$. Using the above notation, we can express F_q as follows:

$$F_q = \bigcup_{i=0}^{2^{q-r-1}-1} \alpha_i F_{q(r+1)} = \bigcup_{j=0}^{2^{q-r}-1} \beta_j F_{qr}.$$

Arranging the elements of $\alpha_i F_{q(r+1)}$ and $\beta_j F_{qr}$ in Yates order, we have the following theorem.

Theorem 4.1　*Suppose that $D = (D_t : D_b)$ is a $2^{n-m} : 2^r$ design.*

　(a) *When $N/2 - 2^{r-1} + 1 \leqslant n \leqslant N/2$, if D_t consists of the last $n_1 - 1$*

columns of $\alpha_i F_{q(r+1)}$ for $i = 0, 1, \cdots, J_1 - 1$, the last n_1 columns of $\alpha_i F_{q(r+1)}$ for $i = J_1, \cdots, 2^{q-r-1} - 1$, and $D_b = H_r$, then D has B-GMC. Here, $n_1 = \lceil \frac{n}{2^{q-r-1}} \rceil$, $J_1 = 2^{q-r-1} n_1 - n$, and $\lceil x \rceil$ denotes the smallest integer which is larger than or equal to x.

(b) When $5N/16 + 1 \leqslant n \leqslant N/2 - 2^{r-1}$ and $\lceil \frac{N/2 - 2^{r-1} - n}{2^{q-r} - 1} \rceil$ is odd (or even), if D_t consists of the last n_2 (or $n_2 - 1$) columns of $\beta_j F_{qr}$ for $j = 1, \cdots, J_2$, the last $n_2 - 1$ (or n_2) columns of $\beta_j F_{qr}$ for $j = J_2 + 1, \cdots, 2^{q-r} - 1$, and $D_b = H_{r-1} \cup F_{qr}$, then D has B-GMC. Here $n_2 = \lceil \frac{n}{2^{q-r} - 1} \rceil$ and $J_2 = n - (2^{q-r} - 1)(n_2 - 1)$ (or $J_2 = (2^{q-r} - 1)n_2 - n$).

The next examples show the usefulness of Theorem 4.1 for the construction of B-GMC designs.

Example 4.2　We first consider the construction of B-GMC $2^{6-2} : 2^2$ design. Here $n = 6$, $m = 2$, $r = 2$, $q = 4$, and $N = 16$. Then $5N/16 + 1 \leqslant n \leqslant N/2 - 2^{r-1}$ and $\lceil \frac{N/2 - 2^{r-1} - n}{2^{q-r} - 1} \rceil = \lceil \frac{8-2-6}{2^{4-2} - 1} \rceil = 0$ is even. Recall that $\beta_0 = I$, $H_{r,q-1} = H_{2,3} = \{\beta_1, \cdots, \beta_3\} = \{2, 3, 23\}$, and $F_{qr} = F_{42} = \{4, 14\}$. Then

$$F_q = F_4 = \bigcup_{j=0}^{3} \beta_j F_{qr} = \left\{ \begin{array}{cc} 4 & 14 \\ 24 & 124 \\ 34 & 134 \\ 234 & 1234 \end{array} \right\}.$$

Note that $n_2 = \lceil \frac{n}{2^{q-r} - 1} \rceil = \lceil \frac{6}{2^{4-2} - 1} \rceil = 2$ and $J_2 = (2^{q-r} - 1)n_2 - n = 0$. By part (b) of Theorem 4.1, $D = (D_t : D_b)$ with

$$D_t = \left\{ \begin{array}{cc} 24 & 124 \\ 34 & 134 \\ 234 & 1234 \end{array} \right\}$$

and $D_b = H_{r-1} \cup F_{qr} = \{1, 4, 14\}$ has B-GMC among all $2^{6-2} : 2^2$ designs.

Suppose that we use b_1 and b_2 to label the first two block factors 1 and 4. After rearranging its rows, the B-GMC $2^{6-2} : 2^2$ design is presented in Table 4.1, in which the 16 runs are divided into four blocks I, II, III, IV, according to $(b_1, b_2) = (-1, -1)$, $(-1, +1)$, $(+1, -1)$, and $(+1, +1)$.　　　　　　□

Example 4.3　We next consider the construction of B-GMC $2^{n-m} : 2^r$ designs with $q = 6$, $N = 64$, $r = 3$, and $5N/16 + 1 \leqslant n \leqslant N/2$.

Table 4.1　The B-GMC $2^{6-2} : 2^2$ design $D = (D_t : D_b)$ with

$$D_t = \{a_1 = 24, a_2 = 34, a_3 = 234, a_4 = 124, a_5 = 134, a_6 = 1234\} \text{ and}$$

$$D_b = \{b_1 = 1, b_2 = 4, b_3 = 14\}$$

Treatment factors						Block factors			Blocks
a_1	a_2	a_3	a_4	a_5	a_6	b_1	b_2	b_3	
+1	+1	−1	−1	−1	+1	−1	−1	+1	I
+1	+1	−1	+1	+1	−1	+1	−1	−1	III
−1	+1	+1	+1	−1	−1	−1	−1	+1	I
−1	+1	+1	−1	+1	+1	+1	−1	−1	III
+1	−1	+1	−1	+1	−1	−1	−1	+1	I
+1	−1	+1	+1	−1	+1	+1	−1	−1	III
−1	−1	−1	+1	+1	+1	−1	−1	+1	I
−1	−1	−1	−1	−1	−1	+1	−1	−1	III
−1	−1	+1	+1	+1	−1	−1	+1	−1	II
−1	−1	+1	−1	−1	+1	+1	+1	+1	IV
+1	−1	−1	−1	+1	+1	−1	+1	−1	II
+1	−1	−1	+1	−1	−1	+1	+1	+1	IV
−1	+1	−1	+1	−1	+1	−1	+1	−1	II
−1	+1	−1	−1	+1	−1	+1	+1	+1	IV
+1	+1	+1	−1	−1	−1	−1	+1	−1	II
+1	+1	+1	+1	+1	+1	+1	+1	+1	IV

If we take $n = 29$, then $N/2 - 2^{r-1} + 1 \leqslant n \leqslant N/2$. We have

$$H_r = H_3 = \{1, 2, 12, 3, 13, 23, 123\}$$

and

$$H_{r+1,q-1} = H_{4,5} = \{\alpha_1, \alpha_2, \alpha_3\} = \{4, 5, 45\}.$$

Note that $\alpha_0 = I$ and $F_{q(r+1)} = F_{64} = \{6, 16, 26, 126, 36, 136, 236, 1236\}$. Then

$$F_6 = \bigcup_{i=0}^{3} \alpha_i F_{64} = \left\{ \begin{array}{llllllll} 6 & 16 & 26 & 126 & 36 & 136 & 236 & 1236 \\ 46 & 146 & 246 & 1246 & 346 & 1346 & 2346 & 12346 \\ 56 & 156 & 256 & 1256 & 356 & 1356 & 2356 & 12356 \\ 456 & 1456 & 2456 & 12456 & 3456 & 13456 & 23456 & 123456 \end{array} \right\}.$$

Further, $n_1 = \lceil \frac{n}{2^{q-r-1}} \rceil = \lceil \frac{29}{2^{6-3-1}} \rceil = 8$ and $J_1 = 2^{q-r-1} n_1 - n = 4 \times 8 - 29 = 3$. By Part (a) of Theorem 4.1, $D_1 = (D_{t1} : D_{b1})$ with

$$D_{t1} = \left\{ \begin{array}{llllllll} & 16 & 26 & 126 & 36 & 136 & 236 & 1236 \\ & 146 & 246 & 1246 & 346 & 1346 & 2346 & 12346 \\ & 156 & 256 & 1256 & 356 & 1356 & 2356 & 12356 \\ 456 & 1456 & 2456 & 12456 & 3456 & 13456 & 23456 & 123456 \end{array} \right\}$$

and $D_{b1} = H_3$ has B-GMC among the $2^{29-23} : 2^3$ designs.

If we take $n = 23$, then $5N/16 + 1 \leqslant n \leqslant N/2 - 2^{r-1}$ and

$$\left\lceil \frac{N/2 - 2^{r-1} - n}{2^{q-r} - 1} \right\rceil = \left\lceil \frac{32 - 4 - 23}{2^{5-3} - 1} \right\rceil = 1$$

is odd. Recall that

$$H_{r-1} = H_2 = \{1, 2, 12\} \text{ and } H_{r,q-1} = H_{3,5} = \{\beta_1, \cdots, \beta_7\} = \{3, 4, 34, 5, 35, 45, 345\},$$

and note that $\beta_0 = I$ and $F_{qr} = F_{63} = \{6, 16, 26, 126\}$. Then

$$F_6 = \bigcup_{j=0}^{7} \beta_j F_{63} = \left\{ \begin{array}{cccc} 6 & 16 & 26 & 126 \\ 36 & 136 & 236 & 1236 \\ 46 & 146 & 246 & 1246 \\ 346 & 1346 & 2346 & 12346 \\ 56 & 156 & 256 & 1256 \\ 356 & 1356 & 2356 & 12356 \\ 456 & 1456 & 2456 & 12456 \\ 3456 & 13456 & 23456 & 123456 \end{array} \right\}.$$

Note that $n_2 = \lceil \frac{n}{2^{q-r}-1} \rceil = \lceil \frac{23}{2^{6-3}-1} \rceil = 4$ and $J_2 = n - (2^{q-r} - 1)(n_2 - 1) = 2$. By part (b) of Theorem 4.1, $D_2 = (D_{t2} : D_{b2})$ with

$$D_{t2} = \left\{ \begin{array}{cccc} 36 & 136 & 236 & 1236 \\ 46 & 146 & 246 & 1246 \\ & 1346 & 2346 & 12346 \\ & 156 & 256 & 1256 \\ & 1356 & 2356 & 12356 \\ & 1456 & 2456 & 12456 \\ & 13456 & 23456 & 123456 \end{array} \right\}$$

and $D_{b2} = H_2 \cup F_{63} = \{1, 2, 12, 6, 16, 26, 126\}$ has B-GMC among the $2^{23-17} : 2^3$ designs.   □

Outline of the proof of Theorem 4.1.

For the rest of this section, we provide an outline of the proof of Theorem 4.1. More details can be found in Zhao, Lin, and Li (2016). The proof of Theorem 4.1 consists of four steps.

In Step 1, we argue that there are two possible choices of D_b up to isomorphism.

Lemma 4.4 *Suppose $D_t \subset F_q$. Up to isomorphism, there are two possibilities for* the block effects D_b: (i) $D_b = H_r$ and (ii) $D_b = H_{r-1} \cup F_{qr}$, where F_{qr} is defined in (3.6).

In Step 2, we define $D^* = (D_t^* : D_b^*)$ with $D_t^* = F_q \backslash D_t$ and $D_b^* = H_{q-1} \cap D_b$, and establish the relation between the B-AENPs of D and D^*. Note that the number of columns in D_t^* is smaller than that of D_t. Hence, the derived relationship is very helpful for constructing B-GMC designs.

Lemma 4.5　*Suppose $D = (D_t : D_b)$ is a $2^{n-m} : 2^r$ design with $D_t \subset F_q$, $q \geqslant 4$, and $n > N/4$. Let $D^* = (D_t^* : D_b^*)$ with $D_t^* = F_q \backslash D_t$ and $D_b^* = H_{q-1} \cap D_b$. Then, we have*

(a) $\#_1 C_2^{(k)}(D) = \begin{cases} n, & \text{if } k = 0, \\ 0, & \text{if } k \geqslant 1; \end{cases}$

(b) $\#_2 C_2^{(k)}(D) = \begin{cases} 0, & \text{if } k < n - N/4 - 1, \\ (k+1)(N/2 - 1 - f(D^*)), & \text{if } k = n - N/4 - 1, \\ (k+1)/(k+1-n+N/4) \#_2 C_2^{(k-n+N/4)}(D^*), & \\ & \text{if } k > n - N/4 - 1, \end{cases}$

where $f(D^*) = |D_b^*| + |\{d : d \in H_q \backslash D_b^*, B_2(D_t^*, d) > 0\}|$;

(c) $\#_2 C_0(D) = \#_2 C_0(D^*) + (n - N/4) |H_{q-1} \backslash D_b^*|$.

Lemma 4.5 implies that a design $D = (D_t : D_b)$ has B-GMC if and only if $D_t \subset F_q$ and the corresponding D^* maximizes

$$\left(\#_2 C_0(D^*) + (n - N/4) |H_{q-1} \backslash D_b^*|, -f(D^*), \#_2 C_2(D^*) \right). \tag{4.6}$$

By Lemma 4.4, there are two classes of blocked designs $D = (D_t : D_b)$ with $D_t \subset F_q$. One has $D_b = H_r$ and the other has $D_b = H_{r-1} \cup F_{qr}$. We will find the B-GMC designs in each class, and then compare the two B-GMC designs to give the B-GMC design among all the $2^{n-m} : 2^r$ designs. In each class, $(n - N/4)|H_{q-1} \backslash D_b^*|$ is a constant and (4.6) can be simplified to

$$(\#_2 C_0(D^*), -f(D^*), \#_2 C_2(D^*)). \tag{4.7}$$

In Step 3, we figure out which class we need to consider when $N/2 - 2^{r-1} + 1 \leqslant n \leqslant N/2$ and when $5N/16 + 1 \leqslant n \leqslant N/2 - 2^{r-1}$.

Lemma 4.6　*Suppose that $D = (D_t : D_b)$ is a $2^{n-m} : 2^r$ design with $D_t \subset F_q$. Let $D^* = (D_t^* : D_b^*)$ with $D_t^* = F_q \backslash D_t$ and $D_b^* = H_{q-1} \cap D_b$.*

(a) *When $N/2 - 2^{r-1} + 1 \leqslant n \leqslant N/2$, D has B-GMC if and only if $D_b = H_r$ and $D^* = (D_t^* : D_b^*)$ maximizes* (4.7).

(b) *When $5N/16 + 1 \leqslant n \leqslant N/2 - 2^{r-1}$, D has B-GMC if and only if $D_b = H_{r-1} \cup F_{qr}$ and $D^* = (D_t^* : D_b^*)$ maximizes* (4.7).

In Step 4, we find the GMC design in each class, and complete the proof of Theorem 4.1.

4.3.2　B-GMC $2^{n-m} : 2^r$ Designs with $n > N/2$

This section presents the theory for constructing B-GMC designs when $n > N/2$. Suppose the number of factors in D_t satisfies

$$2^{l-1} \leqslant N - 1 - n \leqslant 2^l - 1$$

for some l with $r + 1 \leqslant l \leqslant q - 1$. As we discussed at the beginning of Section 4.3, the B-GMC design should maximize ${}_1^\#C_2(D)$ or equivalently ${}_1^\#C_2(D_t)$. By Theorem 3.1 and Part (a) of Theorem 3.2, up to isomorphism, $H_q \backslash D \subset H_l$, or equivalently, $S_{ql} \subset D_t$ and $D_b \subset H_l$, where $S_{ql} = H_q \backslash H_l$ denotes the complementary set of H_l consisting of the last $2^q - 2^l$ columns of H_q. Next, we present the structure of GMC $2^{n-m} : 2^r$ designs with $S_{ql} \subset D_t$ and $D_b \subset H_l$.

Recall α_i's in (4.4) and β_j's in (4.5). When $l \geqslant r + 2$, we can express $H_{r+1,l-1}$ as

$$H_{r+1,l-1} = \{\alpha_1, \cdots, \alpha_{2^{l-r-1}-1}\}.$$

Similarly, when $l \geqslant r + 1$, we can express $H_{r,l-1}$ as

$$H_{r,l-1} = \{\beta_1, \cdots, \beta_{2^{l-r}-1}\}.$$

Furthermore, F_l can be written as

$$F_l = \bigcup_{i=0}^{2^{l-r-1}-1} \alpha_i F_{l(r+1)} = \bigcup_{j=0}^{2^{l-r}-1} \beta_j F_{lr}.$$

Suppose the elements of $\alpha_i F_{l(r+1)}$ and $\beta_j F_{lr}$ are arranged in Yates order. We have the following theorem.

Theorem 4.7　*Suppose that $D = (D_t : D_b)$ is a $2^{n-m} : 2^r$ design with $S_{ql} \subset D_t$ for some l $(r+1 \leqslant l \leqslant q-1)$. Let $\tilde{D}_t = D_t \backslash S_{ql}$.*

(a) *When $2^{l-1} - 2^{r-1} < n - (N - 2^l) < 2^{l-1}$, if $\tilde{D}_t$ consists of the last $n_1 - 1$*

columns of $\alpha_i F_{l(r+1)}$ for $i = 0, 1, \cdots, J_1 - 1$, the last n_1 columns of $\alpha_i F_{l(r+1)}$ for $i = J_1, \cdots, 2^{l-r-1} - 1$, and $D_b = H_r$, then D has B-GMC. Here, $n_1 = \lceil \frac{n-N+2^l}{2^{l-r}-1} \rceil$ and $J_1 = 2^{l-r-1} n_1 - (n - N + 2^l)$.

(b) When $5 \times 2^l/16 + 1 \leqslant n - (N - 2^l) \leqslant 2^{l-1} - 2^{r-1}$ and $\lceil \frac{N-n-2^{l-1}-2^{r-1}}{2^{l-r}-1} \rceil$ is odd (or even), if $\tilde{D}_t$ consists of the last n_2 (or $n_2 - 1$) columns of $\beta_j F_{lr}$ for $j = 1, \cdots, J_2$, the last $n_2 - 1$ (or n_2) columns of $\beta_j F_{lr}$ for $j = J_2 + 1, \cdots, 2^{l-r} - 1$, and $D_b = H_{r-1} \cup F_{lr}$, then D has B-GMC. Here, $n_2 = \lceil \frac{n-N+2^l}{2^{l-r}-1} \rceil$ and $J_2 = (n - N + 2^l) - (2^{l-r} - 1)(n_2 - 1)$ (or $J_2 = (2^{l-r} - 1)n_2 - (n - N + 2^l)$).

The example below demonstrates the application of Theorem 4.7 in constructing B-GMC designs.

Example 4.8　Let us consider the construction of B-GMC $2^{n-m} : 2^r$ designs with $q = 6$, $N = 64$, $r = 3$, and $5 \times 2^l/16 + 1 \leqslant n - (N - 2^l) < 2^{l-1}$.

If we take $n = 45$, then $2^{l-1} - 2^{r-1} < n - (N - 2^l) < 2^{l-1}$ for $l = 5$ and $S_{65} \subset D_t$, where

$$S_{65} = H_6 \backslash H_5 = \left\{ \begin{array}{cccccccc} 6 & 16 & 26 & 126 & 36 & 136 & 236 & 1236 \\ 46 & 146 & 246 & 1246 & 346 & 1346 & 2346 & 12346 \\ 56 & 156 & 256 & 1256 & 356 & 1356 & 2356 & 12356 \\ 456 & 1456 & 2456 & 12456 & 3456 & 13456 & 23456 & 123456 \end{array} \right\}.$$

We have

$$H_r = H_3 = \{1, 2, 12, 3, 13, 23, 123\}$$

and

$$H_{r+1, l-1} = H_{4,4} = \{\alpha_1\} = \{4\}.$$

Note that $\alpha_0 = I$ and $F_{l(r+1)} = F_{54} = \{5, 15, 25, 125, 35, 135, 235, 1235\}$. Then

$$F_5 = \bigcup_{i=0}^{1} \alpha_i F_{54} = \left\{ \begin{array}{cccccccc} 5 & 15 & 25 & 125 & 35 & 135 & 235 & 1235 \\ 45 & 145 & 245 & 1245 & 345 & 1345 & 2345 & 12345 \end{array} \right\}.$$

Further,

$$n_1 = \left\lceil \frac{n - N + 2^l}{2^{l-r-1}} \right\rceil = \left\lceil \frac{45 - 64 + 2^5}{2^{5-3-1}} \right\rceil = 7$$

and

$$J_1 = 2^{l-r-1} n_1 - (n - N + 2^l) = 2^{5-3-1} \times 7 - (45 - 64 + 2^5) = 1.$$

By Theorem 4.7 (a), $D_1 = (D_{t1} : D_{b1}) = (\tilde{D}_{t1} \cup S_{65} : D_{b1})$ with

$$\tilde{D}_{t1} = \left\{ \begin{array}{cccccc} 25 & 125 & 35 & 135 & 235 & 1235 \\ 145 & 245 & 1245 & 345 & 1345 & 2345 & 12345 \end{array} \right\}$$

and $D_{b1} = H_3$ has B-GMC among the $2^{45-39} : 2^3$ designs.

If we take $n = 43$, then $5 \times 2^l/16 + 1 \leqslant n - (N - 2^l) \leqslant 2^{l-1} - 2^{r-1}$ for $l = 5$ and

$$\left\lceil \frac{N - n - 2^{l-1} - 2^{r-1}}{2^{l-r} - 1} \right\rceil = \left\lceil \frac{64 - 43 - 16 - 4}{2^{5-3} - 1} \right\rceil = 1$$

is odd. Recall that

$$H_{r-1} = H_2 = \{1, 2, 12\}$$

and

$$H_{r,l-1} = H_{3,4} = \{\beta_1, \beta_2, \beta_3\} = \{3, 4, 34\}.$$

Note that $\beta_0 = I$ and $F_{lr} = F_{53} = \{5, 15, 25, 125\}$. Then

$$F_5 = \bigcup_{i=0}^{3} \beta_i F_{53} = \left\{ \begin{array}{cccc} 5 & 15 & 25 & 125 \\ 35 & 135 & 235 & 1235 \\ 45 & 145 & 245 & 1245 \\ 345 & 1345 & 2345 & 12345 \end{array} \right\}.$$

Further,

$$n_2 = \left\lceil \frac{n - N + 2^l}{2^{l-r} - 1} \right\rceil = \left\lceil \frac{43 - 64 + 2^5}{2^{5-3} - 1} \right\rceil = 4$$

and

$$J_2 = (n - N + 2^l) - (2^{l-r} - 1)(n_2 - 1) = (43 - 64 + 2^5) - (2^{5-3} - 1)(4 - 1) = 2.$$

By Theorem 4.7 (b), $D_2 = (D_{t2} : D_{b2}) = (\tilde{D}_{t2} \cup S_{65} : D_{b2})$ with

$$\tilde{D}_{t2} = \left\{ \begin{array}{cccc} 35 & 135 & 235 & 1235 \\ 45 & 145 & 245 & 1245 \\ & 1345 & 2345 & 12345 \end{array} \right\}$$

and $D_{b2} = H_2 \cup F_{53} = \{1, 2, 12, 5, 15, 25, 125\}$ has B-GMC among the $2^{43-37} : 2^3$ designs. □

Table 4.2 presents the range of parameter combinations covered by Theorem 4.7 for $N = 32, 64, 128$.

We comment that Zhang and Mukerjee (2009b) used the method of complementary design to construct B-GMC designs with s levels. Their results are applicable to construct B-GMC $2^{n-m} : 2^r$ designs. We refer to Section 9.4 for more details.

Table 4.2   The range of parameter combinations for $N = 32, 64, 128$

N	r	l	n from Theorem 4.7 (a)	n from Theorem 4.7 (b)
32	1	4	-	22-23
32	2	4	23	22
32	3	4	21-23	-
64	1	4	-	54-55
64	1	5	-	43-47
64	2	4	55	54
64	2	5	47	43-46
64	3	4	53-55	-
64	3	5	45-47	43-44
64	4	5	41-47	-
128	1	4	-	118-119
128	1	5	-	107-111
128	1	6	-	85-95
128	2	4	119	118
128	2	5	111	107-110
128	2	6	95	85-94
128	3	4	117-119	-
128	3	5	109-111	107-108
128	3	6	93-95	85-92
128	4	5	105-111	-
128	4	6	89-95	85-88
128	5	6	81-95	-

Outline of the proof of Theorem 4.7.

For the remainder of this section, we provide a brief outline of the proof for Theorem 4.7. Additional details can be found in Zhao and Zhao (2018).

Let $\tilde{D} = (\tilde{D}_t : D_b)$ with $\tilde{D}_t = D_t \backslash S_{ql}$. In the proof of Zhao and Zhao (2018), they first establish the relationship between the B-AENPs of D and $\tilde{D}$.

Lemma 4.9   *Suppose $D = (D_t : D_b)$ is a $2^{n-m} : 2^r$ design with $S_{ql} \subset D_t$ and $D_b \subset H_l$. Let $\tilde{D} = (\tilde{D}_t : D_b)$ with $\tilde{D}_t = D_t \backslash S_{ql}$. Then we have*

(a) $\#_1 C_2^{(k)}(D) = \begin{cases} constant, & if\ k < N/2 - 2^{l-1}, \\ \#_1 C_2^{(k-N/2+2^{l-1})}(\tilde{D}) + constant, & if\ k \geqslant N/2 - 2^{l-1}; \end{cases}$

(b) $\#_2 C_2^{(k)}(D) = \begin{cases} constant, & if\ k < N/2 - 2^{l-1} - 1, \\ (k+1)(2^l - 1 - f(\tilde{D})) + constant, & if\ k = N/2 - 2^{l-1} - 1, \\ (k+1)/(k+1-N/2+2^{l-1})\#_2 C_2^{(k-N/2+2^{l-1})}(\tilde{D}) + constant, \\ \qquad\qquad\qquad\qquad\qquad if\ k > N/2 - 2^{l-1} - 1, \end{cases}$

where $f(\tilde{D}) = |D_b| + |\{d : d \in H_q \backslash D_b, B_2(\tilde{D}_t, d) > 0\}|$;

(c) $\#_2 C_0(D) = constant + \#_2 C_0(\tilde{D})$,

where the constants are nonnegative and only depend on N, k, l, n, and r.

By Lemma 4.9, a design D has B-GMC if and only if the corresponding $\tilde{D}$ maximizes

$$\left({}^{\#}_1 C_2(\tilde{D}), {}^{\#}_2 C_0(\tilde{D}), -f(\tilde{D}), {}^{\#}_2 C_2(\tilde{D}) \right). \tag{4.8}$$

When $2^{l-1} \leqslant N - 1 - n \leqslant 2^l - 1$, the unblocked design $\tilde{D}_t$ contains $n - (N - 2^l)$ columns, where $n - (N - 2^l) < 2^{l-1}$. In this scenario, it is possible to find an unblocked design $\tilde{D}_t \subset H_l$ with a resolution of at least IV and containing $n - (N - 2^l)$ columns. One such design could be constructed by selecting the last $n - (N - 2^l)$ columns of H_l. It is worth noting that the first term ${}^{\#}_1 C_2(\tilde{D})$ in (4.8) is maximized when $\tilde{D}_t$ has a resolution of at least IV. Thus, a design $D = (D_t : D_b)$ has B-GMC if and only if the corresponding $\tilde{D}_t$ has a resolution of at least IV and $\tilde{D} = (\tilde{D}_t : D_b)$ maximizes

$$\left({}^{\#}_2 C_0(\tilde{D}), -f(\tilde{D}), {}^{\#}_2 C_2(\tilde{D}) \right). \tag{4.9}$$

The remaining steps of proving Theorem 4.7 follow a similar approach to proving Theorem 4.1. For further details, we refer to Zhao and Zhao (2018).

4.3.3 Weak B-GMC $2^{n-m} : 2^r$ Designs

In the previous two subsections, we have discussed methods for constructing B-GMC designs when $n \geqslant 5N/16+1$. However, there is currently no general method available for the case where $n \leqslant 5N/16$. Recall that the B-GMC design sequentially maximizes

$$ {}^{\#}C(D) = ({}^{\#}_1 C_2(D), {}^{\#}_2 C_0(D), {}^{\#}_2 C_2(D)). $$

If a design only sequentially maximizes the first two terms $({}^{\#}_1 C_2(D), {}^{\#}_2 C_0(D))$, it is referred to as a weak B-GMC design.

In the following, we discuss a general method to construct the weak B-GMC design when $n \leqslant N/2 - 2^{r-1}$. In this case, by applying the same argument presented at the beginning of Section 4.3.1, the first term ${}^{\#}_1 C_2(D)$ is sequentially maximized if D_t has a resolution of at least IV. Without loss of generality, we assume that $D_b = H_r$ in this subsection.

Note that

$$ {}^{\#}_2 C_0(D) = \binom{n}{2} - A_{21} $$

as we only consider the design with $A_{10} = A_{20} = A_{11} = 0$. In the following theorem, we provide a lower bound for A_{21} and, consequently, an upper bound for $_2^{\#}C_0(D)$. Recall that for a real number x, $\lceil x \rceil$ denotes the smallest integer that is larger than or equal to x.

Theorem 4.10 *Suppose that $D = (D_t : D_b)$ is a $2^{n-m} : 2^r$ design with $D_b = H_r$. Let $n_1 = \lceil n/(2^{q-r} - 1) \rceil$ and $J_1 = n - (2^{q-r} - 1)(n_1 - 1)$. We then have*

$$A_{21}(D) \geqslant J_1 n_1 (n_1 - 1)/2 + (2^{q-r} - 1 - J_1)(n_1 - 1)(n_1 - 2)/2. \qquad (4.10)$$

Proof. Let $D_{tj} = D_t \cap \{a_j, a_j H_r\}$, $a_j \in H_{r+1,q}$, $j = 1, \cdots, 2^{q-r} - 1$. Then

$$D_t = \bigcup_{j=1}^{2^{q-r}-1} D_{tj} \text{ and } \sum_{j=1}^{2^{q-r}-1} |D_{tj}| = n.$$

From the definition of A_{21}, $A_{21}(D)$ is the number of pairs (d_1, d_2) in D_t such that $d_1 d_2 \in H_r$. Note that $d_1 d_2 \in H_r$ if and only if both d_1 and d_2 are from the same D_{tj}. Then, we have

$$A_{21}(D) = \sum_{j=1}^{2^{q-r}-1} |D_{tj}|(|D_{tj}| - 1)/2 = \sum_{j=1}^{2^{q-r}-1} |D_{tj}|^2/2 - n/2.$$

Since $\sum_{j=1}^{2^{q-r}-1} |D_{tj}| = n$ and $|D_{tj}|$ can only be non-negative integers, it can be verified that the value of A_{21} is minimized if and only if the $|D_{tj}|$'s differ by at most one and the minimum value of A_{21} is that provided in (4.10). $\qquad \square$

We would like to emphasize that the lower bound in (4.10) is always tight. This is due to the fact that, for any given values of n, m, and r, there exists a $2^{n-m} : 2^r$ design where the value of A_{21} is equal to the lower bound in (4.10). For more details, we refer to Zhao, Li, and Karunamuni (2013).

The following theorem discusses the construction of weak B-GMC $2^{n-m} : 2^r$ designs.

Theorem 4.11 *Suppose that $D = (D_t : D_b)$ is a $2^{n-m} : 2^r$ design with $D_b = H_r$ and $n \leqslant N/2 - 2^{r-1}$. Let $D_{tj} = D_t \cap \{a_j r, a_j r H_{r-1}\}$, $a_j \in H_{r+1,q}$, $j = 1, \cdots, 2^{q-r} - 1$. If $D_t \subset \cup_{j=1}^{2^{q-r}-1}\{a_j r, a_j r H_{r-1}\}$ and the $|D_{tj}|$'s differ by at most one, then D_t sequentially maximizes $(_1^{\#}C_2(D), _2^{\#}C_0(D))$. That is, the resulting $2^{n-m} : 2^r$ design D is a weak B-GMC design.*

Proof. Because of the structure of the design $\cup_{j=1}^{2^{q-r}-1}\{a_j r, a_j r H_{r-1}\}$, for any two columns d_1 and d_2 in this design, their interaction should not be in this design. With $D_t \subset \cup_{j=1}^{2^{q-r}-1}\{a_j r, a_j r H_{r-1}\}$, it follows that D_t has the resolution of at least IV. Hence, ${}_1^{\#}C_2(D)$ is maximized.

Following the same arguments as in Theorem 4.10, $A_{21}(D)$ achieves the lower bound in (4.10) and hence ${}_2^{\#}C_0(D) = \binom{n}{2} - A_{21}(D)$ is maximized. Therefore, D is a weak B-GMC design.   □

The following example illustrates how to apply the construction method of Theorem 4.11.

Example 4.12   Let us consider the $2^{7-2} : 2^3$ designs with $q = 5$ and $r = 3$. Further let $1, 2, 3, 4, 5$ denote the five independent columns,

$$D_b = H_r = \{1, 2, 12, 3, 13, 23, 123\}, \text{ and } H_{r+1,q} = \{a_1 = 4, a_2 = 5, a_3 = 45\}.$$

Note that $n = 7 < N/2 - 2^{r-1} = 12$.

Let $H_{3-1} = \{1, 2, 12\}$. Then we have

$$\{a_1 r, a_1 r H_{r-1}\} = \{34, 134, 234, 1234\},$$

$$\{a_2 r, a_2 r H_{r-1}\} = \{35, 135, 235, 1235\},$$

$$\{a_3 r, a_3 r H_{r-1}\} = \{345, 1345, 2345, 12345\}.$$

If $D_t = \{34, 134, 35, 135, 345, 1345, 2345\}$, then $D_t \subset \cup_{j=1}^3 \{a_j r, a_j r H_{r-1}\}$ and $|D_{t1}|$, $|D_{t2}|$, and $|D_{t3}|$ differ by at most one. By Theorem 4.11, the design $D = (D_t : D_b)$ is a weak B-GMC $2^{7-2} : 2^3$ design.   □

4.4   Construction of B¹-GMC Designs

Zhao, Li, Zhang, and Karunamuni (2013), Guo, Zhou, and Zhang (2015), Zhao, Zhao, and Liu (2016), and Zhao and Sun (2017) collectively completed the construction of B¹-GMC $2^{n-m} : 2^r$ designs with $n > N/4$. This section provides a summary of their main findings.

Applying the same arguments as presented at the beginning of Section 4.3, we find that when $r = q - 1$, the design $D = (D_t : D_b)$, where D_t consists of the last n columns of F_q and $D_b = H_{q-1}$, is a B¹-GMC $2^{n-m} : 2^r$ design. Consequently, in the following three subsections, our focus will be on the case where $r \leqslant q - 2$.

4.4.1 B^1-GMC $2^{n-m} : 2^r$ Designs with $n \geqslant 5N/16 + 1$

We first present the construction method for the case where $n \geqslant 5N/16 + 1$.

Theorem 4.13   *Let $D = (D_t : D_b)$ denote a $2^{n-m} : 2^r$ design.*

(a) *Suppose $5N/16 + 1 \leqslant n \leqslant N/2$, and D_t consists of the last n columns of F_q or H_q with Yates order. Then D has B^1-GMC if $D_b = H_r$ when $N/2 - 2^{r-1} + 1 \leqslant n \leqslant N/2$, and $D_b = H_{r-1} \cup F_{qr}$ when $5N/16 + 1 \leqslant n \leqslant N/2 - 2^{r-1}$.*

(b) *Suppose $n > N/2$. Then D has B^1-GMC if D_t consists of the last n columns of H_q with Yates order and $D_b = H_r$.*

To illustrate the construction method in Theorem 4.13, we provide the following examples.

Example 4.14   Consider the construction of B^1-GMC $2^{15-10} : 2^2$ and $2^{12-7} : 2^2$ designs. Here, $N = 32$, $q = 5$, and $r = 2$.

First, we have

$$F_5 = \{5, 15, 25, 125, 35, 135, 235, 1235, 45, 145, 245, 1245, 345, 1345, 2345, 12345\},$$

which is from H_5 and has Yates order. For $2^{15-10} : 2^2$ design, we take the last 15 columns of F_5 as D_t, i.e.,

$$D_t = \{15, 25, 125, 35, 135, 235, 1235, 45, 145, 245, 1245, 345, 1345, 2345, 12345\},$$

and take $D_b = \{1, 2, 12\}$ because $n = 15$ is the first case of Theorem 4.13 (a). Then the design $D = (D_t : D_b)$ is a B^1-GMC $2^{15-10} : 2^2$ design.

When $n = 12$, which is the second case of Theorem 4.13 (a), we take the last 12 columns of F_5 as D_t, i.e.,

$$D_t = \{35, 135, 235, 1235, 45, 145, 245, 1245, 345, 1345, 2345, 12345\},$$

and $D_b = \{1, 5, 15\}$. The design $D = (D_t : D_b)$ is just a B^1-GMC $2^{12-7} : 2^2$ design.   □

Example 4.15   Consider the construction of B^1-GMC $2^{20-15} : 2^3$ designs. Here, $N = 32$, $q = 5$, and $r = 3$.

To construct the B^1-GMC design, we need to use the saturated design H_5, which can be written as

$$H_5 = \{1, 2, 12, 3, 13, 23, 123, 4, 14, 24, 124, 34, 134, 234, 1234\} \cup F_5,$$

where F_5 has been given in Example 4.14. By Theorem 4.13 (b), taking the last 20 columns of H_5 as D_t, i.e., $D_t = \{34, 134, 234, 1234\} \cup F_5$, and $D_b = H_3 = \{1, 2, 12, 3, 13, 23, 123\}$, then $D = (D_t : D_b)$ is a B^1-GMC $2^{20-15} : 2^3$ design. □

Outline of the proof of Theorem 4.13.

For the sake of clarity, we provide an outline of the proof. For more details, we refer to Zhao, Li, Zhang, and Karunamuni (2013).

For the B-GMC and B^1-GMC criteria, the first term ${}_1^{\#}C_2(D)$ remains the same. Therefore, some discussion presented in Sections 4.3.1 and 4.3.2 are applicable to this context as well.

We start with part (a). The proof consists of three steps. In Step 1, we apply the results established in the proof of Theorem 4.1 to our current situation. As discussed in Section 4.3.1, when ${}_1^{\#}C_2(D)$ is maximized, we can assume, up to isomorphism, $D_t \subset F_q$. Additionally, as indicated in Lemma 4.4, we need to consider two possibilities for the block effects D_b: (i) $D_b = H_r$ and (ii) $D_b = H_{r-1} \cup F_{qr}$. Note that in the AENP of B^1-GMC in (4.3), ${}_2^{\#}C_0(D)$ is absent. Using Lemma 4.5, we then have the $2^{n-m} : 2^r$ design $D = (D_t : D_b)$ has the B^1-GMC if D^* maximizes

$$(-f(D^*), {}_2^{\#}C_2(D^*)), \tag{4.11}$$

where $D^* = (D_t^* : D_b^*)$ with $D_t^* = F_q \backslash D_t$ and $D_b^* = H_{q-1} \cap D_b$.

In Step 2, we identify the structure of the designs which maximize (4.11).

Lemma 4.16 Let $\tilde{S} = (\tilde{S}_t : S_b)$, where $\tilde{S}_t$ consists of the first or the last s columns of F_q with Yates order and $S_b = H_a$. Then $\tilde{S}$ maximizes

$$(-f(S), {}_2^{\#}C_2(S)) \tag{4.12}$$

among all $S = (S_t : S_b)$ with S_t being an s-subset of F_q.

In Step 3, we apply Lemma 4.16 to complete the proof of Part (a).

Now, let's consider part (b). Suppose that

$$2^{l-1} \leqslant N - 1 - n \leqslant 2^l - 1.$$

If $l = r$, then $N - 1 - n = 2^r - 1$, and all the $2^{n-m} : 2^r$ designs are isomorphic. In the following, we assume that $r + 1 \leqslant l \leqslant q - 1$.

The proof of Part (b) involves two steps. In Step 1, we apply the results and discussions presented in the proof of Theorem 4.7 to the current scenario. Following the discussion at the beginning of Section 4.3.2, we may assume that $S_{ql} \subset D_t$ and $D_b \subset H_l$. Denote $D_t^* = D_t \backslash S_{ql}$ and $D^* = (D_t^* : D_b)$. By the definition of B^1-GMC design, Lemma 4.9 implies that a design D has B^1-GMC if and only if the corresponding D^* maximizes

$$({}_1^\#C_2(D^*), -f(D^*), {}_2^\#C_2(D^*)). \tag{4.13}$$

Note that when $2^{l-1} \leqslant N - 1 - n \leqslant 2^l - 1$, there are l independent factors in H_l and $n - (N - 2^l)$ $(< 2^{l-1})$ factors in D_t^*. Therefore, in H_l, we can find an unblocked design with $n - (N - 2^l)$ factors that has a resolution of at least *IV*. Additionally, note that the first term ${}_1^\#C_2(D^*)$ in (4.13) is maximized if D_t^* has a resolution of at least *IV*. Hence, the design D has B^1-GMC if and only if D_t^* has a resolution of at least *IV* and D^* maximizes

$$(-f(D^*), {}_2^\#C_2(D^*)). \tag{4.14}$$

In Step 2, we apply Lemma 4.16 to complete the proof of Part (b).

4.4.2   B^1-GMC $2^{n-m} : 2^r$ Designs with $9N/32 + 1 \leqslant n \leqslant 5N/16$

In this section, we present the method to construct the B^1-GMC $2^{n-m} : 2^r$ design with $9N/32 + 1 \leqslant n \leqslant 5N/16$ and $r \leqslant q - 2$.

Recall that the SOS design with $5N/16$ runs in Example 3.8 is given by

$$S_{(5N/16)} = D^{q-4}(X) = (D^{q-4}(x_1), D^{q-4}(x_2), D^{q-4}(x_3), D^{q-4}(x_4), D^{q-4}(x_5)),$$

where $X = (1, 2, 3, 4, 1234)_{2^4} = (x_1, x_2, x_3, x_4, x_5)$. The detailed forms of $D^{q-4}(x_i)$ for $i = 1, \cdots, 5$ are given in (3.15).

The following result from Zhao, Zhao, and Liu (2016) indicates that if D has B^1-GMC, then the unblocked design D_t should have GMC, and the block effects D_b needs to take some specific forms. The ideas of the proof are close to those of Theorems 3.16 and Part (a) of Theorem 4.13. For more detailed information, readers can refer to Zhao, Zhao, and Liu (2016).

Theorem 4.17   *Suppose* $D = (D_t : D_b)$ *is a* $2^{n-m} : 2^r$ *design with* $9N/32 + 1 \leqslant n \leqslant 5N/16$. *Then,* D *has* B^1-*GMC if* D_t *consists of the last* n *columns of* $S_{(5N/16)}$ *with RC-Yates order (i.e.,* D_t *is a* 2^{n-m} *GMC design), and*

(a) *when* $r \leqslant q - 4$ *and* $5N/16 - 2^{r-1} + 1 \leqslant n \leqslant 5N/16$, $D_b = H_{5,r+4}$;

(b) *when* $r \leqslant q-4$ *and* $9N/32+1 \leqslant n \leqslant 5N/16-2^{r-1}$, $D_b = (H_{5,r+3}, 1, 1H_{5,r+3})$;

(c) *when* $r = q - 3$, $D_b = (H_{5,q}, 23, 23H_{5,q})$;

(d) *when* $r = q - 2$, $D_b = (H_{5,q}, 23, 23H_{5,q}, 24, 24H_{5,q}, 34, 34H_{5,q})$.

The following example illustrates the construction method in Theorem 4.17.

Example 4.18   Consider the construction of $2^{38-31} : 2^r$ B¹-GMC designs. Then, $q = 7$, and $N = 2^7$. Take the last 38 columns of $S_{(5N/16)}$ as D_t.

Next, we consider the block effects matrices D_b for $r = 1, 2, 3, 4, 5$, respectively. For $r = 1, 2$, which correspond to case (b) of Theorem 4.17, we can get $D_b = 1$ for $r = 1$ and $D_b = (5, 1, 15)$ for $r = 2$.

For $r = 3, 4, 5$, which correspond to cases (a), (c), and (d) of Theorem 4.17 respectively, we can get $D_b = H_{5,7}$ for $r = 3$, $D_b = (H_{5,7}, 23, 23H_{5,7})$ for $r = 4$, and

$$D_b = (H_{5,7}, 23, 23H_{5,7}, 24, 24H_{57}, 34, 34H_{5,7})$$

for $r = 5$. The constructed designs are all B¹-GMC designs by Theorem 4.17.   □

4.4.3   B¹-GMC $2^{n-m} : 2^r$ Designs with $N/4 + 1 \leqslant n \leqslant 9N/32$

In this section, we consider the construction of B¹-GMC $2^{n-m} : 2^r$ designs with $N/4+1 \leqslant n \leqslant 9N/32$ and $r \leqslant q - 2$. We only present the construction results. The main ideas of the proof in this section closely follow those presented in Section 3.4. Interested readers can refer to Zhao and Sun (2017) for further details.

We begin with the case where $n = N/4 + 1$. Recall that in (3.25), we introduce a special matrix:

$$\Phi(t) = (t, t(t - 1), (t - 1)H_{1,t-2}^t)_{2^t} = (a_1, \cdots, a_{2^{t-2}+1})$$

for $4 \leqslant t \leqslant q$. In Theorem 3.20, we stated that $\Phi(q)$ is a GMC 2^{n-m} design with $n = N/4 + 1$ factors. The following theorem tells that by selecting $\Phi(q)$ as D_t and assigning suitable $2^r - 1$ columns of H_q to D_b, the resulting design $D = (D_t : D_b)$ is a B^1-GMC $2^{n-m} : 2^r$ design.

Theorem 4.19   *For $n = N/4 + 1$ and $r \leqslant q - 2$, let $D_t = \Phi(q)$ and $D_b = H_r$. Then, the design $D = (D_t : D_b)$ has B^1-GMC among all the $2^{n-m} : 2^r$ designs.*

The design constructed in Theorem 4.19 is isomorphic to the design in Theorem 9 of Chen, Li, Liu, and Zhang (2006) and the design in Theorem 2 of Li, Chen, Liu, and Zhang (2006), where they discussed the construction of block designs with the maximum number of clear 2fi's. The following example illustrates the method in Theorem 4.19.

Example 4.20   Consider the construction of B^1-GMC $2^{9-4} : 2^2$ design. Here, $n = 9$, $m = 4$, $q = 5$, $N = 32$, and $r = 2$. Let

$$D_t = \Phi(5) = (5, 45, 14, 24, 124, 34, 134, 234, 1234)_{2^5}$$

and $D_b = H_2 = (1, 2, 12)_{2^5}$. Then, the design $D = (D_t : D_b)$ is a B^1-GMC $2^{9-4} : 2^2$ design.   □

Next, we consider the construction of B^1-GMC $2^{n-m} : 2^r$ designs with $n = (2^{t-2} + 1)N/2^t$, where $5 \leqslant t \leqslant q - 1$. The following theorem shows that the design obtained by optimally blocking the GMC 2^{n-m} design $D_t = D^{q-t}(\Phi(t))$ has B^1-GMC.

Theorem 4.21   *Let $n = (2^{t-2}+1)N/2^t$, where $5 \leqslant t \leqslant q-1$. The $2^{n-m} : 2^r$ design $D = (D_t : D_b)$ has B^1-GMC if $D_t = D^{q-t}(\Phi(t))$ and*

   (a) when $r \leqslant q - t$, $D_b = H_{t+1,t+r}$;

   (b) when $q - t < r \leqslant q - 2$, D_b is the closed subset generated by $1, \cdots, r - (q - t), t + 1, \cdots, q$.

The following example illustrates the construction method in Theorem 4.21.

Example 4.22   Consider the construction of B^1-GMC $2^{36-29} : 2^r$ design. Here, $n = 36$, $m = 29$, $q = 7$, $N = 128$, $t = 5$, and $q - t = 2$.

If $r = 2$, by Theorem 4.21 (a), let $D_t = D^2(\Phi(5))$ and $D_b = H_{6,7}$, then the design $D = (D_t : D_b)$ is a B^1-GMC $2^{36-29} : 2^2$ design.

If $r = 3$, by Theorem 4.21 (b), let $D_t = D^2(\Phi(5))$ and $D_b = (1, 6, 16, 7, 17, 67, 167)$, then the design $D = (D_t : D_b)$ is a B^1-GMC $2^{36-29} : 2^3$ design.   □

Now, let us consider the construction of B^1-GMC $2^{n-m} : 2^r$ designs, where $(2^{t-1} + 1)N/2^{t+1} < n < (2^{t-2} + 1)N/2^t$ for $t = 5, \cdots, q - 1$. The following Theorem demonstrates that the design obtained by optimally blocking the GMC 2^{n-m} design

D_t still has B¹-GMC.

Theorem 4.23   *Let $l_t = (2^{t-2} + 1)N/2^t - n$. Suppose $(2^{t-1} + 1)N/2^{t+1} < n <$*
$(2^{t-2} + 1)N/2^t$ and $2^{z-1} \leqslant l_t \leqslant 2^z - 1$, where $5 \leqslant t \leqslant q - 1$ and $1 \leqslant z \leqslant q - t - 1$.
Then, the $2^{n-m} : 2^r$ design $D = (D_t : D_b)$ has B¹-GMC if D_t consists of the last n
columns of $D^{q-t}(\Phi(t))$ with RC-Yates order and

  (a) *when $r \leqslant z$, $D_b = H_{t,t+r-1}$;*

  (b) *when $z < r \leqslant q - t$, $D_b = H_{t+1,t+r}$;*

  (c) *when $q - t < r \leqslant q - 2$, D_b is the closed subset generated by $1, \cdots, r - (q -$*
$t), t + 1, \cdots, q$.

The following example illustrates the construction method in Theorem 4.23.

Example 4.24   Consider the construction of B¹-GMC $2^{70-62} : 2^r$ design. Here,
$n = 70$, $m = 62$, $q = 8$, $N = 256$, $N(2^{t-1} + 1)/2^{t+1} < n < N(2^{t-2} + 1)/2^t$ for $t = 5$,
$l_t = 2$, and $z = 2$. Hence, $q - t = 3$. Let D_t consist of the last 70 columns of $D^3(\Phi(5))$
with RC-Yates order.

When $r = 2$, let $D_b = H_{5,6}$. Then, by Theorem 4.23 (a), the design $D = (D_t : D_b)$
is a B¹-GMC $2^{70-62} : 2^2$ design.

When $r = 3$, let $D_b = H_{6,8}$. Then, by Theorem 4.23 (b), the design $D = (D_t : D_b)$
is a B¹-GMC $2^{70-62} : 2^3$ design.

When $r = 4$, let

$$D_b = (1, H_{6,8}, 1H_{6,8}).$$

Then, by Theorem 4.23 (c), the design $D = (D_t : D_b)$ is a B¹-GMC $2^{70-62} : 2^4$
design.   □

4.5   Construction of B²-GMC Designs

This section discusses the construction of B²-GMC designs with multi block variables.
We continue to use the notation $2^{n-m} : 2^r$ to denote a regular blocked design $D =$
$(D_t : D_b)$ with $N = 2^q$ runs, n treatment factors, and r block factors. In this
notation, D_t refers to the unblocked 2^{n-m} design, while D_b denotes a $2^q \times r$ blocking
scheme matrix in which each column represents a block factor.

Two $2^{n-m} : 2^r$ designs, denoted as $D^1 = (D_t^1 : D_b^1)$ and $D^2 = (D_t^2 : D_b^2)$, are considered isomorphic if there exists an isomorphism mapping that maps D_t^1 onto D_t^2 and D_b^1 onto D_b^2. Suppose that effects involving three or more treatment (block) factors can be ignored. Recall that B^2-GMC designs sequentially maximize the pattern (4.3).

Zhao, Zhao, and Liu (2018) as well as Zhao (2021a, b) discussed the construction of B^2-GMC designs with multiblock variables. In this section, we provide a summary of these results. For detailed proofs and further information, please refer to the aforementioned three papers.

4.5.1 B^2-GMC $2^{n-m} : 2^r$ Designs with $n \geqslant 5N/16 + 1$

In this section, we focus on the constructions of B^2-GMC $2^{n-m} : 2^r$ designs with $n \geqslant 5N/16 + 1$. We begin by considering the case where $5N/16 + 1 \leqslant n \leqslant N/2$ and $N \geqslant 16$.

Theorem 4.25   *Suppose $D = (D_t : D_b)$ is a $2^{n-m} : 2^r$ design with $2^p \leqslant N/2 - n \leqslant 2^{p+1} - 1$ for some $p \leqslant q - 3$ and $2^l \leqslant r \leqslant 2^{l+1} - 1$ for some $l \leqslant q - 2$. The design $D = (D_t : D_b)$ is a B^2-GMC design if D_t consists of the last n columns of F_q and*

(a) *D_b is any r-projection of $H_l \cup F_{q(l+1)}$ when $1 \leqslant l \leqslant p$,*

(b) *D_b is any r-projection of H_{l+1} when $p + 1 \leqslant l \leqslant q - 2$.*

In the following, an example is provided to illustrate the construction of B^2-GMC $2^{n-m} : 2^r$ designs with $5N/16 + 1 \leqslant n \leqslant N/2$.

Example 4.26   Let us consider the construction of B^2-GMC $2^{12-7} : 2^2$ and $2^{12-7} : 2^9$ designs. For both B^2-GMC designs to be constructed, we have $n = 12$, $m = 7$, $q = 5$, $N = 32$ and $p = 2$ as $2^2 \leqslant N/2 - n \leqslant 2^3 - 1$. The values of the parameters N and n satisfy $5N/16 + 1 \leqslant n \leqslant N/2$. Therefore, to construct these two B^2-GMC designs, D_t should be the last 12 columns of F_5 in Yates order, i.e.,

$$D_t = \{35, 135, 235, 1235, 45, 145, 245, 1245, 345, 1345, 2345, 12345\}.$$

For the case $2^{12-7} : 2^2$, we have $r = 2$ which gives $l = 1$. Therefore, we should choose D_b according to Theorem 4.25 (a) as $l < p$. From Theorem 4.25 (a), without loss of generality, we choose $D_{b1} = \{1, 5\}$ which is a 2-projection of $H_1 \cup F_{52}$. Then,

$D = (D_t : D_{b1})$ is a B²-GMC $2^{12-7} : 2^2$ design.

For the case $2^{12-7} : 2^9$, we have $r = 9$ which gives $l = 3$. Therefore, we should choose D_b according to Theorem 4.25 (b) as $l > p$. From Theorem 4.25 (b), without loss of generality, we choose $D_{b2} = \{1, 2, 12, 3, 13, 23, 123, 4, 14\}$ which is a 9-projection of H_4. Then $D = (D_t : D_{b2})$ is a B²-GMC $2^{9-4} : 2^9$ design.   □

Now, we consider the construction of B²-GMC $2^{n-m} : 2^r$ designs with $n > N/2$. Following a similar approach to the construction of B-GMC and B¹-GMC designs with $n > N/2$, we should also first consider to maximize ${}^\#_1 C_2(D_t)$. Suppose the number of columns in $H_q \backslash D_t$ satisfies

$$2^p \leqslant N - 1 - n \leqslant 2^{p+1} - 1$$

for some $p \leqslant q - 2$. Based on Part (a) of Theorem 3.2 and the discussions in Sections 4.3.2 and 4.4.1, when $n > N/2$, if D_t maximizes ${}^\#_1 C_2(D_t)$, then $H_q \backslash D_t \subset H_{p+1}$ up to isomorphism. This implies that $D_b \subset H_{p+1}$.

Suppose $2^l \leqslant r \leqslant 2^{l+1} - 1$ for some $l \leqslant q - 2$. In the case where $l = p$ with $N - 1 - n = 2^{l+1} - 1$, the construction is trivial. We have $D_t = H_q \backslash H_{l+1}$, and thus $D_b \subset H_{l+1}$. This implies that the design $D = (D_t : D_b)$, where $D_t = H_q \backslash H_{l+1}$ and D_b is any r-projection of H_{l+1}, is a B²-GMC design. The following theorem considers the construction of B²-GMC designs for the case of $l < p$.

Theorem 4.27   *Suppose $D = (D_t : D_b)$ is a $2^{n-m} : 2^r$ design with $2^p \leqslant N-1-n \leqslant 2^{p+1} - 1$ for some $p \leqslant q - 2$ and $2^l \leqslant r \leqslant 2^{l+1} - 1$ for some $l < p$. The design $D = (D_t : D_b)$ is a B²-GMC design if D_t consists of the last n columns of H_q and D_b is any r-projection of H_{l+1}.*

In the following, an example is provided to illustrate the construction of B²-GMC $2^{n-m} : 2^r$ designs with $n > N/2$.

Example 4.28   Let us consider the construction of B²-GMC $2^{9-5} : 2^2$ and $2^{12-8} : 2^3$ designs.

For the case $2^{9-5} : 2^2$, we have $n = 9$, $m = 5$, $q = 4$, $N = 16$ and $p = 2$ as $2^2 \leqslant N - n - 1 \leqslant 2^3 - 1$. Since $r = 2$, we obtain $l < p$ as $l = 1$. According to Theorem 4.27, let

$$D_{t1} = \{123, 4, 14, 24, 124, 34, 134, 234, 1234\}$$

be the last 9 columns of H_4 in Yates order, and $D_{b1} = \{1, 2\}$ be a 2-projection of H_2. Then $D = (D_{t1} : D_{b1})$ is a B²-GMC $2^{9-5} : 2^2$ design.

For the case $2^{12-8} : 2^3$, we have $n = 12$, $m = 8$, $q = 4$, $N = 16$ and $p = 1$ as $2^1 \leqslant N - n - 1 \leqslant 2^2 - 1$. Since $r = 3$, we obtain $l = p$ as $l = 1$. As discussed in the paragraph before Theorem 4.27, let

$$D_{t2} = \{3, 13, 23, 123, 4, 14, 24, 124, 34, 134, 234, 1234\}$$

be the last 12 columns of H_4, and $D_{b2} = \{1, 2, 12\} = H_2$. Then $D = (D_{t2} : D_{b2})$ is a B²-GMC $2^{12-8} : 2^3$ design.   □

4.5.2   B²-GMC $2^{n-m} : 2^r$ Designs with $N/4 + 1 \leqslant n \leqslant 5N/16$

This section summaries the construction results of B²-GMC $2^{n-m} : 2^r$ designs with $N/4 + 1 \leqslant n \leqslant 5N/16$. We begin by considering the construction of B²-GMC $2^{n-m} : 2^r$ designs with $n = N/4 + 1$.

Recall the notation

$$\Phi(t) = (t, t(t-1), (t-1)H_{1,t-2}^t)_{2^t} = (a_1, \cdots, a_{2^{t-2}+1})$$

for $4 \leqslant t \leqslant q$. Furthermore, $\Phi(q)$ is the GMC 2^{n-m} design with $n = N/4 + 1$. Theorem 4.29 provides the construction of B²-GMC $2^{n-m} : 2^r$ designs with $n = N/4 + 1$.

Theorem 4.29   *Suppose $D = (D_t : D_b)$ is a $2^{n-m} : 2^r$ design with $n = N/4 + 1$ and $2^l \leqslant r \leqslant 2^{l+1} - 1$ for some l $(0 \leqslant l \leqslant q - 3)$, then $D = (D_t : D_b)$ is a B²-GMC design if $D_t = \Phi(q)$ and D_b is any r-projection of H_{l+1}.*

The following example illustrates the construction method in Theorem 4.29.

Example 4.30   Let us consider the constuction of a B²-GMC $2^{9-4} : 2^5$ design. Here, $n = 9, m = 4, q = 5$, $N = 32$, and $r = 5$, which leads to $l = 2$. By applying Theorem 4.29, let $D_t = \{5, 45, 4H_3\}$ and D_b be any 5-projection of H_3, say $D_b = \{1, 2, 12, 3, 13\}$. Then $D = (D_t : D_b)$ is a B²-GMC $2^{9-4} : 2^5$ design.   □

Now, we consider the construction of B²-GMC $2^{n-m} : 2^r$ designs with $N/4 + 1 < n \leqslant 5N/16$. Write $D^{q-t}(\Phi(t))$ as

$$D^{q-t}(\Phi(t)) = (D^{q-t}(a_1), \cdots, D^{q-t}(a_{2^{t-2}+1})). \tag{4.15}$$

Theorem 4.31 constructs B²-GMC $2^{n-m} : 2^r$ designs with $N/4 + 1 < n \leqslant 5N/16$.

Theorem 4.31 *Let $D = (D_t : D_b)$ be a $2^{n-m} : 2^r$ design with $N(2^{t-1}+1)/2^{t+1} < n \leqslant N(2^{t-2}+1)/2^t$ for $t \geqslant 4$ and $2^l \leqslant r \leqslant 2^{l+1}-1$ for some $0 \leqslant l \leqslant q-3$. Suppose $2^p \leqslant N(2^{t-2}+1)/2^t - n \leqslant 2^{p+1}-1$ for some $0 \leqslant p \leqslant q-t-1$, then D is a B^2-GMC design if D_t consists of the last n columns of $D^{q-t}(\Phi(t))$ and*

    (a) *D_b is any r-projection of $(t, tH_{t+1,t+l})$ when $l \leqslant p \leqslant q-t-2$;*

    (b) *D_b is any r-projection of $H_{t+1,q}$ when $p+1 \leqslant l \leqslant q-t-1$;*

    (c) *D_b is any r-projection of H_{q-2} when $q-t-1 < l \leqslant q-3$.*

Remark 4.32 According to Theorem 4.31, when constructing B²-GMC designs with $N/4+1 < n \leqslant 5N/16$, we can first partition the range $(N/4+1, 5N/16]$ into $q-4$ sequential subranges as $(N(2^{t-1}+1)/2^{t+1}, N(2^{t-2}+1)/2^t]$ with $t = 4, 5, \cdots$, $q-1$, and then obtain the B²-GMC designs according to Theorem 4.31.

In the following, an example is provided to illustrate the constructions of B²-GMC $2^{n-m} : 2^r$ designs with $N/4+1 < n \leqslant 5N/16$.

Example 4.33 Let us consider the construction of B²-GMC $2^{19-13} : 2^r$ designs with $r = 1, 3, 4$. Here, we have $n = 19, m = 13, q = 6$, and $N = 64$. It is worth noting that the values of parameters N and n satisfy $N/4+1 < n \leqslant 5N/16$.

From Remark 4.32, we can observe that $n = 19$ falls within the range $(18, 20]$ with $t = 4$. According to Theorem 4.31, D_t should be the last 19 columns of $D^{q-t}(\Phi(4))$. Since $5N/16 - n = 20 - 19 = 1$, we have $p = 0$. Now, we proceed to choose D_b for $r = 1, 3, 4$.

For $r = 1$, we have $l = 0$. According to Theorem 4.31 (a), $D_b = t$ as $H_{5,4} = \varnothing$.

For $r = 3$, we have $l = 1$. According to Theorem 4.31 (b), D_b should be a 3-projection of $H_{5,6}$.

For $r = 4$, we have $l = 2$. According to Theorem 4.31 (c), D_b should be a 4-projection of H_4. Without loss of generality, we choose $D_b = \{1, 2, 12, 3\}$. $\qquad\square$

5 Factor Aliased and Blocked Factor Aliased Effect-Number Patterns

Zhou, Balakrishnan, and Zhang (2013) extended the AENP to the factor aliased effect-number pattern (F-AENP) for ranking the columns of a regular design. Subsequently, Wang, Ye, Zhou, and Zhang (2017) further extended the AENP to the blocked factor aliased effect-number pattern (B-F-AENP) for ranking the columns of a blocked regular design. This chapter provides a summary of their findings.

5.1 Factor Aliased Effect-Number Pattern of GMC Designs

In an experiment, it is important to assign the factors to appropriate columns within the design. This section introduces the F-AENP as a ranking method for the columns of a regular design, with the goal of achieving efficient implementation of GMC designs in practice. We provide the best F-AENP columns for any GMC 2^{n-m} design, where $5N/16 \leqslant n \leqslant N - 1$.

5.1.1 Factor Aliased Effect-Number Pattern

When an experimenter selects a design for their experiment, a crucial consideration is how to allocate the factors to the columns of the design so that the important effects and related models can be best estimated. In practice, experimenters often have a prior understanding of the relative importance of factors in the experiment and intend to prioritize the effects associated with these important factors. To do this, the experimenter needs to know, for a given design, which columns are "good" ones that are suitable for assigning the important factors and the remaining ones are for the others.

Example 5.1　Consider the 2^{6-2} design $\{1, 12, 123, 4, 134, 234\}$ taken from H_4. Denote the 6 factors (columns) of the design by $d_1, \cdots, d_6$, respectively. Its defining relation is

$$I = d_1 d_2 d_3 d_4 d_5 = d_1 d_3 d_4 d_6 = d_2 d_5 d_6.$$

Through a simple computation, we get the confounding between the main effects and 2fi's of the six factors, as shown in Table 5.1. From the table, we can see that d_1, d_3, and d_4 are equally the best ones, d_2 and d_5 are equally good but worse than d_1, d_3, and d_4, and d_6 is the worst one as far as the lower-order confounding between them is concerned.　　　　　□

Table 5.1　Lower-order confounding situations relating to the six factors of the 2^{6-2} design in terms of factor interactions

Factor	Main effects aliased with 2fi's	Related 2fi's aliased with main effect	Related 2fi's aliased with other 2fi's
d_1	Non	Non	$d_1 d_3 = d_4 d_6, d_1 d_4 = d_3 d_6, d_1 d_6 = d_3 d_4$
d_3	Non	Non	$d_3 d_6 = d_1 d_4, d_3 d_4 = d_1 d_6, d_3 d_1 = d_4 d_6$
d_4	Non	Non	$d_4 d_1 = d_3 d_6, d_4 d_3 = d_1 d_6, d_4 d_6 = d_1 d_3$
d_2	$d_2 = d_5 d_6$	$d_2 d_5 = d_6, d_2 d_6 = d_5$	Non
d_5	$d_5 = d_2 d_6$	$d_5 d_2 = d_6, d_5 d_6 = d_2$	Non
d_6	$d_6 = d_2 d_5$	$d_6 d_2 = d_5, d_6 d_5 = d_2$	$d_6 d_1 = d_3 d_4, d_6 d_3 = d_1 d_4, d_6 d_4 = d_1 d_3$

Consider a 2^{n-m} regular design D corresponding to an n-subset of H_q. Suppose n factors are assigned to the columns of the designs. For a $\gamma \in D$, there are $\binom{n-1}{i-1}$ ith-order effects containing γ. Let ${}_i^{\#}C_j^{(k)}(D, \gamma)$ denote the number of ith-order effects involving γ that are aliased with k jth-order effects. Recall that $K_j = \binom{n}{j}$. The vector

$${}_i^{\#}C_j(D, \gamma) = ({}_i^{\#}C_j^{(0)}(D, \gamma), {}_i^{\#}C_j^{(1)}(D, \gamma), \cdots, {}_i^{\#}C_j^{(K_j)}(D, \gamma))$$

describes the distribution of the $\binom{n-1}{i-1}$ ith-order effects involving γ, according to their severity degrees being aliased with jth-order effects, from the least to the most. By the effect hierarchy principle, following the idea of the GMC criterion for designs, we rank $^\#_iC_j(D,\gamma)$'s in the following sequence and denote it as

$$^\#C(D,\gamma) = (^\#_1C_1(D,\gamma), ^\#_1C_2(D,\gamma), ^\#_2C_1(D,\gamma), ^\#_2C_2(D,\gamma), \cdots) \qquad (5.1)$$

for $\gamma \in D$.

We refer to (5.1) as a *factor-AENP* of design D (F-AENP, in short). Since we will only consider designs with resolution at least *III*, the term $^\#_1C_1(D,\gamma)$ in (5.1) can be omitted. Furthermore, in most practical situations, one can suppose that the third and higher-order effects are negligible and so the terms after $^\#_2C_2(D,\gamma)$ can also be omitted. Thus, (5.1) can be simplified as

$$^\#C(D,\gamma) = (^\#_1C_2(D,\gamma), ^\#_2C_1(D,\gamma), ^\#_2C_2(D,\gamma)) \qquad (5.2)$$

for $\gamma \in D$.

For the sake of simplicity in notation, we also refer to (5.2) as an F-AENP of design D. For a given design D, each $\gamma \in D$ has its corresponding F-AENP. As a result, the F-AENP can be used to rank the columns of a design. Now, we present the definition of column ordering as follows.

Definition 5.2   For $\gamma, \gamma' \in D$, let $^\#C_l(D,\gamma)$ and $^\#C_l(D,\gamma')$ be the l-th components of $^\#C(D,\gamma)$ and $^\#C(D,\gamma')$, respectively. If $^\#C_l(D,\gamma) = {}^\#C_l(D,\gamma')$ for all l, then we say γ and γ' have the same F-AENP, and denote it by $\gamma \equiv \gamma'$. Otherwise, suppose l is the smallest number such that $^\#C_l(D,\gamma) \neq {}^\#C_l(D,\gamma')$. If $^\#C_l(D,\gamma) > {}^\#C_l(D,\gamma')$, then we say that γ has better F-AENP than γ', and denote it by $\gamma \succ \gamma'$. This means that, in the design D, the column γ is better than the column γ'.

Based on the definition, it is evident that when γ has a better F-AENP compared to γ', the severe degree of lower-order effects involving γ being aliased with other lower-order effects is less than that involving γ'. Moreover, it is important to note that all the columns in any regular design have an F-AENP ordering.

Example 5.3   Considering the 2^{6-2} design in Example 5.1, and denoting it by D, we have

$$^\#C(D,d_1) = {}^\#C(D,d_3) = {}^\#C(D,d_4) = ((1),(5),(2,3)),$$

$$^\#C(D,d_2) = {}^\#C(D,d_5) = ((0,1),(3,2),(5)),$$

$$^{\#}C(D, d_6) = ((0, 1), (3, 2), (2, 3)).$$

Thus, we have $d_1 \equiv d_3 \equiv d_4 \succ d_2 \equiv d_5 \succ d_6$. □

Clearly, for a regular design, its AENP describes the whole confounding property between the columns of the design, while its F-AENP describes the confounding property of each column with other columns in the design for main effects and two-factor interactions. By the definitions of AENP and F-AENP, it is easy to observe the relationships between them as

$$^{\#}_1C_2(D) = \sum_{\gamma \in D} {}^{\#}_1C_2(D, \gamma) \text{ and } {}^{\#}_2C_2(D) = \sum_{\gamma \in D} {}^{\#}_2C_2(D, \gamma)/2.$$

5.1.2 The F-AENP of GMC Designs

This section applies the notion of F-AENP to GMC designs and gives the F-AENPs and column orderings for all the GMC 2^{n-m} designs with $5N/16 + 1 \leqslant n \leqslant N - 1$. For convenience of presentation, we omit the proofs in this section. The details can be found in Zhou, Balakrishnan, and Zhang (2013).

Recall from Theorem 3.10 that we have established the result that any GMC 2^{n-m} designs with $5N/16 + 1 \leqslant n \leqslant N - 1$ can be represented isomorphically by the last n columns of H_q in (1.6). To gain a better understanding of their structure, we define $q + 1$ different partitions of $\{I, H_q\}$ as follows:

- 0-th partition $\mathcal{D}_0$:

$$\{\{I\}, \{1\}, \{2\}, \cdots, \{12\cdots(q-1)\}; \{q\}, \{1q\}, \cdots, \{1\cdots(q-1)q\}\},$$

- i-th partition $\mathcal{D}_i$:

$$\left\{ \begin{array}{l} \{(I, H_i)\}, \{(I, H_i)(i+1)\}, \{(I, H_i)(i+2)\}, \cdots; \\ \{(I, H_i)q\}, \{(I, H_i)(i+1)q\}, \cdots, \{(I, H_i)(i+1)(i+2)\cdots q\} \end{array} \right\},$$

$i = 1, \cdots, q-2,$

- $(q-1)$-th partition $\mathcal{D}_{q-1}$:

$$\{\{(I, H_{q-1})\}; \{(I, H_{q-1})q\}\},$$

- q-th partition $\mathcal{D}_q$:

$$\{(I, H_q)\},$$

where the semicolon ";" divides every partition into two parts with the second half involving q but the first half not. Clearly, the i-th partition $\mathcal{D}_i$ consists of 2^{q-i} disjoint subsets of $\{I, H_q\}$ with each subset containing 2^i columns.

Thus, for any GMC 2^{n-m} design D with $5N/16 + 1 \leqslant n \leqslant N - 1$ given above, we can represent n using the unique expression $n = \sum_{i=0}^{q-1} j_i 2^i$, where j_i is either 1 or 0. Using this representation, we can denote D as $\{\mathcal{A}_0, \cdots, \mathcal{A}_{q-1}\}$, where $\mathcal{A}_i = \varnothing$ if $j_i = 0$, while $\mathcal{A}_i$ with $j_i = 1$ consists of 2^i columns, which is one subset within $\mathcal{D}_i$. Also, we observe that if $n < N/2$, then all the $\mathcal{A}_i$'s with $j_i = 1$ are respectively located in the second half of $\mathcal{D}_i$'s. On the other hand, if $n \geqslant N/2$, except for $\mathcal{A}_{q-1} = \{(I, H_{q-1})q\}$ in the second half of $\mathcal{D}_{q-1}$, all the other $\mathcal{A}_i$'s with $j_i = 1$ are respectively situated in the first half of $\mathcal{D}_i$'s.

Example 5.4   From H_6, let us take the GMC 2^{21-15} design

$$D = \{1246, 346, 1346, 2346, 12346,$$
$$(I, 1, 2, 12, 3, 13, 23, 123, 4, 14, 24, 124, 34, 134, 234, 1234)56\}.$$

Here, $q = 6, N = 64$, and $N/2 > n = 21 = \sum_{i=0}^{5} j_i 2^i$, where $j_1 = j_3 = j_5 = 0$ and $j_0 = j_2 = j_4 = 1$. We have $\mathcal{A}_1 = \mathcal{A}_3 = \mathcal{A}_5 = \varnothing$, and $\mathcal{A}_0 = \{1246\}$, $\mathcal{A}_2 = \{(I, H_2)346\}$ and $\mathcal{A}_4 = \{(I, H_4)56\}$ are respectively in the second half of $\mathcal{D}_0, \mathcal{D}_2$, and $\mathcal{D}_4$.

Consider the GMC 2^{46-40} design from H_6:

$$D = \{25, 125, 35, 135, 235, 1235, 45, 145, 245, 1245, 345, 1345, 2345, 12345, (I, H_5)6\}.$$

Here, $q = 6, N = 64$, and $N/2 \leqslant n = 46 = \sum_{i=0}^{5} j_i 2^i$ with $j_0 = j_4 = 0$ and $j_1 = j_2 = j_3 = j_5 = 1$. We have $\mathcal{A}_0 = \mathcal{A}_4 = \varnothing$, and $\mathcal{A}_1 = \{25, 125\}$, $\mathcal{A}_2 = \{(I, H_2)35\}$, $\mathcal{A}_3 = \{(I, H_3)45\}$ are respectively in the first half of $\mathcal{D}_1, \mathcal{D}_2$ and $\mathcal{D}_3$, and $\mathcal{A}_5 = \{(I, H_5)6\}$ is in the second half of $\mathcal{D}_5$.   □

Next, we consider the computation of the F-AENP of GMC designs. We need some notation. Let

$$D = \{\mathcal{A}_0, \cdots, \mathcal{A}_{q-1}\}$$

be a GMC 2^{n-m} design as shown above and $(j_0, \cdots, j_{q-1})$ denote the vector of the j_t's in $n = \sum_{t=0}^{q-1} j_t 2^t$. Consider a function

$$f(D, p) = \sum_{t=p+1}^{q-1} j_t 2^{t-1} + j_p \sum_{t=0}^{p-1} j_t 2^t, \tag{5.3}$$

$p = 0, \cdots, q - 1$, with the convention that $\sum_{t=u}^{s} j_t 2^t = 0$ if $u > s$. By noting

$$f(D,p) = \sum_{t=p+2}^{q-1} j_t 2^{t-1} + j_p \sum_{t=0}^{p-1} j_t 2^t + j_{p+1} 2^p,$$

$$f(D,p+1) = \sum_{t=p+2}^{q-1} j_t 2^{t-1} + j_{p+1} \sum_{t=0}^{p-1} j_t 2^t + j_{p+1} j_p 2^p,$$

and comparing the values of $f(D,p)$ for $p = 0, \cdots, q-1$, we have the following relation:

$$\begin{cases} f(D,p) > f(D,p+1), & \text{if } (j_p, j_{p+1}) = (0,1) \text{ or } (1,0) \text{ with } \sum_{t=0}^{p-1} j_t > 0, \\ f(D,p) = f(D,p+1), & \text{otherwise.} \end{cases} \tag{5.4}$$

The relation (5.4) establishes the decreasing order for the $f(D,p)$ values:

$$f(D,0) \geqslant \cdots \geqslant f(D,q-1).$$

Let $(n_1, \cdots, n_f)$ denote the f successive change points of $(f(D,0), \cdots, f(D,q-1))$ with respect to p, where $f(D,n_f) > 0$. That is, we have

$$f(D,p) = f(D,n_1)$$

for $p = 0, \cdots, n_1$,

$$f(D,p) = f(D,n_i)$$

for $p = n_{i-1}+1, \cdots, n_i$,

$$f(D,n_{i-1}) > f(D,n_i),$$

for $i = 2, \cdots, f$, and

$$f(D,p) = 0$$

if $n_f < p \leqslant q-1$. Therefore, there are only n_f distinct values of k, given by $k = f(D,p) - 1$. It is evident that both the values $(n_1, \cdots, n_f)$ and the number of possible distinct k values are solely determined by n.

With the above preparations, the following theorem provides the explicit forms of the F-AENP of GMC designs.

Theorem 5.5 *Suppose $D = \{A_0, \cdots, A_{q-1}\}$ is a GMC 2^{n-m} design with $5N/16 + 1 \leqslant n \leqslant N - 1$ as given above, and the j_t's are as defined in $n = \sum_{t=0}^{q-1} j_t 2^t$. Let r be the number such that $j_r = 0$ and $j_{r+1} = \cdots = j_{q-1} = 1$ and $^{\#}_u C_v^{(k)}(D, (\gamma, i))$ denote the F-AENP of $\gamma \in A_i$. Then,*

  (a) for $\gamma \in A_i$, $i = r+1, \cdots, q-1$, we have

$$
{}^{\#}_1 C_2^{(k)}(D,(\gamma,i)) = \begin{cases} 1, & for\ k = \sum_{t=r+2}^{q-1} 2^{t-1} + \sum_{t=0}^{r-1} j_t 2^t, \\ 0, & otherwise; \end{cases} \tag{5.5}
$$

for $\gamma \in \mathcal{A}_i$ with $i = 0, \cdots, r-1$ and $j_i = 1$, we have

$$
{}^{\#}_1 C_2^{(k)}(D,(\gamma,i)) = \begin{cases} 1, & for\ k = \sum_{t=r+1}^{q-1} 2^{t-1}, \\ 0, & otherwise; \end{cases} \tag{5.6}
$$

(b) for $\gamma \in \mathcal{A}_i$ with $j_i = 1$ and $i = 0, 1, \cdots, q-1$, we have

$$
{}^{\#}_2 C_2^{(k)}(D,(\gamma,i)) = \begin{cases} \sum_{p=n_{v-1}+1}^{n_v} y_i(D,p), & for\ k = f(D,n_v) - 1, v = 1, \cdots, f, \\ 0, & otherwise, \end{cases} \tag{5.7}
$$

where

$$
f(D,p) = \sum_{t=p+1}^{q-1} j_t 2^{t-1} + j_p \sum_{t=0}^{p-1} j_t 2^t
$$

with the convention that $\sum_{t=s}^{u} j_t 2^t = 0$ if $s > u$, $n_0 = -1$ and

$$
y_i(D,p) = \begin{cases} 2^p, & for\ p = 0, 1, \cdots, i-1, i \neq 0, \\ \sum_{t=0}^{i-1} j_t 2^t, & for\ p = i, \\ j_p 2^p, & for\ p = i+1, \cdots, q-1. \end{cases} \tag{5.8}
$$

From Theorem 5.5, we can see that, for any i, the different γ's within an $\mathcal{A}_i$ share the same F-AENP. Therefore, ${}^{\#}_1 C_2^{(k)}(D,(\gamma,i))$ and ${}^{\#}_2 C_2^{(k)}(D,(\gamma,i))$ can be denoted respectively as ${}^{\#}_1 C_2^{(k)}(D,i)$ and ${}^{\#}_2 C_2^{(k)}(D,i)$, or as ${}^{\#}_1 C_2^{(k)}(D,\mathcal{A}_i)$ and ${}^{\#}_2 C_2^{(k)}(D,\mathcal{A}_i)$, representing the F-AENP of $\mathcal{A}_i$. Therefore, the F-AENP ordering of the γ's in GMC 2^{n-m} designs with $5N/16 + 1 \leqslant n \leqslant N - 1$, from the best to the worst, follows that of $\mathcal{A}_i$'s. For the F-AENP ordering of $\mathcal{A}_i$'s, we have the following theorem.

Theorem 5.6　Suppose $D = \{\mathcal{A}_0, \cdots, \mathcal{A}_{q-1}\}$ is a GMC 2^{n-m} design with $5N/16 \leqslant n \leqslant N - 1$ as given above, and the j_t's are as defined in $n = \sum_{t=0}^{q-1} j_t 2^t$.

(a) If $5N/16 + 1 \leqslant n < N/2$, then the F-AENP ordering of the $\mathcal{A}_i$'s is

$$
\{\mathcal{A}_0, \mathcal{A}_1, \cdots, \mathcal{A}_{q-2}, \mathcal{A}_{q-1}\}, \tag{5.9}
$$

where $\mathcal{A}_{q-1} = \varnothing$.

(b) When $N/2 \leqslant n \leqslant N - 1$, let r be the number such that $j_r = 0$ and $j_{r+1} = \cdots = j_{q-1} = 1$, then the F-AENP ordering of the $\mathcal{A}_i$'s is

$$\{\mathcal{A}_{q-1}, \mathcal{A}_{q-2}, \cdots, \mathcal{A}_{r+1}, \mathcal{A}_0, \mathcal{A}_1, \cdots, \mathcal{A}_r\}. \tag{5.10}$$

The following example serves as an illustration of Theorems 5.5 and 5.6.

Example 5.7   Consider the GMC 2^{21-15} design D in Example 5.4. In this case, since $5N/16 + 1 \leqslant 21 < N/2$ with $N = 64$, by the results in Example 5.4 and Theorem 5.6 (a), the column F-AENP ordering of the design is

$$D = \{\overbrace{1246}^{\mathcal{A}_0}, \overbrace{346, 1346, 2346, 12346}^{\mathcal{A}_2}, \overbrace{(I, H_4)56}^{\mathcal{A}_4}\}.$$

From Theorem 5.5, it is easy to see that $(j_0, \cdots, j_{6-1}) = (1, 0, 1, 0, 1, 0)$, $n_f = 4$, $(n_1, n_2, n_3, n_4) = (1, 2, 3, 4)$, and $f(D, 0) = f(D, 1) = 10$, $f(D, 2) = 9$, $f(D, 3) = 8$, $f(D, 4) = 5$, and $f(D, 5) = 0$, and so $k = 9, 8, 7, 4$. Table 5.2 compares ${}^{\#}_2 C_2^{(k)}(D, \mathcal{A}_i)$ for $i = 0, 2, 4$. This shows that

$$\#_2 C_2(D, \mathcal{A}_0) \succ \#_2 C_2(D, \mathcal{A}_2) \succ \#_2 C_2(D, \mathcal{A}_4). \qquad \square$$

Table 5.2   A comparison of ${}^{\#}_2 C_2^{(k)}(D, \mathcal{A}_i)$, $i = 0, 2, 4$

k	4	7	8	9	other k's
${}^{\#}_2 C_2^{(k)}(D, \mathcal{A}_0)$	16	4	0	0	0
${}^{\#}_2 C_2^{(k)}(D, \mathcal{A}_2)$	16	1	3	0	0
${}^{\#}_2 C_2^{(k)}(D, \mathcal{A}_4)$	5	8	4	3	0

5.1.3   Application of the F-AENP

In this section, we explore how the F-AENP results of GMC designs can be utilized to arrange the factors within a GMC design. Considering the definition of the F-AENP, one significant application of these results becomes apparent. If an experimenter has prior knowledge regarding the relative importance of factors in their experiment and is primarily interested in studying each factor and the lower-order effects associated with it separately, then the optimal approach for the experimenter is to organize the factors in the selected GMC design's columns based on the F-AENP ordering provided in Theorem 5.6. This enables the experimenter to prioritize the factors according to their importance rank.

However, in practice, this may not always be the case. Sometimes, the experimenter may need to handle the first k important factors as a group, considering that all the effects of these k factors are equally important. Suppose there are q factors in an experiment that are considered the most important and require special attention. As an application of the F-AENP, we can employ it sequentially to select the first $q = n - m$ best columns of a GMC 2^{n-m} design, aiming to identify and prioritize the q most important factors. To ensure minimal confounding between their lower-order effects, it is important to require that the selected q columns are independent.

However, it is important to note that no two sets of q independent columns that are selected play the same role in arranging the q important factors. This is because the degree of severity of the lower-order effects associated with the q important factors, which are to be aliased, is influenced not only by the F-AENP of each selected column but also by the confounding structure among the selected columns and the confounding structure between the selected columns and other columns. The following example illustrates this point.

Example 5.8   Let us consider the design $\{1, 12, 123, 4, 134, 234\}$ again, and denote $d_1 = 1, d_2 = 12, d_3 = 123, d_4 = 4, d_5 = 134$, and $d_6 = 234$ as in Example 5.3. Clearly, the maximum number of independent columns in the design is 4.

Let us consider two selected sets, each consisting of four independent columns: $\{d_1, d_2, d_3, d_4\}$ and $\{d_1, d_2, d_3, d_6\}$. These sets are chosen for the purpose of arranging the four most important factors.

Although there is no confounding between the main effects and 2fi's of the four factors for both sets, we can observe the following difference. When considering the two cases d_1, d_2, d_3, d_4 and d_5, d_6, and d_1, d_2, d_3, d_6 and d_4, d_5, it becomes apparent that in the latter case, there are two main effects, d_2 and d_6, that are aliased with the 2fi's $d_5 d_6$ and $d_2 d_5$, respectively. On the other hand, in the former case, there is only one main effect, d_2, being aliased with the 2fi $d_5 d_6$. For more information on their difference, see Table 5.1. $\qquad\qquad\square$

Thus, we need to select the q best independent columns from a 2^{n-m} design. Utilizing the results of F-AENP from Theorems 5.5 and 5.6, we present a procedure below for selecting the q best independent columns from GMC 2^{n-m} designs in a sequential manner. This procedure is applicable to two cases: when $5N/16 + 1 \leqslant n < N/2$ and when $N/2 \leqslant n \leqslant N - 1$. Let $D = \cup_{t=0}^{q-1} \mathcal{A}_t$ as indicated in Section 5.1.2.

For the case $5N/16 + 1 \leqslant n \leqslant N/2 - 1$, we can follow the order specified in (5.9) for $\mathcal{A}_i$'s, which is $\{\mathcal{A}_0, \cdots, \mathcal{A}_{q-1}\}$. We rank all the columns γ's of the design D accordingly, and sequentially select q independent columns, as required.

For the case $N/2 \leqslant n \leqslant N - 1$, we can follow the order specified in (5.10) for $\mathcal{A}_i$'s, which is $\{\mathcal{A}_{q-1}, \cdots, \mathcal{A}_{r+1}, \mathcal{A}_0, \cdots, \mathcal{A}_r\}$. We rank all the columns γ's of the design D accordingly, and sequentially select q independent columns, as required.

Obviously, in the selected set obtained by the above procedure, the first part from $\mathcal{A}_0$ ($\mathcal{A}_{q-1}$) must be the maximum number of independent columns in $\mathcal{A}_0$ ($\mathcal{A}_{q-1}$). Similarly, the second part from $\mathcal{A}_1$ ($\mathcal{A}_{q-2}$) must be the maximum number of independent columns in $\mathcal{A}_1$ ($\mathcal{A}_{q-2}$) that are independent of the γ's in the first part. This pattern continues for each subsequent part. Clearly, based on the results of Theorems 5.5 and 5.6, it is evident that assigning the first q important factors in the same ordering to the corresponding q selected columns is the best choice, up to isomorphism.

5.2 Blocked Factor Aliased Effect-Number Pattern of B^1-GMC Designs

5.2.1 Blocked Factor Aliased Effect-Number Pattern

Similar to the unblocked case, the columns of a blocked design may not be equally effective for estimating factorial effects. Therefore, it is necessary to have a measure to assess the columns of a blocked design. To address this, we introduce an extension of the F-AENP called the blocked factor aliased effect-number pattern (B-F-AENP) in this section.

Consider a $2^{n-m} : 2^r$ design $D = (D_t : D_b)$. The $2^n - 1$ treatment effects are partitioned into four classes: g-, b-, m-, and ϕ-class. These classes respectively consist of the effects located in the defining contrast subgroup, the alias sets containing a block effect, a treatment main effect, and none of the three kinds of effects. For any

$\gamma \in D_t$, we partition the effects involving γ in D into four classes: g-, b-, m-, and ϕ-class. We use $^{\#*}_iC^{(k)}_j(D, \gamma)$, or $^{\#*}_iC^{(k)}_j(\gamma)$ for short, to denote the number of ith-order effects containing γ aliased with k jth-order effects in $*$-class, where $* = g, m, b, \phi$ and k indicates the aliased severity degree.

The set of numbers

$$^{\#B}C(D, \gamma) = \{^{\#*}_iC_j(D, \gamma), i, j = 1, \cdots, n, * = g, b, m, \phi\} \tag{5.11}$$

is called a B-F-AENP of column γ in D_t, and

$$^{\#B}C(D) = \{^{\#*}_iC_j(D, \gamma), i, j = 1, \cdots, n, * = g, b, m, \phi, \gamma \in D_t\} \tag{5.12}$$

is called a B-F-AENP of design D. Here,

$$^{\#*}_iC_j(D, \gamma) = (^{\#*}_iC^{(0)}_j(D, \gamma), \cdots, ^{\#*}_iC^{(K_j)}_j(D, \gamma))$$

describes the distribution of the $\binom{n-1}{i-1}$ ith-order effects involving γ in $*$-class on the aliased severe degrees with jth-order effects, from the least to the most.

Example 5.9　Consider the $2^{6-2} : 2^1$ design D with defining relation

$$I = 12345 = 1346 = 256 = 123b_1 = 45b_1 = 246b_1 = 1356b_1.$$

Its g-, b-, m-, and ϕ-class effects are

g-class:　$\{I, 256, 1346, 12345\}$,

b-class:　$\{45, 123, 246, 1356(= b_1)\}$,

m-class:　$\{1, 346, 2345, 1256; 2, 56, 1345, 12346; 3, 146, 1245, 2356; 4, 136, 1235, 2456;$
　　　　　　$5, 26, 1234, 13456; 6, 25, 134, 123456\}$,

ϕ-class:　$\{12, 345, 156, 2346; 13, 46, 245, 12356; 14, 36, 235, 12456; 15, 234, 126, 3456;$
　　　　　　$16, 34, 125, 23456; 23, 145, 356, 1246; 24, 135, 456, 1236; 35, 124, 236, 1456\}$.

By the definition of $^{\#*}_iC_j(D, \gamma)$, we have $^{\#m}_1C_2(D, 1) = (1)$, $^{\#m}_2C_2(D, 1) = (0)$, $^{\#b}_2C_2(D, 1)$ $= (0)$, $^{\#\phi}_2C_2(D, 1) = (2, 3)$, and so on. Similarly, we can obtain $^{\#*}_iC_j(D, \gamma)$ for $\gamma = 2, \cdots, 6$.　$\square$

When we only consider the regular designs with resolution at least III and assume that the third or higher-order interactions are negligible, we can simplify the B-F-AENPs (5.11) and (5.12) by dropping unnecessary terms. They can be expressed as

$$^{\#B}C(D, \gamma) = \{^{\#*}_iC_j(D, \gamma), i + j \geqslant 3, i, j = 1, 2, * = m, b, \phi\}$$

and

$$^{\#B}C(D) = \{^{\#*}_iC_j(D,\gamma), i+j \geqslant 3, i,j = 1,2, * = m,b,\phi,\ \gamma \in D_t\}.$$

Now, we use $^{\#B}C(D)$ to define a criterion for ranking the columns of D_t in D. We note that, for a column $\gamma \in D_t$, the lower the aliased degrees of the main effect and the 2fi's involving γ with other lower-order effects are, the better the column γ is.

Let us first consider the main effect of column γ, whose information is contained in the vectors $^{\#b}_1C_2(D,\gamma)$ and $^{\#m}_1C_2(D,\gamma)$. Clearly, $^{\#b}_1C_2(D,\gamma)$ should be ignored, since only the blocked designs with resolution at least III are considered so that none of the main effects are in b-class. According to the effect hierarchy principle, a good column γ should sequentially maximize the components of $^{\#m}_1C_2(D,\gamma)$ first.

We then consider the 2fi's involving γ. Since there is no 2fi in the g-class, all the information of the 2fi's aliased with other effects is contained in the m-, b-, or ϕ-class. Note that $^{\#m}_2C_1(D,\gamma)$ is determined by the previous term $^{\#m}_1C_2(D,\gamma)$ and can thus be ignored. Therefore, what remains is to consider $^{\#m}_2C_2(D,\gamma)$, $^{\#b}_2C_2(D,\gamma)$, and $^{\#\phi}_2C_2(D,\gamma)$. Comparing the aliased severity degrees of a 2fi in the three classes, being in the b-class has the highest severity, while being in the ϕ-class has the lowest severity. It follows that after considering $^{\#m}_1C_2(D,\gamma)$, we should prioritize $^{\#b}_2C_2(D,\gamma)$ first, followed by $^{\#m}_2C_2(D,\gamma)$, and finally $^{\#\phi}_2C_2(D,\gamma)$.

For any 2fi in the b-class, its information is completely lost. Thus, instead, we consider the total number of 2fi's involving γ not in the b-class, which is given by

$$n - 1 - \sum_k {}^{\#b}_2C_2^{(k)}(D,\gamma).$$

This value should be maximized. At last, we should sequentially maximize the components of $^{\#m}_2C_2(D,\gamma)$ and $^{\#\phi}_2C_2(D,\gamma)$. Based on all the above analyses, we arrive at the pattern

$$^{\#B}C(D,\gamma) = ({}^{\#m}_1C_2(D,\gamma), n-1-\sum_k {}^{\#b}_2C_2^{(k)}(D,\gamma), {}^{\#m}_2C_2(D,\gamma), {}^{\#\phi}_2C_2(D,\gamma)). \quad (5.13)$$

We sequentially compare the components of the pattern (5.13) as a criterion to rank the columns of D_t. For simplicity, we also call the pattern (5.13) as a B-F-AENP.

The following defines how to compare any two columns of D_t in $D = (D_t : D_b)$.

Definition 5.10　For $\gamma, \gamma' \in D_t$, let $^{\#B}C_l(D,\gamma)$ and $^{\#B}C_l(D,\gamma')$ be the l-th com-

ponents of $^{\#B}C(D,\gamma)$ *and* $^{\#B}C(D,\gamma')$, *respectively. If* $^{\#B}C_l(D,\gamma) = {}^{\#B}C_l(D,\gamma')$ *for all l, then* γ *and* γ' *are said to have the same B-F-AENP. Otherwise, suppose l is the smallest number such that* $^{\#B}C_l(D,\gamma) \neq {}^{\#B}C_l(D,\gamma')$. *If* $^{\#B}C_l(D,\gamma) > {}^{\#B}C_l(D,\gamma')$, *then* γ *is said to have a better B-F-AENP than* γ', *denoted as* $^{\#B}C(D,\gamma) \succ {}^{\#B}C(D,\gamma')$ *or* $\gamma \succ \gamma'$. *That is, in the design D, column* γ *is better than column* γ'. *If column* γ *sequentially maximizes the components of the sequence (5.13), then it is said to be the best in* D_t *according to the B-F-AENP.*

Example 5.11   Let us consider the $2^{6-2} : 2^1$ design D in Example 5.9. With some calculation, we can get

$$^{\#B}C(D,1) = {}^{\#B}C(D,3) = ((1), 5, (0), (2,3)),$$

$$^{\#B}C(D,2) = ((0,1), 5, (2), (3)),$$

$$^{\#B}C(D,4) = ((1), 4, (0), (1,3)),$$

$$^{\#B}C(D,5) = ((0,1), 4, (2), (2)),$$

$$^{\#B}C(D,6) = ((0,1), 5, (2), (0,3)).$$

By Definition 5.10, we have

$$\{1,3\} \succ 4 \succ 2 \succ 6 \succ 5. \qquad \square$$

5.2.2   The B-F-AENP of B^1-GMC Designs

In this section, we calculate B-F-AENPs and rank the columns of B^1-GMC $2^{n-m} : 2^r$ designs with $5N/16+1 \leqslant n \leqslant N-1$, as constructed in Theorem 4.13. For convenience of presentation, we omit the proofs in this section. All details can be found in Wang, Ye, Zhou, and Zhang (2017).

Recall that the results in Theorem 4.13 can be summarized as follows:

(i) if $5N/16 + 1 \leqslant n \leqslant N/2$, D_t consists of the last n columns of F_{qq}, and

$$D_b = \begin{cases} H_r, & \text{for } N/2 - 2^{r-1} + 1 \leqslant n \leqslant N/2, \\ H_{r-1} \cup F_{qr}, & \text{for } 5N/16+1 \leqslant n \leqslant N/2 - 2^{r-1}, \end{cases}$$

then $D = (D_t : D_b)$ is a GMC $2^{n-m} : 2^r$ design;

(ii) if $n > N/2$, D_t consists of the last n columns of H_q, and $D_b = H_r$, then $D = (D_t : D_b)$ is a GMC $2^{n-m} : 2^r$ design.

The above results indicate that if $D = (D_t : D_b)$ is a B^1-GMC $2^{n-m} : 2^r$ design, then D_t consists of the last n columns of H_q in (1.6), up to isomorphism. That is, D_t is a GMC 2^{n-m} design. Hence, some techniques and results in Section 5.1.2 can be utilized. Recall that in Section 5.1.2, we have defined $q + 1$ different partitions of $\{I, H_q\}$. For the i-th partition $\mathcal{D}_i$, it consists of 2^{q-i} disjoint subsets of $\{I, H_q\}$, each containing 2^i columns. Thus, for any B^1-GMC $2^{n-m} : 2^r$ design $D = (D_t : D_b)$ with $5N/16 + 1 \leqslant n \leqslant N - 1$, by using the $q + 1$ partitions of $\{I, H_q\}$ and the binary expression of n: $n = \sum_{i=0}^{q-1} j_i 2^i$, where $j_i = 0$ or 1, the D_t has the decomposition $\{\mathcal{A}_0, \cdots, \mathcal{A}_{q-1}\}$, where $\mathcal{A}_i$ is a specific group in $\mathcal{D}_i$ that contains 2^i columns if $j_i = 1$ and $\mathcal{A}_i = \varnothing$ if $j_i = 0$. The following is an illustrative example.

Example 5.12　Consider the B^1-GMC $2^{12-7} : 2^2$ design $D = (D_t : D_b)$. Then, $q = 5$, $N = 32, n = 12, r = 2$, $5N/16 + 1 \leqslant n \leqslant N/2 - 2^{r-1}$, $H_{r-1} = \{1\}$ and $F_{qr} = \{5, 15\}$. By Theorem 4.13, we have $D_b = \{1, 5, 15\}$.

Because $12 = \sum_{i=0}^{5-1} j_i 2^i$ with $(j_0, j_1, j_2, j_3, j_4) = (0, 0, 1, 1, 0)$, then the decomposition of D_t is $\{\mathcal{A}_2, \mathcal{A}_3\}$, where $\mathcal{A}_2 = \{(I, H_2)35\}$ and $\mathcal{A}_3 = \{(I, H_3)45\}$, which respectively are the groups in the partitions $\mathcal{D}_2$ and $\mathcal{D}_3$ of $\{I, H_5\}$.　　□

In the following, we define a 2fi in D_t to be of class p if it is aliased with a column in $H_p \setminus H_{p-1}$, meaning its two parent factors are in the same group of $\mathcal{D}_p$ but not in the same group of $\mathcal{D}_{p-1}$.

To compute the B-F-AENP (5.13), it is important to note the differences of the B^1-GMC designs discussed here with the unblocked GMC designs discussed in Section 5.1.2. First, let us calculate the total number of 2fi's involving γ in the b-class of D, $\sum_k {}^{\#b}_2 C_2^{(k)}(D, \gamma)$. To do this, we need to know what 2fi's and how many 2fi's involving a given $\gamma \in D_t$ are aliased with a block effect. We have the following lemma.

Lemma 5.13　Let $D = (D_t : D_b)$ be a B^1-GMC $2^{n-m} : 2^r$ with $r \leqslant q - 2$.

(a) If $5N/16 + 1 \leqslant n \leqslant N/2 - 2^{r-1}$, then in D_t, any 2fi is aliased with a block effect if and only if it is of class p with $1 \leqslant p \leqslant r - 1$.

(b) If $N/2 - 2^{r-1} + 1 \leqslant n \leqslant N - 1$, then in D_t, any 2fi is aliased with a block effect if and only if it is of class p with $1 \leqslant p \leqslant r$.

Based on Lemma 5.13, we have the following theorem.

Theorem 5.14　*Let $D = (D_t : D_b)$ be a B^1-GMC $2^{n-m} : 2^r$ design with $5N/16+1 \leqslant n \leqslant N-1$, where $D_t = \{\mathcal{A}_0, \cdots, \mathcal{A}_{q-1}\}$ and $n = \sum_{t=0}^{q-1} j_t 2^t$.*

(a) If $5N/16 + 1 \leqslant n \leqslant N/2 - 2^{r-1}$, then for $\gamma \in \mathcal{A}_i$ with $j_i = 1$, we have

$$\sum_k {}^{\#b}_2 C_2^{(k)}(D, \gamma) = \begin{cases} \sum_{t=0}^{r-2} j_t 2^t - 1, & \text{if } 0 \leqslant i \leqslant r-2, \\ 2^{r-1} - 1, & \text{if } r-1 \leqslant i \leqslant q-1. \end{cases}$$

(b) If $N/2 - 2^{r-1} + 1 \leqslant n \leqslant N-1$, then for $\gamma \in \mathcal{A}_i$ with $j_i = 1$, we have

$$\sum_k {}^{\#b}_2 C_2^{(k)}(D, \gamma) = \begin{cases} \sum_{t=0}^{r-1} j_t 2^t - 1, & \text{if } 0 \leqslant i \leqslant r-1, \\ 2^r - 1, & \text{if } r \leqslant i \leqslant q-1. \end{cases} \tag{5.14}$$

The following example illustrates Theorem 5.14 and its use.

Example 5.15　Continuing from Example 5.12, let us consider the B^1-GMC 2^{12-7} : 2^2 design $D = (D_t : D_b)$. We have $n = 12, r = 2, D_t = \{\mathcal{A}_2, \mathcal{A}_3\} = \{(I, H_2)35, (I, H_3)45\}$, $D_b = \{1, 5, 15\}$, and $5N/16 + 1 \leqslant n \leqslant N/2 - 2^{r-1}$. Thus, design D belongs to case (a) of Theorem 5.14.

Furthermore, for any $\gamma \in \mathcal{A}_2$ (or $\mathcal{A}_3$), we have $\sum_k {}^{\#b}_2 C_2^{(k)}(D, \gamma) = 1$. This is because there is only one 2fi $\gamma(1\gamma)$ of D_t, only one block effect $1 \in D_b$, and they are aliased with each other.　　　　　　　　　　　　　　　　　　　　　　　□

The following corollary, which provides a method for ranking columns, can be directly derived from Theorem 5.14.

Corollary 5.16　*Let $D = (D_t : D_b)$ be a B^1-GMC $2^{n-m} : 2^r$ design with $r \leqslant q-2$. If we are only concerned with the severity of the main effect, as well as the severity of the 2fi's involving $\gamma \in D_t$ aliased with block effect, then*

(a) if $5N/16 + 1 \leqslant n \leqslant N/2 - 2^{r-1}$, then any $\gamma \in \{\mathcal{A}_0, \cdots, \mathcal{A}_{r-2}\}$ is better than any $\gamma \in \{\mathcal{A}_{r-1}, \cdots, \mathcal{A}_{q-1}\}$;

(b) if $N/2 - 2^{r-1} + 1 \leqslant n \leqslant N-1$, then any $\gamma \in \{\mathcal{A}_0, \cdots, \mathcal{A}_{r-1}\}$ is better than any $\gamma \in \{\mathcal{A}_r, \cdots, \mathcal{A}_{q-1}\}$.

Based on the functions $f(D_t, p)$ in (5.3) and $y_i(D_t, p)$ in (5.8), as well as the decomposition of D_t, we now compute the remaining terms of the B-F-AENP (5.13): ${}^{\#m}_1 C_2^{(k)}(D, \gamma)$, ${}^{\#m}_2 C_2^{(k)}(D, \gamma)$, and ${}^{\#\phi}_2 C_2^{(k)}(D, \gamma)$. For convenience, we still divide the range of n into two parts: (I) $5N/16 + 1 \leqslant n \leqslant N/2$ and (II) $n > N/2$.

First, let us consider case (I) with $5N/16 + 1 \leqslant n \leqslant N/2$. In this case, $D_t \subset F_q$

and the resolution of D_t is IV. Hence, we have

$$^{\#m}_1 C_2(D,\gamma) = (1) \text{ and } ^{\#m}_2 C_2(D,\gamma) = (0), \quad \text{for any } \gamma \in D_t. \tag{5.15}$$

In addition, if $r = q - 1$, then the B^1-GMC designs satisfy $D_b = H_{q-1}$, and furthermore, all the 2fi's in D_t are aliased with block effects. Consequently, we have the following results:

$$\sum_k {}^{\#b}_2 C_2^{(k)}(D,\gamma) = n - 1 \text{ and } {}^{\#\phi}_2 C_2(D,\gamma) = (0), \quad \text{for any } \gamma \in D_t. \tag{5.16}$$

Now, let us consider the case where $r \leqslant q - 2$. In this case, we have the following theorem.

Theorem 5.17   *Let $D = (D_t : D_b)$ be a B^1-GMC $2^{n-m} : 2^r$ design with $5N/16+1 \leqslant n \leqslant N/2$.*

   (a) If $N/2 - 2^{r-1} + 1 \leqslant n \leqslant N/2$, then for $\gamma \in \mathcal{A}_i$ with $j_i \neq 0$ and $0 \leqslant i \leqslant q-1$, we have

$$^{\#\phi}_2 C_2^{(k)}(D,\gamma) = \begin{cases} \sum_{p=n_{v-1}+1}^{n_v} y_i(D_t,p), & \text{for } k = f(D_t,n_v) - 1, \\ 0, & \text{otherwise,} \end{cases} \tag{5.17}$$

where $n_1, \cdots, n_g$ are the successive change points of $f(D_t,r), \cdots, f(D_t, q-2)$, respectively, and $n_0 = r - 1$.

   (b) If $5N/16 + 1 \leqslant n \leqslant N/2 - 2^{r-1}$, then for $\gamma \in \mathcal{A}_i$ with $j_i \neq 0$ and $0 \leqslant i \leqslant q - 1$, we have

$$^{\#\phi}_2 C_2^{(k)}(D,\gamma) = \begin{cases} \sum_{p=n'_{v-1}+1}^{n'_v} y_i(D_t,p), & \text{for } k = f(D_t,n'_v) - 1, \\ 0, & \text{otherwise,} \end{cases}$$

where $n'_1, \cdots, n'_{g'}$ are the successive change points of $f(D_t, r-1), \cdots, f(D_t, q-2)$, respectively, and $n'_0 = r - 2$.

   The following is an illustrative example of case (I) for computing B-F-AENP.

Example 5.18   Continuing with the $2^{12-7} : 2^2$ design from Example 5.12, we calculate $^{\#\phi}_2 C_2(D,\gamma)$ for $\gamma \in D_t$.

   Given that $D_t = \{(I, H_2)35, (I, H_3)45\}$, there are only two 2fi's belonging to classes 1-4, and only the 2fi's from classes 2-4 are in the ϕ-class. Hence, our focus is on the 2fi's of classes 2-4. First, for $p = 1, 2, 3$, we obtain the number $f(D_t,p)$ for the class-$(p+1)$ 2fi's, which are aliased with each other. By the formula

$$f(D_t, p) = \sum_{t=p+1}^{q-1} j_t 2^{t-1} + j_p \sum_{t=0}^{p-1} j_t 2^t$$

and $(j_0, j_1, j_2, j_3, j_4) = (0, 0, 1, 1, 0)$, the calculation is fairly straightforward, resulting in

$$(f(D_t, 1), f(D_t, 2), f(D_t, 3)) = (6, 4, 4).$$

Then, by (5.8), we get

$$(y_2(D_t, 1), y_2(D_t, 2), y_2(D_t, 3)) = (2, 0, 8)$$

and

$$(y_3(D_t, 1), y_3(D_t, 2), y_3(D_t, 3)) = (2, 4, 4).$$

Moreover, for $\gamma \in \mathcal{A}_i, i = 2, 3$, we find that $f(D_t, 2) = f(D_t, 3) = 4$ resulting

$$^{\#\phi}_2 C_2^{(3)}(D, \gamma) = y_i(D_t, 2) + y_i(D_t, 3).$$

Additionally, with $f(D_t, 1) = 6$, we get that

$$^{\#\phi}_2 C_2^{(5)}(D, \gamma) = y_i(D_t, 1).$$

Consequently, we obtain

$$^{\#\phi}_2 C_2^{(3)}(D, \gamma) = 8, \quad ^{\#\phi}_2 C_2^{(5)}(D, \gamma) = 2$$

for $\gamma \in \mathcal{A}_i$ with $i = 2, 3$, and $^{\#\phi}_2 C_2(D, \gamma) = (0^3, 8, 0, 2)$ for $\gamma \in D_t$. Using (5.13) and combining it with the results from (5.15) and Example 5.15, we have

$$^{\#B} C(D, \gamma) = ((1), 10, (0), (0^3, 8, 0, 2))$$

for the design D and $\gamma \in D_t$.　　　　　　　　　　　　　　□

Next, we consider case (II) for computing B-F-AENP: $n > N/2$. Note that for this case, $D_t = \{\mathcal{A}_0, \cdots, \mathcal{A}_{q-1}\}$, $D_b = H_r$, and particularly in $n = \sum_{t=0}^{q-1} j_t 2^t$, there is an s such that $j_s = 0$ and $j_{s+1} = \cdots = j_{q-1} = 1$.

First, we can directly obtain $^{\#m}_1 C_2(D, \gamma)$ from Theorem 5.5, as $^{\#m}_1 C_2(D, \gamma) = {^\#_1} C_2(D_t, \gamma)$. For $\gamma \in \mathcal{A}_i$ with $j_i = 1, i = s+1, \cdots, q-1$, we have

$$^{\#m}_1 C_2^{(k)}(D, \gamma) = \begin{cases} 1, & \text{for } k = \sum_{t=s+2}^{q-1} 2^{t-1} + \sum_{t=0}^{s-1} j_t 2^t, \\ 0, & \text{otherwise,} \end{cases} \tag{5.18}$$

and for $\gamma \in \mathcal{A}_i$ with $j_i = 1$, $i = 0, \cdots, s-1$, we have

$$
{}^{\#m}_1 C_2^{(k)}(D, \gamma) = \begin{cases} 1, & for\ k = \sum_{t=s+1}^{q-1} 2^{t-1}, \\ 0, & otherwise. \end{cases}
\tag{5.19}
$$

For case (II), we compute ${}^{\#m}_2 C_2^{(k)}(D, \gamma)$ and ${}^{\#\phi}_2 C_2^{(k)}(D, \gamma)$ according to the following theorem.

Theorem 5.19   *Let $D = (D_t : D_b)$ be a B^1-GMC $2^{n-m} : 2^r$ design with $n > N/2$. Then, for $\gamma \in \mathcal{A}_i$ with $j_i = 1$, $i = s+1, \cdots, q-1$, we have*

$$
{}^{\#m}_2 C_2^{(k)}(D, \gamma) = \begin{cases} n - 2^{s+1}, & for\ k = \sum_{t=s+2}^{q-1} 2^{t-1} + \sum_{t=0}^{s-1} j_t 2^t - 1, \\ \sum_{t=0}^{s-1} j_t 2^t, & for\ k = \sum_{t=s+1}^{q-1} 2^{t-1} - 1, \end{cases}
\tag{5.20}
$$

and for $\gamma \in \mathcal{A}_i$ with $j_i = 1$, $i = 0, \cdots, s-1$, we have

$$
{}^{\#m}_2 C_2^{(k)}(D, \gamma) = \begin{cases} \sum_{t=s+1}^{q-1} 2^t, & for\ k = \sum_{t=s+2}^{q-1} 2^{t-1} + \sum_{t=0}^{s-1} j_t 2^t - 1, \\ 0, & otherwise. \end{cases}
\tag{5.21}
$$

Furthermore,

$$
{}^{\#\phi}_2 C_2^{(k)}(D, \gamma) = \begin{cases} \sum_{p=n_{v-1}+1}^{n_v} y_i'(D_t, p), & for\ k = f(D_t, n_v) - 1, v = 1, \cdots, g, \\ 0, & otherwise, \end{cases}
\tag{5.22}
$$

where $n_1, \cdots, n_g$ are the successive change points of $f(D_t, r), \cdots, f(D_t, s)$, respectively, $n_0 = r - 1$, and

$$
y_i'(D_t, p) = \begin{cases} y_i(D_t, p), & r \leqslant p < s, 0 \leqslant i \leqslant q-1, i \neq s, \\ 2^s - \sum_{t=0}^{s-1} j_t 2^t, & p = s, s+1 \leqslant i \leqslant q-1, \\ 0, & p = s, 0 \leqslant i \leqslant s-1. \end{cases}
\tag{5.23}
$$

The following is an example of case (II) for computing B-F-AENP.

Example 5.20   Consider the B^1-GMC $2^{20-15} : 2^3$ design D with $D_t = \{\mathcal{A}_2, \mathcal{A}_4\} = \{(I, H_2)34, (I, H_4)5\}$ and $D_b = H_3$. In this design, we have $q = 5$ and express $20 = \sum_{i=0}^{5-1} j_i 2^i$ with $(j_0, j_1, j_2, j_3, j_4) = (0, 0, 1, 0, 1)$. As a result, we determine $s = 3$ because $j_s = 0$ and $j_{s+1} = j_{q-1} = 1$.

Now, we calculate the B-F-AENP for $\gamma \in \mathcal{A}_4$. Firstly, using (5.18), we find

$$
{}^{\#m}_1 C_2(D, \gamma) = (0^4, 1).
$$

Secondly, according to (5.14), we have

$$\sum_k {}^{\#b}_2 C_2^{(k)}(D, \gamma) = 7,$$

which means that

$$n - 1 - \sum_k {}^{\#b}_2 C_2^{(k)}(D, \gamma) = 12.$$

Thirdly, from (5.20), we get that ${}^{\#m}_2 C_2^{(3)}(D, \gamma) = 4$ and ${}^{\#m}_2 C_2^{(7)}(D, \gamma) = 4$, resulting in

$$ {}^{\#m}_2 C_2(D, \gamma) = (0^3, 4, 0^3, 4).$$

Finally, combining the values $f(D_t, 3) = 8$ and $y'_4(D_t, 3) = 4$ in (5.23), we obtain ${}^{\#\phi}_2 C_2(D, \gamma) = (0^7, 4)$. Thus, by (5.13), we get

$$ {}^{\#B}C(D, \gamma) = ((0^4, 1), 12, (0^3, 4, 0^3, 4), (0^7, 4))$$

for $\gamma \in \mathcal{A}_4$. Similarly,

$$ {}^{\#B}C(D, \gamma) = ((0^8, 1), 16, (0^3, 16), (0))$$

for $\gamma \in \mathcal{A}_2$.　　　　　　　　　　　　　　　　　　　　　　□

　　　Based on the B-F-AENP criterion (5.13) and the computation results above, we now rank the columns of D_t for all the B^1-GMC $2^{n-m} : 2^r$ designs $D = (D_t : D_b)$ with $5N/16 + 1 \leqslant n \leqslant N - 1$. It is worth noting that all the columns in the same $\mathcal{A}_i$ have the same B-F-AENP, as observed from the computation results. Therefore, we can conveniently use ${}^{\#B}C(D, \mathcal{A}_i)$ to denote ${}^{\#B}C(D, \gamma)$ with $\gamma \in \mathcal{A}_i$, and ranking columns is equivalent to ranking the $\mathcal{A}_i$'s. We have the following theorem.

Theorem 5.21　*Let $D = (D_t : D_b)$ be a B^1-GMC $2^{n-m} : 2^r$ design with $5N/16+1 \leqslant n \leqslant N - 1$, where $n = \sum_{t=0}^{q-1} j_t 2^t$, D_t has the decomposition $\{\mathcal{A}_0, \cdots, \mathcal{A}_{q-1}\}$, and $q = n - m$.*

　　(a) If $5N/16 + 1 \leqslant n \leqslant N/2$, then we have the B-F-AENP ordering of the $\mathcal{A}_i$'s:

$$\{\mathcal{A}_0, \mathcal{A}_1, \cdots, \mathcal{A}_{q-2}, \mathcal{A}_{q-1}\}, \tag{5.24}$$

where $\mathcal{A}_{q-1} = \varnothing$.

　　(b) If $N/2 < n \leqslant N - 1$, let s be the number such that $j_s = 0$ and $j_{s+1} = \cdots = j_{q-1} = 1$, then we have the B-F-AENP ordering of the $\mathcal{A}_i$'s:

$$\{\mathcal{A}_{q-1}, \mathcal{A}_{q-2}, \cdots, \mathcal{A}_{s+1}, \mathcal{A}_0, \mathcal{A}_1, \cdots, \mathcal{A}_s\}. \tag{5.25}$$

Back to the B^1-GMC 2^{20-15} : 2^3 design in Example 5.20, its construction, in conjunction with conclusions in Theorem 5.21, shows that the column rank is $\{(I, H_4)5, (I, H_2)34\}$. The B-F-AENP presented in Example 5.20 further serves as a confirmation of this result.

5.2.3   Applications of the B-F-AENP

In this section, we explore some applications of B-F-AENP in factor assignment. It is important to note that not all factor assignments to columns are equally desirable. To illustrate this, we consider the B^1-GMC 2^{12-7} : 2^2 design $D = (D_t : D_b)$ from Example 5.12, where $D_t = \{(I, H_2)35, (I, H_3)45\}$ and $D_b = \{1, 5, 15\}$, designed to incorporate three important factors. Let us compare two different factor assignments: $\{12345, 2345, 1345\}$ and $\{12345, 245, 35\}$ for the same set of three factors. Although the columns in both assignments are independent, the latter assignment is clearly superior to the former. This is because the former assignment has a 2fi that is aliased with block effect 1, whereas the latter assignment avoids this aliasing, making it a better choice.

Suppose that an experimenter has prior knowledge regarding the relative importance order of factors in their blocked experiment. Based on the importance order of factors, we typically encounter two cases that need to be considered:

(I) The factors in the importance order are individually addressed. This means that for each individual factor, its main effect and all the 2fi's involving that factor are addressed in the specified order.

(II) The factors in the importance order are addressed in groups. This means that for the first k important factors, their main effects and all the 2fi's between those k factors are of primary concern. The value of k ranges from 1 to the total number of factors, and particularly for $k = 1$, the main effect and all the 2fi's involving the most important factor are given the highest priority.

Clearly, in case (I) mentioned earlier, as a separate factor becomes more important, it becomes crucial to accurately estimate its main effect and the 2fi's involving that factor through the experiment. Theorem 5.21 demonstrates that to achieve the objective set in case (I), the experimenter simply needs to select a B^1-GMC $2^{n-m} : 2^r$ design and assign the factors to the columns based on their priori importance order using the B-F-AENP ordering as illustrated in (5.24) or (5.25).

Next, let us consider case (II) as described earlier. We denote the factors in the importance order as $d_1, d_2, \cdots, d_n$. In this case, we group the factors sequentially as $\{d_1\}$, $\{d_1, d_2\}$, and so on, up to $\{d_1, d_2, \cdots, d_n\}$. Our goal is to ensure that the effect groups $\{d_1, d_1 d_j, j = 2, \cdots, n\}$ and $\{d_1, \cdots, d_k, d_i d_j, i, j = 1, \cdots, k, i < j\}$, with $k = 2, \cdots, n$, can be sequentially estimated with the best precision. To achieve this, we need to assign the factors to the columns of the selected B^1-GMC $2^{n-m} : 2^r$ design in a suitable manner based on the B-F-AENP. The goal is that for $k = 1$, the severity degrees of $\{d_1, d_1 d_j, j = 2, \cdots, n\}$ aliased with block effect and other lower-order effects are sequentially minimized. Then, step by step, for every added factor d_k, we minimize the severity degrees of $\{d_k, d_k d_j, j = 1, \cdots, k-1\}$ aliased with block effect and other lower-order effects sequentially, with $k = 2, \cdots, n$.

In the following, for case (II), we focus on the special case of taking the first q important factors. Obviously, in this case, we only need to sequentially select q independent columns for assigning the q factors. It is important to note that a 2fi aliased with the block effect cannot be estimated. Therefore, we must avoid selecting any column that involves such a 2fi. To achieve this, we need to identify which columns would lead to this situation.

Let us write $D_t = \{\mathcal{B}_0, \mathcal{B}_1, \cdots\}$ as the decomposition defined as follows.

(a) When $5N/16 + 1 \leqslant n \leqslant N/2 - 2^{r-1}$, $\mathcal{B}_0 = \cup_{t=0}^{r-2} \mathcal{A}_t$ and $\mathcal{B}_i$, with $i \geqslant 1$, contains successively 2^{r-1} columns of $\{\mathcal{A}_{r-1}, \cdots, \mathcal{A}_{q-1}\}$.

(b) When $N/2 - 2^{r-1} + 1 \leqslant n \leqslant N - 1$, $\mathcal{B}_0 = \cup_{t=0}^{r-1} \mathcal{A}_t$ and $\mathcal{B}_i$, with $i \geqslant 1$, contains successively 2^r columns of $\{\mathcal{A}_r, \cdots, \mathcal{A}_{q-1}\}$.

Clearly, with case (a), every $\mathcal{B}_i$ with $i \geqslant 1$ is a group of partition $\mathcal{D}_{r-1}$, and $\mathcal{B}_0$ is in a group of partition $\mathcal{D}_{r-1}$. Hence, a 2fi $\alpha_1 \alpha_2$ with $\alpha_1, \alpha_2 \in \mathcal{B}_i$ is of classes 1 to $r - 1$. Additionally, a 2fi $\alpha_1 \alpha_2$ with $\alpha_1 \in \mathcal{B}_i$, $\alpha_2 \in \mathcal{B}_j$, with $i \neq j$ is of class r or higher. With case (b), every $\mathcal{B}_i$ with $i \geqslant 1$ is a group of partition $\mathcal{D}_r$, and $\mathcal{B}_0$ is in a group of partition $\mathcal{D}_r$. Hence, a 2fi $\alpha_1 \alpha_2$ with $\alpha_1, \alpha_2 \in \mathcal{B}_i$ is of classes 1 to r. Furthermore, a 2fi $\alpha_1 \alpha_2$ with $\alpha_1 \in \mathcal{B}_i$, $\alpha_2 \in \mathcal{B}_j$, and $i \neq j$ is of class $r + 1$ or higher.

Based on Lemma 5.13, we have thus established the following corollary.

Corollary 5.22   Let $D = (D_t : D_b)$ be a B^1-GMC $2^{n-m} : 2^r$ with D_t having the decomposition $D_t = \{\mathcal{B}_0, \mathcal{B}_1, \cdots\}$ defined above, for both cases (a) and (b). Then any 2fi $\alpha_1\alpha_2$ with $\alpha_1, \alpha_2 \in \mathcal{B}_i$ is aliased with the block effect, and any 2fi $\alpha_1\alpha_2$ with $\alpha_1 \in \mathcal{B}_i$, $\alpha_2 \in \mathcal{B}_j$, and $i \neq j$ is not aliased with the block effect.

Based on the results in Corollary 5.22 and the B-F-AENP ordering of $\mathcal{A}_i$'s in Theorem 5.21, for case (II), the procedure for selecting q independent columns in D_t is evident and therefore omitted here.

6 General Minimum Lower-Order Confounding Split-plot Designs

This chapter considers fractional factorial split-plot (FFSP) designs, which are particularly useful when changing the levels of certain factors in an experiment is challenging or costly. The GMC criterion for FFSP designs has been explored by Wei, Yang, Li, and Zhang (2010) as well as Sun and Zhao (2021, 2023), and their findings will be discussed in this chapter.

6.1 Introduction

When conducting an experiment, it is often necessary to randomize the experimental runs completely, which may require frequent changes to the levels of the factors. However, in some cases, meeting this requirement may be impractical, especially when changing the levels of specific factors is challenging or costly. In such situations, it is recommended to use fractional factorial split-plot (FFSP) designs, which involve a two-phase randomization process. In FFSP designs, the factors with levels that are difficult to change are referred to as whole plot (WP) factors, while those with relatively easy-to-change levels are known as subplot (SP) factors. The WP factors are denoted by capital letters (A, B, C, etc.) and SP factors are denoted by lowercase letters (p, q, r, s, etc.). Box and Jones (1992) provided a comprehensive and insightful discussion on this type of design.

A regular FFSP design, which consists of n_1 WP factors and n_2 SP factors, is often denoted as $2^{(n_1+n_2)-(m_1+m_2)}$. The design is determined by m_1 WP defining words and m_2 SP defining words. A WP defining word involves only WP factors, while an SP defining word involves at least two SP factors. It is preferable for the WP factors to be included in the SP defining words, but no SP factor should be contained in the WP defining words (Huang, Chen, and Voelkel, 1998). In other words, the split-plot nature of the experiment would not be preserved if any SP defining word contains fewer than two SP factors. If we consider a $2^{(n_1+n_2)-(m_1+m_2)}$ design as a 2^{n-m} design, where $n = n_1 + n_2$ and $m = m_1 + m_2$, then the concepts of fractional factorial designs such as defining word, alias set, resolution, WLP, MA, and clear effects also apply to the former in the usual manner.

The design matrix of an FFSP design appears identical to that of a typical fractional factorial design. However, the key distinction between them lies in the randomization structures employed in the designs. A $2^{(n_1+n_2)-(m_1+m_2)}$ design incorporates a two-phase randomization process, resulting in several unique features that distinguish it from a usual fractional factorial design. Bisgaard (2000) summarizes the most notable of these as follows:

(a) factors do not have equal status;

(b) inference can be made at two different levels of accuracy.

It is important to note that the WP part of a $2^{(n_1+n_2)-(m_1+m_2)}$ design is essentially a $2^{n_1-m_1}$ design. Consequently, the treatment combinations of a $2^{(n_1+n_2)-(m_1+m_2)}$ design involve $2^{n_1-m_1}$ WP factor settings. Each WP factor setting appears in conjunction with $2^{n_2-m_2}$ SP factor settings (Mukerjee and Wu, 2006). To perform a $2^{(n_1+n_2)-(m_1+m_2)}$ design, one often first randomly choose one of the WP factor settings, then run all the $2^{n_2-m_2}$ conjunctive SP factor settings in a random order. This is repeated for each of the $2^{n_1-m_1}$ WP factor settings.

6.2   GMC Criterion for Split-plot Designs

Split-plot designs have their own unique characteristics due to the two-phase randomization scheme employed. This randomization gives rise to two types of random errors: the WP error term and the SP error term. These error terms have different precisions, indicating that the power to detect significant effects in data analysis is not the same for WP and SP effects. Consequently, inferences made about these effects may have two distinct levels of accuracy. Further details and explanations can be found in Bisgaard (2000).

In split-plot designs, effects that involve only WP factors are referred to as *WP-type effects*, while effects that involve at least one SP factor are called *SP-type effects*. An alias set is said to be of *WP-type* if it contains at least one WP-type effect, or of SP-type otherwise. When assessing the significance of an effect within an alias set of WP-type, the WP error term is used. Similarly, the SP error term is employed to assess the significance of an effect within an alias set of SP-type. These rules were initially developed by Bisgaard (2000) and subsequently summarized by Bingham and Sitter (2001).

Let $_{i(s)}^{\#}C_{(w)}^{(1)}$ denote the number of ith-order SP-type effects in WP-type alias sets, and $_{i(s)}^{\#}C_{(w)}^{(0)}$ denote the number of ith-order SP-type effects not in any WP-type alias set. It is evident that

$$_{i(s)}^{\#}C_{(w)}^{(0)} + {}_{i(s)}^{\#}C_{(w)}^{(1)} = \sum_{l=1}^{i} \binom{n_2}{l}\binom{n_1}{i-l}.$$

In particular, $_{1(s)}^{\#}C_{(w)}^{(0)}$ is the number of SP-type main effects that are not aliased with any WP-type effects. Considering the split-plot structure, for a $2^{(n_1+n_2)-(m_1+m_2)}$ design, the value of $_{1(s)}^{\#}C_{(w)}^{(0)}$ must be n_2. Hence, we define the AENP for FFSP designs as:

$$\#^{sp}C = (\,{}_{1(s)}^{\#}C_{(w)}^{(0)} = n_2, {}_{1}^{\#}C_2, {}_{2}^{\#}C_2, {}_{2(s)}^{\#}C_{(w)}^{(0)}, {}_{1}^{\#}C_3, {}_{2}^{\#}C_3, {}_{3}^{\#}C_2, {}_{3}^{\#}C_3, {}_{3(s)}^{\#}C_{(w)}^{(0)}, \cdots). \tag{6.1}$$

In the pattern (6.1), the positioning of $_{2(s)}^{\#}C_{(w)}^{(0)}$ after $_{2}^{\#}C_2$ is based on the following rationale. After considering the confounding of 2fi's, the next concern is the estimation accuracy of these 2fi's. In an FFSP design, all WP-type effects are tested against the WP level error, while SP-type effects are tested against either the WP or SP level error. It is known that the WP level error is typically larger than the SP level error (Bisgaard, 2000). Therefore, a good FFSP design should strive to have as many lower-order SP-type effects not aliased with WP effects as possible. The $_{2(s)}^{\#}C_{(w)}^{(0)}$ just indicates the number of such SP 2fi's and hence it should follow $_{2}^{\#}C_2$. Similarly, $_{3(s)}^{\#}C_{(w)}^{(0)}$ should be placed after $_{3}^{\#}C_3$, and so on.

Definition 6.1 *Suppose that D and D' are two $2^{(n_1+n_2)-(m_1+m_2)}$ designs. Let $^{\#^{sp}}C_l$, which may have the form $^{\#}_iC_j^{(k)}$ or $^{\#}_{i(s)}C_{(w)}^{(0)}$, be the l-th component of $^{\#^{sp}}C$. Suppose $^{\#^{sp}}C_t$ is the first component of $^{\#^{sp}}C$ such that $^{\#^{sp}}C_t(D) \neq {}^{\#^{sp}}C_t(D')$. If $^{\#^{sp}}C_t(D) > {}^{\#^{sp}}C_t(D')$, then D is said to have less lower-order confounding than D'. A $2^{(n_1+n_2)-(m_1+m_2)}$ design D is said to have GMC if no other $2^{(n_1+n_2)-(m_1+m_2)}$ design has less lower-order confounding than D, and also we call such design a GMC-FFSP design.*

Based on the given definition, a GMC-FFSP design aims to maximize the components of $^{\#^{sp}}C$ in (6.1) sequentially. Wei, Yang, Li, and Zhang (2010) proposed an algorithm for searching GMC $2^{(n_1+n_2)-(m_1+m_2)}$ designs. The designs with $n_1+n_2 \leqslant 14$ are tabulated in the appendix of Wei, Yang, Li, and Zhang (2010).

6.2.1　Comparison with MA-MSA-FFSP Criterion

In the literature, most existing results on choosing optimal FFSP designs are of the MA type. In this context, the WP and SP factors in a word are also called *letters*, and the number of letters in a word is called the *length of the word*. Recall that for a design D, $A_i(D)$ denotes the number of defining words with a length i. The vector $(A_1, A_2, \cdots, A_n)$ is referred to as the WLP of the design D. A $2^{(n_1+n_2)-(m_1+m_2)}$ design that sequentially minimizes the A_i's in the WLP is called an *MA-FFSP design*. The rule for selecting FFSP designs is called the *MA-FFSP criterion*. The 2fi's in FFSP designs can be divided into three types: WP2fi, SP2fi, and WS2fi. In this context, a WP2fi or SP2fi refers to a 2fi where both factors are WP or SP factors, respectively. Similarly, a WS2fi indicates a 2fi where one factor is a WP factor and the other is an SP factor.

Huang, Chen, and Voelkel (1998) employed the MA-FFSP criterion to select an optimal regular two-level FFSP design for a thin-film coating experiment. Bingham and Sitter (1999) developed a new sequential construction method and compiled a catalog of MA two-level FFSP designs with 8 and 16 runs, primarily using algorithmic approaches. Continuing with the two-level case, Bingham and Sitter (2001) listed MA-FFSP designs with up to 32 runs. Mcleod and Brewster (2004, 2006) and Mcleod

(2008) discussed split-plot designs with blocking.

It is important to note that split-plot designs do not have interchangeability between WP factors and SP factors, resulting in the presence of multiple non-isomorphic FFSP designs that have MA. In order to address this issue, Mukerjee and Fang (2002) introduced the concept of minimum secondary aberration (MSA) and proposed the MA-MSA-FFSP criterion. This criterion effectively narrows down the class of competing non-isomorphic MA designs and often yields a unique optimal design of MA type. Ai and Zhang (2006) constructed MA-MSA-FFSP designs based on consulting designs. Yang, Zhang, and Liu (2007) constructed weak MA-MSA-FFSP designs. Recognizing the greater importance of the WP factors compared to the SP factors in specific scenarios, Wang, Zhao, and Zhao (2019) introduced the minimum aberration of type WP (WP-MA) criterion. Building upon this criterion, Zhao and Zhao (2020) developed a construction method for WP-MA FFSP designs utilizing complementary designs.

Let $B_i(D)$ be the number of distinct ith-order SP-type factorial effects that appear in the WP-type alias sets. Considering the structure of split-plot designs, we have $B_1(D) = 0$. A good FFSP design should assign as less lower-order SP-type factorial effects as possible to WP-type alias sets (Mukerjee and Fang, 2002). This implies that we should sequentially minimize $B_2(D)$, $B_3(D)$, $\cdots$. Mukerjee and Fang (2002) referred to

$$W^*(D) = (B_2(D), \cdots, B_n(D))$$

as the secondary WLP and used it for further ranking these MA-FFSP designs as follows. For two nonisomorphic MA $2^{(n_1+n_2)-(m_1+m_2)}$ designs, D_1 and D_2, D_1 is said to have less secondary aberration than D_2 if there exists a positive integer r such that $B_r(D_1) < B_r(D_2)$ and $B_i(D_1) = B_i(D_2)$ for $i < r$. An MA-FFSP design has MSA, called an *MA-MSA-FFSP design*, if no other MA design has less secondary aberration. We call the criterion combining the two steps of MA and MSA an MA-MSA-FFSP criterion. Since the MA-MSA-FFSP design is the best among the MA-FFSP designs, we only need to compare the GMC-FFSP criterion with the MA-MSA-FFSP criterion.

By comparing the definitions of B_i and $_{i(s)}^{\#}C_{(w)}^{(k)}$ in (6.1), we can immediately establish the following proposition.

Proposition 6.2 *For a $2^{(n_1+n_2)-(m_1+m_2)}$ FFSP design D, we have*

$$B_i(D) = \sum_{l=1}^{i} \binom{n_2}{l}\binom{n_1}{i-l} - {}_{i(s)}^{\#}C_{(w)}^{(0)}(D)$$

and

$$\sum_{i=2}^{n_1+n_2} B_i(D) = 2^{n_1}(2^{m_2}-1).$$

Proof. The first part of the proposition is evident. Hence, we will focus on the second part.

In a $2^{(n_1+n_2)-(m_1+m_2)}$ FFSP design, there are $2^{n_1-m_1}$ WP-type alias sets, each of which involves $2^{m_1+m_2}-2^{m_1}$ SP-type effects. Therefore, the total number of SP-type effects in these WP-type alias sets is

$$2^{n_1-m_1}(2^{m_1+m_2}-2^{m_1}) = 2^{n_1}(2^{m_2}-1).$$

By the definition of $B_i(D)$, $\sum_{i=2}^{n_1+n_2} B_i(D)$ equals the sum of SP-type effects that are in WP-type alias sets. Therefore, the second equation is established. □

As usual, from the definitions of the WLP of an FFSP design and clear effects, and Lemma 2.10, we also have that, $A_i = {}_i^{\#}C_0^{(1)}$ and the numbers of clear main effects and 2fi's are ${}_1^{\#}C_2^{(0)}$ and ${}_2^{\#}C_2^{(0)} - {}_1^{\#}C_2^{(1)}$, respectively.

Thus, the aforementioned facts indicate that the patterns of MA-FFSP (WLP) and MSA (secondary WLP) are all the functions of the pattern of GMC-FFSP (AENP-FFSP). Therefore, the GMC-FFSP criterion is the most elaborate and explicit one for selecting optimal designs with least lower-order confounding. In the following, we provide some examples to illustrate the comparison.

Example 6.3 Consider the following two $2^{(5+4)-(1+3)}$ designs:

$$D_1 : I = ABCDE = ABDpq = ACDpr = BCDps,$$

$$D_2 : I = ABCDE = ABpq = ACpr = BCps.$$

Here, design D_1 is an MA-MSA-FFSP design, while design D_2 is a GMC-FFSP design. In fact, we have ${}_1^{\#}C_2(D_1) = {}_1^{\#}C_2(D_2) = (9)$, and

$${}_2^{\#}C_2(D_1) = (8, 24, 0, 4), \quad {}_2^{\#}C_2(D_2) = (15, 0, 21).$$

Note that $^{\#}_1 C_2^{(0)}$ and $^{\#}_2 C_2^{(0)}$ are the numbers of clear main effects and clear 2fi's respectively because both designs have resolution IV.

It is obvious that both designs have 9 clear main effects, but D_2 has 7 more clear 2fi's than D_1. Therefore, we can say that D_2 is better than D_1 in the sense of less confounding between the lower-order effects. For more comparisons between them, refer to Table 6.1.　　　　　　　　　　　　　　　　　　　　□

Table 6.1　Comparisons between $2^{(5+4)-(1+3)}$ MA-MSA-FFSP design D_1 and GMC-FFSP design D_2

	D_1	D_2
$^{\#}_1 C_2;\, ^{\#}_2 C_2;\, ^{\#}_{2(s)} C^{(0)}_{(w)}$	9; 8, 24, 0, 4; 20	9; 15, 0, 21; 20
WLP	0, 6, 8, 0, 0, 1, 0	0, 7, 7, 0, 0, 0, 1
Number of clear main effects	9	9
Number of total clear 2fi's	8	15
Numbers of clear WP, WS, and SP 2fi's	4, 4, 0	7, 8, 0

An illustrative representation of the example in Table 6.1 is presented in Figure 6.1. In the figure, factors are denoted by letters, and clear main effects, clear WP 2fi's, and clear WS 2fi's are represented by bold dots, solid lines, and dotted lines, respectively. Therefore, the structures of the clear main effects and various types of clear 2fi's for the $2^{(5+4)-(1+3)}$ MA-MSA-FFSP design D_1 and GMC-FFSP design D_2 are visualized. From the figure, it is evident that D_2 is a better choice compared to D_1 when an experimenter has a prior understanding of the relative importance of factors in experiments, similar to the case without split-plot.

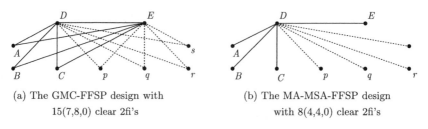

(a) The GMC-FFSP design with　　　　(b) The MA-MSA-FFSP design
　　15(7,8,0) clear 2fi's　　　　　　　　with 8(4,4,0) clear 2fi's

Fig 6.1　A comparison of the $2^{(5+4)-(1+3)}$ GMC-FFSP and MA-MSA-FFSP designs

In the following, we compare the GMC-FFSP and MA-MSA-FFSP designs by the de-aliasing of certain 2fi's.

Example 6.4   Consider the following two $2^{(4+6)-(0+5)}$ designs:

$$D_3 : I = BDpq = ABpr = CDps = ABCDpt = ACpu,$$

$$D_4 : I = BDpq = BCpr = ADps = CDpt = ABpu.$$

Here, we only give the five independent defining words. Design D_3 is an MA-MSA-FFSP design, while D_4 is a GMC-FFSP design. The $({}^{\#}_1C_2; {}^{\#}_2C_2; {}^{\#}_{2(s)}C^{(0)}_{(w)})$'s of D_3 and D_4 are

$$(10; 0, 0, 45; 24) \quad \text{and} \quad (10; 0, 6, 27, 12; 24),$$

respectively.

We observe that although both designs have the same number of clear main effects and clear 2fi's, their confounding degrees between lower-order effects are different. In D_3, 45 2fi's are confounded with two other 2fi's, while in D_4, 6 2fi's are confounded with only one other 2fi's and 27 2fi's are confounded with two other 2fi's. This indicates that the design D_4 has a significantly higher number of 2fi's with less confounding compared to the design D_3.

If we need to de-alias a few 2fi's, say, less than 15, for estimating, it is likely that the number of additional runs required for follow-up experiments will be much lower with design D_4 compared to design D_3.   □

From the two examples above, it is evident that FFSP designs with GMC tend to have more clear effects and less confounding between lower-order effects. The following example demonstrates the application of GMC-FFSP designs in scenarios where prior information is available for the factorial effects.

Example 6.5   Consider the GMC-FFSP $2^{(5+4)-(1+3)}$ design D_2 in Example 6.3. In this design, all the main effects are clear. The 15 clear 2fi's in the design are AD, AE, BD, BE, CD, CE, DE, Dp, Dq, Dr, Ds, Ep, Eq, Er, and Es.

Suppose we want to assign a $2^{(5+4)-(1+3)}$ design with five WP factors (denoted by 1, 2, 3, 4, 5), and four SP factors (denoted by 6, 7, 8, 9). If we have prior information that all 2fi's involving factors 1 or/and 2 are of special interest and need to be estimated clearly, we can assign factor 1 to the column labeled D and factor 2 to the column labeled E in the design matrix. In this sense, it is evidence that the GMC-FFSP design D_2 is better than the MA-MSA-FFSP design D_1 when using the prior information, as the former has more clear 2fi's than the latter.

The same observation applies to the two designs D_3 and D_4 in Example 6.4. Despite having the same number of clear effects, the designs exhibit different levels of confounding between lower-order effects. So, we can also strategically assign the factors to the columns of the GMC design in order to prioritize the important 2fi's with the least confounding. □

6.2.2 Comparison with Clear Effects Criterion

Next, we consider a comparison with the CE criterion, which sequentially maximizes the numbers of clear main effects and clear 2fi's. Yang, Li, Liu, and Zhang (2006) provided necessary and sufficient conditions for the existence of two-level FFSP designs containing various clear effects. Zi, Zhang, and Liu (2006) established the upper and lower bounds on the maximum numbers of clear WP and WS 2fi's for two-level FFSP designs. They also presented methods for constructing the desired FFSP designs. Zhao and Chen (2012a, b), Wang, Yuan, and Zhao (2015), Yuan and Zhao (2016), Han, Chen, Liu, and Zhao (2020), and Han, Liu, Yang, and Zhao (2020) investigated mixed-level FFSP designs. They provided necessary and sufficient conditions for the existence of such designs that contains various clear effects.

Since the definition of clear effect in FFSP designs is the same as that of the usual fractional factorial designs, all the properties of clear effects in the GMC-FFSP criterion remain the same as those of the GMC criterion in usual fractional factorial designs. Therefore, we can draw the following conclusion.

Proposition 6.6 *For given n_1, n_2, m_1, and m_2, if the optimal designs under the CE criterion exist, then the GMC-FFSP design must be the best one among all the optimal designs under the CE criterion, where the meaning of "best" is under the comparison in Definition 6.1 of the GMC-FFSP criterion. Moreover, the GMC-FFSP criterion can be applied to designs that do not have any clear effect.*

Similarly to the case of usual fractional factorial designs, the AENP-FFSP criterion in (6.1) may appear to be complex. However, in practical scenarios where the interactions of three and higher orders are considered negligible, the AENP-FFSP can be simplified as follows:

$$\#^{sp}C = (\ \substack{\#\\1(s)}C^{(0)}_{(w)} = n_2,\ \substack{\#\\1}C_2,\ \substack{\#\\2}C_2,\ \substack{\#\\2(s)}C^{(0)}_{(w)}).$$

A natural question arises regarding whether a GMC-FFSP design can be derived from a GMC fractional factorial design by assigning some factors as WP factors and the remaining factors as SP factors. However, the answer to this question is negative. This can be illustrated through the following example.

Example 6.7   Consider the 2^{10-5} design determined by the following independent defining words

$$I = ABCpq = ABCDr = ABDps = ACDpt = BCDpu.$$

As a fractional factorial design, it is a GMC design. Suppose we are interested in running a $2^{(4+6)-(0+5)}$ FFSP experiment. The 2^{10-5} GMC fractional factorial design, however, does not have split-plot structure since

$$\substack{\#\\1(s)}C^{(0)}_{(w)}(D) < n_2$$

whenever any four factors are considered as WP factors. Therefore, GMC-FFSP designs cannot be obtained from GMC fractional factorial designs by randomly assigning some factors as WP factors and others as SP factors.   □

6.3   WP-GMC Split-plot Designs

6.3.1   WP-GMC Criterion for Split-plot Designs

In most of the literature, the WP factors and the SP factors are typically considered equally important in screening the optimal design. However, in certain circumstances, the WP factors are more important than the SP factors. An example illustrating this scenario is presented by Montgomery (2013) in the context of factors influencing uniformity in a single-wafer plasma etching process (Example 14.3). Three factors on the etching tool are relatively difficult to change from run to run: A=electrode gap, B=gas flow, and C=pressure. Two other factors are easy to change from run to run: D=time and E=RF (radio frequency) power. The presence of hard-to-change factors suggests the need for a split-plot design. The objective of the experimenter was to minimize the uniformity response. The experimenter opted for a 2^{5-1} design, where factors A, B, and C were assigned to the whole plots, while factors D and E were allocated to the subplots. In Montgomery (2013), Figure 14.8 demonstrated that the main effects A, B, and E, as well as the 2fi's AB and AE, had a significant impact on the response variable. Specifically, the combinations of high A, low B, and low E levels, or low A, high B, and high E levels resulted in low levels of the uniformity response. Given that the selection of A levels influenced the selection of E levels, it can be inferred that the WP factors were more important than the SP factors in this particular experiment.

In an FFSP experiment, the levels of WP factors are typically chosen first as they are often more difficult to change compared to SP factors. Consequently, when a WP factor interacts with an SP factor, it indicates that the WP factor is more important than the SP factor. Lawson (2015) provides additional examples supporting this notion. For instance, Figure 8.3 in Lawson (2015) illustrates the significant influence of level combinations of the WP two-factor interaction AB on the selection of the SP factor C in the Saussage-Casting Experiment. This further emphasizes the importance of WP factors over SP factors in certain experimental scenarios.

From the examples above, it is evident that in certain real-world scenarios, some WP factors may be more important than the SP factors. In such circumstance, we are more interested in studying the impact and influence of the WP factors on the experimental outcomes. In light of the importance of WP factors in certain cases, the effect hierarchy principle can be modified as follows:

(i) Lower-Order effects are more likely to be significant than higher-order effects.

(ii) Effects containing more WP factors are more important among the same order effects.

Based on the modified effect hierarchy principle mentioned above, Wang, Zhao, and Zhao (2019) proposed the WP-MA (Minimum Aberration of type WP) criterion for selecting designs in situations where WP factors are considered more important. They successfully constructed 8, 16, and 32 runs WP-MA designs for cases where $k_1 + k_2 \leqslant 4$. Zhao and Zhao (2020) studied the construction of WP-MA FFSP designs using complementary designs.

Sun and Zhao (2021) extended the GMC criterion and introduced the general minimum lower-order confounding of type WP (WP-GMC) criterion for selecting FFSP designs, considering the importance of WP factors over SP factors. Although both the WP-MA criterion and the WP-GMC criterion are based on the prior information that WP factors are more important than SP factors, they are different. The difference between them is essentially the difference between MA and GMC criteria. Moreover, the WP-GMC criterion is more suitable when the experimenter knows the importance ordering of the WP factors. When we want to clearly estimate more lower-order effects involving important WP factors, the WP-GMC criterion has important theoretical significance and practical value in the selection of designs.

Now, we extend the GMC criterion to FFSP designs by incorporating the assumption that WP factors are more important than SP factors. Additionally, we consider the scenario where the experimenter has prior information regarding the order of importance of the WP factors.

Recall that ${}_{1(s)}^{\#}C_{(w)}^{(0)}$ is the number of SP-type main effects that are not aliased with any WP-type effect. Let ${}_{i(w)}^{\#}C_j^{(k)}$ denote the number of ith-order WP-type effects which are fully aliased with k jth-order effects. We define the AENP for FFSP designs with WP factors more important than SP factors (WP-AENP) as:

$$ {}^{\#^{wp}}C = ({}_{1(s)}^{\#}C_{(w)}^{(0)} = n_2, {}_{1(w)}^{\#}C_2, {}_{1}^{\#}C_2, {}_{2(w)}^{\#}C_2, {}_{2}^{\#}C_2, {}_{1(w)}^{\#}C_3, {}_{1}^{\#}C_3, {}_{2(w)}^{\#}C_3, {}_{2}^{\#}C_3, \cdots). \quad (6.2) $$

According to the assumption that WP factors are more important than SP factors, our first priority is to estimate the WP-type main effects. Therefore, we aim to keep the WP-type main effects aliased with the 2fi's as minimally as possible. Consequently, we prioritize placing ${}_{1(w)}^{\#}C_2$ before ${}_{1}^{\#}C_2$ in the WP-AENP. Similarly, we put ${}_{i(w)}^{\#}C_j$ before ${}_{i}^{\#}C_j$. The ordering principle of the remaining terms in (6.2) follows the same logic as explained in detail in Chapter 2 for the pattern (2.4). Based on (6.2), we define the new GMC criterion for FFSP designs as follows.

Definition 6.8   *Suppose that D_1 and D_2 are two $2^{(n_1+n_2)-(m_1+m_2)}$ designs. Under the condition that WP factors are more likely to be significant than SP factors, let ${}^{\#^{wp}}C_l$ be the l-th component of ${}^{\#^{wp}}C$. Suppose ${}^{\#^{wp}}C_t$ is the first component of ${}^{\#^{wp}}C$ such that ${}^{\#^{wp}}C_t(D_1) \neq {}^{\#^{wp}}C_t(D_2)$. If ${}^{\#^{wp}}C_t(D_1) > {}^{\#^{wp}}C_t(D_2)$, then D_1 is said to have less general lower-order confounding of type WP (WP-GLOC) than D_2. A*

$2^{(n_1+n_2)-(m_1+m_2)}$ *design D_1 is said to have general minimum lower-order confounding of type WP (WP-GMC) if no other $2^{(n_1+n_2)-(m_1+m_2)}$ design has less WP-GLOC than D_1, and such an FFSP design is called a WP-GMC FFSP design.*

Remark 6.9　A GMC 2^{n-m} design must have maximum resolution among all 2^{n-m} designs. Similarly, a WP-GMC $2^{(n_1+n_2)-(k_1+k_2)}$ FFSP design must also be a maximum resolution design. When the WP factors are more important, it is not only the WP-type effects are more important, but also the SP-type effects involving the WP factors may be of interest to the experimenter. However, considering the complexity of the actual situation, we adopt a compromise strategy. We give priority to the WP-type effects, assuming that the SP-type effects of the same order are equally important.

6.3.2　Construction of WP-GMC Split-plot Designs

This section considers the construction of WP-GMC split-plot designs using complementary designs. Let $q_1 = n_1 - m_1$, $q_2 = n_2 - m_2$, and $q = q_1 + q_2$. Recall that H_q represents the saturated design defined in (1.6), where the columns $1, \cdots, q$ correspond to the q independent columns of H_q. Throughout this section, we use $1, \cdots, q_1$ to denote the independent WP factors, and $q_1 + 1, \cdots, q = q_1 + q_2$ to denote the independent SP factors.

Recall that H_{q_1} consists of the first $2^{q_1} - 1$ columns of H_q, and the complementary design of H_{q_1} is denoted as $S_{qq_1} = H_q \backslash H_{q_1}$. For more details, refer to (3.5) in Section 3.1. To construct the $2^{(n_1+n_2)-(m_1+m_2)}$ design $D = (T_1, T_2)$, we can select subsets T_1 and T_2 from H_{q_1} and S_{qq_1}, respectively.

Definition 6.10　*A $2^{(n_1+n_2)-(m_1+m_2)}$ design $D = (T_1, T_2)$ is called eligible if*

(a) *T_i has n_i columns $(i = 1, 2)$;*

(b) *$T_1 \subset H_{q_1}$ and $T_2 \subset S_{qq_1}$;*

(c) *the number of independent columns/factors in T_1 is q_1;*

(d) *the number of independent columns/factors in D is q.*

Let N_1 be the number of SP-type main effects that appear in WP-type alias sets. According to Sun and Zhao (2021), a $2^{(n_1+n_2)-(m_1+m_2)}$ design with resolution *III* or higher and $N_1 = 0$ is considered eligible. Additionally, an eligible $2^{(n_1+n_2)-(m_1+m_2)}$ design exists if and only if the following conditions are satisfied:

$$n_1 \leqslant 2^{q_1} - 1, \quad n_2 \leqslant 2^q - 2^{q_1}.$$

Moving forward, we assume that the aforementioned conditions are met.

The concept of isomorphism for FFSP designs is similar to that for 2^{n-m} designs, with the additional consideration of distinguishing between WP and SP factors. Two $2^{(n_1+n_2)-(m_1+m_2)}$ FFSP designs are considered *isomorphic* if the defining contrast subgroup of one design can be obtained from that of the other by permuting the WP factor labels and/or the SP factor labels. It is important to note that isomorphic designs are considered to be the same designs.

Using the concept of complementary designs, Sun and Zhao (2021) derived several general results for constructing WP-GMC split-plot designs. These results can be summarized as follows.

Let

$$\bar{T}_1 = H_{q_1} \backslash T_1, \quad \bar{T}_2 = S_{qq_1} \backslash T_2, \quad \text{and} \quad \bar{D} = (\bar{T}_1, \bar{T}_2).$$

The numbers of columns in $\bar{D}$, $\bar{T}_1$, and $\bar{T}_2$ are denoted as

$$\bar{n} = 2^q - 1 - n, \quad \bar{n}_1 = 2^{q_1} - 1 - n_1, \quad \text{and} \quad \bar{n}_2 = \bar{n} - \bar{n}_1 = 2^q - 2^{q_1} - n_2,$$

respectively. In the first result, we consider the case when $\bar{n}_2$ is either 0 or 1.

Theorem 6.11 *For a $2^{(n_1+n_2)-(m_1+m_2)}$ design $D = (T_1, T_2)$ with $\bar{n}_2 = 0, 1$,*

(a) *if $\bar{n}_1 = 4, 5,$ or 6, then the design D can have WP-GMC only if $\bar{T}_1$ is contained in a closed subset of H_{q_1} generated by 3 independent columns;*

(b) *if $8 \leqslant \bar{n}_1 \leqslant 14$, then the design D can have WP-GMC only if $\bar{T}_1$ is contained in a closed subset of H_{q_1} generated by 4 independent columns;*

(c) *if $\bar{n}_1 = 2^w - 1$, $2 \leqslant w \leqslant n_1 - m_1 - 1$, then the design D can have WP-GMC only if $\bar{T}_1$ is a closed subset of H_{q_1} generated by w independent columns.*

With the results in Theorem 6.11 and those in Zhang and Mukerjee (2009a), Sun and Zhao (2021) obtained all $2^{(n_1+n_2)-(m_1+m_2)}$ WP-GMC designs with $\bar{n}_2 = 0, 1$ and $\bar{n}_1 = 3, \cdots, 15$. The corresponding $\bar{T}_1$'s are summarized in Table 6.2 at the end of this section.

Next, we consider the case where $\bar{n}_1 = 0$. In Theorem 6.12 below, we provide the WP-GMC FFSP designs for $1 \leqslant \bar{n}_2 \leqslant 4$ and $\bar{n}_2 = 2^v - 1$ with $1 \leqslant v \leqslant q_2$ up to isomorphism.

Theorem 6.12   *Let D denote a $2^{(n_1+n_2)-(m_1+m_2)}$ FFSP design with $T_1 = H_{q_1}$, i.e., $\bar{n}_1 = 0$.*

(a) *When $\bar{n}_2 = 1, 2, 3$, or 4, D has WP-GMC if T_2 takes the following forms:*

(a.1) $T_2 = S_{qq_1} \setminus \{q_1 + 1\}$, *if $\bar{n}_2 = 1$ and $q > q_1$;*

(a.2) $T_2 = S_{qq_1} \setminus \{q_1 + 1, 1(q_1 + 1)\}$, *if $\bar{n}_2 = 2$ and $q = q_1 + 1$;*

(a.3) $T_2 = S_{qq_1} \setminus \{q_1 + 1, q_1 + 2\}$, *if $\bar{n}_2 = 2$ and $q \geqslant q_1 + 2$;*

(a.4) $T_2 = S_{qq_1} \setminus \{q_1 + 1, 1(q_1 + 1), 2(q_1 + 1)\}$, *if $\bar{n}_2 = 3$ and $q = q_1 + 1$;*

(a.5) $T_2 = S_{qq_1} \setminus \{q_1 + 1, q_1 + 2, (q_1 + 1)(q_1 + 2)\}$, *if $\bar{n}_2 = 3$ and $q \geqslant q_1 + 2$;*

(a.6) $T_2 = S_{qq_1} \setminus \{q_1 + 1, 1(q_1 + 1), 2(q_1 + 1), 12(q_1 + 1)\}$, *if $\bar{n}_2 = 4$ and $q = q_1 + 1$;*

(a.7) $T_2 = S_{qq_1} \setminus \{q_1 + 1, q_1 + 2, 1(q_1 + 1), 1(q_1 + 1)(q_1 + 2)\}$, *if $\bar{n}_2 = 4$ and $q = q_1 + 2$;*

(a.8) $T_2 = S_{qq_1} \setminus \{q_1 + 1, q_1 + 2, q_1 + 3, (q_1 + 1)(q_1 + 2)\}$, *if $\bar{n}_2 = 4$ and $q \geqslant q_1 + 3$.*

(b) *When $\bar{n}_2 = 2^v - 1$ with $1 \leqslant v \leqslant q_2$, then D has WP-GMC if $\bar{T}_2$ is a closed subset of S_{qq_1}.*

The following theorem constructs WP-GMC FFSP designs with $\bar{n}_1 = 1$ and $\bar{n}_1 = 2$ for small values of $\bar{n}_2$.

Theorem 6.13   *Let D denote a $2^{(n_1+n_2)-(m_1+m_2)}$ FFSP design.*

(a) *When $\bar{n}_1 = 1$ and $\bar{n}_2 = 1, 2$, or 3, the design D given by $T_1 = H_{q_1} \setminus \{1\}$ and T_2 as shown below has WP-GMC:*

(a.1) $T_2 = S_{qq_1} \setminus \{q_1 + 1\}$, *if $\bar{n}_2 = 1$ and $q > q_1$;*

(a.2) $T_2 = S_{qq_1} \setminus \{q_1 + 1, 1(q_1 + 1)\}$, *if $\bar{n}_2 = 2$ and $q > q_1$;*

(a.3) $T_2 = S_{qq_1} \setminus \{q_1 + 1, 1(q_1 + 1), 2(q_1 + 1)\}$, *if $\bar{n}_2 = 3$ and $q = q_1 + 1$;*

(a.4) $T_2 = S_{qq_1} \setminus \{q_1 + 1, q_1 + 2, (q_1 + 1)(q_1 + 2)\}$, *if $\bar{n}_2 = 3$ and $q \geqslant q_1 + 2$.*

(b) *When $\bar{n}_1 = 2$ and $\bar{n}_2 = 1$ or 2, the design D given by $T_1 = H_{q_1} \setminus \{1, 2\}$ and T_2 as shown below has WP-GMC:*

(b.1) $T_2 = S_{qq_1} \setminus \{q_1 + 1\}$, *if $\bar{n}_2 = 1$ and $q > q_1$;*

(b.2) $T_2 = S_{qq_1} \setminus \{q_1 + 1, 12(q_1 + 1)\}$, *if $\bar{n}_2 = 2$ and $q = q_1 + 1$;*

(b.3) $T_2 = S_{qq_1} \setminus \{q_1 + 1, q_1 + 2\}$, *if $\bar{n}_2 = 2$ and $q \geqslant q_1 + 2$.*

According to Theorems 6.12 and 6.13, we have further constructed several WP-GMC FFSP designs presented in Tables 6.3–6.5. Please note that we have used $1, \cdots, q_1$ to denote the independent WP factors, and $q_1 + 1, \cdots, q = q_1 + q_2$ to represent the independent SP factors.

Table 6.2 **The designs $\bar{T}_1$ for WP-GMC $2^{(n_1+n_2)-(m_1+m_2)}$ designs with $\bar{n}_2 = 0, 1$,**
where $\bar{T}_2 = \{q_1 + 1\}$ when $\bar{n}_2 = 1$

$\bar{n}_1$	$\bar{T}_1$
3	$\{1, 2, 12\}$
4	$\{1, 2, 12, 3\}$
5	$\{1, 2, 12, 3, 13\}$
6	$\{1, 2, 12, 3, 13, 23\}$
7	$\{1, 2, 12, 3, 13, 23, 123\}$
8	$\{1, 2, 12, 3, 13, 23, 123, 4\}$
9	$\{1, 2, 12, 3, 13, 23, 123, 4, 14\}$
10 $(q_1 = 4)$	$\{1, 2, 12, 3, 13, 23, 4, 14, 24, 34\}$
10 $(q_1 \geqslant 5)$	$\{1, 2, 12, 3, 13, 23, 123, 4, 14, 24\}$
11	$\{1, 2, 12, 3, 13, 23, 123, 4, 14, 24, 124\}$
12	$\{1, 2, 12, 3, 13, 23, 123, 4, 14, 24, 124, 34\}$
13	$\{1, 2, 12, 3, 13, 23, 123, 4, 14, 24, 124, 134\}$
14	$\{1, 2, 12, 3, 13, 23, 123, 4, 14, 24, 124, 34, 134, 234\}$
15	$\{1, 2, 12, 3, 13, 23, 123, 4, 14, 24, 124, 34, 134, 234, 1234\}$

Table 6.3 **The designs $\bar{T}_2$ for WP-GMC $2^{(n_1+n_2)-(m_1+m_2)}$ designs with $\bar{n}_1 = 0$**

$\bar{n}_2$	q_2	$\bar{T}_2$
1	$\geqslant 1$	$\{q_1 + 1\}$
2	1	$\{q_1 + 1, 1(q_1 + 1)\}$
	$\geqslant 2$	$\{q_1 + 1, q_1 + 2\}$
3	1	$\{q_1 + 1, 1(q_1 + 1), 2(q_1 + 1)\}$
	$\geqslant 2$	$\{q_1 + 1, q_1 + 2, (q_1 + 1)(q_1 + 2)\}$
	1	$\{q_1 + 1, 1(q_1 + 1), 2(q_1 + 1), 12(q_1 + 1)\}$
4	2	$\{q_1 + 1, q_1 + 2, 1(q_1 + 1), 1(q_1 + 1)(q_1 + 2)\}$
	$\geqslant 3$	$\{q_1 + 1, q_1 + 2, q_1 + 3, (q_1 + 1)(q_1 + 2)\}$

Table 6.4   The designs $\bar{T}_2$ for WP-GMC $2^{(n_1+n_2)-(m_1+m_2)}$ designs with $\bar{T}_1 = \{1\}$

$\bar{n}_2$	q_2	$\bar{T}_2$
1	$\geqslant 1$	$\{q_1 + 1\}$
2	$\geqslant 1$	$\{q_1 + 1, 1(q_1 + 1)\}$
3	1	$\{q_1 + 1, 1(q_1 + 1), 2(q_1 + 1)\}$
	$\geqslant 2$	$\{q_1 + 1, q_1 + 2, (q_1 + 1)(q_1 + 2)\}$

Table 6.5   The designs $\bar{T}_2$ for WP-GMC $2^{(n_1+n_2)-(m_1+m_2)}$ designs with
$\bar{T}_1 = \{1, 2\}$

$\bar{n}_2$	q_2	$\bar{T}_2$
1	$\geqslant 1$	$\{q_1 + 1\}$
2	$= 1$	$\{q_1 + 1, 12(q_1 + 1)\}$
2	$\geqslant 2$	$\{q_1 + 1, q_1 + 2)\}$

7 Partial Aliased Effect-Number Pattern and Compromise Designs

Addelman (1962) studied a range of designs that sought to find a compromise between orthogonal main-effect designs and designs that allowed for uncorrelated estimation of all main effects and all 2fi's. These designs were commonly known as compromise plans or compromise designs. Often, experimenters are interested in estimating a few specified factorial effects. A compromise design can effectively achieve this objective. To assess and select compromise designs, this chapter introduces a partial aliased effect-number pattern, which is used to study a class of two-level compromise designs.

7.1 Introduction

Addelman (1962) discussed three classes of compromise designs for estimating all main effects and three classes of specified 2fi's. In addition, Sun (1993) proposed a fourth class of compromise design. These four classes were distinguished based on the specific 2fi's that needed to be estimated in each class:

1. $\{G_1 \times G_1\}$, 2. $\{G_1 \times G_1, G_2 \times G_2\}$, 3. $\{G_1 \times G_1, G_1 \times G_2\}$, 4. $\{G_1 \times G_2\}$.

Here, $\{G_1, G_2\}$ is a partition of the n factors in an experiment, and $G_i \times G_j$ denotes the set of 2fi's between the factors in G_i and those in G_j $(i, j = 1, 2)$. Ke, Tang, and Wu (2005) introduced the concept of clear compromise plans and examined the existence and characteristics of compromise plans in classes one to four. Their analysis assumed that all third- or higher-order interactions are negligible.

Zhao and Zhang (2010) expanded on this research by investigating mixed-level $4^m 2^n$ designs.

Since Addelman (1962), researchers have typically considered the clear estimation of all main effects as a prerequisite for compromise designs. Consequently, in most studies focusing on selecting compromise designs, the range of design candidates has been limited to those with a resolution of at least IV. However, in many practical experiments, experimenters are interested in estimating a few specified factorial effects, which may only include some main effects and some 2fi's. Consequently, it is necessary to extend the original definition of a compromise design, which was based on the precondition of clear estimation of all main effects. In this chapter, we will broadly refer to a design that can achieve this target as a compromise design, removing the original precondition. For the sake of consistency, we will continue to use the term compromise design to refer to this type of design.

With this extension, the limitation that "resolution must be at least IV" should also be removed when seeking optimal compromise designs. Consider a scenario where an experimenter aims to find an experiment with 8 runs and 4 factors that can effectively estimate only one specified factor main effect. Consider two designs $D_1 = \{1, 2, 3, 23\}$ and $D_2 = \{1, 2, 3, 123\}$ with the interested factor respectively assigning to column 1 in D_1 and any column in D_2. Since D_1 has resolution III and D_2 has resolution IV, it might seem that D_2 would be better than D_1. However, with D_1, the specified main effect can be strongly clearly estimated, whereas with D_2, the specified main can only be clearly estimated. This implies that D_1 with resolution III is actually better than D_2 with resolution IV. So, if an experimenter aims to estimate only certain specified effects, then selecting a design with resolution IV is not always superior to selecting one with resolution III. Therefore, in the broader context of compromise design, it becomes necessary to expand the range of design candidates with resolutions from at least IV to at least III in order to select the optimal designs.

We denote the specified main effects and specified 2fi's as G_i and $G_i \times G_j$, respectively. Similarly, we study four classes of extended compromise designs represented by the following sets of specified effects:

1. $\{G_1, G_1 \times G_1\}$, 2. $\{G_1, G_1 \times G_1, G_2 \times G_2\}$,

3. $\{G_1, G_1 \times G_1, G_1 \times G_2\}$, 4. $\{G_1, G_1 \times G_2\}$.

$$(7.1)$$

In this chapter, our focus is primarily on the class one compromise designs. However, it is important to note that the ideas and results presented can be generalized to the other classes as well.

7.2 Partial Aliased Effect-Number Pattern

In order to assess and select optimal compromise designs, Ye, Wang, and Zhang (2019) introduced a measure called the partial aliased effect-number pattern (P-AENP). In the following sections of this chapter, we will provide a summary of their main findings.

We should note that when selecting a regular design that can provide the most accurate estimation of a set of specified effects, it is essential to consider both the column composition of the design and the factor assignment on those columns. Different compositions and factor assignments can lead to varying levels of accuracy in estimating these specific effects. Therefore, it is crucial to choose the design that achieves the best coordination between column composition and factor assignment.

Example 7.1 Let us consider an experiment with seven factors, where the experimenter's interest lies in estimating three main effects from the set of seven main effects and three 2fi's between three specific factors. We can represent this set as

$$\{G_1, G_1 \times G_1\} = \{d_1, d_2, d_3, d_1 d_2, d_1 d_3, d_2 d_3\}.$$

From H_5, the experimenter selects the 2^{7-2} design with the composition

$$\{1, 2, 3, 4, 5, 45, 12345\}.$$

Now let us consider two assignments of the three factors to $\{1, 2, 3\}$ and $\{1, 4, 5\}$, respectively. It can be easily verified that in the former assignment, all the six specified effects are clear, while in the latter assignment, only the main effect d_1 and the 2fi's $d_1 d_2$ and $d_1 d_3$ are clear. This indicates that the former assignment is superior to the latter in terms of estimation accuracy for the specified effects.

If the experimenter selects another 2^{7-2} design with the composition

$$\{1, 2, 3, 4, 5, 123, 45\},$$

it can be observed that none of the six specified effects are clear for any factor assignment. This indicates that the first 2^{7-2} design with the first factor assignment is superior to the second 2^{7-2} design with any factor assignment for this experiment. Therefore, the better design choice would be $\{1, 2, 3 : 4, 5, 45, 12345\}$.　　　□

Thus, we can observe that when estimating the four classes of specified effects in (7.1), selecting a compromise design is equivalent to choosing a 2^{n-m} design with certain defining relations and a specific partition of the n columns, denoted as $\{G_1 : G_2\}$, where $|G_1| = f$ and $|G_2| = n - f$.

We denote the set of all effects as Ω, and the set of specified effects as Ω_1. Obviously, $\Omega_1 \subset \Omega$. Suppose that D is a 2^{n-m} compromise design intended for estimating the effects of Ω_1. Let ${}^{\#}_i P_j^{(k)}(D; \Omega_1)$ denote the number of i-th order effects in Ω_1 aliased with k j-th order effects in Ω. We define a number set as follows:

$$\{{}^{\#}_i P_j^{(k)}(D; \Omega_1), i, j = 1, 2, \cdots, n, \ k = 0, 1, \cdots, K_j\}. \tag{7.2}$$

This set is referred to as the partial aliased effect-number pattern (P-AENP) of D with respect to Ω_1.

Write

$${}^{\#}_i P_j(D; \Omega_1) = ({}^{\#}_i P_j^{(0)}(D; \Omega_1), {}^{\#}_i P_j^{(1)}(D; \Omega_1), \cdots, {}^{\#}_i P_j^{(K_j)}(D; \Omega_1)).$$

For simplicity, we denote it as ${}^{\#}_i P_j$. Suppose that the specified effect set Ω_1 also follows the effect hierarchy principle. Then, in a similar manner to the AENP, we sort the numbers in (7.2) as the sequence

$${}^{\#}P = ({}^{\#}_1 P_1, {}^{\#}_1 P_2, {}^{\#}_2 P_1, {}^{\#}_2 P_2, {}^{\#}_1 P_3, {}^{\#}_2 P_3, {}^{\#}_3 P_1, {}^{\#}_3 P_2, {}^{\#}_3 P_3, \cdots), \tag{7.3}$$

where the ordering of ${}^{\#}_i P_j$'s remains the same as that of the AENP in (2.3). The sequence (7.3) is also referred to as the P-AENP of D with respect to Ω_1. To save space, when writing a P-AENP, we also use the abbreviation notation for trivial zeros, similar to the AENP. As usual, the term ${}^{\#}_1 P_1$ is omitted since we do not consider designs with resolution II.

If we only consider designs with resolution at least III and assume that the fourth or higher-order interactions are negligible, we can follow a similar approach as the AENP to simplify the P-AENP (7.3) by dropping the trivial terms. The simplified form becomes:

$$^\#P = (^\#_1P_2, {}^\#_2P_1, {}^\#_2P_2, {}^\#_1P_3, {}^\#_2P_3).\tag{7.4}$$

We still refer to (7.4) as the P-AENP of D with respect to Ω_1.

In the following, we define the optimal compromise design (OCD) and compare any two compromise designs.

Definition 7.2 *Let $^\#P(D_1; \Omega_1)$ and $^\#P(D_2; \Omega_1)$ be P-AENP's of two compromise designs D_1 and D_2 with respect to Ω_1. Further, let $^\#P_l$ denote the l-th component of $^\#P$ and l^* be the first l such that $^\#P_l(D_1; \Omega_1) \neq {}^\#P_l(D_2; \Omega_1)$. If $^\#P_{l^*}(D_1; \Omega_1) > {}^\#P_{l^*}(D_2; \Omega_1)$, then we say that D_1 is better than D_2. If there is no any other compromise design with respect to Ω_1 that is better than D_1, then we consider D_1 to be an OCD with respect to Ω_1.*

Example 7.3 Consider the specified effect set $\Omega_1 = \{G_1, G_1 \times G_1\} = \{d_1, d_2, d_3,$ $d_1d_2, d_1d_3, d_2d_3\}$ and the two selected 2^{7-2} designs $D_1 = \{1, 2, 3 : 4, 5, 45, 12345\}$ and $D_2 = \{1, 4, 5 : 2, 3, 45, 12345\}$ in Example 7.1. By the definition of P-AENP, we can easily get

$$\left(^\#_1P_2, {}^\#_2P_1, {}^\#_2P_2, {}^\#_1P_3, {}^\#_2P_3\right)(D_1; \Omega_1) = \left((3, 0), (3, 0), (3, 0), (3, 0), (0, 3)\right),$$

$$\left(^\#_1P_2, {}^\#_2P_1, {}^\#_2P_2, {}^\#_1P_3, {}^\#_2P_3\right)(D_2; \Omega_1) = \left((1, 2), (2, 1), (3, 0), (3, 0), (1, 2)\right).$$

From Definition 7.2, it is evident that D_1 is better than D_2. $\qquad\square$

Unlike the AENP, which considers how all the effects in the entire Ω are aliased with each other in a design, the P-AENP focuses specifically on how the effects in Ω_1 are aliased with the effects in the entire Ω. Therefore, when selecting an OCD, the P-AENP is more suitable and efficient than the AENP and other patterns such as the WLP.

Naturally, we may consider a two-step approach to find the OCD: We first find a GMC (or MA) design, and then we select the best factor assignment based on the selected GMC (or MA) design as the OCD. However, this approach does not always work as expected. The following example illustrates this.

Example 7.4 Suppose we aim to select a class one 2^{10-4} OCD with $f = 5$. Using the AENP, we obtain the GMC design

$$\{1, 2, 3, 4, 5, 12345, 6, 1236, 246, 3456\}.$$

We then determine the best factor assignment and obtain the compromise design:

$$D_3 = \{1, 2, 3, 4, 5 : 12345, 6, 1236, 246, 3456\}$$

for estimating $\Omega_1 = \{G_1, G_1 \times G_1\}$ with $|G_1| = 5$. Its P-AENP is

$$({}^{\#}_1 P_2, {}^{\#}_2 P_1, {}^{\#}_2 P_2, {}^{\#}_1 P_3, {}^{\#}_2 P_3)(D_3; \Omega_1) = \big((5), (10), (9, 1), (2, 3), (2, 0, 8)\big).$$

It can be verified that for the specified effects Ω_1, D_3 has five clear main effects and nine clear 2fi's. Additionally, it has two strongly clear main effects and one strongly clear 2fi.

However, by considering the P-AENP directly, we can identify an OCD

$$D_4 = \{1, 2, 3, 4, 5 : 2345, 6, 1246, 1356, 23456\}.$$

Its P-AENP is

$$({}^{\#}_1 P_2, {}^{\#}_2 P_1, {}^{\#}_2 P_2, {}^{\#}_1 P_3, {}^{\#}_2 P_3)(D_4; \Omega_1) = \big((5), (10), (10), (5), (0, 4, 4, 2)\big).$$

In D_4, all the main effects and 2fi's are clear, and notably, five main effects are strongly clear. This means that in terms of both the number of clear effects and the number of strongly clear effects, the OCD D_4 is supervior to D_3.

However, if we use the AENP as the first step to find the OCD, D_4 is not considered as an option. This is because when we evaluate the designs using the AENP, we obtain the following results:

$$({}^{\#}_1 C_2, {}^{\#}_2 C_1, {}^{\#}_2 C_2)(D_4) = \big((5, 4, 1), (39, 6), (39, 6)\big),$$

$$({}^{\#}_1 C_2, {}^{\#}_2 C_1, {}^{\#}_2 C_2)(D_3) = \big((10), (45), (33, 12)\big).$$

These results indicate that according to the AENP, D_4 is considered worse than D_3.

□

7.3　Some General Results of Compromise Designs

Consider a 2^{n-m} compromise design D with the specified effect set Ω_1. We use ${}^{\#}_1 C_{2*}^{(1)}$ to denote the number of main effects in Ω aliased with only one 2fi in Ω_1. Then, we have the following lemma.

Lemma 7.5　*For a 2^{n-m} compromise design D, let c_1 and c_2 respectively denote the numbers of clear specified main effects and clear specified 2fi's. Then, we have*

$$c_1 = {}^{\#}_1 P_2^{(0)} \quad and \quad c_2 = {}^{\#}_2 P_2^{(0)} - {}^{\#}_1 C_{2*}^{(1)}.$$

Proof. It is evident that we have $c_1 = {}^{\#}_1 P_2^{(0)}$, since the design D has a resolution of at least III. We only need to prove the second equation.

Let S denote the set of the specified 2fi's that are not aliased with any other 2fi's, implying that S contains all the clear specified 2fi candidates, and we have $|S| = {}^{\#}_2 P_2^{(0)}$. This also means that there are $|S|$ alias sets each containing only one specified 2fi. Moreover, the $|S|$ alias sets can be divided into two parts: one part where each set contains one main effect, and another part where each set does not contain a main effect. It is evident that the specified 2fi's in the sets of the first part are not clear, while the specified 2fi's in the sets of the second part are clear.

By the definition of notation ${}^{\#}_1 C_{2*}^{(1)}$, the number of sets in the first part, i.e., the number of sets where each set contains one main effect, is exactly ${}^{\#}_1 C_{2*}^{(1)}$. Thus, the second equation is obtained. □

From Lemma 7.5, it is evident that if a 2^{n-m} compromise design D has a resolution of at least IV, then it has $c_1 = {}^{\#}_1 P_2^{(0)}$ and $c_2 = {}^{\#}_2 P_2^{(0)}$. We have the following theorem.

Theorem 7.6 *An OCD for estimating Ω_1 must have maximum numbers of clear specified main effects and clear specified 2fi's.*

Proof. Let D be a 2^{n-m} OCD with $|G_1| = f \leqslant n$. According to the definition of OCD, ${}^{\#}_1 P_2^{(0)}(D)$ is maximum among all the compromise designs. Therefore, based on Lemma 7.5, the number of clear specified main effects of D is also maximum.

Then we consider whether the number of clear specified 2fi's of D is also maximum. First, we note that according to Lemma 7.5, when $n \geqslant N/2$, any compromise design must have ${}^{\#}_2 P_2^{(0)} - {}^{\#}_1 C_{2*}^{(1)} = 0$, as no 2^{n-m} design can have clear 2fi (Chen and Hedayat, 1998). Therefore, when $n \geqslant N/2$, ${}^{\#}_2 P_2^{(0)} - {}^{\#}_1 C_{2*}^{(1)}$ is the number of clear specified 2fi's of D, and it is maximized when it equals 0.

When $n \leqslant N/2$, for any $f \leqslant n$, there exists a compromise 2^{n-m} design of resolution IV such that ${}^{\#}_2 P_1^{(0)}$ is maximum among all the P-AENPs of the compromise designs respect to the same Ω_1. Since ${}^{\#}_2 P_1^{(0)}(D)$ and ${}^{\#}_2 P_2^{(0)}(D)$ are sequentially maximum, and based on the definition of ${}^{\#}_1 C_{2*}^{(1)}$, it follows that D has ${}^{\#}_1 C_{2*}^{(1)}(D) = 0$. Hence, the number ${}^{\#}_2 P_2^{(0)}(D) - {}^{\#}_1 C_{2*}^{(1)}(D)$ is maximum, as implied by Lemma 7.5.

This completes the proof.   □

Clearly, with a substitution of $\{G_1, G_1 \times G_1\}$ by a general Ω_1 to compute ${}_1^{\#}C_{2*}^{(1)}$, Lemma 7.5 and Theorem 7.6 remain valid.

7.4   Class One Compromise Designs

7.4.1   Largest Class One Clear Compromise Designs and Their Construction

A compromise design is said to be clear if all the effects of Ω_1 can be clearly estimated, and we call it a clear compromise design (CCD). In this definition, the requirement for clear estimation applies only to the effects in Ω_1, and we focus on CCDs with a resolution of at least III. It is important to note that according to Theorem 7.6, if a CCD exists for a given parameter, any OCD must also be a CCD.

First, considering by the definition of CCD and Lemma 7.5, for a class one 2^{n-m} CCD $D = \{G_1 : G_2\}$ with $|G_1| = f$, its P-AENP must have

$$({}_1^{\#}P_2, {}_2^{\#}P_1, {}_2^{\#}P_2)(D; \Omega_1) = ((f), (f(f-1)/2), (f(f-1)/2)).$$

Let

$$f^*(q, n) = \max\{f(q, n)\}, \quad n^*(q, f) = \max\{n(q, f)\},$$

where $f(q, n)$ denotes the f that for a given pair of (q, n) there exists a 2^{n-m} CCD with $|G_1| = f$, and $n(q, f)$ denotes the n that for a given pair of (q, f) there exists a 2^{n-m} CCD with $|G_1| = f$.

Especially, for a fixed n, among all the class one CCDs with different f's, the CCDs with larger f values are more powerful. Similarly, for a fixed f, among all the class one CCDs $\{G_1 : G_2\}$ with different n's, the CCDs with larger n values are more powerful.

Let M_q denote the largest 2^{n-m} design with resolution V and $M(q)$ denote the number of columns of M_q. Obviously, we have $n^*(q, f) \geq n^*(q, f+1)$ for class one CCDs, because if $\{G_1 : G_2\}$ is a 2^{n-m} CCD with $|G_1| = f+1$ and $\alpha \in G_1$, then $\{G_1 \backslash \{\alpha\} : G_2 \cup \{\alpha\}\}$ is a 2^{n-m} CCD with $|G_1 \backslash \{\alpha\}| = f$. With a similar argument, we have $f^*(q,n) \leqslant f^*(q,n-1)$ for $n \geqslant M(q)+1$. If a class one 2^{n-m} CCD $D = \{G_1:G_2\}$ with $|D| = n$ has $f = f^*(q,n)$, then it is said to be the largest for f. If a class one 2^{n-m} CCD $D = \{G_1:G_2\}$ with $|G_1| = f$ has $n = n^*(q,f)$, then it is said to be the largest for n.

7.4.2 Supremum $f^*(q,n)$ and Construction of Largest Class One CCDs

By the definition of CCD, the G_1 in a class one 2^{n-m} CCD $D = \{G_1 : G_2\}$ with $f = |G_1|$ must have a resolution of at least V. Therefore, for given q and n, $M(q)$ serves as an upper bound for $f(q,n)$, i.e.,

$$f^*(q,n) \leqslant M(q).$$

Moreover, regarding $f^*(q,n)$, we have the following additional result.

Theorem 7.7 *For a class one 2^{n-m} CCD $D=\{G_1:G_2\}$'s with $|G_1| = f$, we have*

$$f^*(q,n) \begin{cases} = n, & \text{if } n \leqslant M(q), \\ \leqslant M(q) - 2, & \text{if } n \geqslant M(q)+1 \text{ and } q \geqslant 4. \end{cases} \tag{7.5}$$

Proof. The validity of the first equation in (7.5) is evident, so we focus on proving the second equation.

First, let us consider the case where $n = M(q)+1$ with $q \geqslant 4$. By the definition of $M(q)$, any 2^{n-m} design with $n = M(q)+1$ can only have a resolution of III or IV. If the design has a resolution of III, it implies that there are at least three factors whose main effects and 2fi's are not clear. In other words, $f(q, M(q)+1) \leqslant M(q)-2$, which further implies that $f^*(q, M(q)+1) \leqslant M(q) - 2$. If the design has a resolution of IV, it implies that the design must have four factors in a defining word with length four. As a result, at least three of these factors cannot be in G_1 due to the confounding between their 2fi's. Therefore, we have $f(q, M(q) + 1) \leqslant M(q) - 2$ and $f^*(q, M(q) + 1) \leqslant M(q) - 2$.

Next, let us consider the case where $n = M(q)+2$ with $q \geqslant 4$. Suppose we have a class one 2^{n-m} CCD $D = \{G_1:G_2\}$ with $n = M(q) + 2$ and $f = |G_1| = f^*(q,n)$. Since G_1 has a resolution of V, we have $f^*(q,n) \leqslant M(q)$. Additionally, it must hold that $f^*(q,n) \neq M(q) - 1$. If this is not the case, it implies that $|G_2| = 3$, there exists a column $\alpha \in G_2$, and a class one CCD $D' = \{G_1 : \{G_2 \backslash \{\alpha\}\}\}$ with $|D'| = M(q) + 1$ and $f = M(q) - 1$. This contradicts $f^*(q, M(q) + 1) \leqslant M(q) - 2$. Similarly, we can prove $f^*(q,n) \neq M(q)$. Therefore, we conclude that $f^*(q,n) \leqslant M(q) - 2$.

Finally, let us consider the case when $n > M(q) + 2$ with $q \geqslant 4$. Since for $n \geqslant M(q) + 1$ we have $f^*(q,n) \leqslant f^*(q, n-1)$, it follows that for $n > M(q) + 2$ we have $f^*(q,n) \leqslant M(q) - 2$. Therefore, the second equation of (7.5) is proven. $\qquad\square$

Theorem 7.7 relates to the designs with resolution at least III and can be seen as an extension of Lemma 2 in Ke, Tang, and Wu (2005), which only focuses on designs with a resolution of at least IV.

By the definition of CCD, we can derive the following corollary, which is evident.

Corollary 7.8　*A class one 2^{n-m} CCD $D = \{G_1 : G_2\}$ has resolution III if and only if the letters in its defining words with length three are from G_2.*

Theorem 7.7 states that when $n \leqslant M(q)$, $f^*(q,n)$ is equal to n. Furthermore, when $q \geqslant 4$ and $n \geqslant M(q) + 1$, $M(q) - 2$ serves as an upper bound for $f^*(q,n)$. However, it remains to be determined whether $M(q) - 2$ is also the supremum in the second case. In the following, we construct the class one 2^{n-m} CCDs with resolution at least III for the cases where $f = M(q) - 2$, $q = 4, 5, 6, 7$, and $n = M(q) + 1$. Interestingly, this construction coincides with $f^*(q,n) = M(q) - 2$.

Let us assume that the $2^{M(q) - (M(q) - q)}$ design with resolution V can be expressed, up to isomorphism, as

$$M_q = \{1, 2, \cdots, q, t_{q+1}, \cdots, t_{M(q)}\}.$$

Here, $\{1, 2, \cdots, q\}$ are q independent columns, and t_i's are defining columns with defining relations $(q+1) = t_{q+1}, \cdots$, and $M(q) = t_{M(q)}$. Regarding the existence of CCD with $f = M(q) - 2$ and $n = M(q) + 1$, we have the following proposition.

Proposition 7.9　*Let $M_q = \{1, 2, \cdots, q, t_{q+1}, \cdots, t_{M(q)}\}$ be a design of resolution V with $|M_q| = M(q)$. Then,*

(a) if in its defining contrast subgroup there is a pair of letters, say ij, which does not appear in any word with length five, then the design $D = \{M_q \backslash \{i, j\} : i, j, ij\}$ is a class one 2^{n-m} CCD of resolution III with $f = M(q) - 2$ and $n = M(q) + 1$;

(b) *if in its defining contrast subgroup there is a letter triple, say ijk, which does not appear in any word with length five or six, then the design $D = \{M_q\backslash\{i,j\}: i, j, ijk\}$ is a 2^{n-m} class one CCD of resolution IV with $f = M(q) - 2$ and $n = M(q) + 1$.*

Proof. For expression convenience, we denote $1, 2, \cdots, q$ as $t_1, \cdots, t_q$.

For (a), it is evident that $D = M_q \cup \{t_i t_j\}$ has resolution *III* with $f = M(q) - 2$ and $n = M(q) + 1$. If D is not a CCD, then based on M_q having the resolution V, the only possibility is that there exists an s different from i and j such that $t_s(t_i t_j)$ is aliased with some 2fi $t_u t_v$. This means that in the defining contrast subgroup of M_q, there is a length five word $t_u t_v t_s t_i t_j$ that includes the pair $t_i t_j$. However, this contradicts the assumption.

For (b), it is evident that $D = M_q \cup \{t_i t_j t_k\}$ has resolution *IV* with $f = M(q) - 2$ and $n = M(q) + 1$. If it is not a CCD, then, once again, considering that M_q has the resolution V, there are only two possibilities:

(i) there is a 2fi $t_u t_v$ in $G_1 \times G_1$ with $u \neq k$ and $v \neq k$, which is aliased with a 2fi $t_s(t_i t_j t_k)$, where s is different from any one in $\{u, v, i, j, k\}$, and $t_i t_j t_k$ is a column (factor) of D. Moreover, $t_i t_j t_k$ can be treated as a 3fi of M_q. Consequently, this implies that for M_q, there exists a length six word $t_u t_v t_s t_i t_j t_k$ containing the triple $t_i t_j t_k$, which contradicts the assumption;

(ii) there exists a 2fi $t_u t_v$ in $G_1 \times G_1$ with $u \neq k$ and $v \neq k$ that is aliased with the main effect $t_i t_j t_k$ of D. This means that for M_q, there exists a length five word $t_u t_v t_i t_j t_k$ containing the triple $t_i t_j t_k$, which further contradicts the assumption.   □

Furthermore, for these CCDs in Proposition 7.9, we have the following proposition, and the construction method is in the proof.

Proposition 7.10   *For each case of $n = M(q) + 1$ with $q = 4, 5, 6, 7$, there are an M_q satisfying the assumption in Proposition 7.9 and a class one 2^{n-m} CCD with $f = M(q) - 2$ and $n = M(q) + 1$.*

Proof. For $q = 7$, we have $M(7) = 11$ and

$$M_7 = \{1, 2, 3, 4, 5, 6, 7, 1234, 3456, 2367, 12357\}$$

is the largest design with resolution V. It is worth noting that the pair 17 does not appear in any of the six length five words:

$$\{12348, 34569, 2367t_1, 4578t_2, 289t_1t_2, 156t_1t_2\},$$

where $t_1 = 10$, $t_2 = 11$. By Proposition 7.9, the design

$$\{2, 3, 4, 5, 6, 1234, 3456, 2367, 12357 : 1, 7, 17\}$$

is a class one 2^{12-5} CCD of resolution III with $f = 9$ and $n = 12$. Furthermore, it is worth noting that the triple 246 does not appear in any of the six length five words or any of the five length six words of M_7. According to Proposition 7.9, the design

$$\{1, 3, 5, 6, 7, 1234, 3456, 2367, 12357 : 2, 4, 246\}$$

is a class one 2^{12-5} CCD of resolution IV with $f = 9$ and $n = 12$.

For $q = 5$, we have $M(5) = 6$ and its M_5 is $\{1, 2, 3, 4, 5, 2345\}$. The pair 12 does not appear in its only length five word 23456. Consequently,

$$D_1 = \{3, 4, 5, 2345 : 1, 2, 12\}$$

is the largest resolution III CCD with $f = 4$ and $n = 7$. Furthermore, it is easy to verify that $D_2 = \{3, 4, 5, 2345 : 1, 2, 123\}$ is the largest resolution IV CCD with $n = 7$ and $f = 4$. The same result can be obtained for the cases $q = 4, 6$ using a similar approach. Thus, Proposition 7.10 is established.　　　　　　　□

7.4.3　Supremum $n^*(q, f)$ and Construction of Largest Class One CCDs

In this subsection, we investigate the supremum $n^*(q, f)$ and the construction of the largest class one CCDs. First, for $f = 1, 2, 3, 4$, we have

Proposition 7.11　*For class one 2^{n-m} CCD $D = \{G_1 : G_2\}$ with $|G_1| = f$, we have*

$$n^*(q, f) = \begin{cases} N/2, & \text{if } f = 1, \\ N/4 + 1, & \text{if } q \geqslant f, f = 2, 3, \\ N/8 + 3, & \text{if } q \geqslant f, f = 4, \end{cases} \tag{7.6}$$

where $N = 2^{n-m}$.

Proof.　Recall that $H_{r+1,q}$ denotes the closed subset of H_q generated by the independent columns $r+1, r+2, \cdots, q$. The first equation of (7.6) is obtained by considering the design $\{1 : H_{2,q}\}$.

Regarding the second and third equations, it is sufficient to consider the case when $q > 4$ since for $q = 2, 3, 4$, we can directly verify their validity.

Firstly, considering any class one 2^{n-m} CCD $D = \{G_1 : G_2\}$ with $f = 2$ and $q > 4$, it is necessary for the two columns in G_1 to be independent. Therefore, we can assume that $G_1 = \{1, 2\}$, and G_2 can only consist of columns from $\{\{I, 1, 2, 12\}H_{3,q}\}$. Thus, the only requirement for selecting G_2 is to ensure that any 2fi of G_2 does not alias with 1, 2, and 12. To maximize n, the only choice of G_2 is $\{\mathcal{A}_1, 1\mathcal{A}_2, 2\mathcal{A}_3, 12\mathcal{A}_4\}$, where $\mathcal{A}_i \subset H_{3,q}$, $i = 1, 2, 3, 4$. Additionally, $\mathcal{A}_i \cap \mathcal{A}_j = \varnothing$ for $i \neq j$, and $\cup_{i=1}^{4}\mathcal{A}_i = H_{3,q}$. It is easy to see that $n^*(q, 2) = 2^{q-2} - 1 + 2 = N/4 + 1$.

Particularly, if we take $G_2 = H_{3,q}$, then the design is of resolution III. On the other hand, if we take $G_2 = 1H_{3,q}$, then the design D is of resolution IV.

Next, let us consider any class one 2^{n-m} CCD $D = \{G_1 : G_2\}$ with $f = 3$ and $q > 4$. Without loss of generality, we can assume, under isomorphism, that $G_1 = \{1, 2, 3\}$. This assumption is valid since G_1, as a sub-design, must have a resolution of at least V. Consequently, G_2 cannot contain any column from H_3, i.e., it can only be chosen from $H_q \backslash H_3 = \{I, H_3\}H_{4,q}$. The only limitation is that any 2fi of $G_2 \times G_2$ should not alias with any column of H_3 except for 123. To maximize n, the only viable choice for G_2 is

$$\{\{I, 123\}\mathcal{A}_1, \{1, 23\}\mathcal{A}_2, \{12, 3\}\mathcal{A}_3, \{13, 2\}\mathcal{A}_4\},$$

where $\mathcal{A}_i \subset H_{4,q}, i = 1, 2, 3, 4$, $\mathcal{A}_i \cap \mathcal{A}_j = \varnothing$ for $i \neq j$, and $\cup_{i=1}^{4}\mathcal{A}_i = H_{4,q}$. Consequently, we obtain $n^*(q, 3) = 2(2^{q-3} - 1) + 3 = N/4 + 1$.

Finally, let us consider the case of $f = 4$ and $q > 4$. Following the same approach as before, for the design $D = \{G_1 : G_2\}$, we choose $G_1 = \{1, 2, 3, 4\}$. To achieve the largest n, one of the optimal choices for G_2 is $\{1234\} \cup S_1 \cup S_2$, where $S_1 = \{1234\}H_{5,q}$ and S_2 is $\{1\mathcal{A}_1, 2\mathcal{A}_2, 3\mathcal{A}_3, 4\mathcal{A}_4\}$ with $\mathcal{A}_i \cap \mathcal{A}_j = \varnothing$ for $i \neq j$ and $\cup_{i=1}^{4}\mathcal{A}_i = H_{5,q}$. After some calculations, we get $n^*(q, 4) = 2(2^{q-4} - 1) + 5 = N/8 + 3$. Thus, Proposition 7.11 is proved. □

For the values of $n^*(q, f)$ with $f = 5, 6$, we have the following proposition.

Proposition 7.12　*For class one 2^{n-m} CCDs with $f = 5$ and $f = 6$ when $q \geqslant 4$,* we have $n^*(q, 5) = N/8 + 2$ and $n^*(q, 6) = N/8 + 1$.

Proof.   First, let us consider the case of $f = 5$. To ensure that the selected design $D = \{G_1 : G_2\}$ is a CCD, there are only two possible choices for G_1 up to isomorphism $\{1, 2, 3, 4, 1234\}$ or $\{1, 2, 3, 4, 5\}$.

If we choose $G_1 = \{1, 2, 3, 4, 1234\}$, in order to maximize the size of the CCD, G_2 can only consist of one column selected from each $\{\beta\{I, H_4\}\}$, where $\beta \in H_{5,q}$. Therefore, the number of columns of the largest CCD D is $n = |H_{5,q}| + 5 = N/16 + 4$.

If we choose $G_1 = \{1, 2, 3, 4, 5\}$, in order to make $D = \{G_1 : G_2\}$ the largest CCD, G_2 can only take 1234 or 12345 from H_5, and can take $\{I, 123, 145, 2345\}\beta$ from every $\{\beta\{I, H_5\}\}$, where $\beta \in H_{6,q}$. For each β, up to isomorphism, the four columns $\{I, 123, 145, 2345\}\beta$ are the only largest choices from $\{\beta\{I, H_5\}\}$. This is because selecting any additional column from $\{\beta\{I, H_5\}\}$ would result in some 2fi of G_2 aliasing with some 2fi of G_1. Thus, for this case, we have $n = 4|H_{6,q}| + 5 + 1 = N/8 + 2$. Therefore, the choice $G_1 = \{1, 2, 3, 4, 5\}$ results in the largest CCD, and we have $n^*(q, 5) = N/8 + 2$. This establishes the first equality.

Next, let us consider the case of $f = 6$. In order for $\{G_1 : G_2\}$ to be a CCD, G_1 must have one of the following three selections, up to isomorphism: $\{1, 2, 3, 4, 5, 6\}$, $\{1, 2, 3, 4, 5, 1234\}$, and $\{1, 2, 3, 4, 5, 12345\}$.

If we choose $G_1 = \{1, 2, 3, 4, 5, 6\}$, then, in order to make $\{G_1 : G_2\}$ the largest CCD, up to isomorphism, G_2 has the largest selection $\{1234, 1256, 3456\}$ from H_6 and has the largest choice $\{I, 123, 145, 2345, 246, 1346, 1256, 356\}\beta$ from every $\{\beta\{I, H_6\}\}$, where $\beta \in H_{7,q}$, as selecting any additional column from some $\{\beta\{I, H_6\}\}$ would result in aliasing between some 2fi of G_1 and some 2fi of G_2. Thus, the largest possible value of n is $8|H_{7,q}| + 6 + 3 = N/8 + 1$.

If we take G_1 as $\{1, 2, 3, 4, 5, 1234\}$ or $\{1, 2, 3, 4, 5, 12345\}$, the similar argument applies, and G_2 has only one largest choice, $\{I, 125\}\beta$ from every $\{\beta\{I, H_5\}\}$. Thus, for this case, we have the largest possible value of n as $n = 2|H_{6,q}| + 6 = N/16 + 4$.

Hence, the $\{G_1 : G_2\}$ with $G_1 = \{1, 2, 3, 4, 5, 6\}$ and its best corresponding G_2 is the largest class one CCD for $f = 6$ and has $n^*(q, 6) = N/8 + 1$.   □

Summarizing the results of Propositions 7.9-7.12, we have constructed all the largest class one 2^{n-m} CCDs with possible values of f for $q = 4, 5, 6$, and most of the largest CCDs for $q = 7$. Table 7.1 presents the values of $f^*(q, n)$ and $n^*(q, f)$ for $q = 4, 5, 6, 7$.

Table 7.1 $f^*(q, n)$'s and $n^*(q, f)$'s of 2^{n-m} class one CCD $\{G_1 : G_2\}$'s with $f = |G_1|$ for $q = 4, 5, 6, 7$

$q = 4$	$M(4) = 5$	$f^*(4, n)$	5(5)	1(6-8)			
		$n^*(4, f)$	8(1)	5(2-5)			
$q = 5$	$M(5) = 6$	$f^*(5, n)$	6(6)	4(7)	3(8-9)	1(10-16)	
		$n^*(5, f)$	16(1)	9(2-3)	7(4)	6(5-6)	
$q = 6$	$M(6) = 8$	$f^*(6, n)$	8(8)	6(9)	5(10)	4(11)	3(12-17) 1(18-32)
		$n^*(6, f)$	32(1)	17(2-3)	11(4)	10(5)	9(6) 8(7-8)
$q = 7$	$M(7) = 11$	$f^*(7, n)$	11(11)	9(12)	8(13)	6(14-17) 5(18)	4(19) 3(20-33) 1(34-64)
		$n^*(7, f)$	64(1)	33(2-3)	19(4)	18(5) 17(6-7)	13(8) 12(9) 11(10-11)

The numbers in brackets refer to the n's for taking the f^* or the f's for taking the n^*. For example, for $q = 5$, 3(8-9) is $f^*(5, n) = 3$ if $n = 8, 9$; for $q = 6$, 17(2-3) is $n^*(6, f) = 17$ if $f = 2, 3$.

7.4.4　Largest Class One Strongly Clear Compromise Designs

In certain practical trials, some 3fi's may be significant. In such cases, experimenters require special compromise designs which can strong-clearly estimate the specified effects.

Let $D = \{G_1 : G_2\}$ be a class one compromise design. If all the effects of $\Omega_1 = \{G_1, G_1 \times G_1\}$ are strongly clear in design D, then it is referred to as a class one strongly clear compromise design (SCCD). In this subsection, we focus on studying this specific type of designs. By the definition of SCCD, it is evident that the P-AENPs of the class one 2^{n-m} SCCD D's with $f = |G_1|$ must have

$$\left({}^{\#}_1 P_2, {}^{\#}_2 P_1, {}^{\#}_2 P_2, {}^{\#}_1 P_3, {}^{\#}_2 P_3 \right)(D; \Omega_1)$$

$$= \left((f), (f(f-1)/2), (f(f-1)/2), (f), (f(f-1)/2) \right). \tag{7.7}$$

Now, let us examine the relationships between n and f for class one 2^{n-m} SCCDs with a resolution of at least *III*. Additionally, for a fixed $q = n - m$, we will address two problems related to SCCDs:

(i) Given a fixed f, what is the maximum value of n?

(ii) Given a fixed n, what is the maximum value of f?

We introduce similar notation as follows:

$$f_s^*(q, n) = \max\{f_s(q, n)\}, \quad n_s^*(q, f) = \max\{n_s(q, f)\}.$$

Here, $f_s(q, n)$ denotes the f such that there exists a 2^{n-m} SCCD for a given (q, f), and $n_s(q, f)$ follows a similar definition.

First, we study the supremum $f_s^*(q, n)$ and the construction of the largest class one SCCD for f. Let M_q^{VI} denote the largest 2^{n-m} design with resolution VI, and $M^{VI}(q)$ denote the number of columns in M_q^{VI}. For example, we have $M^{VI}(5) = 6$, $M^{VI}(6) = 7$, and $M^{VI}(7) = 9$ (Draper and Lin, 1990). Clearly, if $D = \{G_1 : G_2\}$ is an SCCD, then G_1, as a sub-design of D, must be a design with resolution at least VI. Therefore, for any given n, we must have $f_s^*(q, n) = |G_1| \leqslant M^{VI}(q)$. This implies that $M^{VI}(q)$ serves as an upper bound for $f_s^*(q, n)$, i.e.,

$$f_s^*(q, n) \leqslant M^{VI}(q).$$

Theorem 7.13   *For a class one 2^{n-m} SCCD $D = \{G_1 : G_2\}$'s with $|G_1| = f$, we have*

$$f_s^*(q, n) \begin{cases} = n, & \text{if } n \leqslant M^{VI}(q), \\ \leqslant M^{VI}(q) - 2, & \text{if } q \geqslant 5, n \geqslant M^{VI}(q) + 1 \text{ with resolution } III, \\ \leqslant M^{VI}(q) - 3, & \text{if } q \geqslant 5, n \geqslant M^{VI}(q) + 1 \text{ with resolution } IV \text{ or } V. \end{cases}$$

Proof. If $D = \{G_1 : G_2\}$ is a 2^{n-m} SCCD, then G_1 must have resolution VI. Consider $n \leqslant M^{VI}(q)$ for any q. For $q \leqslant 4$, since $M^{VI}(q) = q$, to achieve the largest f, we can take $G_1 = \{1, \cdots, n\}$. For $q \geqslant 5$ and $5 \leqslant n \leqslant M^{VI}(q)$, to achieve the largest f, we can take a subset of M_q^{VI} as G_1 with $|G_1| = n$ and $G_2 = \varnothing$. Then $\{G_1 : G_2\}$ is a class one 2^{n-m} SCCD with $f = n$. Thus, the first equation is proved.

Next, we consider the case when $n = M^{VI}(q) + 1$ with $q \geqslant 5$. By the definition of $M^{VI}(q)$, any 2^{n-m} design with $n = M^{VI}(q) + 1$ does not have the resolution VI. Therefore, it must be of resolution III, IV, or V.

If the design has resolution III, then it has a defining word of length three. Thus, the main effects and 2fi's of the three factors in the word are not strongly clear. Therefore, we have $f_s(q, M^{VI}(q)+1) \leqslant M^{VI}(q) - 2$, which implies $f_s^*(q, M^{VI}(q)+1) \leqslant M^{VI}(q) - 2$.

If the design has the resolution IV or V, then it has a defining word of length four or five. Consequently, not all the main effects and 2fi's of the four or five factors in the defining word are strongly clear. As a result, among the four or five factors, at least four of them can not be included in G_1. This leads to $f_s(q, M^{VI}(q)+1) \leqslant M^{VI}(q) - 3$ and $f_s^*(q, M^{VI}(q) + 1) \leqslant M^{VI}(q) - 3$.

Finally, using similar arguments as in the proof of Theorem 7.7, we can easily prove that the second and third equations hold for $n > M^{VI}(q) + 1$ and $q \geqslant 5$ as well. This completes the proof. □

Example 7.14 Consider all the non-isomorphic class one compromise 2^{7-2} designs with resolution IV: $D_5 = \{1, 2 : 3, 4, 1234, 5, 345\}$, $D_6 = \{1, 2 : 3, 4, 134, 5, 235\}$, and $D_7 = \{1, 2 : 3, 4, 134, 5, 135\}$. None of them is an SCCD, since their P-AENPs, given by:

$$\left(^\#_1 P_2, ^\#_2 P_1, ^\#_2 P_2, ^\#_1 P_3, ^\#_2 P_3\right)(D_5; \Omega_1) = \left((2), (1), (1), (2, 0, 0), (0, 0, 1)\right),$$

$$\left(^\#_1 P_2, ^\#_2 P_1, ^\#_2 P_2, ^\#_1 P_3, ^\#_2 P_3\right)(D_6; \Omega_1) = \left((2), (1), (1), (0, 2, 0), (1, 0, 0)\right),$$

$$\left(^\#_1 P_2, ^\#_2 P_1, ^\#_2 P_2, ^\#_1 P_3, ^\#_2 P_3\right)(D_7; \Omega_1) = \left((2), (1), (1), (1, 0, 1), (1, 0, 0)\right),$$

do not match the P-AENP $\left((2), (1), (1), (2), (1)\right)$ in the (7.7). This equality is a necessary condition of class one SCCD for $f = 2$ and $n = 7$. However, we can check that among the resolution III 2^{7-2} designs, $D = \{1, 2 : 3, 4, 5, 34, 45\}$ is an SCCD. □

Next, we consider $n_s^*(q, f)$ and construction of the largest class one SCCDs for $f = 1, 2, \cdots, 6$.

Proposition 7.15 *For a class one 2^{n-m} SCCD $D = \{G_1 : G_2\}$ with $|G_1| = f$, we have*

$$n_s^*(q, f) = \begin{cases} N/2, & \text{if } f = 1, \\ N/4 + 1, & \text{if } q \geqslant 2 \text{ and } f = 2, \\ N/8 + 2, & \text{if } q \geqslant 3 \text{ and } f = 3, 4, \end{cases} \tag{7.8}$$

where $N = 2^{n-m}$.

Proof. The first equation of (7.8) is obvious. Now let us consider the second equation. For any 2^{n-m} class one SCCD $D = \{G_1 : G_2\}$ with $f = 2$, the two columns in G_1 must be independent. Thus, up to isomorphism, $G_1 = \{1, 2\}$ and G_2 must be from $\{\{I, 1, 2, 12\}H_{3,q}\}$. Similar to the proof of the largest class one CCD when

$f = 2$, we can determine that the largest n is achieved when G_2 is $\{\mathcal{A}_1, 1\mathcal{A}_2, 2\mathcal{A}_3,$ $12\mathcal{A}_4\}$, where $\mathcal{A}_i \subset H_{3,q}$, $i = 1, 2, 3, 4$, $\mathcal{A}_i \cap \mathcal{A}_j = \varnothing$ for $i \neq j$, and $\cup_{i=1}^4 \mathcal{A}_i = H_{3,q}$. By constructing such a G_2, we have $n_s^*(q, 2) = 2^{q-2} - 1 + 2 = N/4 + 1$.

Next, we consider the third equality of (7.8). Let $D = \{G_1 : G_2\}$ be a class one 2^{n-m} SCCD with $f = 3$. Without loss of generality, let us assume that $G_1 = \{1, 2, 3\}$ and consider the SCCD $D = \{G_1 : G_2\}$. Since D is an SCCD with $f = 3$, it follows that any column in H_3 cannot appear in G_2. Therefore, G_2 can only take columns from $\{\{I, H_3\}H_{4,q}\}$. With the same reasoning as before, we can determine the largest choice for G_2 to be $\{\mathcal{A}_1, 1\mathcal{A}_2, 2\mathcal{A}_3, 12\mathcal{A}_4, 3\mathcal{A}_5, 13\mathcal{A}_6, 23\mathcal{A}_7, 123\mathcal{A}_8\}$, where $\mathcal{A}_i \subset H_{4,q}$, $i = 1, 2, \cdots, 8$, $\mathcal{A}_i \cap \mathcal{A}_j = \varnothing$ for $i \neq j$, and $\cup_{i=1}^8 \mathcal{A}_i = H_{4,q}$. By a simple calculation, we obtain $n_s^*(q, 3) = 2^{q-3} - 1 + 3 = N/8 + 2$.

For $f = 4$, we can assume, without loss of generality, that $G_1 = \{1, 2, 3, 4\}$ up to isomorphism, since G_1 must have a resolution of at least VI. Considering $D = \{G_1 : G_2\}$ is an SCCD, we observe that no column in H_4 can appear in G_2. Therefore, G_2 can only consist of columns from $\{\{I, H_4\}H_{5,q}\}$, and the largest selection is given by $\{\{I, 1234\}\mathcal{A}_1, \{1, 234\}\mathcal{A}_2, \{2, 134\}\mathcal{A}_3, \{12, 34\}\mathcal{A}_4, \{3, 124\}\mathcal{A}_5, \{13, 24\}\mathcal{A}_6, \{23, 14\}\mathcal{A}_7, \{4, 123\}\mathcal{A}_8\}$, where $\mathcal{A}_i \subset H_{5,q}$, $i = 1, 2, \cdots, 8$, $\mathcal{A}_i \cap \mathcal{A}_j = \varnothing$ for $i \neq j$, and $\cup_{i=1}^8 \mathcal{A}_i = H_{5,q}$. By calculation, we find that $n_s^*(q, 4) = 2(2^{q-4} - 1) + 4 = N/8 + 2$.
□

Proposition 7.16　*For class one 2^{n-m} SCCDs with $f = 5, 6$ when $q \geqslant 4$, we have $n_s^*(q, 5) = N/16 + 4$ and $n_s^*(q, 6) = N/32 + 5$.*

Proof.　First, we consider $f = 5$. To ensure that $\{G_1 : G_2\}$ is an SCCD, up to isomorphism, we have only one choice for G_1, which is $\{1, 2, 3, 4, 5\}$. For G_2, we can select 12345 from H_5 and choose two columns $\{\beta\{I, 5\}\}$ from every $\{\beta\{I, H_5\}\}$, where $\beta \in H_{6,q}$. By calculation, we find that $n_s^*(q, 5) = 2|H_{6,q}| + 5 + 1 = N/16 + 4$.

Next, we consider $f = 6$. To ensure that $\{G_1 : G_2\}$ is an SCCD, the G_1 has two possible selections: $\{1, 2, 3, 4, 5, 12345\}$ and $\{1, 2, 3, 4, 5, 6\}$ up to isomorphism. For $G_1 = \{1, 2, 3, 4, 5, 12345\}$, G_2 can only select the column 6 from H_6 and the two columns $\{I, 6\}\beta$ from every $\{\beta\{I, H_6\}\}$, where $\beta \in H_{7,q}$. For $G_1 = \{1, 2, 3, 4, 5, 6\}$, G_2 can only select the column 12345 (or 123456) of H_6 and the two columns $\{I, 12345\}\beta$

(or $\{I, 123456\}\beta$) from every $\{\beta\{I, H_6\}\}$, where $\beta \in H_{7,q}$. Thus, in both cases, we have $n_s^*(q, 6) = 2|H_{7,q}| + 6 + 1 = N/32 + 5$. This completes the proof.   □

Based on Propositions 7.15 and 7.16, we have constructed all the class one 2^{n-m} SCCDs with $f = |G_1|$ for $q = 5, 6, 7$. Table 7.2 provides the values of $f_s^*(q, n)$ and $n_s^*(q, f)$ for $q = 5, 6, 7$.

Table 7.2 $f_s^*(q, n)$'s and $n_s^*(q, f)$'s of 2^{n-m} class one SCCD $\{G_1 : G_2\}$'s with $f = |G_1|$ for $q = 5, 6, 7$

$q = 5$	$M^{VI}(5) = 6$	$f_s^*(5, n)$	6(6)	2(7-9)	1(10-16)		
		$n_s^*(5, f)$	16(1)	9(2)	6(3-6)		
$q = 6$	$M^{VI}(6) = 7$	$f_s^*(6, n)$	6(7)	5(8)	4(9-10)	2(11-17)	1(18-32)
		$n_s^*(6, f)$	32(1)	17(2)	10(3-4)	8(5)	7(6)
$q = 7$	$M^{VI}(7) = 9$	$f_s^*(7, n)$	9(9)	5(10-12)	4(13-18)	2(19-33)	1(34-64)
		$n_s^*(7, f)$	64(1)	33(2)	18(3-4)	12(5)	9(6-9)

The numbers indicate the same as in Table 7.1 with substituting f_s^* and n_s^* for f^* and n^*.

For practical applications, we provide a collection of class one 2^{n-m} CCDs and SCCDs with 8-, 16-, 32-, and 64-run, having resolutions III and IV, for various values of n and f in Tables 7.3 and 7.4. It is evident from the tables that, in many cases, a CCD with resolution III is also an SCCD, whereas a CCD with resolution IV is not. Additionally, we notice that there are cases where neither CCD with resolution III nor resolution IV is an SCCD. However, among these cases, the CCD with resolution III tends to have more strongly clear effects. Based on these findings, it can be concluded that a CCD of resolution III often outperforms a CCD of resolution IV.

7.4.5   Class One General Optimal Compromise Designs

From the previous section, we observed that not all parameter combinations have corresponding 2^{n-m} SCCDs or CCDs. In fact, for a significant number of parameters, neither an SCCD nor a CCD exists. We refer to an OCD that is neigther an SCCD nor a CCD as a general optimal compromise design (GOCD). To address the issue of constructing GOCDs, we discuss it in this subsection.

For $f = 2$, we have the following two theorems to construct 2^{n-m} GOCDs for the respective ranges of $N/4 + 2 \leqslant n \leqslant N/2$ and $N/2 \leqslant n \leqslant N - 2$.

Theorem 7.17　*For $N/4 + 2 \leqslant n \leqslant N/2$ and $f = 2$, the 2^{n-m} design*

$$D = \{1, 2 : \mathcal{A}_1, 1\mathcal{A}_2, 2\mathcal{A}_3, 12\mathcal{A}_4\}$$

with $\cup_{i=1}^4 \mathcal{A}_i \subseteq H_{3,q}$, $(\mathcal{A}_1 \cup \mathcal{A}_4) \cap (\mathcal{A}_2 \cup \mathcal{A}_3) = \varnothing$, and $|\mathcal{A}_1 \cap \mathcal{A}_4| + |\mathcal{A}_2 \cap \mathcal{A}_3| = n - N/4 - 1$ is a class one GOCD, and has

$$({}_1^\#P_2, {}_2^\#P_1, {}_2^\#P_2)(D; \Omega_1) = ((2), (1), (0^{n-N/4-1}, 1)).$$

Proof.　First, according to Proposition 7.11, we know that for $N/4 + 2 \leqslant n \leqslant N/2$ and $f = 2$, there is no class one 2^{n-m} CCD, but there do exist GOCDs. By the P-AENP, the GOCD must have the form $D = \{G_1 : G_2\} = \{1, 2 : \mathcal{A}_1, 1\mathcal{A}_2, 2\mathcal{A}_3, 12\mathcal{A}_4\}$ up to isomorphism. Here, $\cup_{i=1}^4 \mathcal{A}_i \subseteq H_{3,q}$ and $\mathcal{A}_1 \cap \mathcal{A}_2 = \mathcal{A}_1 \cap \mathcal{A}_3 = \varnothing$, such that for $\Omega_1 = \{G_1, G_1 \times G_1\}$, it has $({}_1^\#P_2, {}_2^\#P_1)(T; \Omega_1) = ((2), (1))$, which sequentially maximizes the $({}_1^\#P_2, {}_2^\#P_1)$.

Thus, to prove Theorem 7.17, we only need to prove that if the D satisfies the conditions $(\mathcal{A}_1 \cup \mathcal{A}_4) \cap (\mathcal{A}_2 \cup \mathcal{A}_3) = \varnothing$ and $|\mathcal{A}_1 \cap \mathcal{A}_4| + |\mathcal{A}_2 \cap \mathcal{A}_3| = n - N/4 - 1$, then it also sequentially maximizes ${}_2^\#P_2$.

Note that it must hold

$$ {}_2^\#P_2(D; \Omega_1) = (0, \cdots, 0, {}_2^\#P_2^{(k)}) $$

for some k, since there are only two cases in which the 2fi 12 is aliased: (i) $\alpha_1 \alpha_2 = 12$ with $\alpha_1 \in \mathcal{A}_1$ and $\alpha_2 \in 12\mathcal{A}_4$, and (ii) $\beta_1 \beta_2 = 12$ with $\beta_1 \in 1\mathcal{A}_2$ and $\beta_2 \in 2\mathcal{A}_3$. From the structure of D and $(\mathcal{A}_1 \cup \mathcal{A}_4) \cap (\mathcal{A}_2 \cup \mathcal{A}_3) = \varnothing$, we can deduce that $\mathcal{A}_1 \cap \mathcal{A}_2 = \mathcal{A}_1 \cap \mathcal{A}_3 = \varnothing$ and $k = |\mathcal{A}_1 \cap \mathcal{A}_4| + |\mathcal{A}_2 \cap \mathcal{A}_3|$.

Since $\cup_{i=1}^4 \mathcal{A}_i \subseteq H_{3,q}$ and $(\mathcal{A}_1 \cup \mathcal{A}_4) \cap (\mathcal{A}_2 \cup \mathcal{A}_3) = \varnothing$, we have

$$\sum_{i=1}^4 |\mathcal{A}_i| - |\mathcal{A}_1 \cap \mathcal{A}_4| - |\mathcal{A}_2 \cap \mathcal{A}_3| \leqslant 2^{q-2} - 1.$$

Thus, we have

$$k = |\mathcal{A}_1 \cap \mathcal{A}_4| + |\mathcal{A}_2 \cap \mathcal{A}_3| \geqslant n - 2 - (2^{q-2} - 1) = n - N/4 - 1, \qquad (7.9)$$

and $n - N/4 - 1$ is the minimum value that k can reach. Therefore, D is a GOCD and has $({}_1^\#P_2, {}_2^\#P_1, {}_2^\#P_2)(T; \Omega_1) = ((2), (1), (0^{n-N/4-1}, 1))$.　□

Theorem 7.18　*For $N/2 \leqslant n \leqslant N - 2$ and $f = 2$, the design D with the form*

$$\{1, 2 : \{H_{3,q} \backslash \mathcal{A}_1\}, \{1H_{3,q} \backslash 1\mathcal{A}_2\}, \{2H_{3,q} \backslash 2\mathcal{A}_3\}, \{12H_{3,q} \backslash 12\mathcal{A}_4\}\}$$

is a class one 2^{n-m} *GOCD with*

$$({}^{\#}_1P_2, {}^{\#}_2P_1, {}^{\#}_2P_2)(D; \Omega_1) = \begin{cases} ((0^{n-N/2}, 2), (1), (0^{N/4-1}, 1)), & \text{if } N/2 \leqslant n \leqslant 3N/4-1, \\ ((0^{n-N/2}, 2), (1), (0^{n-N/2}, 1)), & \text{if } 3N/4-1 < n \leqslant N-2, \end{cases}$$

$$(7.10)$$

where $\cup_{i=1}^4 \mathcal{A}_i \subseteq H_{3,q}$ *and* $(\mathcal{A}_1 \cup \mathcal{A}_4) \cap (\mathcal{A}_2 \cup \mathcal{A}_3) = \varnothing$.

Proof. Let $\bar{D}$ denote the complementary set of the D, i.e., $\bar{D} = H_q \backslash D$, where

$$H_q = \{1, 2, 12, H_{3,q}, 1H_{3,q}, 2H_{3,q}, 12H_{3,q}\}.$$

Recall that in (3.3), it is shown that for any $\gamma \in D$,

$$B_2(D, \gamma) = \frac{1}{2}(n - f - 1) + B_2(\bar{D}, \gamma),$$

where f is the number of columns in $\bar{D}$. Hence,

$$B_2(D, 1) = n - N/2 + B_2(\bar{D}, 1) \text{ and } B_2(D, 2) = n - N/2 + B_2(\bar{D}, 2). \quad (7.11)$$

To prove that D is a GOCD, we first need to demonstrate that the ${}^{\#}_1P_2(D; \Omega_1)$ is sequentially maximized, which means we need show that the $B_2(D, 1) + B_2(D, 2)$ is minimized. By (7.11), we only need to prove that both $B_2(\bar{D}, 1)$ and $B_2(\bar{D}, 2)$ are minimized. Since the $\bar{D}$ has the form $\{12, \mathcal{A}_1, 1\mathcal{A}_2, 2\mathcal{A}_3, 12\mathcal{A}_4\}$ and $(\mathcal{A}_1 \cup \mathcal{A}_4) \cap (\mathcal{A}_2 \cup \mathcal{A}_3) = \varnothing$, we have $B_2(\bar{T}, 1) = B_2(\bar{T}, 2) = 0$. By (7.11) and the definition of P-AENP, ${}^{\#}_1P_2(D; \Omega_1)$ is sequentially maximized and we have ${}^{\#}_1P_2(D; \Omega_1) = (0^{n-N/2}, 2)$.

Furthermore, considering that $N/2 \leqslant n \leqslant N-2$ and $12 \notin D$, we have ${}^{\#}_2P_1(D; \Omega_1)$ $= (1)$. This indicates that ${}^{\#}_2P_1(D; \Omega_1)$ is also maximized.

Finally, we consider ${}^{\#}_2P_2(D; \Omega_1)$. Due to $(\mathcal{A}_1 \cup \mathcal{A}_4) \cap (\mathcal{A}_2 \cup \mathcal{A}_3) = \varnothing$, we have $B_2(\bar{D}, 12) = |\mathcal{A}_1 \cap \mathcal{A}_4| + |\mathcal{A}_2 \cap \mathcal{A}_3|$. Recall that in (3.4), we have shown that for any $\gamma \notin D$

$$B_2(D, \gamma) = \frac{1}{2}(n - f + 1) + B_2(\bar{D}, \gamma).$$

Since $12 \notin D$, we have

$$B_2(D, 12) = n - N/2 + 1 + B_2(\bar{D}, 12).$$

Furthermore, the fact that ${}^{\#}_2P_2(D; \Omega_1)$ is sequentially maximized is equivalent to $B_2(D, 12)$ being minimized. Let us examine if $|\mathcal{A}_1 \cap \mathcal{A}_4| + |\mathcal{A}_2 \cap \mathcal{A}_3|$ is minimized.

There are only two cases to consider:

(i) $\mathcal{A}_1 \cap \mathcal{A}_4 = \mathcal{A}_2 \cap \mathcal{A}_3 = \varnothing$;

(ii) $(\mathcal{A}_1 \cap \mathcal{A}_4) \cup (\mathcal{A}_2 \cap \mathcal{A}_3) \neq \varnothing$.

For Case (i), it implies that $\mathcal{A}_i \cap \mathcal{A}_j = \varnothing$ for any $i \neq j$, and hence $B_2(\bar{D}, 12) = 0$. Thus, we have $B_2(D, 12) = n - N/2 + 1$. However, we note that for this case we have $|\bar{D}| = 1 + \sum_{i=1}^{4} |\mathcal{A}_i| \leqslant N/4$. Therefore, by using the relation $n + |\bar{D}| = N - 1$, we obtain $_2^{\#}P_2(D; \Omega_1) = (0^{n-N/2}, 1)$ only for $n \geqslant 3N/4 - 1$.

Then consider Case (ii). Let $\bar{D}^*$ denote $\bar{D} \backslash \{12\} \cup \{1, 2\}$, we have $|\bar{D}^*| = (N - 1 - n) + 1$. Since $\cup_{i=1}^{4} \mathcal{A}_i \subseteq \bar{H}_2$, $N/4 + 2 \leqslant |\bar{D}^*| \leqslant N/2$. By applying (7.9) in the proof of Theorem 7.17 to $\bar{D}^*$, we have

$$B_2(\bar{D}, 12) = B_2(\bar{D}^*, 12) = |\mathcal{A}_1 \cap \mathcal{A}_4| + |\mathcal{A}_2 \cap \mathcal{A}_3| = 3N/4 - 1 - n,$$

which is minimum because of $\cup_{i=1}^{4} \mathcal{A}_i \subseteq H_{3,q}$ and $(\mathcal{A}_1 \cup \mathcal{A}_4) \cap (\mathcal{A}_2 \cup \mathcal{A}_3) = \varnothing$. Thus, we have $n \leqslant 3N/4 - 1$ and we obtain $_2^{\#}P_2(D; \Omega_1) = (0^{N/4-1}, 1)$ for $n \leqslant 3N/4 - 1$.

In summary, based on the reasoning above, we can conclude that the given design D is a class one GOCD, and its P-AENP satisfies (7.10). Thus, Theorem 7.18 is proved. □

Example 7.19　For $q = 4$ and $f = 2$, we take $\mathcal{A}_1 = \mathcal{A}_4 = \{3, 4\}$ and $\mathcal{A}_2 = \mathcal{A}_3 = \{34\}$ from $H_{3,q}$, then the design

$$\{1, 2 : \mathcal{A}_1, 1\mathcal{A}_2, 2\mathcal{A}_3, 12\mathcal{A}_4\} = \{1, 2 : 3, 4, 134, 234, 123, 124\}$$

is a 2^{n-m} GOCD of Ω_1 with $n = N/2 = 8$. □

Tables 7.3 and 7.4 also present several examples of class one 2^{n-m} GOCDs for $f = 3, 4, 5$ with 16-, 32-, and 64-run, respectively. These designs were obtained using Definition 7.2 and computer searching.

For a set of given parameters N, n, and f that is not in Tables 7.3 and 7.4, the following steps can be used to find optimal designs:

(i) Compute the P-AENPs of all the possible designs with the given parameters.

(ii) Compare the P-AENPs of all designs using Definition 7.2 to determine the best one.

According to Definition 7.2 and Theorem 7.6, the design with the best P-AENP must be the OCD. If all specified effects are clear, then the design must be a CCD. If all specified effects are strongly clear, then the design must be an SCCD. Otherwise, the design must be a GOCD.

7.5   Discussion

In this chapter, we have extended the concept of compromise designs, and introduced the pattern P-AENP as a measure to assess and select the extended compromise designs. Specifically, we have expanded the range of design candidates from at least resolution IV to at least resolution III in order to select such compromise designs. Furthermore, we have introduced the notions of SCCDs and GOCDs, which offer superior performance compared to CCDs and OCDs respectively. This improvement is achieved under a weaker assumption that all fourth- or higher-order effects are negligible.

For the class one 2^{n-m} CCDs and SCCDs, we obtain the suprema $f^*(q,n)$'s, $f_s^*(q,n)$'s, $n^*(q,f)$'s and $n_s^*(q,f)$'s for a number of parameter (q,f,n)'s, and construct the largest class one CCD's and SCCD's in which f and n are at their respective suprema. For applications, a large number of CCDs, SCCDs, and GOCDs are tabulated for 8, 16, 32, and 64 runs with both resolution III and IV.

Furthermore, the following findings are interesting and notable:

1. If there exists a class one 2^{n-m} CCD of resolution IV for a set of parameters (q,n,f), then there also exists a CCD of resolution III. Based on the P-AENP, the CCD of resolution III is generally better than, or at least equally good as, the CCD of resolution IV. This means that the CCD of resolution III is mostly an SCCD, while the CCD of resolution IV is not (refer to Tables 7.3 and 7.4).

For instance, when $(q,n,f) = (6,10,4)$, the 2^{10-4} class one CCD with resolution III is also an SCCD (refer to Table 7.4), whereas the 2^{10-4} CCD with resolution IV is not. This implies that for certain parameter combinations in designs with resolution IV, there are no SCCDs available, whereas in designs with resolution III, SCCDs do exist.

2. For a wide range of parameters, the CCD with resolution III has more strongly clear effects compared to the CCD with resolution IV. For instance, when $(q,n,f) = (5,9,3)$, the numbers of strongly clear main effects and 2fi's of the 2^{9-4} class one CCD of resolution III are $(3,0)$ (see Table 7.3), while those of the CCD of resolution IV are $(2,0)$.

Table 7.3 Some class one 2^{n-m} CCDs, SCCDs, and GOCDs for 8, 16, and 32 runs

n	f	Design $T = \{G_1 : G_2\}$	$^{\#}_1P_2; {}^{\#}_2P_1; {}^{\#}_2P_2; {}^{\#}_1P_3; {}^{\#}_2P_3$	Cs	SCs	R	SC?
8-run							
4	1	$1:2,4,6$	$1; -; -; 1; -$	1,0	1,0	III	yes
		$1:2,4,7$	$1; -; -; 0,1; -$	1,0	0,0	IV	no*
16-run							
5	1	$1:2,4,8,12$	$1; -; -; 1; -$	1,0	1,0	III	yes
		$1:2,4,8,15$	$1; -; -; 1; -$	1,0	1,0	IV	yes
	2	$1,2:4,8,12$	$2; 1; 1; 2; 1$	2,1	2,1	III	yes
		$1,2:4,8,15$	$2; 1; 1; 2; 0,1$	2,1	2,0	IV	no*
6	1	$1:2,4,6,8,10$	$1; -; -; 1; -$	1,0	1,0	III	yes
		$1:2,4,8,11,13$	$1; -; -; 0^2,1; -$	1,0	0,0	IV	no*
	2	$1,2:4,8,11,13$	$2; 1; 0,1; 0^2,2; 1$	2,0	0,0	IV	no
	3	$1,2,4:8,11,13$	$3; 3; 0,3; 0^2,3; 3$	3,0	0,0	IV	no
7	1	$1:2,4,6,8,10,12$	$1; -; -; 1; -$	1,0	1,0	III	yes
		$1:2,4,8,11,13,14$	$1; -; -; 0^4,1; -$	1,0	0,0	IV	no*
	2	$1,2:4,8,11,13,14$	$2; 1; 0^2,1; 0^4,2; 1$	2,0	0,0	IV	no
	3	$1,2,4:8,11,13,14$	$3; 3; 0^2,3; 0^4,3; 3$	3,0	0,0	IV	no
8	1	$1:2,4,6,8,10,12,14$	$1; -; -; 1; -$	1,0	1,0	III	yes
		$1:2,4,7,8,11,13,14$	$1; -; -; 0^7,1; -$	1,0	0,0	IV	no*
	2	$1,2:4,7,8,11,13,14$	$2; 1; 0^3,1; 0^7,2; 1$	2,0	0,0	IV	no
	3	$1,2,4:7,8,11,13,14$	$3; 3; 0^3,3; 0^7,3; 3$	3,0	0,0	IV	no
	4	$1,2,4,7:8,11,13,14$	$4; 6; 0^3,6; 0^7,4; 6$	4,0	0,0	IV	no
9	2	$1,2:4,5,7,8,11,12,15$	$0,2; 1; 0^3,1; 0^5,2; 0^6,1$	0,0	0,0	III	no
	3	$1,2,4:7,8,9,10,12,15$	$0,3; 3; 0^3,3; 0^7,3; 0^4,3$	0,0	0,0	III	no
	4	$1,2,4,7:8,9,10,12,15$	$0,4; 6; 0^3,6; 0^7,4; 0^4,6$	0,0	0,0	III	no
10	2	$1,2:4,7,8,9,11,12,14,15$	$0^2,2; 1; 0^3,1; 0^7,2; 0^9,1$	0,0	0,0	III	no
	3	$1,2,4:7,8,9,11,12,14,15$	$0^2,3; 3; 0^3,3; 0^7,3; 0^9,3$	0,0	0,0	III	no
	4	$1,2,4,7:8,11,12,13,14,15$	$0^2,4; 6; 0^3,4,2; 0^8,4; 0^8,6$	0,0	0,0	III	no
	5	$1,2,4,7,8:11,12,13,14,15$	$0^2,5; 8,2; 0^3,8,2; 0^8,5; 0^4,2,0^3,8$	0,0	0,0	III	no
32-run							
7	2	$1,2:4,8,12,16,20$	$2; 1; 1; 2; 1$	2,1	2,1	III	yes
		$1,2:4,8,15,16,23$	$2; 1; 1; 2; 0^2,1$	2,1	2,0	IV	no*
	3	$1,2,4:8,16,23,24$	$3; 3; 3; 3; 0,3$	3,3	3,0	III	no*
		$1,2,4:8,15,16,23$	$3; 3; 3; 3; 0^2,3$	3,3	3,0	IV	no*
8	2	$1,2:4,8,12,16,20,24$	$2; 1; 1; 2; 1$	2,1	2,1	III	yes
		$1,2:4,8,15,16,27,28$	$2; 1; 1; 2; 0^4,1$	2,1	2,0	IV	no*
	3	$1,2,4:8,16,23,24,31$	$3; 3; 3; 3; 0^2,3$	3,3	3,0	III	no*
		$1,2,4:8,15,16,27,28$	$3; 3; 3; 2,0,1; 0^2,2,0,1$	3,3	2,0	IV	no*
	4	$1,2,4,8:15,16,27,28$	$4; 6; 5,1; 2,0,2; 0,1,4,0,1$	4,5	2,0	IV	no
9	2	$1,2:4,8,12,16,20,24,28$	$2; 1; 1; 2; 1$	2,1	2,1	III	yes
		$1,2:4,8,15,16,23,27,28$	$2; 1; 1; 2; 0^7,1$	2,1	2,0	IV	no*
	3	$1,2,4:8,15,16,23,24,31$	$3; 3; 3; 3; 0^3,3$	3,3	3,0	III	no*
		$1,2,4:8,15,16,23,27,28$	$3; 3; 3; 2,0^3,1; 0^3,2,0^3,1$	3,3	2,0	IV	no*
	4	$1,2,4,8:15,16,23,27,28$	$4; 6; 5,0,1; 2,0^3,2; 0,1,0,4,0^3,1$	4,5	2,0	IV	no
10	2	$1,2:4,7,8,15,16,23,24,31$	$2; 1; 0,1; 0,2; 0^3,1$	2,0	0,0	III	no
	3	$1,2,4:7,8,15,16,23,24,31$	$3; 3; 0,3; 0,3; 0^3,3$	3,0	0,0	III	no
	4	$1,2,4,8:15,16,19,21,25,30$	$4; 6; 0,6; 0^4,4; 0^4,6$	4,0	0,0	IV	no
	5	$1,2,4,8,15:16,19,21,25,30$	$5; 10; 0,10; 0^4,5; 0^4,10$	5,0	0,0	IV	no
11	2	$1,2:4,8,11,12,15,16,20,24,28$	$2; 1; 0^2,1; 0^2,2; 0^6,1$	2,0	0,0	III	no
	3	$1,2,4:7,8,11,14,16,23,25,30$	$3; 3; 0^2,3; 0^4,1,0,2; 0^2,1,0,2$	3,0	0,0	III	no
	4	$1,2,4,8:7,11,14,16,22,27,29$	$4; 6; 0^2,5,0,1; 0^6,4; 0^2,1,0,5$	4,0	0,0	III	no
	5	$1,2,4,8,11:7,14,16,23,25,30$	$5; 10; 0^2,8,0,2; 0^4,1,0,4; 0^2,4,0,6$	5,0	0,0	III	no
12	2	$1,2:4,8,12,16,19,20,23,24,27,28$	$2; 1; 0^3,1; 0^3,2; 0^9,1$	2,0	0,0	III	no
	3	$1,2,4:8,11,13,16,19,21,24,27,29$	$3; 3; 0^3,3; 0^6,3; 0^6,1,2$	3,0	0,0	III	no
	4	$1,2,4,8:16,15,19,21,22,25,26,28$	$4; 6; 0^3,6; 0^9,4; 0^4,6$	4,0	0,0	III	no
	5	$1,2,4,8,16:15,19,21,22,25,26,28$	$5; 10; 0^3,10; 0^9,4,1; 0^3,4,6$	5,0	0,0	III	no

Note: In Tables 7.3 and 7.4, "Cs" refers numbers of clear main effects and 2fi's, "SCs" refers numbers of strongly-clear main effects and 2fi's, "R" refers resolution, and "SC?" stands for asking if the design is a SCCD, "no*" refers a CCD and "no" refers a GOCD.

Table 7.4 Some class one 2^{n-m} CCDs, SCCDs, and GOCDs for 64 runs

n	f	Design $T = \{G_1 : G_2\}$	$\#P_2; \#P_{1,2}; \#P_{2,1}; \#P_{3,1}; \#P_{3,2}^3$	Cs	SCs	R	SC?
8	2	$1,2:4,8,16,31,32,63$	$2;1;1;2;1$	$2,1$	$2,1$	III	yes
		$1,2:4,8,16,31,32,47$	$2;1;1;2;1$	$2,1$	$2,1$	IV	yes
	3	$1,2,4:8,16,31,32,63$	$3;3;3;3;3$	$3,3$	$3,3$	III	yes
		$1,2,4:8,16,31,32,47$	$3;3;3;3;3$	$3,3$	$3,3$	IV	yes
	4	$1,2,4,8:16,31,32,63$	$4;6;6;4;6$	$4,6$	$4,6$	III	yes
		$1,2,4,8:16,31,32,47$	$4;6;6;4;6$	$4,6$	$4,6$	IV	yes
	5	$1,2,4,8,16:31,32,63$	$5;10;10;5;10$	$5,10$	$5,10$	III	no*
		$1,2,4,8,16:31,32,47$	$5;10;10;4,1;10$	$5,10$	$4,10$	IV	no*
9	2	$1,2:4,8,16,32,47,48,63$	$2;1;1;2;1$	$2,1$	$2,1$	III	yes
		$1,2:4,8,16,32,47,54,57$	$2;1;1;2;1$	$2,1$	$2,1$	IV	yes
	3	$1,2,4:8,16,32,47,48,63$	$3;3;3;3;3$	$3,3$	$3,3$	III	yes
		$1,2,4:8,16,32,47,54,57$	$3;3;3;3;2,0,1$	$3,3$	$3,2$	IV	no*
	4	$1,2,4,8:16,32,47,48,63$	$4;6;6;4;6$	$4,6$	$4,6$	III	yes
		$1,2,4,8:16,32,47,54,57$	$4;6;6;4,4,0,2$	$4,6$	$4,4$	IV	no*
	5	$1,2,4,8,16:32,43,55$	$5;10;10;5;0,8,2$	$5,10$	$5,0$	III	no*
		$1,2,4,8,16:32,47,54,57$	$5;10;10;5;4,0,6$	$5,10$	$5,4$	IV	no*
10	2	$1,2:4,8,16,31,32,47,48,63$	$2;1;1;2;1$	$2,1$	$2,1$	III	yes
		$1,2:4,8,16,30,32,46,55,57$	$2;1;1;2;1$	$2,1$	$2,1$	IV	yes
	3	$1,2,4:8,16,31,32,47,48,63$	$3;3;3;3;3$	$3,3$	$3,3$	III	yes
		$1,2,4:8,16,30,32,47,48,63$	$3;3;3;3;2,0^2,1$	$3,3$	$3,2$	IV	no*
	4	$1,2,4,8:16,31,32,47,48,63$	$4;6;6;4;6$	$4,6$	$4,6$	III	yes
		$1,2,4,8:16,31,32,47,51,60$	$4;6;6;4,0^3,2$	$4,6$	$4,4$	IV	no*
	5	$1,2,4,8,16:30,32,43,53,62$	$5;10;10;5;0,4,4,2$	$5,10$	$5,0$	III	no*
		$1,2,4,8,16:31,32,47,51,60$	$5;10;10;4,0,1;4,0,4,0,2$	$5,10$	$4,4$	IV	no*

Table 7.4 (continued)

n	f	Design $T = \{G_1 : G_2\}$	${}_1^{\#}P_2; {}_2^{\#}P_1; {}_2^{\#}P_2; {}_1^{\#}P_3; {}^{\#}P_3; {}_2^{\#}P_3$	Cs	SCs	R	SC?
11	2	1, 2 : 28, 32, 36, 40, 44, 48, 52, 56, 60	2; 1; 1; 2; 1	2, 1	2, 1	III	yes
	3	1, 2, 4 : 8, 15, 16, 23, 32, 39, 57, 62	2; 1; 1; 2; 0⁴, 1	2, 1	2, 0	IV	no*
		1, 2, 4 : 8, 15, 16, 31, 32, 47, 48, 63	3; 3; 3; 3; 0, 3	3, 3	3, 0	III	no*
		1, 2, 4 : 8, 15, 16, 23, 32, 39, 57, 62	3; 3; 3; 3; 0⁴, 3	3, 3	3, 0	IV	no*
	4	1, 2, 4, 8 : 15, 16, 31, 32, 47, 48, 63	4; 6; 6; 4; 0, 6	4, 6	4, 0	III	no*
		1, 2, 4, 8 : 15, 16, 23, 32, 39, 57, 62	4; 6; 3, 0², 1; 0, 2, 0², 3, 1	4, 6	3, 0	IV	no*
	5	1, 2, 4, 8, 16 : 15, 23, 32, 39, 57, 62	5; 10; 9, 1; 3, 0², 2; 0, 4, 1, 0, 3, 2	5, 9	3, 0	IV	no
12	2	1, 2 : 24, 28, 32, 36, 40, 44, 48, 52, 56, 60	2; 1; 1; 2; 1	2, 1	2, 1	III	yes
	3	1, 2, 4 : 8, 15, 16, 23, 28, 32, 39, 56, 63	2; 1; 1; 2; 0⁸, 1	2, 1	2, 0	IV	no*
		1, 2, 4 : 8, 15, 16, 23, 24, 32, 47, 55, 56	3; 3; 3; 3; 0², 3	3, 3	3, 0	III	no*
		1, 2, 4 : 8, 15, 16, 23, 28, 32, 39, 56, 63	3; 3; 3; 2, 0³, 1; 0⁴, 2, 0³, 1	3, 3	2, 0	IV	no*
	4	1, 2, 4, 8 : 15, 16, 25, 30, 32, 47, 48, 63	4; 6; 5, 1; 2, 0, 1, 0, 1; 0², 4, 1, 0², 1	4, 5	2, 0	III	no
	5	1, 2, 4, 8, 16 : 23, 27, 32, 45, 46, 55, 59	5; 10; 8, 1, 1; 1, 0, 2, 2; 0², 1, 4, 5	5, 8	1, 0	III	no
13	2	1, 2 : 20, 24, 28, 32, 36, 40, 44, 48, 52, 56, 60	2; 1; 1; 2; 1	2, 1	2, 1	III	yes
	3	1, 2, 4 : 8, 15, 16, 23, 28, 32, 39, 44, 56, 63	2; 1; 1; 2; 0¹², 1	2, 1	2, 0	IV	no*
		1, 2, 4 : 8, 15, 16, 23, 24, 31, 32, 40, 48, 56	3; 3; 3; 3; 0³, 3	3, 3	3, 0	III	no*
		1, 2, 4 : 8, 15, 16, 23, 28, 32, 39, 44, 56, 63	3; 3; 3; 2, 0⁷, 1; 0⁴, 2, 0⁷, 1	3, 3	2, 0	IV	no*
	4	1, 2, 4, 8 : 15, 16, 23, 28, 32, 39, 44, 56, 63	4; 6; 5, 0, 1; 2, 0⁷, 1, 0, 1, 0, 2, 2, 0⁷, 1	4, 5	2, 0	IV	no
	5	1, 2, 4, 8, 16 : 23, 27, 30, 32, 37, 46, 50, 55, 57	5; 10; 8, 0, 1, 1, 1; 1, 0², 2, 0², 2; 2, 1, 0, 1, 1, 4, 0², 2, 0³, 2	5, 8	1, 0	IV	no
14	2	1, 2 : 16, 20, 24, 28, 32, 36, 40, 44, 48, 52, 56, 60	2; 1; 1; 2; 1	2, 1	2, 1	III	yes
	3	1, 2, 4 : 8, 15, 16, 27, 28, 32, 43, 44, 52, 56, 63	2; 1; 1; 2; 0¹⁶, 1	2, 1	2, 0	IV	no*
		1, 2, 4 : 8, 15, 16, 23, 24, 31, 32, 39, 40, 48, 56	3; 3; 3; 3; 0⁴, 3	3, 3	3, 0	III	no*
		1, 2, 4 : 8, 15, 16, 27, 28, 32, 43, 44, 52, 56, 63	3; 3; 3; 2, 0¹², 1; 0⁴, 2, 0¹¹, 1	3, 3	2, 0	IV	no*
	4	1, 2, 4, 8 : 15, 16, 27, 28, 32, 43, 44, 52, 56, 63	4; 6; 5, 0², 1; 2, 0¹², 2; 0, 1, 0², 4, 0¹¹, 1	4, 5	2, 0	IV	no
	5	1, 2, 4, 8, 16 : 23, 30, 32, 38, 41, 51, 53, 58, 60	5; 10; 8, 0², 1, 1, 1; 0³, 2, 0⁴, 2; 1, 0, 1, 0, 4, 0³, 2, 0⁴, 2	5, 8	1, 0	IV	no

Table 7.4 (continued)

n	f	Design $T = \{G_1 : G_2\}$	$\#P_2; \#P_1; \#P_2; \#P_2; \#P_3; \#P_3$	Cs	SCs	R	SC?
15	2	$1, 2 : 12, 16, 20, 24, 28, 32, 36, 40, 44, 48, 52, 56, 60$	$2; 1; 1; 2; 1$	2, 1	2, 1	*III*	yes
	3	$1, 2 : 4, 8, 15, 16, 23, 27, 28, 32, 39, 51, 52, 56, 63$	$2; 1; 1; 2; 0^{22}, 1$	2, 1	2, 0	*IV*	no*
		$1, 2, 4 : 8, 15, 16, 23, 24, 31, 32, 39, 40, 47, 48, 56$	$3; 3; 3; 3; 0^5, 3$	3, 3	3, 0	*III*	no*
	4	$1, 2, 4 : 8, 15, 16, 23, 27, 28, 32, 39, 51, 52, 56, 63$	$3; 3; 3; 2, 0^{15}; 1; 0^6, 2, 0^{15}, 1$	3, 3	2, 0	*IV*	no*
	4	$1, 2, 4, 8 : 15, 16, 23, 27, 28, 32, 39, 51, 52, 56, 63$	$4; 6; 5, 0^3, 1; 2, 0^{15}, 1; 1; 0, 1, 0^3, 2, 2, 0^{15}, 1$	4, 5	2, 0	*IV*	no
	5	$1, 2, 4, 8, 16 : 23, 30, 32, 38, 41, 47, 51, 53, 58, 60$	$5; 10; 8, 0^3, 1, 1; 1, 0^4, 2, 0^6, 2; 1, 0, 1, 0^2, 4, 0^4, 2, 0^6, 2$	5, 8	1, 0	*IV*	no
16	2	$1, 2 : 8, 12, 16, 20, 24, 28, 32, 36, 40, 44, 48, 52, 56, 60$	$2; 1; 1; 2; 1$	2, 1	2, 1	*III*	yes
	3	$1, 2 : 4, 8, 15, 16, 23, 27, 28, 32, 43, 44, 51, 52, 56, 63$	$2; 1; 1; 2; 0^{28}, 1$	2, 1	2, 0	*IV*	no*
		$1, 2, 4 : 8, 15, 16, 23, 24, 31, 32, 39, 40, 47, 48, 55, 56$	$3; 3; 3; 3; 0^6, 3$	3, 3	3, 0	*III*	no*
	4	$1, 2, 4 : 8, 15, 16, 23, 27, 28, 32, 43, 44, 51, 52, 56, 63$	$3; 3; 3; 2, 0^{21}; 1; 0^6, 2, 0^{21}, 1$	3, 3	2, 0	*IV*	no*
	4	$1, 2, 4, 8 : 15, 16, 23, 27, 28, 32, 43, 44, 51, 52, 56, 63$	$4; 6; 5, 0^4, 1; 2, 0^{21}; 2; 0, 1, 0^4, 4, 0^{21}, 1$	4, 5	2, 0	*IV*	no
	5	$1, 2, 4, 8, 16 : 15, 23, 27, 28, 32, 43, 44, 51, 52, 56, 63$	$5; 10; 7, 0^4, 3; 2, 0^{21}; 3; 0, 3, 0^4, 6, 0^{21}, 1$	5, 7	2, 0	*IV*	no
17	2	$1, 2 : 4, 8, 12, 16, 20, 24, 28, 32, 36, 40, 44, 48, 52, 56, 60$	$2; 1; 1; 2; 1$	2, 1	2, 1	*III*	yes
	3	$1, 2 : 4, 8, 15, 16, 23, 27, 28, 32, 39, 43, 44, 51, 52, 56, 63$	$2; 1; 1; 2; 0^{35}, 1$	2, 1	2, 0	*IV*	no*
		$1, 2, 4 : 8, 15, 16, 23, 24, 31, 32, 39, 40, 47, 48, 55, 56, 63$	$3; 3; 3; 3; 0^7, 3$	3, 3	3, 0	*III*	no*
	3	$1, 2, 4 : 8, 15, 16, 23, 27, 28, 32, 39, 43, 44, 51, 52, 56, 63$	$3; 3; 3; 2, 0^{27}; 1; 0^7, 2, 0^{27}, 1$	3, 3	2, 0	*IV*	no*
	4	$1, 2, 4, 8 : 15, 16, 23, 27, 28, 32, 39, 43, 44, 51, 52, 56, 63$	$4; 6; 5, 0^5, 1; 2, 0^{27}, 2; 0, 1, 0^5, 4, 0^{27}, 1$	4, 5	2, 0	*IV*	no
	5	$1, 2, 4, 8, 16 : 15, 23, 27, 28, 32, 39, 43, 44, 51, 52, 56, 63$	$5; 10; 7, 0^5, 3; 2, 0^{27}; 3; 0, 3, 0^5, 6, 0^{27}, 1$	5, 7	2, 0	*IV*	no

For $13 \leqslant n \leqslant 17$ and $f = 4, 5$ of 64 runs, we have not obtained the OCDs with resolution *III* yet. Therefore, we only list the OCDs with resolution *IV* here.

3. There are, however, a few exceptions to the aforementioned conclusions. For example, when $(q, n, f) = (6, 9, 5)$, the 2^{9-3} class one CCD of resolution IV has the numbers $(5, 4)$ of strongly clear main effects and 2fi's (see Table 7.4). However, the 2^{9-3} CCD of resolution III has the numbers $(5, 0)$, indicating that the CCD of resolution III is worse than the one of resolution IV.

8 General Minimum Lower-Order Confounding Criteria for Robust Parameter Designs

Robust parameter design is an approach to plan experimentation aimed at reducing process variation. It was originally proposed by Taguchi (1987). In this approach, factors considered in the design are categorized into two types: control factors and noise factors. Control factors are adjustable and set at fixed levels once chosen during the regular process, while noise factors are difficult to control within the normal process. Ren, Li, and Zhang (2012) extended the GMC criterion to effectively identify the optimal combination of control factors. This chapter summarizes their findings.

8.1 Introduction

Robust parameter design, a fundamental strategy pioneered by Taguchi (Taguchi 1986, 1987) in the field of quality engineering, has been the subject of extensive study by statisticians over the past four decades. In a parameter design experiment, factors are classified into two types: control factors and noise factors. Control factors are adjustable but remain fixed once chosen, while noise factors are difficult to control. The objective of the experiment is to determine the optimal settings for the control factors, ensuring that the system not only meets a specified target but also exhibits minimal sensitivity to variations caused by noise. For more detailed information, reference can be made to Wu and Hamada (2000) and Mukerjee and Wu (2006).

Taguchi (1987) suggested employing a cross array methodology that utilizes two distinct designs: the control array and the noise array. The control array is used to determine the level settings for the control factors, while the noise array determines the level settings for the noise factors. The experiment is conducted for each combination of control array and noise array settings. Subsequently, the experiment results are analyzed using location-dispersion modeling. This modeling approach involves separately modeling location measure and dispersion measure to understand the impact of control factor level combinations on system performance.

In response to concerns regarding the run size and flexibility associated with cross arrays, Welch, Yu, Kang, and Sacks (1990) and Shoemaker, Tsui, and Wu (1991) proposed the use of single arrays as an alternative approach.

A single array is an ordinary orthogonal array that accommodates both control and noise factors. In this approach, the response modeling technique is utilized to establish the relationship between the response and the control and noise factors. The mean response and transmitted variance models are employed to analyze location and dispersion effects. It is worth noting that cross arrays can be viewed as a specific type of single array.

Researchers have made efforts to identify optimal single arrays that yield the best results for robust parameter experiments. Studies such as Bingham and Sitter (2003) and Wu and Zhu (2003) have explored this area. Many of the existing criteria are based on the WLP or its generalized form.

Examples illustrate that in numerous cases, the optimal designs obtained through these criteria do not achieve the maximum number of clear interested effects. Kulahci, Ramírez, and Tobias (2006) raised concerns about the effectiveness of the MA criterion employed in designs involving different types of factors. They suggested that experimenters need to ensure that the chosen designs are suitable for the specific problem at hand.

In Section 8.2, we explore alternative methods for identifying optimal designs that are tailored to fit the specific problem at hand. Our focus will be on selecting designs that exhibit minimal lower-order confounding and allow for accurate estimation of the maximum number of interested effects. We will consider two rank-orders of effects: one based on the experimenters' interests and the other following the effect hierarchy principle. Furthermore, we propose a new criterion for selecting optimal designs that takes these factors into account.

8.2   Selection of Optimal Regular Robust Parameter Designs

As discussed in Wu and Zhu (2003), it has been observed that cross arrays may not exist for small run sizes and specific combinations of control and noise factors. While our current focus is on selecting a single array, it is important to be aware that the optimal designs may ultimately involve a cross array structure.

We use $2^{l_1+l_2-m}$ to represent a single array for a robust parameter design involving l_1 control factors and l_2 noise factors. This type of array appears similar to an ordinary 2^{n-m} design (where $n = l_1 + l_2$), but with the first l_1 columns reserved for control factors and the remaining l_2 columns for noise factors. We refer the main effects of the l_1 control factors as C type effects, and those of the l_2 noise factors as N type effects.

Given the presence of various types of main effects, it becomes essential to discern their interactions, especially when dealing with varying numbers of control factors and noise factors. Interactions involving two factors, with one being a control factor and the other a noise factor, are referred to as CN type effects. Similarly, we can denote the remaining type of interactions.

Factorial effects, such as the CN type of factorial effects, often play a vital role in achieving robustness in a process. Therefore, when selecting designs, experimenters should carefully consider these effects and ensure that they can be easily estimated.

The main effects of C type are crucial for adjusting the mean response, while the main effects of N type, along with CN type 2fi's, are valuable for reducing variation. Therefore, these three types of effects should be considered equally important. Of course, the grand mean I is most important. Following the arguments of Wu and Zhu

(2003), experimenters can use a numerical rule to determine the ranking of effects based on their relevance and the level of interest. Let us denote a factorial interaction involving i control factors and j noise factors as $e_{i,j}$. Its weight is defined as follows:

$$W(e_{i,j}) = \begin{cases} \max\{i,j\}, & \text{if } \max\{i,j\} \leqslant 1, \\ i, & \text{if } i > j \text{ and } i > 1, \\ j + \frac{1}{2}, & \text{if } j \geqslant i \text{ and } j > 1. \end{cases} \tag{8.1}$$

We can then rank $e_{i,j}$ based on its weight, as presented in Table 8.1.

Table 8.1   Factorial effects ranked with the interest of experimenters

Rank	Weight	Factorial effect
(0)	0	I
(1)	1	C, CN, N
(2)	2	CC, CCN
(3)	2.5	$CCNN, CNN, NN$
(4)	3	$CCC, CCCN, CCCN$
(5)	3.5	$CCCNN, CCNNN, CNNN, NNN$
(6)	4	$CCCC, CCCCN, CCCCNNN, CCCCNNN$
$\cdots$	$\cdots$	$\cdots$

In this manner, all factorial effects can be categorized into different groups denoted as (0), (1), (2), and so on, as illustrated in Table 8.1. The i-th set is referred to as the (i)th-order set, and the effects within each set are of equal interest to experimenters. Particularly, the effects positioned at the top of the ranking are the ones that experimenters are most interested in and desire to estimate.

Assuming that the 3rd or higher order effects are negligible, then (1)st-set is $\{C, N, CN\}$, (2)nd-set is $\{CC\}$, and (3)rd-set is $\{NN\}$. Wu and Zhu (2003) defines the concept of J-aberration as the vector

$$J = (J_1, J_2, J_3, J_4, J_5, J_6),$$

where $J_1, J_2, J_3, J_4, J_5, J_6$ represent the numbers of alias pairs in (1)st-set, between (1)st-set and (2)nd-set, between (1)st-set and (3)rd-set, in (2)nd-set, between (2)nd-set and (3)rd-set, and in (3)rd-set, respectively. Note that J is a generalized form of the WLP since it is a function of it. The minimum J-aberration criterion is to select the designs that sequentially minimize the entries of J.

The following example shows that sometimes a minimum J-aberration design cannot reach the maximum number of interested effects to be clearly estimated.

Example 8.1 Consider the 2^{6-2} array:

$$I = 125 = 2346 = 13456.$$

From it we can obtain two 2^{4+2-2} single arrays, D_1 and D_2, respectively, by assigning factors 1 and 2 to noise factors and by assigning factors 4 and 6 to noise factors.

The J-aberrations of D_1 and D_2 are $(4,3,0,0,1,0)$ and $(4,0,1,6,0,0)$, respectively. Therefore, D_2 is better than D_1 under the minimum J-aberration criterion. However, D_1 contains 5 clear effects in (1)st-set: one C type, two N type and two CN type, while D_2 contains only three C type clear effects in (1)st-set. Therefore, it is evident that D_1 is better than D_2 for clearly estimating interested effects. □

Also, we find that it is not necessary for effects of the same interest to have the same potential significance, as supposed in Wu and Zhu (2003). The following example illustrates this fact.

Example 8.2 Let us consider the case study used in Bingham and Sitter (2003), taken from Lewis, Hutchens, and Smith (1997).

The experiment examines the effect of customer usage factors on the time between failures of a robotic wafer handling subsystem in an optical recognition process used for positioning a wafer under a repair laser. The response variable of primary interest is a measure of correlation system and the expected image. A larger value of this variable indicates better performance.

The experiment has eight control factors that describe the system design options, each at two levels: A = training box size, B = corner orientation, C = binary threshold, D = illumination level, E = illumination angle, F = illumination uniformity, G = teach scene angle, and H = train condition. Additionally, there are three noise factors that represent customer usage, each at two levels: j = ambient light intensity, k = initial wafer displacement, and l = initial wafer orientation. The original analysis of the experiment was conducted using location-dispersion modeling. For more details, we refer to Bingham and Sitter (2003).

Based on the above arguments, it is evident that the effect Aj is in the (1)st-order interest set with main effects. However, if we assume a rule stating that effects in the same interest set have the same potential significance, a contradiction arises when considering the following hypothetical scenario.

In the new hypothetical scenario, the response is from a tiny workshop instead of a subsystem. Here, the ambient light is considered as a control factor since it is part of the workshop. In this case, the effect Aj is included in the (2)nd-order interest set, rather than having the same potential significance as the main effects, as suggested by the rule. However, this presents a contradiction because the two factorial systems are identical.   □

To improve the results of Wu and Zhu (2003), we propose an alternative rank-ordering of effects based on their likely significance. It is important to note that, in general, during the planning stage, aside from adhering to the effect hierarchy principle, we often lack prior information regarding which factorial effects are more likely to be significant than others.

For a $2^{l_1+l_2-m}$ design, we present two rank-orders of the factorial effects: the rank-order of interest denoted as (i)th-order, and the rank-order of likely significance denoted as ith-order. In the following, we extend the idea discussed in Chapter 2 and introduce a new approach for selecting optimal designs in robust parameter experiments.

Definition 8.3   *If a factorial effect is aliased exactly with k jth-order factorial effects different from it, it is called to be aliased with jth-order effects at degree k. The notation $^{\#}_{(i)}C_j^{(k)}$ is used to denote the number of (i)th-order factorial effects which aliased with jth-order factorial effects at degree k.*

The following vector distributes all (i)th-order factorial effects into K_j+1 groups in order:

$$^{\#}_{(i)}C_j = (^{\#}_{(i)}C_j^{(0)},\ ^{\#}_{(i)}C_j^{(1)}, \cdots, \ ^{\#}_{(i)}C_j^{(K_j)}),$$

where $K_j = \binom{n}{j}$.

Let D_1 and D_2 be any two different $2^{l_1+l_2-m}$ designs. Compare the two vectors $^{\#}_{(i)}C_j(D_1)$ and $^{\#}_{(i)}C_j(D_2)$. If k is the smallest number such that

$$^{\#}_{(i)}C_j^{(k)}(D_1) \neq \ ^{\#}_{(i)}C_j^{(k)}(D_2)$$

and

$$\mathop{\#}_{(i)}C_j^{(k)}(d_1) > \mathop{\#}_{(i)}C_j^{(k)}(d_2),$$

then it is said that (i)th-order factorial effects of D_1 have less severely aliased with its jth-order factors than that of D_2, or $\mathop{\#}_{(i)}C_j(D_1)$ is said to be better than $\mathop{\#}_{(i)}C_j(D_2)$, denoted by $\mathop{\#}_{(i)}C_j(D_1) \succ \mathop{\#}_{(i)}C_j(D_2)$.

To rank the importance of $\mathop{\#}_{(i)}C_j$'s with different i and j, a compromise between the (i)th-order of interest and the jth-order of likely significance has to be made. The following example illustrates the concept of this compromise.

Example 8.4   Let us compare the importance of $\mathop{\#}_{(2)}C_3$ and $\mathop{\#}_{(3)}C_3$. Based on the meanings of (i)th-order interest of effects, it is evident that estimating (2)nd-order effects is more desirable. Therefore, $\mathop{\#}_{(2)}C_3$ is considered more important than $\mathop{\#}_{(3)}C_3$.

Next, Let us compare the importance of $\mathop{\#}_{(2)}C_2$ and $\mathop{\#}_{(2)}C_3$. The answer is also apparent because, based on the the meanings of jth-order likely significance, the presence of 2nd-order effects can have a more significant impact on estimating other (2)nd-order effects compared to the influence of 3rd-order effects do. Hence, $\mathop{\#}_{(2)}C_2$ is considered more important than $\mathop{\#}_{(2)}C_3$.

Lastly, Let us compare the importance of $\mathop{\#}_{(2)}C_3$ and $\mathop{\#}_{(3)}C_2$. The answer to this comparison will depend on whether all (2)nd-order and (3)rd-order effects are desired and if all 2nd-order and 3rd-order effects are non-negligible. If there is a greater desire to estimate (2)nd-order effects compared to (3)rd-order effects, we may consider $\mathop{\#}_{(2)}C_3$ as more important. If the desires to estimate (2)nd-order effects and (3)rd-order effects are very similar and the influence of 2nd-order and 3rd-order effects is the primary concern, then $\mathop{\#}_{(3)}C_2$ should be chosen as more important one.   □

The above examples demonstrate the need for a compromise between the two rank-orders when ranking the importance of $\mathop{\#}_{(i)}C_j$'s. In this section, we adopt a ranking sequence similar to Chapter 2, but we acknowledge that other preferences may also be justified. It is important to note that even if alternative ranking sequences for $\mathop{\#}_{(i)}C_j$'s are used, the approach presented in this section can still be applied in a similar manner.

Definition 8.5   *Define the vector*

$$
\begin{aligned}
{}^{\#}C = \ & ({}^{\#}_{(1)}C_1, {}^{\#}_{(0)}C_2, {}^{\#}_{(1)}C_2, {}^{\#}_{(2)}C_0, {}^{\#}_{(2)}C_1, {}^{\#}_{(2)}C_2, {}^{\#}_{(0)}C_3, {}^{\#}_{(1)}C_3, {}^{\#}_{(2)}C_3, {}^{\#}_{(3)}C_0, {}^{\#}_{(3)}C_1, \\
& {}^{\#}_{(3)}C_2, {}^{\#}_{(3)}C_3, {}^{\#}_{(0)}C_4, {}^{\#}_{(1)}C_4, {}^{\#}_{(2)}C_4, {}^{\#}_{(3)}C_4, {}^{\#}_{(4)}C_0, {}^{\#}_{(4)}C_1, {}^{\#}_{(4)}C_2, {}^{\#}_{(4)}C_3, {}^{\#}_{(4)}C_4, \cdots)
\end{aligned}
\tag{8.2}
$$

with the rules: (i) *if* $\max\{i,j\} < \max\{s,t\}$, *then* ${}^{\#}_{(i)}C_j$ *is placed ahead of* ${}^{\#}_{(s)}C_t$; (ii) *if* $\max\{i,j\} = \max\{s,t\}$ *and* $i < s$, *then* ${}^{\#}_{(i)}C_j$ *is placed ahead of* ${}^{\#}_{(s)}C_t$; (iii) *if* $\max\{i,j\} = \max\{s,t\}$, $i = s$ *and* $j < t$, *then* ${}^{\#}_{(i)}C_j$ *is placed ahead of* ${}^{\#}_{(s)}C_t$. *The vector in* (8.2) *is called the aliased interested-effect-number pattern (denoted by AIENP).*

Note that if hth-order effects and higher (where $3 \leqslant h \leqslant j_1 + j_2$) are considered negligible, then contents of some (i)th-order sets in (8.2) can differ. The corresponding (8.2) is called an aliased interested effect-number pattern with hth- and higher order effects neglected (denoted by h-AIENP). From now on, we will use the notation h-AIENP, as it is the same as AIENP when $h > j_1 + j_2$.

Definition 8.6   *Suppose D_1 and D_2 are two different $2^{l_1+l_2-m}$ designs, and ${}^{\#}C_l(D_1)$ and ${}^{\#}C_l(D_2)$ are the first entries of h-AIENPs ${}^{\#}C(D_1)$ and ${}^{\#}C(D_2)$ such that ${}^{\#}C_l(D_1) \neq {}^{\#}C_l(D_2)$. If ${}^{\#}C_l(D_1) > {}^{\#}C_l(D_2)$, then we say D_1 to have less hth-lower order confounding as per interest than D_2. If there are no other $2^{l_1+l_2-m}$ designs which have less hth-lower order confounding as per interest than D_1, then we call D_1 to be a minimum h-lower order confounding as per interest (h-MLOCI, for short) design. The criterion for selecting h-MLOCI designs is referred to as h-MLOCI criterion.*

The following discussion highlights differences between the 3-MLOCI and CE criteria.

In the case of resolution IV designs, the CE criterion aims to maximize the number of clear 2fi's, while 3-MLOCI criterion focuses on discriminating among those 2fi's.

Since all 3rd-order and higher-order effects are considered negligible, only three (i)th-order sets are non-empty: (1)st-order set containing C, CN, N type effects, (2)nd-order set containing CC type effects and (3)rd-order set containing NN type effects. Therefore, the 3-AIENP is as follows:

$$
{}^{\#}C = ({}^{\#}_{(1)}C_1, {}^{\#}_{(0)}C_2, {}^{\#}_{(1)}C_2, {}^{\#}_{(2)}C_0, {}^{\#}_{(2)}C_1, {}^{\#}_{(2)}C_2, {}^{\#}_{(3)}C_0, {}^{\#}_{(3)}C_1, {}^{\#}_{(3)}C_2).
$$

If the 3-MLOCI design is of resolution IV, then some entries of $^{\#}C$ remain fixed:

$$\underset{(1)}{^{\#}}C_1 = (l_1 + l_2 + l_1 l_2, 0, \cdots, 0),$$

$$\underset{(0)}{^{\#}}C_2 = (1, 0, \cdots, 0),$$

$$\underset{(2)}{^{\#}}C_0 = (\tbinom{l_1}{2}, 0),$$

$$\underset{(2)}{^{\#}}C_1 = (\tbinom{l_1}{2}, 0, \cdots, 0),$$

$$\underset{(3)}{^{\#}}C_0 = (\tbinom{l_2}{2}, 0),$$

$$\underset{(3)}{^{\#}}C_1 = (\tbinom{l_2}{2}, 0, \cdots, 0).$$

The other three are

$$\underset{(1)}{^{\#}}C_2 = (l_1 + l_2 + \text{clear}\,(CN), \cdots,),$$

$$\underset{(2)}{^{\#}}C_2 = (\text{clear}\,(CC), \cdots,),$$

$$\underset{(3)}{^{\#}}C_2 = (\text{clear}\,(NN), \cdots,).$$

So, for resolution IV designs, the 3-MLOCI criterion first minimizes the confounding to CN type effects rather than confounding to all 2fi's simultaneously.

8.3   An Algorithm for Searching Optimal Arrays

In this section, an algorithm for searching h-AIENP designs is provided using an example.

In this section, any set of words or effects arranges its members in an order $\vartriangleleft$ as defined below. Suppose $i_1 \cdots i_k$ and $j_1 \cdots j_l$ are two words. We say $i_1 \cdots i_k$ is "smaller" than $j_1 \cdots j_l$ (denoted by $i_1 \cdots i_k \vartriangleleft j_1 \cdots j_l$) if either $k < j$ or when $k = j$ and $i_1 \cdots i_k$ is lexicographically ahead of $j_1 \cdots j_l$.

Consider a $2^{l_1 + l_2 - m}$ design D. Let $\mathbf{D}_0$ be a $2^m \times (l_1 + l_2)$ matrix that represents the contrast subgroup G. The (i, j)-entry of $\mathbf{D}_0$ equals 1 if the i-th word in G contains the letter j, and it equals 0 otherwise. We call $\mathbf{D}_0$ the *defining structure matrix* of the design.

Let $\mathbf{S}$ denote the set of n-dimensional row vectors, where each vector represents an effect of the $2^{l_1 + l_2 - m}$ design. In each row vector, the jth entry equals 1 if it involves the j-th factor, and 0 otherwise.

Let $\mathbf{S}_0$ be the set of row vectors of $\mathbf{D}_0$.

Set $\mathbf{S}_1 = \mathbf{S} \backslash \mathbf{S}_0$. Select the first vector of $\mathbf{S}_1$, and add it to every row of $\mathbf{D}_0$. Then, rearrange the order of rows according to the order defined by $\lhd$. The resulting matrix $\mathbf{D}_1$ is called the aliased-effect matrix.

Set $\mathbf{S}_2 = \mathbf{S}_1 \backslash \mathbf{S}_0$. Select the first vector of $\mathbf{S}_2$, and add it to every row of $\mathbf{D}_0$. Then, rearrange the order of rows according to the order defined by $\lhd$. The resulting matrix $\mathbf{D}_2$ is another aliased-effect matrix.

Following the above steps, we obtain all $2^{l_1 + l_2 - m}$ matrices. Using this information, we can calculate the h-AENPI. By comparing the h-AENPI of all non-isomorphic $2^{l_1 + l_2 - m}$ designs, we can identify the optimal h-MLOCI designs.

Let us consider a 2^{5+3-3} design with 5 control factors $\{1, 2, 3, 4, 5\}$ and 3 noise factors $\{6, 7, 8\}$. The design is determined by:

$$6 = 123, \quad 7 = 124, \quad 8 = 135.$$

Its defining contrast subgroup G for this design is

$$\{I, 1236, 1247, 1358, 3467, 145678, 234578\}.$$

The corresponding defining structure matrix $\mathbf{D}_0$ is shown in Table 8.2.

Table 8.2   Defining structure matrix $\mathbf{D}_0$ and relevant information

1	2	3	4	5	6	7	8	W	C	N	$(i)_{h=3}$	$(i)_{h=4}$
0	0	0	0	0	0	0	0	0	0	0	(0)	(0)
1	1	1	0	0	1	0	0	4	3	1	—	—
1	1	0	1	0	0	1	0	4	3	1	—	—
1	0	1	0	1	0	0	1	4	3	1	—	—
0	1	0	0	1	1	0	1	4	2	2	—	—
0	0	1	1	0	1	1	0	4	2	2	—	—
1	0	0	1	1	1	1	1	6	3	3	—	—
0	1	1	1	1	0	1	1	6	4	2	—	—

In the right part of the table, some information are needed for calculating the h-AIENP. We denote the wordlength of the corresponding row by W and use C and N to denote the numbers of control and noise factors involved in the corresponding row, respectively. The notation (i) represents the interest set to which the relevant row belongs.

We initially set all $_{(i)}^{\#} C_j^{(k)}$ values to 0. In the above table, the columns labeled

(i) are empty, so no further action is required in this case.

Then $\mathbf{D}_1$ can be obtained by add $(1,0,\cdots,0)$ to every rows of $\mathbf{D}_0$, as in Table 8.3.

Table 8.3   Aliased effect matrix $\mathbf{D}_1$ and relevant information

1	2	3	4	5	6	7	8	W	C	N	$(i)_{h=3}$	$(i)_{h=4}$
1	0	0	0	0	0	0	0	1	1	0	(1)	(1)
0	1	1	0	0	1	0	0	3	2	1	—	(2)
0	1	0	1	0	0	1	0	3	2	1	—	(2)
0	0	1	0	1	0	0	1	3	2	1	—	(2)
1	1	0	0	1	1	0	1	5	3	2	—	—
1	0	1	1	0	1	1	0	5	3	2	—	—
0	0	0	1	1	1	1	1	5	2	3	—	—
1	1	1	1	1	0	1	1	7	5	2	—	—

For $h = 3$, there is one (1)st-order effect, but it is aliased with no effect with order lower than 3. Therefore, ${}_{(1)}^{\#}C_j^{(0)}(h = 3) = {}_{(1)}^{\#}C_j^{(0)}(h = 3) + 1$ for $j = 0, 1, 2$. For $h = 4$, there is a (1)st-order effect which is aliased with three 3-order effects. Therefore, ${}_{(1)}^{\#}C_3^{(3)}(h = 4) = {}_{(1)}^{\#}C_3^{(3)}(h = 4) + 1$. Additionally, ${}_{(1)}^{\#}C_j^{(0)}(h = 4) = {}_{(1)}^{\#}C_j^{(0)}(h = 4) + 1$ for $j = 0, 1, 2$. There are also three (2)nd-order effects which are aliased with one 1st-order effect and two 3rd-order effects. Therefore, ${}_{(2)}^{\#}C_1^{(1)}(h = 4) = {}_{(2)}^{\#}C_1^{(1)}(h = 4) + 3$, ${}_{(2)}^{\#}C_3^{(2)}(h = 4) = {}_{(2)}^{\#}C_3^{(2)}(h = 4) + 3$, and ${}_{(2)}^{\#}C_j^{(0)}(h = 4) = {}_{(2)}^{\#}C_j^{(0)}(h = 4) + 3, j = 0, 2$.

By repeating the above procedure for every $\mathbf{D}_i$, $i = 0, 1, \cdots, 2^{l_1+l_2-m} - 1$, we can obtain ${}_{(i)}^{\#}C_j^{(k)}(h = 3)$ and ${}_{(i)}^{\#}C_j^{(k)}(h = 4)$. Using this information, we can get the 3-AIENP and 4-AIENP.

The optimal single arrays of 16-, 32-, and 64-run under the 3-MLOCI criterion, along with some optimal minimum J-aberration single arrays for comparison, are provided in Tables 8.4–8.6.

In the tables, the notations C, N, and m represent the numbers of control and noise factors and independent generators in a design respectively. "add.columns" refers to the m independent generators of the regular fraction by turning the binary numbers into the denary numbers. "n" indicates the array's columns assigned to noise factors, and "α" represents for a vector of 5 entries that denote the numbers of clear C, N, CN, CC, and NN type effects in order. We can observe that in most cases the α's of 3-MLOCI arrays are more desirable for the purpose of robust parameter designs than that of minimum J-aberration arrays. From Table 8.6, it is evident that the 3-MLOCI criterion elaborates the results of minimum J-aberration criterion in some cases.

Table 8.4 16-run 3-MLOCI arrays and comparisons with minimum J-aberration arrays

$C\ N\ m$ add.columns	n	$^{\#}_{(1)}C_1; ^{\#}_{(1)}C_2; ^{\#}_{(2)}C_1; ^{\#}_{(2)}C_2;$ $^{\#}_{(3)}C_1; ^{\#}_{(3)}C_2$	J-aberration	α	Orders M, J
4 1 1 15	1	9; 9; 6; 6; ;	0 0 0 0 0 0	4 1 6 4 0	1 1
3 2 1 15	1 2	11; $11,0^5,14,15$; 3; $3,0^5,91$; 1; 1	0 0 0 0 0 0	3 2 3 6 1	1 1
2 3 1 15	1 2 3	11;$11,0^5,26,15$; 1; $0^5,78$; 3; $3,0^5,1$	0 0 0 0 0 0	2 3 1 6 3	1 1
5 1 2 14 7	1	11; 6,4,1; 10; 0,8,2;;	0 6 0 6 0 0	5 1 0 0 0	1 2
5 1 2 14 3	1	11; 5,6; 7,3; 7,3;;	0 6 0 0 0 0	2 1 4 2 0	4 1
4 2 2 14 3	1 2	14;$7,7,0^4,14,15$;3,3;$5,1,0^4,91$; 1; 0,1	4 3 0 0 1 0	1 2 2 4 0	1 2
4 2 2 14 3	4 6	$12,2;11,3,0^4,14,15;6;0,6,0^4,91;0,1;1$	4 0 1 6 0 0	3 0 0 6 0	6 1
3 3 2 14 3	3 4 6	$15;9,6,0^4,26,15;3;0,3,0^4,78;0,3;3,0^5,1$	0 3 3 0 0 0	3 0 0 6 0	1 1
6 1 3 14 7 11	1	13; 7,0,6; 15; $0^2,15$;;	0 12 0 18 0 0	6 1 0 0 0	1 2
6 1 3 14 7 3	1	13; 3,8,2; 9,6; 5,8,2;;	0 12 0 6 0 0	1 1 1 1 0	4 1
5 2 3 14 7 11	1 2	$17;7,0,10;10;0^2,10;1;0^2,1$	8 12 0 6 2 0	5 2 0 0 0	1 12
5 2 3 14 7 3	1 5	$17;4,12,1;4,6;4,4,2;1;0^2,1$	8 6 0 6 2 0	0 2 0 2 0	4 1
4 3 3 14 7 11	1 2 3	19; 7,0,12,6; $0^2,6,3; 0^2,3$	12 9 3 0 3 0	4 3 0 0 0	1 21
4 3 3 14 7 3	2 6 7	17,2; 6,10,3; 5,1; 0,5,1; 0,3; 2,1	8 7 3 0 1 0	2 0 0 2 0	8 1
7 1 4 14 7 11 13	1	15; $8,0^2,7$; 21; $0^3,21$;;	0 21 0 42 0 0	7 1 0 0 0	1 3
7 1 4 14 7 11 3	5	15; 2,6,6,1; 12,9; 6,0,15;;	0 21 0 18 0 0	0 1 0 1 0	4 1
6 2 4 14 7 11 13	1 2	20; $8,0^2,12$; 15; $0^3,15$; 1; $0^3,1$	12 24 0 18 3 0	6 2 0 0 0	1 20
6 2 4 14 7 3 5	1 5	20; 2,12,6; 3,12; 0,12,0,3; 1; $0^3,1$	12 12 0 18 3 0	0 2 0 0 0	4 1
5 3 4 14 7 11 3	1 5 7	21,2; 4,6,12,1; 4,6; 4,0,6; 2,1; $0^2,3$	28 6 1 6 6 0	0 1 0 1 0	1 75
5 3 4 14 7 3 12	1 2 8	19,4; 2,13,8; 5,5; 1,7,2; 0,3; 1,2	16 14 3 0 2 0	0 0 0 0 0	16 1
8 1 5 14 7 11 13 3	1	15,2; 1,8,0,7,1; 18,10; $7,0^2,21$;;	4 31 0 42 0 0	0 0 0 0 0	1 2
8 1 5 14 7 11 3 6	5	15,2; 0,4,10,3; 12,16; 2,10,13,3;;	4 31 0 30 0 0	0 0 0 0 0	5 1
7 2 5 12 6 10 14 3	4 9	21,2; 2,14,0,6,1; 0,21; $0^2,18,3; 0,1; 0^3,1$	16 21 1 42 3 0	0 0 0 0 0	1 1
6 3 5 14 7 11 13 3	1 2 6	23,4; 3,8,0,15,1; 8,7;$5,0^2,10$; 2,1; $0^3,3$	32 25 4 6 6 0	0 0 0 0 0	1 46
6 3 5 14 7 11 3 6	1 5 9	21,6; 1,8,14,4; 6,9; 0,5,8,2; 0,3; 1,1,1	24 27 3 6 3 0	0 0 0 0 0	13 1
9 1 6 14 7 11 13 3 6	1	15,4; 0,2,8,6,3; 16,20; 0,14,0,18,4;;	8 44 0 60 0 0	0 0 0 0 0	1 2
9 1 6 14 7 3 12 9 6	7	15,4; $0^2,9,10$; 13,23; 0,6,21,9;;	8 44 0 54 0 0	0 0 0 0 0	6 1
8 2 6 12 6 10 14 3 5	4 9	20,6; 0,4,13,6,3; 5,23; 0,2,17,9; 0,1; $0^3,1$	24 41 1 42 3 0	0 0 0 0 0	1 1
7 3 6 12 6 10 14 3 5	4 9 10	25,6; 0,6,18,4,3; 0,21; $0^2,12,9; 0,3; 0^3,3$	48 21 3 42 9 0	0 0 0 0 0	1 62
7 3 6 14 7 11 13 3 6	1 8 9	19,12; 0,8,8,12,3; 11,10; 0,6,0,12,3; 1,2; $0,2,0^2,1$	36 43 5 18 3 0	0 0 0 0 0	25 1
10 1 7 14 7 11 13 3 6 12	1	15,6; $0^2,3,12,6$; 15,30; $0^2,21,12,12$;;	12 60 0 96 0 0	0 0 0 0 0	1 1
10 1 7 14 7 3 12 9 6 5	1	15,6; $0^2,3,12,6$; 12,33; $0^2,12,33$;;	12 60 0 96 0 0	0 0 0 0 0	5 1
9 2 7 14 7 3 12 9 6 5	1 5	19,10; $0^2,6,17,6$; 8,28; $0^2,9,27; 0,1; 0^3,1$;	32 64 1 60 3 0	0 0 0 0 0	1 1
8 3 7 14 7 3 12 9 6 5	1 5 8	23,12; $0^2,9,20,6$; 4,24; $0^2,6,22; 0,3; 0^3,3$	60 51 3 42 9 0	0 0 0 0 0	1 38
8 3 7 14 7 11 13 3 6 12	1 3 10	19,16; $0^2,10,16,9$; 10,18; $0^2,12,8,8; 1,2; 0^2,2,0,1$	52 63 5 30 5 0	0 0 0 0 0	20 1
11 1 8 14 7 11 13 3 6 12 9	1	15,8; $0^3,8,12,3$; 15,40; $0^3,40,0,15$;;	16 79 0 156 0 0	0 0 0 0 0	1 1
11 1 8 14 7 11 13 3 6 12 5	11	15,8; $0^3,8,12,3$; 12,43; $0^3,28,27$;;	16 79 0 156 0 0	0 0 0 0 0	4 1
10 2 8 14 7 11 13 3 6 12 9	1 2	18,14; $0^3,14,12,6$; 12,33; $0^3,33,0,12; 0,1; 0^3,1$	40 93 1 96 3 0	0 0 0 0 0	1 1
10 2 8 14 7 11 13 3 6 12 5	1 11	18,14; $0^3,11,18,3$; 9,36; $0^3,24,21; 0,1; 0^3,1$	40 93 1 96 3 0	0 0 0 0 0	4 1
9 3 8 14 7 11 13 3 6 12 9	1 2 9	21,18; $0^3,18,12,9$; 9,27; $0^3,27,0,9; 0,3; 0^3,3$	72 90 3 54 9 0	0 0 0 0 0	1 23
9 3 8 14 7 11 13 3 6 12 5	1 5 9	19,20; $0^3,14,22,3$; 8,28; $0^3,20,16; 0,3; 0^3,2,1$	68 91 6 54 7 0	0 0 0 0 0	21 1
12 1 9 14 7 11 13 3 6 12 9 5	1	15,10; $0^4,9,15,1$; 10,56; $0^4,51,15$;;	20 107 0 228 0 0	0 0 0 0 0	1 1
11 2 9 14 7 11 13 3 6 12 9 5	1 8	17,18; $0^4,18,16,1$; 8,47; $0^4,42,13; 0,1; 0^5,1$	56 119 1 156 5 0	0 0 0 0 0	1 4
11 2 9 14 7 11 13 3 6 12 9 5	1 2	17,18; $0^4,16,18,1$; 8,47; $0^4,43,12; 0,1; 0^4,1$	52 125 1 150 4 0	0 0 0 0 0	4 1
10 3 9 14 7 11 13 3 6 12 9 5	1 2 4	19,24; $0^4,23,19,1$; 6,39; $0^4,35,10; 0,3; 0^4,2,1$	88 123 6 96 10 0	0 0 0 0 0	1 4
10 3 9 14 7 11 13 3 6 12 9 5	1 2 12	19,24; $0^4,21,21,1$; 6,39; $0^4,36,9; 0,3; 0^4,3$	84 129 6 90 9 0	0 0 0 0 0	5 1
13 1 10 14 7 11 13 3 6 12 9 5 101		15,12; $0^5,12,15$; 6,72; $0^5,72,6$;;	24 138 0 330 0 0	0 0 0 0 0	1 1
12 2 10 14 7 11 13 3 6 12 9 5 101 2		16,22; $0^5,22,16$; 5,61;$0^5,61,5$; 0,1; $0^5,1$	164 163 1 228 5 0	0 0 0 0 0	1 1
11 3 10 14 7 11 13 3 6 12 9 5 101 2 3		17,30; $0^5,30,17$; 4,51;$0^5,51,4$; 0,3; $0^5,3$	108 168 6 150 12 0	0 0 0 0 0	1 1

Table 8.5   32-run 3-MLOCI arrays and comparisons with minimum J-aberration arrays

$C\ Nm$ add.columns	n	$^{\#}_{(1)}C_1;\,{}^{\#}_{(1)}C_2;\,{}^{\#}_{(2)}C_1;\,{}^{\#}_{(2)}C_2;$ $^{\#}_{(3)}C_1;\,{}^{\#}_{(3)}C_2$	J-aberration	α	Orders M, J
5 1 1 31	1	11;11;10;10;;	0 0 0 0 0 0	5 1 10 5 0	1 1
4 2 1 31	1 2	14;14,0^2,8,1,3;6;6,0^2,40,0,15;1;1	0 0 0 0 0 0	4 2 6 8 1	1 1
4 2 1 15	1 2	14;14,0^2,8,1,3;6;6,0^2,40,0,15;1;1	0 0 0 0 0 0	4 2 6 8 1	2 1
3 3 1 31	1 2 3	15;15,0,11,13,1;3;3,0,9,24,4;3;3,0^3,1	0 0 0 0 0 0	3 3 3 9 3	1 1
3 3 1 15	2 3 4	15;15,0,11,13,1;3;3,0,9,24,4;3;3,0^3,1	0 0 0 0 0 0	3 3 3 9 3	2 1
6 1 2 30 7	1	13;13;15;9,6;;	0 0 0 6 0 0	6 1 9 6 0	1 1
5 2 2 30 7	1 2	17;17,0^3,1,3;10;4,6,0^3,15;1;1	0 0 0 6 0 0	5 2 4 10 1	1 1
4 3 2 30 7	1 2 6	19;19,0^3,1;6;0,6,0^2,4;3;3,0^3,1	0 0 0 6 0 0	4 3 0 12 3	1 1
7 1 3 30 7 11	1	15;15;21;6,12,3;;	0 0 0 18 0 0	7 1 6 7 0	1 1
6 2 3 30 7 11	1 6	20;20;15;0,12,3;1;1	0 0 0 18 0 0	6 2 0 12 1	1 1
5 3 3 30 7 11	1 2 6	23;18,4,1;10;0,8,2;3;3	0 6 0 6 0 0	5 3 0 10 3	1 1
8 1 4 30 7 11 13	1	17;17;28;7,0,21;;	0 0 0 42 0 0	8 1 7 8 0	1 2
8 1 4 30 7 11 19	6	17;17;28;0,24,0,4;;	0 0 0 36 0 0	8 1 0 8 0	2 1
7 2 4 30 7 11 13	1 6	23;23;21;0^2,21;1;1	0 0 0 42 0 0	7 2 0 14 1	1 1
6 3 4 30 7 3 5	1 2 6	27;21,0,6;3;12;0,12,3;3;3	0 12 0 18 0 0	0 3 0 18 3	1 1
9 1 5 30 7 11 19 29	9	19;10,8,0^2,1;36;0,32,0^2,4;;	0 12 0 36 0 0	9 1 0 0 0	1 1
8 2 5 30 7 11 13 3	1 6	26;15,10,0,1;19,9,6,1,21;1;0,1	4 9 0 42 1 0	1 2 0 12 0	1 2
8 2 5 28 14 22 26 3	5 10	24,2;23,3;28;0^3,28;0;1;1	4 0 1 84 0 0	7 0 0 14 0	36 1
7 3 5 30 7 11 13 3	1 6 9	31;15,9,6,1;12,9,6,0,15;3;0,3	0 21 3 18 0 0	0 3 0 12 0	1 1
101 6 30 7 11 19 6 5	6	21;9,0,12;33,12;0,28,12,0,5;;	0 24 0 60 0 0	4 1 0 4 0	1 7
101 6 30 7 11 19 6 12	6	21;5,8,8;33,12;4,26,11,4;;	0 24 0 48 0 0	2 1 0 2 0	12 1
9 2 6 30 7 11 13 3 6	1 6	29;12,10,5,2;18,18;2,10,20,4;1;0^2,1	8 18 0 60 2 0	0 2 0 10 0	1 4
9 2 6 28 14 22 26 6 3	5 11	27,2;14,13,1,0,1;24,12;7,1,0,28; 0,1;0,1	8 12 1 84 1 0	0 0 0 12 0	16 1
8 3 6 30 7 11 24 5 3	1 2 9	33,2;8,16,9,2;15,13;0,22,3,3;0,3;2,1	8 31 3 18 1 0	1 0 0 6 0	1 1
11 1 7 28 14 7 19 25 11 6	1	23;6,6,3,8;46,9;10,0,12,33;;	0 36 0 96 0 0	4 1 4 1 0	1 1
10 2 7 28 14 22 26 7 11 3	1 6	32;7,6,6,9,4;36,9;9,0,18,8,10;1;0^4,1	16 45 0 60 4 0	3 2 3 2 0	1 164
10 2 7 28 14 22 26 6 12 3	5 12	30,2;12,10,7,1,2;21,24;0,14,2,24,5; 0,1;0^2,1	12 24 1 108 2 0	0 0 0 10 0	5 1
9 3 7 28 14 7 19 11 6 3	1 6 9	37,2;7,10,20,1,1;18,18;2,12,9,13; 2,1;0^3,3	40 18 1 60 9 0	0 1 0 4 0	1 454
9 3 7 30 7 11 19 14 6 3	1 6 10	35,4;5,14,16,3,1;19,17;1,17,12,6; 0,3;1,2	16 44 3 30 2 0	0 0 0 4 0	7 1
121 8 28 14 22 26 7 11 13 3	1	25;5,8,0,8,1,3;54,12;11,0^2,40,0,15;;	0 51 0 156 0 0	3 1 3 1 0	1 9
121 8 30 7 11 19 6 12 9 3	6	25;2,8,6,8,1;36,30;2,18,24,22;;	0 48 0 114 0 0	0 1 0 1 0	6 1
112 8 28 14 7 19 25 11 6 3	6 10	35;2,8,11,13,1;34,21;6,12,9,24,4;;	16 57 0 78 4 0	0 2 2 0 0	1 31
112 8 28 14 22 26 7 11 6 3	11 13	29,6;5,12,12,3,2,1;38,17;5,5,14,18,13; 0,1;0,1	16 47 1 108 1 0	0 0 0 4 0	602 1
103 8 30 7 11 24 12 5 6 3	1 6 9	39,4;4,22,9,4,4;15,30;0,4,23,18; 1,2;0^2,1,2	40 30 2 96 8 0	0 0 0 2 0	1 168
103 8 30 7 11 24 21 12 6 3	1 2 9	37,6;0,12,24,7;24,21;1,13,28,3; 0,3;1,1,1	24 60 3 36 3 0	0 0 0 0 0	10 1
131 9 28 14 7 19 11 6 13 5 3	6	27;4,2,8,8,2,2,1;36,42;2,4,40,8,18,6;;	0 66 0 186 0 0	0 1 0 3 0	1 5
131 9 30 7 11 24 5 19 12 10 3	6	27;1,3,10,9,4;42,36;0,19,20,35,4;;	0 66 0 150 0 0	0 1 0 0 0	5 1
122 9 28 14 7 19 25 11 13 6 3	6 10	38;2,6,8,16,5,1;39,27; 4,16,0,20,21,5;1;0^5,1	20 75 0 132 5 0	0 2 2 0 0	1 19
122 9 28 14 7 19 25 11 13 6 3	6 13	30,8;4,12,8,8,3,3;47,19; 2,9,0,28,23,4;1;0,1	20 67 0 156 1 0	1 1 0 2 0	602 1
113 9 28 14 7 19 11 17 12 6 3	1 9 11	39,8;2,11,16,14,4;27,28;0,6,23,22,4; 0,3; 0^2,1,2	48 58 3 96 8 0	0 0 0 1 0	1 158
113 9 30 7 11 24 21 14 12 6 3	6 8 10	39,8;0,9,18,16,4;27,28;0,8,28,16,3; 0,3;1,0,2	32 82 3 66 4 0	0 0 0 0 0	9 1
141 10 28 14 22 26 7 11 13 19 6 36		27,2;2,4,9,0,9,4,1;60,31;;;	4 82 0 258 0 0	0 0 1 1 0	1 10
141 10 30 7 11 24 5 19 12 17 6 3 6		27,2;0,1,8,14,5,1;45,46;1,4,33,48,5;;	4 82 0 198 0 0	0 0 0 0 0	15 1
132 10 28 14 22 26 7 11 13 19 6 36 9		39,2;4,4,9,0,18,5,1;48,30;2,20,0^2,37,19; 0,1;0^5,1	24 102 1 186 5 0	0 0 0 2 0	1 22
132 10 28 14 22 26 7 11 13 19 6 3 13	15	31;10;3,14,9,0,11,3,1;56,22; 3,9,0^2,44,22;0,1;0,1	24 82 1 234 1 0	0 0 0 2 0	602 1
123 10 30 7 11 24 5 19 12 10 6 3	1 6 9	43,8;1,8,18,14,8,2;25,41;0,3,14,33,16; 1,2;0^3,1,2	60 74 2 150 11 0	0 0 0 0 0	1 216
123 10 30 7 11 24 21 12 10 5 6 3	6 8 10	41,10;0,4,20,13,13,1;28,38;0,6,14,36,10; 0,3;0,2,0,1	40 107 3 108 5 0	0 0 0 0 0	7 1

Table 8.6   64-run 3-MLOCI arrays and comparisons with minimum J-aberration arrays

C	N	m	add.columns	n	${}^{\#}_{(1)}C_1; {}^{\#}_{(1)}C_2; {}^{\#}_{(2)}C_1; {}^{\#}_{(2)}C_2; {}^{\#}_{(3)}C_1; {}^{\#}_{(3)}C_2$	J-aberration	α	Orders M, J
6	1	1	63	1	13;13;15;15;;	0 0 0 0 0 0	6 1 15 6 0	1 1
6	1	1	31	1	13;13;15;15;;	0 0 0 0 0 0	6 1 15 6 0	2 1
6	1	1	31	2	13;13;15;15;;	0 0 0 0 0 0	6 1 15 6 0	3 1
6	1	1	15	1	13;13;15;15;;	0 0 0 0 0 0	6 1 15 6 0	4 1
6	1	1	15	3	13;13;15;15;;	0 0 0 0 0 0	6 1 15 6 0	5 1
5	2	1	63	1 2	17;17,0,4;10;10,0,6;1;1	0 0 0 0 0 0	5 2 10 10 1	1 1
5	2	1	31	1 2	17;17,0,4;10;10,0,6;1;1	0 0 0 0 0 0	5 2 10 10 1	2 1
5	2	1	31	2 3	17;17,0,4;10;10,0,6;1;1	0 0 0 0 0 0	5 2 10 10 1	3 1
5	2	1	15	1 2	17;17,0,4;10;10,0,6;1;1	0 0 0 0 0 0	5 2 10 10 1	4 1
5	2	1	15	1 3	17;17,0,4;10;10,0,6;1;1	0 0 0 0 0 0	5 2 10 10 1	5 1
5	2	1	15	3 4	17;17,0,4;10;10,0,6;1;1	0 0 0 0 0 0	5 2 10 10 1	6 1
4	3	1	63	1 2 3	19;19,0,4;6;6,0,6;3;3	0 0 0 0 0 0	4 3 6 12 3	1 1
4	3	1	31	1 2 3	19;19,0,4;6;6,0,6;3;3	0 0 0 0 0 0	4 3 6 12 3	2 1
4	3	1	31	2 3 4	19;19,0,4;6;6,0,6;3;3	0 0 0 0 0 0	4 3 6 12 3	3 1
4	3	1	15	1 2 3	19;19,0,4;6;6,0,6;3;3	0 0 0 0 0 0	4 3 6 12 3	4 1
4	3	1	15	3 4 5	19;19,0,4;6;6,0,6;3;3	0 0 0 0 0 0	4 3 6 12 3	5 1
4	3	1	15	1 3 4	19;19,0,4;6;6,0,6;3;3	0 0 0 0 0 0	4 3 6 12 3	6 1
7	1	2	60 15	5	15;15;21;21;;	0 0 0 0 0 0	7 1 21 7 0	1 1
7	1	2	60 15	1	15;15;21;21;;	0 0 0 0 0 0	7 1 21 7 0	1 1
7	1	2	60 15	3	15;15;21;21;;	0 0 0 0 0 0	7 1 21 7 0	3 1
6	2	2	60 15	1 2	20;20;15;15;1;1	0 0 0 0 0 0	6 2 15 12 1	1 1
6	2	2	60 15	1 5	20;20;15;15;1;1	0 0 0 0 0 0	6 2 15 12 1	2 1
6	2	2	60 15	1 3	20;20;15;15;1;1	0 0 0 0 0 0	6 2 15 12 1	3 1
6	2	2	60 15	3 4	20;20;15;15;1;1	0 0 0 0 0 0	6 2 15 12 1	4 1
5	3	2	60 15	1 2 7	23;23;10;10;3;3	0 0 0 0 0 0	5 3 10 15 3	1 1
5	3	2	60 15	1 2 3	23;23;10;10;3;3	0 0 0 0 0 0	5 3 10 15 3	2 1
5	3	2	60 15	1 2 5	23;23;10;10;3;3	0 0 0 0 0 0	5 3 10 15 3	3 1
5	3	2	60 15	1 3 5	23;23;10;10;3;3	0 0 0 0 0 0	5 3 10 15 3	4 1
5	3	2	60 15	1 3 4	23;23;10;10;3;3	0 0 0 0 0 0	5 3 10 15 3	5 1
8	1	3	60 15 22	6	17;17;28;22;6;;	0 0 0 6 0 0	8 1 22 8 0	1 1
8	1	3	60 15 22	1	17;17;28;22;6;;	0 0 0 6 0 0	8 1 22 8 0	1 1
8	1	3	60 15 22	3	17;17;28;22;6;;	0 0 0 6 0 0	8 1 22 8 0	3 1
7	2	3	60 15 22	1 7	23;23;21;15;6;1;1	0 0 0 6 0 0	7 2 15 14 1	1 1
7	2	3	60 15 22	1 6	23;23;21;15;6;1;1	0 0 0 6 0 0	7 2 15 14 1	2 1
7	2	3	60 15 22	1 3	23;23;21;15;6;1;1	0 0 0 6 0 0	7 2 15 14 1	3 1
6	3	3	60 15 22	1 3 7	27;27;15;9;6;3;3	0 0 0 6 0 0	6 3 9 18 3	1 1
6	3	3	60 15 22	1 6 7	27;27;15;9;6;3;3	0 0 0 6 0 0	6 3 9 18 3	2 1
6	3	3	60 15 22	1 3 6	27;27;15;9;6;3;3	0 0 0 6 0 0	6 3 9 18 3	3 1
9	1	4	60 15 22 39	6	19;19;36;24;12;;	0 0 0 12 0 0	9 1 24 9 0	1 1
9	1	4	60 15 22 26	1	19;19;36;21,12,3;;	0 0 0 18 0 0	9 1 21 9 0	2 2
9	1	4	60 15 22 26	6	19;19;36;21,12,3;;	0 0 0 18 0 0	9 1 21 9 0	2 2
8	2	4	60 15 22 39	6 7	26;26;28;16,12;1;1	0 0 0 12 0 0	8 2 16 16 1	1 1
8	2	4	60 15 22 26	1 7	26;26;28;13,12,3;1;1	0 0 0 18 0 0	8 2 13 16 1	2 2
7	3	4	60 14 13 7	1 2 7	31;31;21;0^2,21;3;3	0 0 0 42 0 0	7 3 0 21 3	1 1
7	3	4	56 28 44 7	5 6 10	31;28,3;21;0^2,21;3;0,3	0 0 3 42 0 0	7 3 0 18 0	2 2
10	1	5	60 14 7 6 3	1	21;13,2,5,1;30;15;21,18,6;;	0 15 0 30 0 0	2 1 19 10 0	1 1
10	1	5	56 11 12 6 3	1	21;10,7,4;33,12;18,21,6;;	0 15 0 30 0 0	2 1 14 7 0	2 1
9	2	5	60 14 7 6 3	1 2	29;21,2,5,1;21,15;12,18,6;1;1	0 15 0 30 0 0	1 2 10 18 1	1 1
9	2	5	56 11 12 6 3	1 2	29;17,8,4;24,12;11,19,6;1;0,1	4 12 0 30 1 0	1 2 7 14 0	2 2
8	3	5	60 14 7 6 3	1 2 7	35;27,2,5,1;13,15;4,18,6;3;3	0 15 0 30 0 0	0 3 2 24 3	1 2
8	3	5	56 11 12 6 3	1 2 7	35;24,7,4;16,12;4,18,6;3;0,3	0 12 3 30 0 0	0 3 0 21 0	2 1

9 General Minimum Lower-Order Confounding Criterion for s^{n-m} Designs

Fractional factorial designs with factors at $s(\geqslant 3)$ levels are commonly used in practical experiments. These designs are particularly useful when investigating the curvature effects of quantitative factors or when dealing with qualitative factors that have s levels. Zhang and Mukerjee (2009a) extended the GMC criterion to s^{n-m} designs, where s is a prime or prime power. In another study, Zhang and Mukerjee (2009b) explored the application of the GMC criterion to blocked s^{n-m} designs. Subsequently, Li, Zhang, and Zhang (2013) examined the GMC criterion in the three-level designs, while Li, Zhao, and Zhang (2015) focused on s-level designs. Additionally, Li, Teng, Wu, and Zhang (2018) constructed GMC 3^{n-m} designs with $n = (N - 3^r)/2 + i$, where i ranges from 0 to 3, and $N = 3^{n-m}$. This chapter provides a summary of the key findings from these studies.

9.1 Introduction to s^{n-m} Designs

Similarly to the two-level designs, denote $q = n - m$ and $N = s^q$, where s is a prime or prime power. Let $H_1 = \{1\}$ and

$$H_r = \{H_{r-1}, r, (r, r^2, \cdots, r^{s-1})H_{r-1}\}, \tag{9.1}$$

for $r = 2, \cdots, q$. Here, $1, \cdots, q$ are independent columns and

$$1_{s^q} = (0, 1, \cdots, s-1, \cdots, 0, 1, \cdots, s-1)',$$

$$2_{s^q} = \underbrace{(0, \cdots, 0,}_{s} \underbrace{1, \cdots, 1,}_{s} \cdots, \underbrace{s-1, \cdots, s-1,}_{s} \cdots, \underbrace{s-1, \cdots, s-1)'}_{s},$$

$$\cdots$$

$$q_{s^q} = \underbrace{(0, \cdots, 0,}_{s^{q-1}} \underbrace{1, \cdots, 1,}_{s^{q-1}} \cdots, \underbrace{s-1, \cdots, s-1)'}_{s^{q-1}}.$$

The remaining columns are obtained by performing component-wise operations (modulus s or mod s) on these q independent columns. Let us consider 12 and 12^2 as examples:

$$(12)_{s^q} = 1_{s^q} + 2_{s^q} \pmod{s}, \quad (12^2)_{s^q} = 1_{s^q} + 2 \cdot 2_{s^q} \pmod{s}.$$

Then, H_q is the saturated design with N rows and $(s^q - 1)/(s - 1)$ columns. Each column in H_q has $s - 1$ degrees of freedom. For instance, in the case of $s = 3$ and $q = 3$, we have:

$$H_3 = \{1, 2, 12, 12^2, 3, 13, 13^2, 23, 23^2, 123, 123^2, 12^2 3, 12^2 3^2\}.$$

For convenience, we let the power of the first "letter" of each column label to be 1.

Similar to the 2^{n-m} designs defined in Section 1.2, we can consider an s^{n-m} design D as an n-projection of H_q, denoted as $D \subset H_q$. These designs are commonly referred to as regular s^{n-m} designs. Among the n columns, q of them are independent and generate the s^q runs. The remaining m columns are obtained through component-wise operations (mod s) applied to the q independent columns, and they determine m independent defining words. In the s^{n-m} design where $s \geqslant 3$, we use I to represent the column consisting of 0's.

To illustrate, let us consider a 3^{4-1} design with three independent factors/-columns represented by 1, 2, and 3. The fourth factor/column is defined as $4 = 123$, which can be expressed as follows:

$$4_{3^3} = 1_{3^3} + 2_{3^3} + 3_{3^3} \pmod{3}.$$

Note that in modulus 3 calculus, any multiple of 3 equals zero. Therefore, $4 = 123$ implies that

$$1_{3^3} + 2_{3^3} + 3_{3^3} + 2 \cdot 4_{3^3} \pmod{3} = 0_{3^3},$$

which leads to

$$I = 1234^2.$$

Here, 1234^2 is called a defining word.

Suppose that the s^{n-m} design is defined using m independent defining words v_i for $i = 1, \cdots, m$. Specifically, we have:

$$I = v_1 = \cdots = v_m.$$

The defining contrast subgroup is defined as the set that includes I and distinct words formed by $v_1^{a_1} \cdots v_m^{a_m}$, where a_i takes values from $\{0, \cdots, s-1\}$. Each term within the defining contrast subgroup, excluding I, is referred to as a defining word. It is important to note that within the defining contrast subgroup, the word v and its power

$$v^a \text{ for any } a \in \{2, \cdots, s-1\}$$

are considered to be the same. For instance, in the aforementioned 3^{4-1} design where $4 = 123$, we treat the word 1234^2 as identical to $(1234^2)^2 = 1^2 2^2 3^2 4^4 = 1^2 2^2 3^2 4$ (note that in modulus 3 calculus, any multiple of 3 equals zero). Therefore, the defining contrast subgroup of an s^{n-m} design consists of I and $(s^m - 1)/(s - 1)$ distinct defining words. It is worth noting that since the word v and its power v^a with $a \in \{2, \cdots, s-1\}$ are considered the same, we only include the words in the defining contrast subgroup where the power of the first letter is 1.

For example, in the 3^{4-1} design with $4 = 123$, the words 1234^2 and $1^2 2^2 3^2 4$ are considered the same. The defining contrast subgroup for this design contains only one distinct defining word, which is 1234^2. For convenience, we include 1234^2 only in the defining contrast subgroup as shown below:

$$I = 1234^2.$$

This is because the power of the first letter, "1", in "1234^2" is one.

Next, we discuss the aliasing relations of s^{n-m} design. Let $d_1, \cdots, d_i$ denote i factors in a s^{n-m} design. The ith-order factorial effect $d_1 \times \cdots \times d_i$ has $(s-1)^i$ degrees of freedom. It is represented by $(s-1)^{i-1}$ orthogonal ith-order component effects, each with $s-1$ degrees of freedom. These component effects are denoted as

$$d_1 d_2^{a_2} \cdots d_i^{a_i}, \quad a_2, \cdots, a_i \in \{1, \cdots, s-1\}.$$

For example, in a 3^{n-m} design, a main effect has only $1 = (3-1)^0$ component, which will be referred to as the main effect in the following. The two factor interaction 1×2 has $2 = (3-1)^{2-1}$ orthogonal component effects, which are denoted as 12 and 12^2. Similarly, the three factor interaction $1 \times 2 \times 3$ has $4 = (3-1)^{3-1}$ orthogonal component effects, denoted as 123, 123^2, 12^23, and 12^23^2.

Generally speaking, for an s^{n-m} design, there are a total of $(s^n-1)/(s-1)$ component effects. The defining contrast subgroup contains $(s^m-1)/(s-1)$ component effects as the defining words, denoted as $v_1, \cdots, v_{(s^m-1)/(s-1)}$. The remaining $(s^n-s^m)/(s-1)$ component effects are divided into $(s^q-1)/(s-1)$ alias sets, with each set containing s^m component effects that are aliased with each other. Let $1, \cdots, q$ be q independent factors that can be used to generate $(s^q-1)/(s-1)$ component effects. By multiplying these component effects with I and $v_i^{a_i}$ for $a_i \in \{1, \cdots, s-1\}$ and $i = 1, \cdots, (s^m-1)/(s-1)$, we obtain all alias sets. Each component effect corresponds to one alias set.

Consider the 3^{4-1} design mentioned above with the defining contrast subgroup $I = 1234^2$. We still use $1, 2, 3$ to denote the independent factors, which generates a total of $13 = (3^3-1)/(3-1)$ component effects:

$$1, 2, 12, 12^2, 3, 13, 13^2, 23, 23^2, 123, 123^2, 12^23, 12^23^2.$$

It is worth noting that the labels for these thirteen component effects are the same as those of H_3. By multiplying the component effect 12 to I, 1234^2, and $(1234^2)^2$, we obtain:

$$12 = 1^22^234^2 = 3^24^4.$$

Recall that in modulus 3 calculus, any multiple of 3 equals zero, and any positive power of a word is the same as that word. Then, we further have

$$12 = 123^24(= (1^22^234^2)^2) = 34^2(= (3^24^4)^2).$$

By applying the same techniques, we can derive all thirteen alias sets:

$$1 \quad = \quad 234^2 \quad = \quad 12^23^24,$$

$$2 \quad = \quad 134^2 \quad = \quad 12^234^2,$$

$$12 \quad = \quad 34^2 \quad = \quad 123^24,$$

$$12^2 \quad = \quad 13^24 \quad = \quad 23^24,$$

$$
\begin{aligned}
3 &= 124^2 &&= 123^2 4^2, \\
13 &= 24^2 &&= 12^2 34, \\
13^2 &= 12^2 4 &&= 23^2 4^2, \\
23 &= 14^2 &&= 12^2 3^2 4^2, \\
23^2 &= 12^2 4^2 &&= 13^2 4^2, \\
123 &= 4 &&= 1234, \\
123^2 &= 34 &&= 124, \\
12^2 3 &= 24 &&= 134, \\
12^2 3^2 &= 14 &&= 234.
\end{aligned}
\tag{9.2}
$$

9.2   GMC Criterion and Relationship with Other Criteria

In this section, we introduce the GMC criterion for the s^{n-m} design and explore its relationship with other criteria.

Let ${}^{\#}_{i}C^{(k)}_{j}$ be the number of ith-order component effects aliased with k jth-order component effects in an s^{n-m} design D. Based on the component effect hierarchy principle, i.e., (i) lower-order component effects are more likely to be important than higher-order ones, and (ii) component effects of the same order are equally likely to be important, Zhang and Mukerjee (2009a) introduced the *aliased component-number pattern* (ACNP) as follows:

$$
{}^{\#}C = ({}^{\#}_{1}C_2, {}^{\#}_{2}C_2, {}^{\#}_{1}C_3, {}^{\#}_{2}C_3, {}^{\#}_{3}C_2, {}^{\#}_{3}C_3, \cdots),
\tag{9.3}
$$

where

$$
{}^{\#}_{i}C_j = ({}^{\#}_{i}C^{(0)}_{j}, {}^{\#}_{i}C^{(1)}_{j}, \cdots, {}^{\#}_{i}C^{(K_j)}_{j}),
$$

and $K_j = \binom{n}{j}$. An s^{n-m} design D that maximizes (9.3) sequentially is called a GMC design. We would like to emphasize that Zhang and Mukerjee (2009a) originally defined $K_j = \binom{n}{j}(s-1)^{j-1}$. However, upon considering the orthogonality of $(s-1)^{j-1}$ component effects of jth-order factorial effect, it becomes evident that there are at most $\binom{n}{j}$ jth-order component effects in an alias set. As a result, in this chapter, we choose to define $K_j = \binom{n}{j}$ to align with this insight.

Similar to 2^{n-m} designs, the length of a defining word in an s^{n-m} design refers to the number of letters it contains. Let A_i be the number of defining words of length i in design D. The resolution of D is defined as the smallest i such that $A_i(D) > 0$. As usual, only designs of resolution III or higher are considered. The following theorem follows immediately from the definition of $_i^{\#}C_j^{(k)}$.

Theorem 9.1 *The resolution of an s^{n-m} design equals the smallest integer i such that $_i^{\#}C_0^{(1)} > 0$.*

Now, let us use resolution to classify s^{n-m} designs and examine the relationship between resolution and $_i^{\#}C_j$'s.

(i) *Resolution III designs.* For a resolution III design, it does not have any main effect that is aliased with another main effect. However, it does have main effects that are aliased with certain two-factor interaction components (2fic's), and the 2fic's themselves are also aliased with each other. Furthermore, we have

$$_0^{\#}C_1 = (1), \quad _1^{\#}C_0 = (n), \quad _1^{\#}C_1 = (n). \tag{9.4}$$

(ii) *Resolution IV designs.* For a resolution IV design, it does not have any main effect that is aliased with another main effect or any 2fic. However, it does have 2fic's that are aliased with other 2fic's. In addition to (9.4), the following results also hold:

$$_0^{\#}C_2 = (1), \quad _1^{\#}C_2 = (n). \tag{9.5}$$

(iii) *Resolution V designs.* For a resolution V design, it does not have any main effect or 2fic that is aliased with any other main effect or 2fic. In addition to (9.4) and (9.5), we further have

$$_2^{\#}C_2 = (\binom{n}{2}(s - 1)).$$

The above results (i), (ii) and (iii) establish the connection between resolution and ACNP. The following theorem extends these results, and its proof follows directly from the definition of resolution.

Theorem 9.2 *For an s^{n-m} design D of resolution $R \geqslant III$, if $i + j < R$, then*

$$_i^{\#}C_j^{(0)}(D) = \binom{n}{i}(s - 1)^{i-1} \text{ and } _i^{\#}C_j^{(k)}(D) = 0 \text{ for } k \geqslant 1.$$

The following corollary can be directly obtained from Theorem 9.2, highlighting the relationship between GMC designs and maximum resolution designs.

Corollary 9.3   *A GMC s^{n-m} design must have maximum resolution among all s^{n-m} designs.*

Note that for an s^{n-m} design D with resolution at least *III*, we have $A_1(D) = A_2(D) = 0$. When comparing two designs, D_1 and D_2, D_1 is said to have less aberration than D_2 if $A_i(D_1) = A_i(D_2)$ for $i = 3, \cdots, j-1$ and $A_j(D_1) < A_j(D_2)$. A design D is said to *have MA* if no other design has less aberration than D.

According to the definition of the MA criterion, an MA design sequentially minimizes the WLP given by:

$$W = (A_3, A_4, \cdots, A_n).$$

Li, Zhang, and Zhang (2013) and Li, Zhao, and Zhang (2015) investigated the relationship between the ACNP and WLP of s^{n-m} designs. The following results can be derived directly from the definitions of A_i and ${}_i^{\#}C_j^{(k)}$.

Theorem 9.4   *For an s^{n-m} design D with resolution at least III,*

$$A_i = {}_i^{\#}C_0^{(1)} \quad or \quad A_i = \binom{n}{i}(s-1)^{i-1} - {}_i^{\#}C_0^{(0)} \quad for \quad i = 1, 2, \cdots, n.$$

Part (c) of Theorem 2.5 revealed an exact expression of the average minimum lower-order confounding property of two-level MA designs. The following theorem generalizes this property to s-level designs.

Theorem 9.5   *For any s^{n-m} design D with resolution at least III, it has*

(a) $A_3 = \frac{1}{3} \sum_{k=1}^{K_2} k\, {}_1^{\#}C_2^{(k)}$, *and*

(b) $A_4 = \frac{1}{6} \sum_{k=1}^{K_2} k\, {}_2^{\#}C_2^{(k)}$ *when $A_3 = 0$.*

Proof.   Denote the n factors of D as $d_1, \cdots, d_n$.

(a) From each defining word of length three, say $d_1 d_2 d_3$, we can identify three 2fic's $d_1 d_2$, $d_1 d_3$, and $d_2 d_3$, which are aliased with the main effects d_3, d_2, d_1, respectively. By the definition of ${}_1^{\#}C_2^{(k)}$, $\sum_{k=1}^{K_2} k\, {}_1^{\#}C_2^{(k)}$ equals the number of 2fic's aliased with main effects. Therefore, we have $3A_3 = \sum_{k=1}^{K_2} k\, {}_1^{\#}C_2^{(k)}$, which leads to (a).

(b) Each defining word of length four, say $d_1 d_2 d_3 d_4$, includes six pairs of components, and each pair is aliased with one another. Specifically,

$$d_1 d_2 = d_3^{s-1} d_4^{s-1}, \quad d_1 d_3 = d_2^{s-1} d_4^{s-1}, \quad d_2 d_3 = d_1^{s-1} d_4^{s-1}.$$

By the definition of ${}^{\#}_2C_2^{(k)}$, $\sum_{k=1}^{K_2} k {}^{\#}_2C_2^{(k)}$ equals the number of pairs of 2fic's aliased with each other. Therefore, we have $\sum_{k=1}^{K_2} k {}^{\#}_2C_2^{(k)} = 6A_4$. Consequently, (b) follows immediately. □

Theorem 9.5 shows that, for an s-level design, A_3 reflects the average of the confounding severity between main effects and 2fic's. When $A_3 = 0$, A_4 reflects to the average severity of confounding of 2fic's.

A main effect is called clear if it is not aliased with any other main effect or any 2fic. A two-factor interaction has $s - 1$ orthogonal 2fic's. A 2fic is called clear if it is not aliased with any main effect or any other 2fic. A two-factor interaction is called clear if all of its 2fic's are clear. Ai and Zhang (2004b) studied the conditions of an s^{n-m} design that contains clear two-factor interactions. Let C_1 be the number of clear main effects, and CC be the number of clear 2fic's. The following result directly follows from the definitions.

Theorem 9.6 *For any s^{n-m} design D with resolution III or higher, we have*

$$C_1 = {}^{\#}_1C_2^{(0)}, \quad CC = {}^{\#}_2C_2^{(0)} - {}^{\#}_1C_2^{(1)}.$$

As discussed in Section 9.1, an s^{n-m} design D has $(s^{n-m} - 1)/(s-1)$ alias sets, and there are n alias sets, each containing one main effect. Let $f = (s^{n-m} - 1)/(s - 1) - n$ denote the number of the remaining alias sets in D. If $f = 0$, there is only one choice for D, namely, the saturated design. To avoid trivialities, we assume that $f \geqslant 1$ hereafter. Let $m_1(D), \cdots, m_f(D)$ be the number of 2fic's in the f alias sets that are not aliased with main effects, and $E_r(D)$ denote the number of models containing all the main effects and r 2fic's that can be estimated by the design D, where $1 \leqslant r \leqslant \binom{n}{2}(s-1)$. A design that maximizes $E_r(D)$ for all r is said to have maximum estimation capacity (MEC).

Lemma 9.7 *For a regular s^{n-m} design D, any alias set of D contains at most* $\min\{n(n-1)/2, s^m\}$ *2fic's.*

Proof. Note that in an s^{n-m} design, each alias set contains s^m components. Therefore, there are at most s^m 2fic's in each alias set. On the other hand, any two-factor interaction $d_1 \times d_2$ can be split into $s - 1$ orthogonal 2fic's. Due to orthogonality of these component effects, an alias set contains at most one of the $s - 1$ component effects. Therefore, there are at most $n(n-1)/2$ 2fic's in each alias set. Thus, the result follows immediately.   □

Based on Lemma 9.7, all the alias sets containing 2fic's but none of the main effects can be partitioned into $l = \min\{n(n-1)/2, s^m\}$ classes. The ith class, denoted by $\mathcal{C}_i$, consists of the alias sets that contain i 2fic's, where $i = 1, 2, \cdots, l$. Recall that for a set $\mathcal{C}$, its cardinality is denoted as $|\mathcal{C}|$.

Lemma 9.8   *For* $i = 1, 2, \cdots, l$,

$$|\mathcal{C}_i| = {}^{\#}_2 C_2^{(i-1)}/i - {}^{\#}_1 C_2^{(i)}.$$

Proof.   For an s^{n-m} design D, let us consider the total number of 2fic's contained in the alias sets, each of which has i 2fic's.

By the definition of ${}^{\#}_i C_j^{(k)}$, there are a total of ${}^{\#}_2 C_2^{(i-1)}$ 2fic's in these alias sets. Note that these alias sets of D can be divided into two classes: (i) the first class consists of the alias sets that contain no main effect, i.e. $\mathcal{C}_i$, and (ii) the second class consists of the alias sets that contain main effects. In the first class, there are a total of $i|\mathcal{C}_i|$ 2fic's, and in the second class, there are $i {}^{\#}_1 C_2^{(i)}$ 2fic's. Thus, we have ${}^{\#}_2 C_2^{(i-1)} = i(|\mathcal{C}_i| + {}^{\#}_1 C_2^{(i)})$ for $i = 1, 2, \cdots, l$. Hence, the result follows immediately.   □

Any model involving all the main effects and r 2fic's is estimable in D if and only if the r 2fic's are contained in different alias sets of the f ones that do not contain any main effect. Therefore, $E_r(D)$ is equal to the number of ways of choosing r 2fic's from these f alias sets such that no two of them belong to the same alias set.

By applying Lemmas 9.7 and 9.8, we can get the following result.

Theorem 9.9   *For an* s^{n-m} *design* D,

$$E_r(D) = \begin{cases} \displaystyle\sum_{r_1+\cdots+r_l=r} \prod_{i=1}^{l} i^{r_i}\binom{|\mathcal{C}_i|}{r_i}, & \text{if } r \leqslant f, \\ 0, & \text{otherwise}, \end{cases}$$

where $0 \leqslant r_i \leqslant |\mathcal{C}_i|$ *and* $|\mathcal{C}_i| = {}^{\#}_2 C_2^{(i-1)}/i - {}^{\#}_1 C_2^{(i)}$ *for* $i = 1, 2, \cdots, l$.

Proof.   If $r > f$, it is evident that $E_r(D) = 0$.

Next, we consider the case $0 \leqslant r \leqslant f$. By the definitions of $\mathcal{C}_i$ and $E_r(D)$, $E_r(D)$ equals the number of ways of choosing r 2fic's from the classes $\{\mathcal{C}_i, i = 1, 2, \cdots, l\}$

such that no two of them are chosen from the same alias set.

For a given r, let us suppose that there are r_i 2fic's chosen from $\mathcal{C}_i$, where $0 \leqslant r_i \leqslant |\mathcal{C}_i|$ $(i = 1, 2, \cdots, l)$ and $r_1 + r_2 + \cdots + r_l = r$. For a given i, since each alias set of $\mathcal{C}_i$ contains i 2fic's, there are $i^{r_i} \binom{|\mathcal{C}_i|}{r_i}$ ways to choose r_i 2fic's from $\mathcal{C}_i$. Thus, for the given $r_1, r_2, \cdots, r_l$, there are a total of $\prod_{i=1}^{l} i^{r_i} \binom{|\mathcal{C}_i|}{r_i}$ methods to choose 2fic's from $\mathcal{C}_i$ $(i = 1, 2, \cdots, l)$. Note that $E_r(D)$ is the sum over r_i under the conditions $0 \leqslant r_i \leqslant |\mathcal{C}_i|$ and $r_1 + r_2 + \cdots + r_l = r$. Then the result follows directly. $\qquad\square$

Cheng and Mukerjee (1998) pointed out that a design D will behave well under the MEC criterion if $\sum_{i=1}^{f} m_i(D)$ is large and $m_1(D), \cdots, m_f(D)$ are close to one another. In other words, a design D does well under the MEC criterion if $\sum_{i=1}^{f} m_i(D)$ is large and $\sum_{i=1}^{f} \{m_i(D)\}^2$ is small. The following theorem presents another approach for selecting better designs based on the MEC criterion.

Theorem 9.10 *For any s^{n-m} design D and $l = \min\{n(n-1)/2, s^m\}$, we have*

(a) $\sum_{i=1}^{f} m_i(D) = \sum_{i=1}^{l} (\#_2 C_2^{(i-1)} - i\#_1 C_2^{(i)});$

(b) $\sum_{i=1}^{f} \{m_i(D)\}^2 = \sum_{i=1}^{l} i(\#_2 C_2^{(i-1)} - i\#_1 C_2^{(i)}).$

Proof. (a) By the definitions of $m_i(D)$ and $\mathcal{C}_i$, both $\sum_{i=1}^{f} m_i(D)$ and $\sum_{i=1}^{l} i|\mathcal{C}_i|$ represent the number of 2fic's that are not aliased with main effects. Therefore

$$\sum_{i=1}^{f} m_i(D) = \sum_{i=1}^{l} i|\mathcal{C}_i|.$$

By Lemma 9.7, we have

$$\sum_{i=1}^{l} i|\mathcal{C}_i| = \sum_{i=1}^{l} i(\#_2 C_2^{(i-1)}/i - \#_1 C_2^{(i)}) = \sum_{i=1}^{l} (\#_2 C_2^{(i-1)} - i\#_1 C_2^{(i)}).$$

Then (a) follows immediately.

(b) Again, by the definitions of $m_i(D)$ and $\mathcal{C}_i$, we can directly obtain that

$$\sum_{i=1}^{f} \{m_i(D)\}^2 = \sum_{i=1}^{l} i^2 |\mathcal{C}_i|.$$

Also, by Lemma 9.7, we have

$$\sum_{i=1}^{l} i^2 |\mathcal{C}_i| = \sum_{i=1}^{l} i^2 (\#_2 C_2^{(i-1)}/i - \#_1 C_2^{(i)}) = \sum_{i=1}^{l} i(\#_2 C_2^{(i-1)} - i\#_1 C_2^{(i)}).$$

This proves (b). $\qquad\square$

Theorem 9.10 demonstrates that a design D performs well under the MEC criterion if it maximizes

$$\sum_{i=1}^{l}({}_{2}^{\#}C_{2}^{(i-1)} - i{}_{1}^{\#}C_{2}^{(i)})$$

and then minimizes

$$\sum_{i=1}^{l} i({}_{2}^{\#}C_{2}^{(i-1)} - i{}_{1}^{\#}C_{2}^{(i)}).$$

The ACNP of a design may appear complex. However, from the perspective of practical applications, it is often sufficient to consider only the anterior parts ${}_{1}^{\#}C_{2}$ and ${}_{2}^{\#}C_{2}$ of the ACNP rather than the entire pattern. Therefore, the ACNP is not as complicated as it may initially appear.

Example 9.11 (A seat-belt experiment, Wu and Hamada, 2009)

Consider an experiment to study the effect of four factors on the pull strength of truck seat belts following a crimping operation that joins an anchor and cable. The four factors under study are hydraulic pressure of the crimping machine (A), die flat middle setting (B), length of crimp (C), and anchor lot (D). Each of these factors was examined at three levels.

Usually, it is more efficient to use a one-third of the 3^4 factorial, that is, a 3^{4-1} design. There exist two non-isomorphic 3^{4-1} designs, denoted as D_1 and D_2 respectively. These designs are determined by the defining words $v_1 = 1234^2$ and $v_2 = 124^2$ (Mukerjee and Wu, 2006). The alias sets of D_1 are given in (9.2). By the definition of ${}_{i}^{\#}C_j$, we can get that, for example,

$${}_{1}^{\#}C_2(D_1) = (4) \text{ and } {}_{2}^{\#}C_2(D_1) = (6, 6). \tag{9.6}$$

Using the same method, we can calculate ${}_{1}^{\#}C_2(D_2) = (1, 3)$ and ${}_{2}^{\#}C_2(D_2) = (9, 0, 3)$. According to the GMC criterion, the design D_1 is the GMC design.

By Theorem 9.5 and (9.6), we have

$$A_3(D_1) = \frac{1}{3}\sum_{k=1}^{K_2} k{}_{1}^{\#}C_2^{(k)}(D_1) = 0 \text{ and } A_4(D_1) = \frac{1}{6}\sum_{k=1}^{K_2} k{}_{2}^{\#}C_2^{(k)}(D_1) = 1.$$

This result demonstrates that the WLP is a function of the ACNP.

To compare the two designs D_1 and D_2 under the MEC criterion, we need to calculate $E_r(D_1)$ and $E_r(D_2)$ for all values of r. In this case, we have $n = 4$ and

$f = 9$. By Lemma 9.8, we obtain

$$|\mathcal{C}_1(D_1)| = {}^{\#}_2C_2^{(0)}(D_1) - {}^{\#}_1C_2^{(1)}(D_1) = 6,$$

$$|\mathcal{C}_2(D_1)| = {}^{\#}_2C_2^{(1)}(D_1)/2 - {}^{\#}_1C_2^{(2)}(D_1) = 3,$$

and $|\mathcal{C}_i(D_1)| = 0$ for $i \geqslant 3$. Applying Theorem 9.9, we can calculate $E_r(D_1)$ for different values of r as follows:

$$E_r(D_1) = \begin{cases} \sum\limits_{r_1+r_2=r} 2^{r_2} \binom{6}{r_1}\binom{3}{r_2}, & if \ r \leqslant 9, \\ 0, & \text{otherwise,} \end{cases} \tag{9.7}$$

where $0 \leqslant r_i \leqslant |\mathcal{C}_i(D_1)|$ for $i = 1, 2$.

Similarly, for the design D_2, we can obtain that $|\mathcal{C}_1(D_2)| = 6$, $|\mathcal{C}_3(D_2)| = 1$, and $|\mathcal{C}_i(D_2)| = 0$ for other i's. Then, we can calculate $E_r(D_2)$ for different values of r as follows:

$$E_r(D_2) = \begin{cases} \sum\limits_{r_1+r_3=r} 3^{r_3} \binom{6}{r_1}\binom{1}{r_3}, & if \ r \leqslant 9, \\ 0, & \text{otherwise.} \end{cases} \tag{9.8}$$

By (9.7) and (9.8), we can calculate the values of $E_r(D_1)$ and $E_r(D_2)$ for all relevant values of r. The results are listed in Table 9.1 below. Since $E_r(D_1) > E_r(D_2)$ for all r, we can conclude that design D_1 outperforms design D_2 under the MEC criterion.   □

Table 9.1   Comparison of $E_r(D_i)$ of the designs D_i $(i = 1, 2)$ for $r = 1, 2, \cdots, 9$

r	1	2	3	4	5	6	7	8	9
$E_r(D_1)$	12	63	190	363	456	377	198	60	8
$E_r(D_2)$	9	33	65	75	51	19	3	0	0

Based on the discussion above, both the WLP and $E_r(D)$ are functions of the ACNP, which indicates that the ACNP contains more information about a design D compared to the WLP and $E_r(D)$. In the case of the seat-belt experiment mentioned earlier, since D_1 outperforms D_2 under the MA, MEC, and GMC criteria, it is advisable to choose D_1 for conducting the experiment. The factors A, B, C, and D should be allocated to the four columns of D_1, respectively.

9.3 GMC s^{n-m} Designs Using Complementary Designs

This section provides a brief overview of the construction of GMC s^{n-m} designs, focusing on key findings. For more detailed information, please refer to Zhang and Mukerjee (2009a), Li, Zhang, and Zhang (2013), and Li, Teng, Wu, and Zhang (2018).

Ai and Zhang (2004b) obtained the confounding information among columns in H_q as follows.

Lemma 9.12 *For a given γ corresponding to a column in H_q, the remaining $(s^q - 1)/(s-1) - 1$ columns can be classified into $(s^{q-1} - 1)/(s-1)$ disjoint sets*

$$\{d_i, \gamma d_i, \gamma d_i^2, \cdots, \gamma d_i^{s-2}, \gamma d_i^{s-1}\}, \quad i = 1, 2, \cdots, (s^{q-1} - 1)/(s-1),$$

where $d_i \in H_q$. Each set consists of s columns such that among the 2fic's of any two columns in the same set, there always exists one which is aliased with γ. Furthermore, there are $(s^q - s)/2$ 2fic's aliased with γ.

Consider an s^{n-m} design $D \subset H_q$. Let $\bar{D} = H_q \backslash D$ with a cardinality of $f = (s^q - 1)/(s-1) - n$, which is referred to as the *complementary design* of D. Zhang and Mukerjee (2009a) developed a theory for the GMC criterion using the complementary design, which is particularly useful when f is small. They obtained the confounding relationship between D and $\bar{D}$. In this section, we will extend their results and present an alternative method to demonstrate the confounding information between D and $\bar{D}$.

Let $B_2(D, \gamma)$ be the number of 2fc's in D that are aliased with γ. This definition extends the one given in (3.1) from two-level designs to s-level designs. The following lemma generalizes the results in Part (a) of Theorem 3.1 from $s = 2$ to arbitrary s.

Lemma 9.13 *Let $D \subset H_q$ be an s^{n-m} design. Then*

$$B_2(D, \gamma) = \begin{cases} B_2(\bar{D}, \gamma) + n_1, & \text{if } \gamma \in D, \\ B_2(\bar{D}, \gamma) + n_2, & \text{if } \gamma \in \bar{D}, \end{cases}$$

where

$$n_1 = (s-1)(n-1) - (s^q - s)/2, \quad n_2 = (s-1)n - (s^q - s)/2. \tag{9.9}$$

Proof.   Based on Lemma 9.12, the set H_q can be partitioned into $(s^{q-1} - 1)/(s - 1)$ disjoint sets $\{d_i, \gamma d_i, \gamma d_i^2, \cdots, \gamma d_i^{s-1}\}$ for a fixed factor γ. Let a_j be the number of sets that contain exactly j columns from design D, where $j = 1, 2, \cdots, s$. For $j > 1$, among the j columns, there are $\binom{j}{2}$ pairs of columns whose products are aliased with γ. We can calculate $B_2(D, \gamma)$ as follows:

$$B_2(D, \gamma) = \sum_{j=2}^{s} \binom{j}{2} a_j.$$

Furthermore, we have the relationship:

$$B_2(D, \gamma) + B_2(\bar{D}, \gamma) + \sum_{j=1}^{s} j(s - j)a_j = (s^q - s)/2.$$

Moreover,

$$\sum_{j=1}^{s} j(s - j)a_j = \sum_{j=1}^{s} j(s - 1)a_j - \sum_{j=1}^{s} j(j - 1)a_j = (s - 1)\sum_{j=1}^{s} ja_j - 2B_2(D, \gamma).$$

If $\gamma \in D$, then $\sum_{j=1}^{s} ja_j = n - 1$. We have

$$B_2(D, \gamma) = B_2(\bar{D}, \gamma) + (s - 1)(n - 1) - (s^q - s)/2.$$

If $\gamma \in \bar{D}$, then $\sum_{j=1}^{s} ja_j = n$. We have

$$B_2(D, \gamma) = B_2(\bar{D}, \gamma) + (s - 1)n - (s^q - s)/2.$$

This completes the proof.   □

Let

$$\bar{g}(\bar{D}) = |\{\gamma : \gamma \in D, B_2(\bar{D}, \gamma) > 0\}|,$$

which generalizes the definition of $\bar{g}(\cdot)$ in (3.2) from the two-level design to a general s-level design. Furthermore, let

$$\bar{g}_k(\bar{D}) = |\{\gamma : \gamma \in D, B_2(\bar{D}, \gamma) = k\}|, \quad k = 0, 1, 2, \cdots, K_2.$$

Recall that $K_2 = \binom{n}{2}$. Clearly,

$$\bar{g}(\bar{D}) = \sum_{k=1}^{K_2} \bar{g}_k(\bar{D}),$$

which reflects the confounding relation among factors of D and 2fic's of $\bar{D}$.

As demonstrated in Theorem 3.1, minimizing $\bar{g}(\bar{D})$ is an important step in searching for a GMC design. Hereafter, we call a subset of H_q closed if the 2fic of any two columns is still within the subset. For example, H_r is a closed subset of H_q.

Lemma 9.14   *Suppose $\bar{D}$ is contained in a closed subset of $(s^r-1)/(s-1)$ columns, and $(s^r - s)/(2(s-1)) < f \leqslant (s^r - 1)/(s-1)$. Then, for $r < q$,*

$$\bar{g}(\bar{D}) = (s^r - 1)/(s-1) - f.$$

Proof.   Without loss of generality, suppose $\bar{D} \subset H_r$. Denote $D = (H_q \backslash H_r) \cup D_1$, where $D_1 \subset H_r$. Clearly, we have

$$
\begin{aligned}
\bar{g}(\bar{D}) &= |\{\gamma : \gamma \in H_q \backslash H_r, B_2(\bar{D}, \gamma) > 0\}| + |\{\gamma : \gamma \in D_1, B_2(\bar{D}, \gamma) > 0\}| \\
&= |\{\gamma : \gamma \in D_1, B_2(\bar{D}, \gamma) > 0\}|.
\end{aligned}
$$

Since $D_1 \cup \bar{D} = H_r$, according to Lemma 9.13 and given $\gamma \in D_1$, we have

$$B_2(\bar{D}, \gamma) = B_2(D_1, \gamma) + (s-1)f - (s^r - s)/2 > 0.$$

This implies that

$$\bar{g}(\bar{D}) = |D_1| = (s^r - 1)/(s-1) - f.$$

Thus, the proof is completed.   □

According to Lemma 9.13, we have

$$\#_1 C_2^{(k)}(D) = |\{\gamma : \gamma \in D, (s-1)(n-f-1)/2 + B_2(\bar{D}, \gamma) = k\}|.$$

If the complementary design $\bar{D}$ with $(s^r - s)/(2(s-1)) < f \leqslant (s^r - 1)/(s-1)$ is contained in a closed subset with $(s^r - 1)/(s-1)$ columns, then there are $n - ((s^r - 1)/(s-1) - f)$ 2fic's aliased with $\gamma \in D$ such that $B_2(\bar{D}, \gamma) = 0$. Hence, the following result immediately follows.

Theorem 9.15   *Suppose $\bar{D}$ is contained in a closed subset of $(s^r-1)/(s-1)$ columns and $(s^r - s)/(2(s-1)) < f \leqslant (s^r - 1)/(s-1)$. Then*

(a) $\#_1 C_2^{(n_1)}(D) = n - ((s^r - 1)/(s-1) - f)$,

(b) $\#_1 C_2^{(k)}(D) = 0$, $0 \leqslant k < n_1$,

where $n_1 = (s-1)(n-1) - (s^q - s)/2$.

In general, we establish the confounding relationship between D and $\bar{D}$.

Theorem 9.16   *Let $D \subset H_q$ be an s^{n-m} design. Then*

(a) $\#_1 C_2^{(k)}(D) = \begin{cases} 0, & \text{if } k < n_1, \\[2mm] \bar{g}_{k-n_1}(\bar{D}), & \text{if } k \geqslant n_1; \end{cases}$

$$\text{(b) } {}_2^{\#}C_2^{(k)}(D) = \begin{cases} 0, & \text{if } k < n_1 - 1, \\ (k+1)\bar{g}_{k+1-n_1}(\bar{D}), & \text{if } n_1 - 1 \leqslant k < n_2 - 1, \\ (k+1)(\bar{g}_{k+1-n_1}(\bar{D}) + {}_1^{\#}C_2^{(k+1-n_2)}(\bar{D})), & \text{if } k \geqslant n_2 - 1, \end{cases}$$

where

$$n_1 = (s-1)(n-1) - (s^q - s)/2, \quad n_2 = (s-1)n - (s^q - s)/2.$$

Proof.   For (a), it is worth noting that

$$\tfrac{\#}{1}C_2^{(k)}(D) = |\{\gamma : \gamma \in D, B_2(D, \gamma) = k\}|.$$

According to Lemma 9.13, we have

$$\tfrac{\#}{1}C_2^{(k)}(D) = |\{\gamma : \gamma \in D, B_2(\bar{D}, \gamma) = k - n_1\}|.$$

If $k < n_1$, then ${}_1^{\#}C_2^{(k)}(D) = 0$. If $k \geqslant n_1$, then ${}_1^{\#}C_2^{(k)}(D) = \bar{g}_{k-n_1}(\bar{D})$.

For (b), using Lemma 9.13 and

$$\tfrac{\#}{2}C_2^{(k)}(D) = (k+1)|\{\gamma : \gamma \in H_q, B_2(D, \gamma) = k + 1\}|,$$

we obtain the following:

$$\begin{aligned} {}_2^{\#}C_2^{(k)}(D) &= (k+1)(|\{\gamma : \gamma \in D, B_2(D, \gamma) = k + 1\}| \\ &\quad + |\{\gamma : \gamma \in \bar{D}, B_2(D, \gamma) = k + 1\}|) \\ &= (k+1)(|\{\gamma : \gamma \in D, B_2(\bar{D}, \gamma) = k + 1 - n_1\}| \\ &\quad + |\{\gamma : \gamma \in \bar{D}, B_2(\bar{D}, \gamma) = k + 1 - n_2\}|). \end{aligned}$$

If $k < n_1 - 1$, we have ${}_2^{\#}C_2^{(k)}(D) = 0$. If $n_1 - 1 \leqslant k < n_2 - 1$, we obtain

$$\begin{aligned} {}_2^{\#}C_2^{(k)}(D) &= (k+1)|\{\gamma : \gamma \in D, B_2(\bar{D}, \gamma) = k + 1 - n_1\}| \\ &= (k+1)\bar{g}_{k+1-n_1}(\bar{D}). \end{aligned}$$

If $k \geqslant n_2 - 1$, we have

$$\tfrac{\#}{2}C_2^{(k)}(D) = (k+1)(\bar{g}_{k+1-n_1}(\bar{D}) + {}_1^{\#}C_2^{(k+1-n_2)}(\bar{D})).$$

Thus, the proof is completed.   □

Let

$$G(D) = (\bar{g}_0(\bar{D}), \bar{g}_1(\bar{D}), \cdots, \bar{g}_{K_2}(\bar{D})).$$

Based on Theorem 9.16, we have

$$\tfrac{\#}{1}C_2(D) = ({}_1^{\#}C_2^{(0)}, {}_1^{\#}C_2^{(1)}, \cdots, {}_1^{\#}C_2^{(K_2)}) = (0^{n_1}, G(D)). \tag{9.10}$$

By (9.10), D maximizes ${}_1^{\#}C_2(D)$ if and only if it maximizes the sequence $G(D)$. Based on Part (b) of Theorem 9.16, D maximizes ${}_2^{\#}C_2(D)$ if and only if it maximizs the sequence $(G(D), {}_1^{\#}C_2(\bar{D}))$. Therefore, we obtain the following result.

Theorem 9.17   *Let $D \subset H_q$ be an s^{n-m} design. Then, the design D has GMC if and only if it is the unique design that maximizes*

$$(G(D), {}_1^{\#}C_2(\bar{D})).$$

Example 9.18   There are only two non-isomorphic 3^{10-7} designs, denoted as D_1 and D_2, corresponding to the complementary designs $\bar{D}_1 = H_3 \backslash D_1$ and $\bar{D}_2 = H_3 \backslash D_2$, respectively. These designs are:

$$D_1 = \{1, 2, 12, 12^2, 3, 13, 23, 23^2, 123, 123^2\}, \qquad \bar{D}_1 = \{13^2, 12^2 3, 12^2 3^2\},$$

$$D_2 = \{1, 2, 12, 12^2, 3, 13, 23^2, 123, 123^2, 12^2 3^2\}, \quad \bar{D}_2 = \{13^2, 23, 12^2 3\}.$$

According to Theorem 9.17, we begin by comparing the elements of the vector

$$G(D_i) = (\bar{g}_0(\bar{D}_i), \bar{g}_1(\bar{D}_i), \cdots, \bar{g}_{K_2}(\bar{D}_i)), \ i = 1, 2.$$

For the complementary design $\bar{D}_1$, we observe:

$$13^2 \cdot 12^2 3 = 12, \quad 13^2 \cdot 1^2 23^2 = 23, \quad 13^2 \cdot 12^2 3^2 = 123^2,$$

$$13^2 \cdot 1^2 23 = 2, \quad 12^2 3 \cdot 12^2 3^2 = 12^2, \quad 12^2 3 \cdot 1^2 23 = 3.$$

Therefore, $G(D_1) = (4, 6)$. Similarly, for $\bar{D}_2$, we have $G(D_2) = (7, 1, 1)$. Thus, the design D_1 corresponds to a GMC design.   □

Example 9.18 highlights the convenience of obtaining GMC designs by comparing the corresponding complementary designs, which typically consist of a smaller number of columns. Table 9.2 presents a summary of the complementary designs for GMC 3^{n-m} designs with $f \leqslant 13$. These results are from Zhang and Mukerjee (2009a).

9.4   B-GMC Criterion for Blocked s^{n-m} Designs

In this section, we extend the GMC criterion for blocked s^{n-m} designs, specifically focusing on the single block variable problem and the B-GMC criterion proposed by Zhang and Mukerjee (2009b).

Let $(D_t : D_b)$ denote an $s^{n-m} : s^r$ design, which is a regular s^{n-m} design with s^r

Table 9.2   The complementary designs $\bar{D}$ for GMC 3^{n-m} designs

f	$\bar{D}$
3	$\{1, 2, 12\}$
4	$\{1, 2, 12, 12^2\}$
5	$\{1, 2, 12, 12^2, 3\}$
6	$\{1, 2, 12, 12^2, 3, 13\}$
7	$\{1, 2, 12, 12^2, 3, 12^2 3, 12^2 3^2\}$
8	$\{1, 2, 12, 12^2, 3, 23^2, 12^2 3, 12^2 3^2\}$
9	$\{1, 2, 12^2, 3, 13^2, 23^2, 123^2, 12^2 3, 12^2 3^2\}$
10	$\{1, 2, 12, 12^2, 3, 13, 13^2, 23, 23^2, 123\}$
11	$\{1, 2, 12, 12^2, 3, 13, 13^2, 23, 23^2, 123, 123^2\}$
12	$\{1, 2, 12, 12^2, 3, 13, 13^2, 23, 23^2, 123, 123^2, 12^2 3^2\}$
13	$\{1, 2, 12, 12^2, 3, 13, 13^2, 23, 23^2, 123, 123^2, 12^2 3, 12^2 3^2\}$

blocks. In this design, D_t is an $s^q \times n$ matrix for treatments, where $D_t \subset H_q$; D_b is an $s^q \times (s^r - 1)/(s - 1)$ matrix for blocking, where $D_b \subset H_q$. We can define the $s^{n-m} : s^r$ design similar to the $2^{n-m} : 2^r$ designs discussed in Section 4.2. Specifically, out of the n factors in D_t, $q = n - m$ factors are independent, while the remaining m factors are determined by m treatment-defining words. Similarly, out of the $(s^r - 1)/(s - 1)$ columns in D_b, r columns are considered to be independent block factors. These block factors are also expressed by the q independent treatment columns and determine r independent block-defining words.

Following the procedure outlined in Section 9.1, the m treatment-defining words generate the treatment-defining contrast subgroup, which consists of $(s^m - 1)/(s - 1)$ treatment-defining words. Each treatment-defining word has a length, which refers to the number of letters it contains. Let A_{i0} be the number of treatment-defining words of length i in D_t, and let A_{i1} be the number of ith-order treatment component effects that are aliased with a block effect, where $1 \leqslant i \leqslant n$.

Following Section 4.2, we assume that all treatment component effects involving three or more factors are negligible, and that no treatment main effect is aliased with another treatment main effect or block effect. This implies that $A_{10} = A_{20} = A_{11} = 0$. We define ${}_1^\#C_2^{(k)}(D)$ as the number of main effects that are aliased with k 2fic's, and ${}_2^\#C_0(D) = K_2 - A_{21}$ as the number of 2fic's that are not aliased with the block effects. Among the ${}_2^\#C_0(D)$ component effects that might be estimated, we denote ${}_2^\#C_2^{(k)}(D)$ as the number of those that are aliased with k 2fic's. Furthermore, let

$$_i^{\#}C_j(D) = (_i^{\#}C_j^{(0)}(D), _i^{\#}C_j^{(1)}(D), \cdots, _i^{\#}C_j^{(K_j)}(D)).$$

We refer to

$$^{\#}C(D) = (_1^{\#}C_2(D), _2^{\#}C_0(D), _2^{\#}C_2(D)) \tag{9.11}$$

as the *aliased component-number pattern of blocked designs* (B-ACNP). A design D is said to have B-GMC if it maximizes the components of (9.11) sequentially.

As we illustrated in Section 9.3, the idea of complementary design is powerful for constructing the GMC s^{n-m} designs. This idea has also been applied to construct B-GMC designs by Zhang and Mukerjee (2009b).

Let $\tilde{D}_t = H_q \backslash (D_t \cup D_b)$ be the complement of D_t in $H_q \backslash D_b$, and let $\bar{D} = (\tilde{D}_t : D_b)$. Furthermore, let f be the number of columns in $\tilde{D}_t$, and $u = f + (s^r - 1)/(s-1)$. Using a similar method as in Section 9.3, Zhang and Mukerjee (2009b) established the relationships between the B-ACNPs of D and $\bar{D}$ and utilized them to construct some B-GMC $2^{n-m} : 2^r$ and $3^{n-m} : 3^r$ designs. The results of their constructions are summarized in Tables 9.3–9.5, where $D_b = H_r$. For more detailed information, we refer to Zhang and Mukerjee (2009b).

Table 9.3　B-GMC $2^{n-m} : 2^r$ designs for $u \leqslant 15$ with $D_b = H_r$

r	f	$\tilde{D}_t$
1	1	$\{2\}$
1	2	$\{2, 12\}$
1	3	$\{2, 3, 23\}$
1	4	$\{2, 12, 3, 23\}$
1	5	$\{2, 12, 3, 13, 23\}$
1	6	$\{2, 12, 3, 13, 23, 123\}$
1	7	$\{2, 3, 23, 4, 24, 34, 234\}$
1	8	$\{2, 3, 23, 4, 24, 34, 234, 12\}$
1	9	$\{2, 3, 23, 4, 24, 34, 234, 12, 13\}$
1	10	$\{2, 12, 3, 13, 23, 123, 4, 24, 34, 234\}$
1	11	$\{2, 3, 23, 4, 14, 24, 124, 34, 134, 234, 1234\}$
1	12	$\{2, 12, 3, 13, 23, 123, 4, 14, 24, 124, 134, 234\}$
1	13	$\{2, 12, 3, 13, 23, 123, 4, 14, 24, 124, 34, 134, 234\}$
1	14	$\{2, 12, 3, 13, 23, 123, 4, 14, 24, 124, 34, 134, 234, 1234\}$
2	1	$\{3\}$
2	2	$\{3, 13\}$
2	3	$\{3, 13, 23\}$
2	4	$\{3, 13, 23, 123\}$
2	5	$\{3, 13, 23, 123, 4\}$
2	6	$\{3, 13, 4, 14, 34, 134\}$
2	7	$\{3, 13, 23, 4, 14, 34, 134\}$
2	8	$\{3, 13, 23, 4, 14, 24, 34, 134\}$
2	9	$\{3, 13, 23, 4, 14, 24, 34, 134, 234\}$
2	10	$\{3, 13, 23, 123, 4, 14, 124, 34, 134, 234\}$
2	11	$\{3, 13, 23, 123, 4, 14, 24, 124, 34, 134, 234\}$
2	12	$\{3, 13, 23, 123, 4, 14, 24, 124, 34, 134, 234, 1234\}$

Table 9.3 (continued)

r	f	$\tilde{D}_t$
3	1	$\{4\}$
3	2	$\{4, 14\}$
3	3	$\{4, 14, 24\}$
3	4	$\{4, 14, 24, 34\}$
3	5	$\{4, 14, 24, 124, 34\}$
3	6	$\{4, 14, 24, 124, 134, 234\}$
3	7	$\{4, 14, 24, 124, 34, 134, 234\}$
3	8	$\{4, 14, 24, 124, 34, 134, 234, 1234\}$

Table 9.4   B-GMC 2^{n-m} : 2^4 designs for $f \leqslant 16$ with $D_b = H_4$

f	$\tilde{D}_t$
1	$\{5\}$
2	$\{5, 15\}$
3	$\{5, 15, 25\}$
4	$\{5, 15, 25, 35\}$
5	$\{5, 15, 25, 35, 1235\}$
6	$\{5, 15, 25, 125, 35, 135\}$
7	$\{5, 15, 25, 125, 35, 135, 235\}$
8	$\{5, 15, 25, 35, 1235, 45, 1245, 1345\}$
9	$\{5, 15, 25, 125, 35, 135, 45, 145, 2345\}$
10	$\{5, 15, 25, 125, 35, 135, 45, 245, 345, 12345\}$
11	$\{5, 15, 25, 125, 35, 135, 235, 45, 145, 245, 345\}$
12	$\{5, 15, 25, 125, 35, 135, 235, 1235, 45, 145, 245, 345\}$
13	$\{5, 15, 25, 125, 35, 135, 235, 1235, 45, 145, 245, 1245, 345\}$
14	$\{5, 15, 25, 125, 35, 135, 235, 1235, 45, 145, 245, 1245, 345, 1345\}$
15	$\{5, 15, 25, 125, 35, 135, 235, 1235, 45, 145, 245, 1245, 345, 1345, 2345\}$
16	$\{5, 15, 25, 125, 35, 135, 235, 1235, 45, 145, 245, 1245, 345, 1345, 2345, 12345\}$

Table 9.5   B-GMC 3^{n-m} : 3^r designs for $u \leqslant 13$ with $D_b = H_r$

r	f	$\tilde{D}_t$
1	1	$\{2\}$
1	2	$\{2, 12\}$
1	3	$\{2, 12, 12^2\}$
1	4	$\{2, 3, 23, 23^2\}$
1	5	$\{2, 3, 23, 23^2, 13\}$
1	6	$\{2, 12, 12^2, 3, 23, 23^2\}$
1	7	$\{2, 3, 23, 23^2, 13, 123, 12^2 3\}$
1	8	$\{2, 12^2, 3, 13^2, 23^2, 123^2, 12^2 3, 12^2 3^2\}$
1	9	$\{2, 12, 12^2, 3, 13, 23, 23^2, 12^2 3, 12^2 3^2\}$
1	10	$\{2, 12, 12^2, 3, 13, 13^2, 23, 23^2, 123, 123^2\}$
1	11	$\{2, 12, 12^2, 3, 13, 13^2, 23, 23^2, 123, 123^2, 12^2 3\}$
1	12	$\{2, 12, 12^2, 3, 13, 13^2, 23, 23^2, 123, 123^2, 12^2 3, 12^2 3^2\}$
2	1	$\{3\}$
2	2	$\{3, 13\}$
2	3	$\{3, 13, 13^2\}$
2	4	$\{3, 13, 13^2, 23^2\}$
2	5	$\{3, 13, 13^2, 23, 23^2\}$
2	6	$\{3, 13, 13^2, 23, 23^2, 123\}$
2	7	$\{3, 13, 13^2, 23, 23^2, 123, 123^2\}$
2	8	$\{3, 13, 13^2, 23, 23^2, 123, 123^2, 12^2 3\}$
2	9	$\{3, 13, 13^2, 23, 23^2, 123, 123^2, 12^2 3, 12^2 3^2\}$

10 General Minimum Lower-Order Confounding Criterion for Orthogonal Arrays

General orthogonal designs are widely employed in practical experiments due to their versatility and flexibility. This chapter extends the GMC criterion to general orthogonal arrays/designs.

10.1 Introduction

In this section, we provide a concise introduction to orthogonal arrays/designs (OAs) and present an overview of various existing criteria used for selecting OAs.

An *orthogonal array/design*, denoted as $OA(N, s_1^{m_1} \cdots s_\gamma^{m_\gamma}, t)$, with strength t, is an $N \times n$ matrix, where $n = m_1 + \cdots + m_\gamma$. In this matrix, m_i columns have s_i levels. An important property of an orthogonal array is that for any set of t columns, all possible combinations of levels appear an equal number of times. Throughout this section, we will focus on orthogonal arrays with a minimum strength of two. We will use the notation $OA(N, s_1^{m_1} \cdots s_\gamma^{m_\gamma})$ to represent orthogonal arrays without explicitly mentioning the strength.

All the designs we have examined in previous chapters are orthogonal arrays with a minimum strength of two and are categorized as regular designs. In a regular design, any two effects are either orthogonal or fully aliased. However, in the case of a general orthogonal array, it is possible for at least two effects to be partially aliased. This type of aliasing structure is referred to as complex aliasing (Hamada and Wu, 1992).

Deng and Tang (1999) extended the MA criterion and introduced the concepts of generalized resolution and minimum G-aberration (MGA) criterion. These criteria were designed to rank two-level orthogonal arrays based on their confounding frequency vectors (CFV). Subsequently, they proposed a relaxed version of the MGA criterion called the minimum G_2-aberration (MG_2A) criterion (Tang and Deng, 1999). Xu and Wu (2001) introduced the generalized wordlength pattern (GWLP) and the generalized minimum aberration (GMA) criterion, utilizing the concepts of orthonormal contrast basis (OCB) and ANOVA models. The GMA criterion is applicable to general orthogonal arrays. It reduces to the MA criterion for regular designs and the MG_2A criterion for two-level orthogonal arrays.

Cheng and Tang (2005) noted that the MA design is appropriate when the experimenter possesses limited or no knowledge about potentially significant effects. Similarly, the GMA and MGA designs, as generalizations of MA, are also suitable for such situations. This section introduces the generalized GMC (G-GMC) criterion specifically tailored for general orthogonal arrays. The G-GMC designs are well-suited for situations where the experimenter has prior knowledge about the importance ordering of factors. For convenience of presentation, we omit the proofs in this chapter. Interested readers can refer to Zhou and Zhang (2014) as well as Cheng and Zhang (2023) for further details.

10.2 ANOVA Models and Confounding Between Effects

To begin, let us revisit the OCB and ANOVA models introduced in Xu and Wu (2001). We consider an experiment with n factors, where the ith factor has s_i levels. Let $G_i = 0, 1, \cdots, s_i - 1$, and define $H = G_1 \times \cdots \times G_n$.

For a full factorial experiment with $s_1 \times \cdots \times s_n$ design, where the ith factor has

s_i levels, we consider the following general model:

$$E(Y(\boldsymbol{x})) = \sum_{\boldsymbol{u} \in H} C_{\boldsymbol{u}}(\boldsymbol{x})\beta_{\boldsymbol{u}}. \tag{10.1}$$

Here, $Y(\boldsymbol{x})$ is the response of treatment combination $\boldsymbol{x} \in H$, $C_{\boldsymbol{u}}$ are contrast coefficients, and $\beta_{\boldsymbol{u}}$ are treatment contrasts (or factorial effects). For $\boldsymbol{u} \in H$, let $wt(\boldsymbol{u})$ represent the number of nonzero elements in $\boldsymbol{u}$. When $wt(\boldsymbol{u}) = i$, $\beta_{\boldsymbol{u}}$ (or $\boldsymbol{u}$) is an ith-order interaction (or ith-order component effect, or simply, ith-order effect).

Throughout this chapter, we consider the level contrasts for the ith factor, which has s_i levels, to be real orthogonal polynomials denoted as $\{C_{u_i}^{(s_i)}, u_i \in G_i\}$. The contrast coefficients $C_{\boldsymbol{u}}(\boldsymbol{x})$ are then through tensor products as follows:

$$C_{\boldsymbol{u}}(\boldsymbol{x}) = \prod_{i=1}^{n} C_{u_i}^{(s_i)}(x_i), \text{ for } \boldsymbol{u} = (u_1, \cdots, u_n) \in H \text{ and } \boldsymbol{x} = (x_1, \cdots, x_n) \in H.$$

The set of $C_{\boldsymbol{u}}(\boldsymbol{x})$ is referred to as the *orthogonal polynomial basis* (OPB). For example, let us consider the orthogonal array $OA(18, 2^1 3^2)$ and use the following orthogonal polynomials for a three-level factor:

$$\{\sqrt{1/2}(-1, 0, 1)', \sqrt{1/6}(-1, 2, -1)'\}.$$

The resulting OPB $\{C_{\boldsymbol{u}}(\boldsymbol{x})\}$, up to a column scale transformation, is tabulated in Table 10.1.

Table 10.1　OPB $\{C_{\boldsymbol{u}}(\boldsymbol{x})\}$ of $OA(18, 2^1 3^2)$ up to a column scale transformation

1	1	-1	-1	-1	-1	-1	-1	-1	-1	-1	-1	-1	-1	-1	-1	-1	-1
1	1	-1	-1	0	2	0	2	1	-1	-1	-1	0	2	0	2	1	-1
1	1	-1	-1	1	-1	1	-1	0	2	-1	-1	1	-1	1	-1	0	2
1	1	0	2	-1	-1	0	2	1	-1	0	2	-1	-1	0	2	1	-1
1	1	0	2	0	2	1	-1	-1	-1	0	2	0	2	1	-1	-1	-1
1	1	0	2	1	-1	-1	-1	0	2	0	2	1	-1	-1	-1	0	2
1	1	1	-1	-1	-1	1	-1	0	2	1	-1	-1	-1	1	-1	0	2
1	1	1	-1	0	2	-1	-1	1	-1	1	-1	0	2	-1	-1	1	-1
1	1	1	-1	1	-1	0	2	-1	-1	1	-1	1	-1	0	2	-1	-1
1	-1	-1	-1	-1	-1	-1	-1	-1	1	1	1	1	1	1	1	1	1
1	-1	-1	-1	0	2	0	2	1	-1	1	1	0	-2	0	-2	-1	1
1	-1	-1	-1	1	-1	1	-1	0	2	1	1	-1	1	-1	1	0	-2
1	-1	0	2	-1	-1	0	2	1	-1	0	-2	1	1	0	-2	-1	1
1	-1	0	2	0	2	1	-1	-1	-1	0	-2	0	-2	-1	1	1	1
1	-1	0	2	1	-1	-1	-1	0	2	0	-2	-1	1	1	1	0	-2
1	-1	1	-1	-1	-1	1	-1	0	2	-1	1	1	1	1	1	0	-2
1	-1	1	-1	0	2	-1	-1	1	-1	-1	1	0	-2	-1	1	1	1
1	-1	1	-1	1	-1	0	2	-1	-1	-1	1	-1	1	0	-2	1	1

We consider only the OPB that satisfies the following condition:

$$\sum_{\boldsymbol{x}\in H} C_{\boldsymbol{u}}(\boldsymbol{x})C_{\boldsymbol{v}}(\boldsymbol{x}) = \left(\prod_{i=1}^{n} s_i\right) \delta_{\boldsymbol{u},\boldsymbol{v}}, \text{ for any } \boldsymbol{u}, \boldsymbol{v} \in H,$$

where $\delta_{\boldsymbol{u},\boldsymbol{v}}$ equals 1 if $\boldsymbol{u} = \boldsymbol{v}$ and 0 otherwise. The OCB is called *orthonormal* and can be obtained by applying a column scale transformation from the one above.

Let $OA(N, s_1 \cdots s_n)$ denote an orthogonal array with N runs and n factors, denoted by D, where $N < \prod_{i=1}^{n} s_i$, and D consists of a set of treatment combinations selected from H. Let $\{L_{\boldsymbol{u}}(\boldsymbol{x})\}$ denote the $N \times \prod_{i=1}^{n} s_i$ matrix with elements defined as

$$L_{\boldsymbol{u}}(\boldsymbol{x}) = C_{\boldsymbol{u}}(\boldsymbol{x}) \Big/ \left(\sum_{\boldsymbol{x}\in D} C_{\boldsymbol{u}}(\boldsymbol{x})^2\right)^{1/2}.$$

Consider the ANOVA model similar to (10.1):

$$E(Y(\boldsymbol{x})) = \sum_{\boldsymbol{u}\in H} L_{\boldsymbol{u}}(\boldsymbol{x})\beta_{\boldsymbol{u}}.$$

In this case, it is possible that in the matrix $\{L_{\boldsymbol{u}}(\boldsymbol{x})\}$ there are some columns that are not orthogonal to each other. To select good designs, we define $K_{\boldsymbol{u},\boldsymbol{v}}(D)$ for any pair $\boldsymbol{u}$ and $\boldsymbol{v}$ as follows:

$$K_{\boldsymbol{u},\boldsymbol{v}}(D) = \left| \sum_{\boldsymbol{x}\in D} L_{\boldsymbol{u}}(\boldsymbol{x})L_{\boldsymbol{v}}(\boldsymbol{x}) \right|^2.$$

This serves as a natural description of the confounding severity between $\boldsymbol{u}$ and $\boldsymbol{v}$.

Definition 10.1 *Let k denote $K_{\boldsymbol{u},\boldsymbol{v}}(D)$. The value k is said to be the confounding severity degree between effects $\boldsymbol{u}$ and $\boldsymbol{v}$ or the effect $\boldsymbol{u}$ (effect $\boldsymbol{v}$) is said to be aliased with effect $\boldsymbol{v}$ (effect $\boldsymbol{u}$) at severity degree k.*

Clearly, we have $0 \leqslant K_{\boldsymbol{u},\boldsymbol{v}}(D) \leqslant 1$ for any $\boldsymbol{u}$ and $\boldsymbol{v}$. If D is a two-level regular design, $K_{\boldsymbol{u},\boldsymbol{v}}(D)$ can only take the values of either 0 or 1. Let

$$\Omega_{i,j} = \{k_l, l = 0, \cdots, w_{ij} - 1\}$$

denote the set of all the possible confounding severity degrees between its ith-order and jth-order effects for all the being considered designs. The set $\Omega_{i,j}$ is ranked as $0 = k_0 < k_1 < \cdots < k_{w_{ij}-1} = 1$. As an example, for the designs $OA(N, 2^n)$ with $N = 4t$, the confounding severity set of the ith-order and jth-order effects can be easily obtained as

$$\Omega_{i,j} = \left(0, \left(\frac{1}{t}\right)^2, \left(\frac{2}{t}\right)^2, \cdots, \left(\frac{t-1}{t}\right)^2, 1\right).$$

In particular, the confounding severity of an effect u with the grand mean $0 = (0, \cdots, 0)$ is given by:

$$K_{u,0}(D) = \left|\sum_{x \in D} L_u(x)L_0(x)\right|^2 = N^{-1}\left|\sum_{x \in D} L_u(x)\right|^2,$$

since $L_0(x) = N^{-1/2}$ for every $x \in D$. For a two-level design D, $K_{u,0}(D)$ is equivalent to $J_j^2(S)$, where $J_j(S)$ is the J-characteristic proposed in Deng and Tang (1999) with $wt(u) = j$ and S being the set of factors corresponding to the nonzero elements of u. Let $f_j^{(k_l)}$ denote the number of jth-order effects aliased with the grand mean at degree k_l, where $k_l \in \Omega_{j,0}$ and $l = 0, 1, \cdots, w_{j0-1}$. We define

$$f_j = \left(f_j^{(k_{wj0}-1)}, f_j^{(k_{wj0}-2)}, \cdots, f_j^{(k_1)}\right),$$

and the vector

$$F(D) = (f_3, f_4, \cdots, f_n).$$

For two-level designs, $F(D)$ correponds to the CFV introduced in Deng and Tang (1999). Based on the CFV, we can get a equivalent definition of MGA as follows.

Definition 10.2   *Let f_l denote the l-th component of the CFV F. Consider the CFVs of designs D_1 and D_2, denoted as $F(D_1)$ and $F(D_2)$, respectively. Suppose f_l is the first component where $F(D_1) \neq F(D_2)$. If $f_l(D_1) < f_l(D_2)$, then D_1 is said to have less G-aberration than D_2. If there is no other design which has less G-aberration than D_1, then D_1 is said to have minimum G-aberration.*

Based on the ANOVA model (10.1), Xu and Wu (2001) proposed GMA criterion for general designs. Define

$$A_j(D) = N^{-2}\sum_{wt(v)=j}\left|\sum_{x \in D} C_v(x)C_0(x)\right|^2 = N^{-2}\sum_{wt(v)=j}\left|\sum_{x \in D} C_v(x)\right|^2,$$

for $j = 1, 2, \cdots, n$. The vector

$$(A_1(D), A_2(D), \cdots, A_n(D))$$

is called *generalized wordlength pattern* (GWLP). The *generalized minimum aberration* (GMA) criterion is to sequentially minimize $A_j(D)$ for $j = 1, 2, \cdots, n$. It is worth noting that for two-level orthogonal arrays, GMA is actually a relaxed version of MGA, and designs with the same CFV must have the same GWLP. Therefore, both CFV and GWLP only contain information about the confounding between component effects and the grand mean.

10.3 Generalized AENP and GMC Criterion

For a component effect $\boldsymbol{u}$ of a general design D, there may be many related nonzero $K_{\boldsymbol{u},\boldsymbol{v}}(D)$'s due to the complex aliasing structure associated with $\boldsymbol{u}$ (Wu and Hamada, 2000). To precisely estimate more lower-order effects for a general design, we first extend the AENP to the case of general orthogonal arrays. Subsequently, we establish a generalized GMC criterion.

Consider a general $OA(N, s_1 \cdots s_n)$ D. Suppose $\boldsymbol{u}$ is an ith-order effect of D. In the general case, we introduce a counterpart to the severity degree, which measures the degree to which the ith-order effect is aliased with all the K_j jth-order effects, where K_j represents the total number of jth-order effects in D.

Let $n_l^{\boldsymbol{u},j}$ denote the number of jth-order component effects which are aliased with $\boldsymbol{u}$ at degree k_l, where $k_l \in \Omega_{i,j}$ and $l = 0, \cdots, w_{ij} - 1$. It is evident that

$$\sum_{l=0}^{w_{ij}-1} n_l^{\boldsymbol{u},j} = K_j.$$

We can use the vector

$$A_{i,j}^{\boldsymbol{u},j} = (n_0^{\boldsymbol{u},j}, n_1^{\boldsymbol{u},j}, \cdots, n_{w_{ij}-1}^{\boldsymbol{u},j})$$

to describe the manner in which $\boldsymbol{u}$ is aliased with all the jth-order effects.

Definition 10.3 *We refer to $A_{i,j}^{\boldsymbol{u},j}$ as the confounding severity degree vector of the ith-order effect $\boldsymbol{u}$ being aliased with all the jth-order effects. The set of all possible $A_{i,j}^{\boldsymbol{u},j}$'s with $wt(\boldsymbol{u}) = i$ for the considered $OA(N, s_1 \cdots s_n)$ designs is denoted as $\{A_{i,j}^r\}$.*

The number of elements in $A_{i,j}^r$ is finite, allowing us to consider a ranking based on the following ordering:

$$A_{i,j}^0 \prec A_{i,j}^1 \prec \cdots \prec A_{i,j}^{K_{i,j}-1},$$

where $K_{i,j}$ denotes the number of the vectors in $\{A_{i,j}^r\}$. In this ranking, $A_{i,j}^r \prec A_{i,j}^{r+1}$ indicates that there exists an integer l such that $n_q^r = n_q^{r+1}$ for $q < l$ and $n_l^r > n_l^{r+1}$. That is, for two ith-order effects $\boldsymbol{u}_1$ and $\boldsymbol{u}_2$, if $A_{i,j}^{\boldsymbol{u}_1,j} \prec A_{i,j}^{\boldsymbol{u}_2,j}$, we say that $\boldsymbol{u}_1$ has a less severity degree with ith-order effects in design D compared to $\mathbf{u}_2$.

Recall the case of two-level regular designs. In this case, we have $\Omega_{i,j} = 0, 1$ and $w_{ij} = 2$. Moreover, $A^0_{i,j} = (K_j, 0)$ and $A^k_{i,j} = (K_j - k, k)$ for $k = 1, \cdots, K_j$. Thus, the severity degree vectors are ranked as

$$\{(K_j, 0), (K_j - 1, 1), \cdots, (0, K_j)\},$$

which is consistent with the ranked aliased degrees as $\{0, 1, \cdots, K_j\}$ in the AENP.

The second consideration in the AENP is how many ith-order effects are aliased with jth-order component effects at a given severity degree. To generalize this point, we introduce the notation ${}^{\#}_i C^{(r)}_j$ to represent the number of the ith-order component effects that are aliased with jth-order effects at the severity degree vector $A^r_{i,j}$, where $r = 0, 1, \cdots, K_{i,j} - 1$. Similarly, the vector

$$ {}^{\#}_i C_j = ({}^{\#}_i C^{(0)}_j, {}^{\#}_i C^{(1)}_j, \cdots, {}^{\#}_i C^{(K_{(i,j)} - 1)}_j) $$

describes the severity of the aliasing between the ith-order effects and jth-order effects.

Following the same order of ${}^{\#}_i C_j$'s in the AENP (2.3), we define

$$ {}^{\#}C = ({}^{\#}_1 C_2, {}^{\#}_2 C_2, {}^{\#}_0 C_3, {}^{\#}_1 C_3, {}^{\#}_2 C_3, {}^{\#}_3 C_2, {}^{\#}_3 C_3, \cdots). \tag{10.2}$$

Note that we exclude the terms ${}^{\#}_1 C_1$ and ${}^{\#}_0 C_2$, since they have no practical meaning for orthogonal arrays. Additionally, we omit the terms ${}^{\#}_j C_1$'s and ${}^{\#}_j C_0$'s, since they can be determined by ${}^{\#}_1 C_j$'s and ${}^{\#}_0 C_j$'s, respectively. The pattern (10.2) is called a generalized aliasing effect-number pattern (G-AENP).

According to the effect hierarchy principle, a design is considered better when it has fewer lower-order effects that are severely aliased. Building upon this idea, we generalize the GMC criterion to general orthogonal designs as follows.

Definition 10.4   *Let ${}^{\#}C_l$ be the l-th component of ${}^{\#}C$, and let ${}^{\#}C(D_1)$ and ${}^{\#}C(D_2)$ be the G-AENPs of two designs D_1 and D_2 respectively. Suppose ${}^{\#}C_l$ is the first component for which ${}^{\#}C_l(D_1) \neq {}^{\#}C_l(D_2)$. If ${}^{\#}C_l(D_1) > {}^{\#}C_l(D_2)$, then D_1 is said to have less generalized general lower-order confounding than D_2. A design D is said to have generalized general minimum lower order confounding (G-GMC) if no other design has less generalized general lower-order confounding than D.*

The above definition implies that the G-GMC criterion aims to find designs that maximize the inclusion of lower-order effects while minimizing the severity of aliasing among them. The following example illustrates this point.

Example 10.5 Consider two $OA(16, 2^6)$, namely D_1 and D_2. Design D_1 is obtained as the projection of the Type II Hall design with the columns 1, 4, 6, 8, 11, and 12 (Appendix 8B in Wu and Hamada, 2000). On the other hand, design D_2 is obtained as the projection of the Type III Hall design with the columns 1, 2, 4, 8, 10, and 12.

For the $OA(16, 2^6)$, we have

$$\Omega_{1,2} = \{0, 1/16, 1/4, 9/16, 1\}.$$

By a calculation, we can get the possible confounding severity degree vectors that indicate that the main effects are aliased with the 2fi's in the following:

$$A^0_{1,2} = (15, 0, 0, 0, 0), A^1_{1,2} = (13, 2, 0, 0, 0), A^2_{1,2} = (12, 3, 0, 0, 0), A^3_{1,2} = (11, 4, 0, 0, 0).$$

Clearly, we have

$$A^0_{1,2} \prec A^1_{1,2} \prec A^2_{1,2} \prec A^3_{1,2}.$$

According to the definition of $A^r_{i,j}$, the vector $A^0_{1,2}$ means that the main effect is orthogonal to any 2fi. Similarly, $A^1_{1,2}$ means that the main effect is respectively aliased with two 2fi's at degree 1/4 and orthogonal to any other 2fi's, and so on.

For design D_1, there is one main effect aliased with 2fi's as $A^0_{1,2}$, four main effects aliased with 2fi's as $A^1_{1,2}$ and one main effect aliased with 2fi's as $A^3_{1,2}$. On the other hand, for design D_2, there is also one main effect aliased with 2fi's as $A^0_{1,2}$, but three main effects aliased with 2fi's as $A^1_{1,2}$ and two main effect aliased with 2fi's as $A^2_{1,2}$. Therefore, we have

$$^\#_1 C_2(D_1) = (1, 4, 0, 1) \quad \text{and} \quad ^\#_1 C_2(D_2) = (1, 3, 2, 0).$$

According to Definition 10.4, design D_1 has less general lower-order confounding than D_2. $\qquad\square$

10.4 Relationship with Other Criteria

In this section, we examine the relationship between the G-GMC criterion and other existing criteria.

Deng and Tang (1999) introduced the concept of generalized resolution. For a design D, let r be the smallest integer such that

$$\max_{wt(\boldsymbol{u})=r} K_{\boldsymbol{u},\boldsymbol{0}}(D) > 0.$$

The generalized resolution of the design is defined as $R(D) = r + \delta$, where

$$\delta = 1 - K_{\boldsymbol{u}_r,\boldsymbol{0}}(D)^{1/2}.$$

It should be noted that for a design with resolution R, an ith-order effect should never be aliased with any jth-order effect, where $j < \lfloor R \rfloor - i$. Here, $\lfloor R \rfloor$ denotes the largest integer not larger than R.

The following theorem explores the relationship between the G-GMC criterion and the maximum resolution criterion.

Theorem 10.6   *A G-GMC $OA(N, s_1 \cdots s_n)$ must have a generalized resolution R that satisfies $\lfloor R \rfloor = \lfloor R_0 \rfloor$, where R_0 is the maximum generalized resolution.*

For $OA(N, s_1 \cdots s_n)$, a main component effect or two-factor interaction component effect is said to be clear if it is not aliased with any other main component effects or two-factor interaction component effects. The CE criterion aims to select designs that maximize the number of clear main component effects and two-factor interaction component effects in a sequential manner. The following theorem reveals the connection between the G-GMC criterion and the CE criterion.

Theorem 10.7   *A G-GMC $OA(N, s_1 \cdots s_n)$ with generalized resolution R is guaranteed to maximize the number of the clear main component effects. Furthermore, if $\lfloor R \rfloor \geqslant IV$, it also maximizes the number of the clear 2fi component effects.*

According to the definitions, $f_j^{(k_l)}$ is just $_j^{\#}C_0^{(l)}$, which is determined by $_0^{\#}C_j$ in (10.2). Therefore, the CFV of a design is determined by its G-AENP and can be treated as a function of the G-AENP. The following theorem directly follows from this observation.

Theorem 10.8   *Designs with the same G-AENP must have the same CFV.*

However, the converse of the theorem does not hold, i.e., designs with the same CFV may have different G-AENPs. This is because CFV only captures the information on the confounding between certain component effects and the grand mean. CFV does not include information on component effects that are not aliased with the grand mean, nor does it provide details on how an effect is aliased with other effects apart from the grand mean. Therefore, the MGA criterion may not be able to identify designs that can effectively estimate a maximum number of lower-order effects. This limitation can be illustrated through the following example.

Example 10.9　Tang and Deng (1999) noted that while it was anticipated that the MGA criterion and the GMA criterion (which is reduced to MG_2A in two-level cases) would yield similar rankings, there are counterexamples that demonstrate otherwise. An example of such counterexamples can be found in Deng and Tang (1998), specifically designs D_1 and D_2 (referred to as 9.57 and 9.58 in their paper).

The design D_1 is considered superior to D_2 according to the MGA criterion because

$$F(D_1) = ((3, 0, 18, 0), (5, 0, 18, 0), \cdots)$$

and

$$F(D_2) = ((4, 0, 0), (14, 0, 0, 0), \cdots).$$

However, under the GMA criterion, D_2 is considered superior to D_1. Despite the fact that D_1 has one less 3rd-order effect aliased with the grand mean at the worst degree compared to D_2, D_2 has seventeen additional 3rd-order effects that are not aliased with the grand mean, which is significantly beneficial. Consequently, D_2 has less generalized aberration than D_1, indicating that the MGA criterion fails to identify optimal designs in this case.　　　　　　　　　　　　　　　□

For two-level designs, the GMA criterion can be regarded as a relaxed version of the MGA criterion. Additionally, designs with the same CFV will have the same GWLP. As a result, we can directly obtain the following result from Theorem 10.8.

Corollary 10.10　*The two-level designs with the same G-AENP must have the same GWLP.*

To investigate the relationship between the G-GMC criterion and the GMA criterion, we extend a result from Zhang and Park (2000) that was originally established for two-level regular designs. Considering the ith-order and jth-order effects of a design D, we introduce the notation:

$$_iC_j(D) = N^{-2} \sum_{wt(\boldsymbol{u})=i, wt(\boldsymbol{v})=j} \left| \sum_{\boldsymbol{x}\in D} C_{\boldsymbol{u}}(\boldsymbol{x})C_{\boldsymbol{v}}(\boldsymbol{x}) \right|^2.$$

This quantity measures the overall confounding between ith-order and jth-order effects. The following theorem is a generalization of the result (7) in Zhang and Park (2000) for regular designs.

Theorem 10.11 *For a symmetrical $OA(N, s^n)$ D,*

$$_iC_j(D) = \sum_{l=0}^{i} \sum_{h=0}^{l} a_{\delta_{l,h}} A_{\delta_{l,h}}(D),$$

where $\delta_{l,h} = j + i - l - h$ and $a_{\delta_{l,h}} = (s-1)^h (s-2)^{l-h} \binom{n-\delta_{l,h}}{h} \binom{j-h}{l-h} \binom{\delta_{l,h}}{i-l}$.

Note that this result aligns with Lemma 1 in Xu and Wu (2001) when considering the case of $i = 1$. Furthermore, it can be straightforwardly extended to asymmetrical designs as well.

Corollary 10.12 *For asymmetrical $OA(N, s_1 \cdots s_n)$s, we have*

$$_iC_j = \sum_{l=0}^{i} \sum_{h=0}^{l} a_{\delta_{l,h}} A_{\delta_{l,h}},$$

where $\delta_{l,h} = i + j - l - h$ and $a_{\delta_{l,h}}$ is a nonnegative integer determined by the values of i, j, h, l and s_k for $k = 1, 2, \cdots, n$.

Define

$$C = (_1C_2, {}_2C_2, {}_1C_3, {}_2C_3, {}_3C_3, {}_1C_4, {}_2C_4, {}_3C_4, {}_4C_4, \cdots).$$

According to Corollary 10.12, it is easy to show that C and GWLP can be determined each other. Consequently, the following corollary holds.

Corollary 10.13 *Sequentially minimizing the components of C is equivalent to sequentially minimizing the components of GWLP.*

Based on the above discussion, we establish the following relationship between the G-AENP and the GWLP.

Theorem 10.14 *Designs with the same G-AENP must have the same A_3 and A_4.*

According to Corollary 10.13, GWLP only captures information about the overall confounding between different order component effects. Therefore, similar to the limitations of the MGA criterion, the GMA criterion may also fail to consistently select specific optimal designs. The following example illustrates this point.

Example 10.15 Consider design D_1: 18-$2^1 3^3$.1 and D_2: 18-$2^1 3^3$.3 given in Table

10.2. These designs have the the same CFV and GWLP. However, their G-AENPs are different since $^\#_1 C_2^{(0)}(D_1) = 2$ while $^\#_1 C_2^{(0)}(D_2) = 1$. □

10.5   Some G-GMC Designs

Through computer search, Cheng and Zhang (2023) have identified the top two or three projections of the saturated design $OA(18, 2^1 3^7)$ based on the G-GMC criterion. The results are summarized in Tables 10.2 and 10.3. For a $18\text{-}2^1 3^m.l$ or $18\text{-}3^m.l$ design, the value of l denotes its rank-order. We also provide the first three elements of $^\#_1 C_2$ and $^\#_2 C_2$ for each design. Additionally, we include their CFVs and GWLPs for comparison. The notation **C**, **M**, and **G** represent the orders of the projection under the G-GMC, MGA, and GMA criteria, respectively. "N. CE" refers to the numbers of clear effects, and l_1 and l_2 denote the numbers of clear main component effects and clear two-factor interaction component effects, respectively.

Table 10.2   Projection designs $OA(18, 2^1 3^m)$ with G-GMC criterion from $OA(18, 2^1 3^7)$

Design	Columns	Order C, M, G	G-AENP $^\#_1 C_2$; $^\#_2 C_2$	N. CE l_1; l_2	CFV f_3; f_4	GWLP $A_3, \cdots, A_m$
$18\text{-}2^1 3^2.1$	6 7	1,1,1	5; 8	5; 8	0^4; —	0
$18\text{-}2^1 3^2.2$	5 7	2,3,2	0,4,0; 0,8,	0; 0	0,2; —	$\frac{2}{3}$
$18\text{-}2^1 3^2.3$	7 8	3,2,2	0^2,4,0; 0^2,8	0; 0	0^2,2,2; —	$\frac{2}{3}$
$18\text{-}2^1 3^3.1$	2 3 7	1,10,2	2,0,4; 1,0^3,4	2; 1	0,2,0; 0,2,0	1, 1
$18\text{-}2^1 3^3.2$	2 5 8	2,2,1	1,6; 0^5,6	1; 0	0^4,4,0; 0,4,0	0.5,1.5
$18\text{-}2^1 3^3.3$	2 6 7	3,10,2	1,1,4; 0^3,1,0^4	1; 0	0,2,0; 0,2,0	1,1
$18\text{-}2^1 3^3.4$	4 5 8	4,1,1	1,0^6,6; 0^{16},6	1; 0	0^5,4,0; 0^3,4,0	0.5,1.5
$18\text{-}2^1 3^4.1$	2 3 6 7	1,16,1	1,0^2,1; 0^3,1	1; 0	0,4,2; 0^2,4,0	3.5,4.5,0
$18\text{-}2^1 3^4.2$	2 4 5 8	2,8,1	1,0^9,2; 0^5,8	1; 0	0,4,0; 0^2,4,0	3.5,4.5,0
$18\text{-}2^1 3^4.3$	2 3 5 7	3,11,2	0,1,1; 0^5,8	0; 0	0,4,0; 0^2,2,0	$3\frac{5}{6}, 3\frac{5}{6}, \frac{1}{3}$
$18\text{-}2^1 3^4.18$	2 4 7 8	18,1,2	0^7,1,0; 0^{20},1,0	0; 0	0^2,2,4; 0^4,4,0	$3\frac{5}{6},3\frac{5}{6},\frac{1}{3}$
$18\text{-}2^1 3^5.1$	2 3 6 7 8	1,15,5	0,1,0; 0^4,1	0; 0	0,10,4; 0,2,4	9,10.5,4.5,2
$18\text{-}2^1 3^5.2$	2 3 4 6 7	2,3,1	0,1,0; 0^8,1	0; 0	0,6,2; 0,2,6	8.5,12,3,2.5
$18\text{-}2^1 3^5.3$	2 3 5 6 7	3,2,1	0,1,0; 0^{10},1	0; 0	0,6,2; 0,2,4	0.5,12,3,2.5
$18\text{-}2^1 3^6.1$	2 4 5 6 7 8	1,4,2	0,1,1; 0^2,2,0	0; 0	0,12,2; 0,10,8	17,24.5,19.5,15,4
$18\text{-}2^1 3^6.2$	2 3 5 6 7 8	2,6,2	0,1,1; 0^2,2,0	0; 0	0,12,4; 0,10,8	17,24.5,19.5,15,4
$18\text{-}2^1 3^6.7$	3 4 5 6 7 8	7,1,1	0,1,0; 0^4,2,0	0; 0	0,6,12; 0,30,0	16,28.5,13.5,19,3

From Tables 10.2 and 10.3, it is evident that the G-GMC criterion consistently selects the optimal design with the maximum number of clear main component effects and two-factor interaction component effects.

Table 10.3   Projection designs $OA(18, 3^m)$ with G-GMC criterion from $OA(18, 2^1 3^7)$.

Design	Columns	Order C, M, G	G-AENP $_1^\# C_2$; $_2^\# C_2$	N. CE l_1; l_2	CFV f_3; f_4	GWLP $A_3, \cdots, A_m$
18-3^3.1	2 6 8	1,4,2	1,0,4; 0,4,0	1; 0	0,2,0; —	1
18-3^3.2	2 5 8	2,2,1	0,6; 0^2,12	0; 0	0^3,4; —	0.5
18-3^3.3	2 6 7	3,4,2	0,1,4; 0^3,4,4	0; 0	0,2,0; —	1
18-3^3.4	6 7 8	4,1,1	0^5,6; 0^7,12	0; 0	0^4,4,4; —	0.5
18-3^4.1	2 5 6 8	1,4,2	0,1,0; 0^3,4,0	0; 0	0,2,0; 0^2,1,0	2.5,1
18-3^4.2	2 6 7 8	2,7,3	0^2,1,0; 0,2,2	0; 0	0,4,2; 0^7	3.5,0
18-3^4.7	5 6 7 8	7,1,1	0^{15},8; 0^{30},4,8	0; 0	0^4,16,16; 0,2,0	2,1.5
18-3^5.1	2 3 6 7 8	1,7,4	0,1,0; 0,8,0	0; 0	0,8,4; 0,2,0	8,1.5,3
18-3^5.2	2 4 6 7 8	2,3,2	0^2,1,0; 0^4,2,2	0; 0	0,4,2; 0,2,1	6.5,4.5,1.5
18-3^5.7	4 5 6 7 8	7,1,1	0^{20},10; 0^{70},20,0	0; 0	0^4,40,40; 0,10,0	5,7.5,0
18-3^6.1	2 3 5 6 7 8	1,3,2	0,1,0; 0,4,0	0; 0	0,8,4; 0,10,2	13,13.5,9,4
18-3^6.2	2 4 5 6 7 8	2,2,2	0^2,1,1; 0^2,2,0	0; 0	0,8,2; 0,10,2	13,13.5,9,4
18-3^6.3	3 4 5 6 7 8	3,1,1	0^{11},12; 0^{41},30,30	0; 0	0^4,80,80; 0,30,0	10,22.5,0,7

Example 10.16   (Continued to Example 10.15) Consider the designs D_1: 18-$2^1 3^3$.1 and D_3: 18-$2^1 3^3$.4 in Table 10.2. D_1 is a G-GMC projection while D_3 is an MGA and GMA projection with $_1^\# C_2^{(0)}(D_3) = 1$. It can be observed that D_1 has two clear main component effects while D_3 only has one. Thus, neither the MGA nor the GMA criterion identifies such an optimal projection.   □

Tables 10.4 and 10.5 list the numbers of designs distinguished by G-AENP, CFV, and GWLP. It can be observed that G-AENP outperforms the other patterns in terms of distinguishing designs.

Table 10.4   Numbers of $OA(18, 2^1 3^m)$'s projection designs distinguished by patterns G-AENP, CFV, and GWLP

Pattern	$m=2$	$m=3$	$m=4$	$m=5$	$m=6$
CFV	3	15	21	15	6
GWLP	2	6	15	5	2
G-AENP	3	16	23	16	7

Table 10.5   Numbers of $OA(18, 3^m)$'s projection designs distinguished by patterns G-AENP, CFV, and GWLP

Pattern	$m=3$	$m=4$	$m=5$	$m=6$
CFV	5	7	7	3
GWLP	3	3	4	2
G-AENP	6	7	7	3

References

Addelman S, 1962. Symmetrical and asymmetrical factional factorial plans. Technometrics, 4: 47-58.

Ai M Y and Zhang R C, 2004a. Theory of minimum aberration blocked regular mixed factorial designs. Journal of Statistical Planning and Inference, 126: 305-323.

Ai M Y and Zhang R C, 2004b. s^{n-m} designs containing clear main effects or two-factor interactions. Statistics and Probability Letters, 69: 151-160.

Ai M Y and Zhang R C, 2006. Minimum secondary abberation fractional factorial split-plot designs in terms of consulting designs. Science in China Series A: Mathematics, 49: 494-512.

Bingham D and Sitter R R, 1999. Minimum aberration two-level fractional factorial split-plot designs. Technometrics, 41: 62-70.

Bingham D and Sitter R R, 2001. Design issues in fractional factorial split-plot experiments. Journal of Quality Technology, 33: 2-15.

Bingham D and Sitter R R, 2003. Fractional factorial split-plot designs for robust parameter experiments. Technometrics, 45: 80-89.

Bisgaard S, 1994. A note on the definition for blocked 2^{n-p} designs. Technometrics, 36: 308-311.

Bisgaard S, 2000. The design and analysis of $2^{k-p} \times 2^{q-r}$ split-plot experiments. Journal of Quality Technology, 32: 39-56.

Block R M and Mee R W, 2003. Second order saturated resolution IV designs. Journal of Statistical Theory and Applications, 2: 96-112.

Box G E P and Hunter J S, 1961a, b. The 2^{k-p} fractional factorial designs. Technometrics, 3: 311-351 and 449-458.

Box G E P and Jones S, 1992. Split-plot designs for robust product experimentation. Journal of Applied Statistics, 19: 3-26.

Bruen A A, Haddad L and Wehlau D L, 1998. Binary codes and caps. Journal of Combinatorial Designs, 6: 275-284.

Butler N A, 2003. Some theory for constructing minimum aberration fractional factorial designs. Biometrika, 90: 233-238.

Butler N A, 2007. Results for two-level fractional factorial designs of resolution IV or more. Journal of Statistical Planning and Inference, 137: 317-323.

Chen B J, Li P F, Liu M Q and Zhang R C, 2006. Some results on blocked regular 2-level fractional factorial designs with clear effects. Journal of Statistical Planning and Inference, 136: 4436-4449.

Chen H and Cheng C S, 2006. Doubling and projection: a method of constructing two-level designs of resolution IV. Annals of Statistics, 34: 546-558.

Chen H and Cheng C S, 1999. Theory of optimal blocking of 2^{n-m} designs. Annals of Statistics, 27: 1948-1973.

Chen H and Hedayat A S, 1996. 2^{n-l} designs with weak minimum aberration. Annals of Statistics, 24: 2536-2548.

Chen H and Hedayat A S, 1998. 2^{n-m} designs with resolution III and IV containing clear two-factor interactions. Journal of Statistical Planning and Inference, 75: 147-158.

Chen J, 1992. Some results on 2^{n-k} fractional factorial designs and search for minimum aberration designs. Annals of Statistics, 20: 2124-2141.

Chen J and Liu M Q, 2011. Some theory for constructing general minimum lower order confounding designs. Statistica Sinica, 21: 1541-1555.

Chen J, Sun D X and Wu C F J, 1993. A catalogue of two-level and three-level fractional factorial designs with small runs. International Statistical Review, 61: 131-145.

Chen J and Wu C F J, 1991. Some results on s^{n-k} fractional factorial designs with minimum aberration or optimal moments. Annals of Statistics, 19: 1028-1041.

Cheng C S, 2014. Theory of Factorial Design: Single- and Multi-Stratum Experiments. Boca Raton: CRC Press.

Cheng C S and Mukerjee R, 1998. Regular fractional factorial designs with minimum aberration and maximum estimation capacity. Annals of Statistics, 26: 2289-2300.

Cheng C S, Steinberg D M and Sun D X, 1999. Minimum aberration and model robustness for two-level fractional factorial designs. Journal of the Royal Statistical Society Series B, 61: 85-93.

Cheng C S and Tang B, 2005. A general theory of minimum aberration and its applications. Annals of Statistics, 33: 944-958.

Cheng S W and Wu C F J, 2002. Choice of optimal blocking schemes in two-level and three-level designs. Technometrics, 44: 269-277.

Cheng Y and Zhang R C, 2010. On construction of general minimum lower order confounding 2^{n-m} designs with $N/4 + 1 \leqslant n \leqslant 9N/32$. Journal of Statistical Planning and Inference, 140: 2384-2394.

Cheng Y and Zhang R C, 2023. A generalized general minimum lower order confounding criterion for general orthogonal designs. Communications in Statistics-Theory and Methods, 52: 4799-4814.

Davydov A A and Tombak L M, 1990. Quasi-perfect linear binary codes with distance 4 and complete caps in projective geometry. Problems of Information Transmission, 25: 265-275.

Deng L Y and Tang B, 1998. Design selection and classification for Hadamard matrices using generalized minimum aberration criterion. Unpublished manuscript.

Deng L Y and Tang B, 1999. Generalized resolution and minimum aberration criteria for Plackett-Burman and other nonregular factorial designs. Statistica Sinica, 9: 1071-1082.

Draper N R and Lin D J K, 1990. Capacity considerations for two-level fractional factorial designs. Journal of Statistical Planning and Inference, 24: 25-35.

Franklin M F, 1984. Constructing tables of minimum aberration p^{n-m} designs. Technometrics, 26: 225-232.

Fries A and Hunter W G, 1980. Minimum aberration 2^{k-p} designs. Technometrics, 22: 601-608.

Guo B, Zhou Q and Zhang R C, 2014. Some results on constructing general minimum lower order confounding 2^{n-m} designs for $n \leqslant 2^{n-m-2}$. Metrika, 77: 721-732.

Guo B, Zhou Q and Zhang R C, 2015. On construction of blocked general minimum lower-order confounding $2^{n-m} : 2^r$ designs with $N/4 + 1 \leqslant n \leqslant 5N/16$. Journal of Complexity, 31: 98-109.

Hamada M and Wu C F J, 1992. Analysis of designed experiments with complex aliasing. Journal of Quality Technology, 24: 130-137.

Han X X, Chen J B, Liu M Q and Zhao S L, 2020. Asymmetrical split-plot designs with clear effects. Metrika, 83: 779-798.

Han X X, Liu M Q, Yang J F and Zhao S L, 2020. Mixed 2- and 2^r-level fractional factorial split-plot designs with clear effects. Journal of Statistical Planning and Inference, 204: 206-216.

Hu J and Zhang R C, 2011. Some results on two-level regular designs with general minimum lower-order confounding. Journal of Statistical Planning and Inference, 141: 1774-1782.

Huang P, Chen D and Voelkel J, 1998. Minimum aberration two-level split-plot designs. Technometrics, 40: 314-326.

Ke W M, Tang B X and Wu H Q, 2005. Compromise plans with clear two-factor interactions. Statistica Sinica, 15: 709-715.

Kulahci M, Ramírez J G and Tobias R, 2006. Split-plot fractional designs: is minimum aberration enough? Journal of Quality Technology, 38: 56-64.

Lawson J, 2015. Design and Analysis of Experiments with R. Boca Raton: Taylor & Francis Group.

Lewis D K, Hutchens C and Smith J M, 1997. Experimentation for Equipment Reliability Improvement//Czitrom, V., Spagon, P. D. Statistical Case Studies for Industrial Process Improvement, Philadelphia: SIAM: 387-401.

Li P F, Chen B J, Liu M Q and Zhang R C, 2006. A note on minimum aberration and clear criteria. Statistics and Probability Letters, 76: 1007-1011.

Li P F, Zhao S L and Zhang R C, 2011. A theory on constructing 2^{n-m} designs with general minimum lower-order confounding. Statistica Sinica, 21: 1571-1589.

Li Z M, Teng Z D, Wu L J and Zhang R C, 2018. Construction of some 3^{n-m} regular designs with general minimum lower order confounding. Journal of Statistical Theory and Practice, 12: 336-355.

Li Z M, Zhang T F and Zhang R C, 2013. Three-level regular designs with general minimum lower-order confounding. The Canadian Journal of Statistics, 41: 192-210.

Li Z M, Zhao S L and Zhang R C, 2015. On general minimum lower order confounding criterion for s-level regular designs. Statistics and Probability Letters, 99: 202-209.

Mcleod R G, 2008. Optimal block sequences for blocked fractional factorial split-plot designs. Journal of Statistical Planning and Inference, 138: 2563-2573.

Mcleod R G and Brewster J F, 2004. The design of blocked fractional factorial split-plot experiments. Technometrics, 46: 135-146.

Mcleod R G and Brewster J F, 2006. Blocked fractional factorial split-plot experiments for robust parameter design. Journal of Quality Technology, 38: 267-279.

Montgomery D C, 2013. Design and Analysis of Experiments. 8th ed. New York: Wiley.

Mukerjee R and Fang K T, 2002. Fractional factorial split-plot designs with minimum aberration and maximum estimation capacity. Statistica Sinica, 12: 885-903.

Mukerjee R and Wu C F J, 2006. A Modern Theory of Factorial Designs. Springer Series in Statistics. New York: Springer.

Ren J B, Li P and Zhang R C, 2012. An optimal selection of two-level regular single arrays for robust parameter experiments. Journal of Statistical Planning and Inference, 142: 3037-3046.

Robillard P, 1968. Combinatorial problems in the theory of factorial designs and error correcting codes. Institute of Statistics Mimeo Series 594, Univ. of North Carolina, Chapel Hill.

Shoemaker A C, Tsui K L and Wu C F J, 1991. Economical experimentation methods for robust design. Technometrics, 33: 415-427.

Sitter R R, Chen J and Feder M, 1997. Fractional resolution and minimum aberration in blocked 2^{n-k} designs. Technometrics, 39: 382-390.

Suen C Y, Chen H and Wu C F J, 1997. Some identities on q^{n-m} designs with application to minimum aberrations. Annals of Statistics, 25: 1176-1188.

Sun D X, 1993. Estimation Capacity and Related Topics in Experimental Designs. Ph.D. dissertation, University of Waterloo.

Sun T and Zhao S L, 2021. General minimum lower-order confounding split-plot designs when the whole plot factors are important. Metrika, under review.

Sun T and Zhao S L, 2023. General minimum lower-order confounding three-level split-plot designs when the whole plot factors are important. The Canadian Journal of Statistics, 51: 1210-1231.

Taguchi G, 1986. Introduction to Quality Engineering:Designing Quality into Products and Processes. Tokyo: Asian Productivity Organization.

Taguchi G, 1987. System of Experimental Designs. New York: Unipub/Kraus International Publication.

Tan Y L and Zhang R C, 2013. Construction of two-level blocked minimum lower order confounding designs. Pakistan Journal of Statistics, 29: 351-367.

Tang B and Deng L Y, 1999. Minimum G_2-aberration for nonregular fractional factorial designs. Annals of Statistics, 27: 1914-1926.

Tang B, Ma F, Ingram D and Wang H, 2002. Bounds on the maximum number of clear two-factor interactions for 2^{m-p} designs of resolution III and IV. The Canadian Journal of Statistics, 30: 127-136.

Tang B and Wu C F J, 1996. Characterization of minimum aberration 2^{n-k} designs in terms of their complementary designs. Annals of Statistics, 25: 1176-1188.

Wang C C, Zhao Q Q and Zhao S L, 2019. Optimal fractional factorial split-plot designs when the whole plot factors are important. Journal of Statistical Planning and Inference, 199: 1-13.

Wang D Y, Ye S L, Zhou Q and Zhang R C, 2017. Blocked factor aliased effect-number pattern and column rank of blocked regular designs. Metrika, 80: 133-152.

Wang J X, Yuan Y and Zhao S L, 2015. Fractional factorial split-plot designs with two- and four-level factors containing clear effects. Communications in Statistics-Theory and Methods, 44: 671-682.

Wei J L, Li P and Zhang R C, 2014. Blocked two-level regular designs with general minimum lower order confounding. Journal of Statistical Theory and Practice, 8: 46-65.

Wei J L, Yang J F, Li P and Zhang R C, 2010. Split-plot designs with general minimum lower-order confounding. Science in China Series A: Mathematics, 53: 939-952.

Welch W J, Yu T K, Kang S M and Sacks J, 1990. Computer experiments for quality control by parameter design. Journal of Quality Technology, 22: 15-22.

Wu C F J and Chen Y, 1992. A graph-aided method for planning two-level experiments when certain interactions are important. Technometrics, 34: 162-175.

Wu C F J and Hamada M, 2000. Experiments: Planning, Analysis, and Parameter Design Optimization. 1st ed. New York: Wiley.

Wu C F J and Hamada M, 2009. Experiments: Planning, Analysis, and Optimization. 2nd ed. New York: Wiley.

Wu C F J and Zhu Y, 2003. Optimal Selection of Single Arrays for Parameter Design Experiments. Statistica Sinica, 13: 1179-1199.

Wu H Q and Wu C F J, 2002. Clear two-factor interactions and minimum aberration. Annals of Statistics, 30: 1496-1511.

Xu H, 2006. Blocked regular fractional factorial designs with minimum aberration. Annals of Statistics, 34: 2534-2553.

Xu H and Cheng C S, 2008. A complementary design theory for doubling. Annals of Statistics, 36: 445-457.

Xu H and Mee R W, 2010. Minimum aberration blocking schemes for 128-run designs. Journal of Statistical Planning and Inference, 140: 3213-3229.

Xu H and Wu C F J, 2001. Generalized minimum aberration for asymmetrical fractional factorial designs. Annals of Statistics, 29: 1066-1077.

Yang J F, Li P F, Liu M Q and Zhang R C, 2006. $2^{(n_1+n_2)-(k_1+k_2)}$ fractional factorial split-plot designs with clear effects. Journal of Statistical Planning and Inference, 136: 4450-4458.

Yang J F, Zhang R C and Liu M Q, 2007. Construction of fractional factorial split-plot designs with weak minimum aberration. Statistics and Probability Letters, 77: 1567-1573.

Yates F, 1935. Complex experiments. Journal of the Royal Statistical Society, 2: 181-247.

Yates F, 1937. The design and analysis of factorial experiments. Technical Communication, 35. Harpenden: Imperial Bureau of Soil Science.

Ye S L, Wang D Y and Zhang R C, 2019. Partial aliased effect number pattern and selection of optimal compromise designs. Metrika, 82: 269-293.

Yuan Y and Zhao S L, 2016. Mixed two- and eight-level fractional factorial split-plot designs containing clear effects. Acta Mathematicae Applicatae Sinica, 32: 995-1004.

Zhang R C and Cheng Y, 2010. General minimum lower order confounding designs: An overview and a construction theory. Journal of Statistical Planning and Inference, 140: 1719-1730.

Zhang R C, Li P and Wei J L, 2011. Optimal two-level regular designs with multi block variables. Journal of Statistical Theory and Practice, 5: 161-178.

Zhang R C, Li P, Zhao S L and Ai M Y, 2008. A general minimum lower-order confounding criterion for two-level regular designs. Statistica Sinica, 18: 1689-1705.

Zhang R C and Mukerjee R, 2009a. Characterization of general minimum lower order confounding via complementary sets. Statistica Sinica, 19: 363-375.

Zhang R C and Mukerjee R, 2009b. General minimum lower order confounding in block designs using complementary sets. Statistica Sinica, 19: 1787-1802.

Zhang R C and Park D K, 2000. Optimal blocking of two-level fractional factorial designs. Journal of Statistical Planning and Inference, 91: 107-121.

Zhang R C and Shao Q, 2001. Minimum aberration $(s^2)s^{n-k}$ designs. Statistica Sinica, 11: 213-223.

Zhao Q Q and Zhao S L, 2020. Constructing minimum aberration split-plot designs via complementary sets when the whole plot factors are important. Journal of Statistical Planning and Inference, 209: 123-143.

Zhao S L and Chen X F, 2012a. Mixed two- and four-level fractional factorial split-plot designs with clear effects. Journal of Statistical Planning and Inference, 142: 1789-1793.

Zhao S L and Chen X F, 2012b. Mixed-level fractional factorial split-plot designs containing clear effects. Metrika, 75: 953-962.

Zhao S L, Li P F and Karunamuni R, 2013. Blocked two-level regular factorial designs with weak minimum aberration. Biometrika, 100: 249-253.

Zhao S L, Li P F, Zhang R C and Karunamuni R, 2013. Construction of blocked two-level regular designs with general minimum lower order confounding. Journal of Statistical Planning and Inference, 143: 1082-1090.

Zhao S L, Lin D K J and Li P F, 2016. A note on the construction of blocked two-level designs with general minimum lower order confounding. Journal of Statistical Planning and Inference, 172: 16-22.

Zhao S L and Sun Q, 2017. On constructing general minimum lower order confounding two-level block designs. Communications in Statistics-Theory and Methods, 46: 1261-1274.

Zhao S L and Zhang R C, 2010. Compromise $4^m 2^n$ plans with clear two-factor interactions. Acta Mathematicae Applicatae Sinica, 26: 99-106.

Zhao S L and Zhao Q Q, 2018. Some results on constructing two-level block designs with general minimum lower order confounding. Communications in Statistics-Theory and Methods, 47: 2227-2237.

Zhao Y N, 2021a. Construction of blocked designs with multi block variables. AIMS Mathematics, 6: 6293-6308.

Zhao Y N, 2021b. General minimum lower-order confounding designs with multi-block variables. Mathematical Problems in Engineering 2021. https://doi.org/10.1155/2021/5548102.

Zhao Y N, Zhao S L and Liu M Q, 2016. A theory on constructing blocked two-level designs with general minimum lower order confounding. Frontiers of Mathematics in China, 11: 207-235.

Zhao Y N, Zhao S L and Liu M Q, 2018. On construction of optimal two-level designs with multi block variables. Journal of Systems Science and Complexity, 31: 773-786.

Zhou Q, Balakrishnan N and Zhang R C, 2013. The factor aliased effect number pattern and its application in experimental planning. The Canadian Journal of

Statistics, 41: 540-555.

Zhou Z Y and Zhang R C, 2014. A generalized general minimum lower order confounding criterion for nonregular designs. Journal of Statistical Planning and Inference, 148: 95-100.

Zhu Y and Zeng P, 2005. On the coset pattern matrices and minimum M-aberration of 2^{n-p} designs. Statistica Sinica, 15: 717-730.

Zi X M, Zhang R C and Liu M Q, 2006. Bounds on the maximum numbers of clear two-factor interactions for $2^{(n_1+n_2)-(k_1+k_2)}$ fractional factorial split-plot designs. Science in China Series A: Mathematics, 49: 1816-1829.

Index

"统计与数据科学丛书"已出版书目